I'll Be Right Back, *My Dear*

Cassady Rhodes

Seventh Arc Press

First Edition

ISBN 979-8-9934883-0-1 (paperback)

Published by
Seventh Arc Press
Summerville, SC, USA

Cover design by Seventh Arc Press
Cover illustration © Savannah Cassady
Interior design and typesetting by Joshua Hindman

Library of Congress Control Number: 2025922180

For permissions or inquiries, contact:
info.seventharcpress@gmail.com

Printed in the United States of America
10 9 8 7 6 5 4 3 2 1

For Mama.

"I'll be right back, my dear." She wrote it in a poem once—but I know now that sometimes people *can't* come back.

I still talk to her in my quiet moments, and I tell her I'm okay. This time, I mean it with all my heart.

Chapter One

I've heard people say the ache of death calms in time. That it steps away quietly, unnoticed. But not for me. When the pain tried to leave my body, it wasn't a fading symphony. What came was a choir of every beautiful voice collapsing as it fell. My fingers clung to any scrap of their presence left behind. A whisper in the silent part of my memory. A song. A smell. A single rain cloud on a sunny day. I grappled with the reality of my past and tried to endure the unraveling truth of my present.

Only then did I understand my mother's suffering.

I was born in the shadow of the child my mother lost. A daughter, Mama said she knew. She always had a way of sensing things. She saw glimpses of her in me, though she rarely spoke of her. Not to me, and never to my father. But there were times her presence gripped me. Moments when my eyes were closed or the room turned still. I didn't know it then, not in a way I could say out loud, but I carried her with me. A memory that wasn't mine but lived inside me anyway.

Some nights, she came to me in dreams I couldn't remember. Her fingertips brushed against mine when I was alone. A warm gift from the sister I'd never know in this life, yet I craved her all the same.

I think Mama felt that invisible thread between us. Maybe that's why she often lingered before she walked away. Could she ever tell which daughter she was trying to save?

Mama stepped into the hallway and pulled my door closed. I'd been sleeping then. If I had known what would happen to her, to *us*, I would have suffered through my boredom and skipped that nap.

She paused outside my bedroom. Maybe she wanted to grab me, walk me right through the front door, and never look back. But my father would've stopped her. Even drowning in whiskey, he never let anything escape. Not even the air in her lungs.

He'd pass out soon. That was her plan; to wait until he slept and take her chance. Maybe she believed we could get away from him. Maybe.

My father had stolen her strength, her dignity, her name. She wouldn't let him steal the freedom she knew I deserved.

We were trapped beneath him, in the house, and in our own skin. She tried to show me an everyday world, to let me live as other children did. But mostly she ushered me into the safety of my bedroom. It'd been over a week of loneliness. I was getting restless.

I did what I assume most children did to pass the time; I imagined a different life. Mama's books rested on my desk: her old, tattered Bible, and collections of fairy tales by Hans Christian Andersen. I could have been the subject of one of those stories. A child in another realm. Stashed away. Trapped in the highest tower, waiting for a savior to storm the walls. They would rescue me and save the day. Except this shack was no castle. And my only salvation came in the form of a mother too consumed with enduring every blow meant for me to get us out.

It tore her in half to look at me sometimes. I think she hated herself for not being stronger and freeing us sooner. But the only way she knew to protect me was by maintaining some semblance of peace with my father. So she stayed. I never blamed her. She'd made a promise long before to somebody we'd never know. The child before me.

Her hope had been lost when her first child's life ended. Every second of the horror, every piece of shattered glass, every punch, kick and shove lay etched in her mind, branded into the depths of her brain. She lay bleeding on the floor when it was over. Her body was bruised, but intact. That wasn't the case for the baby she'd carried in secret.

She curled up inside an empty bathtub overcome with pain and grief. The tiny life left her body unformed, leaving behind only blood and silent tears.

Six months later, she found herself pregnant again. This time she told my father as soon as she knew. Her hand covered her stomach as though she could shield this fragile hope. As though she could protect me. When I came in the spring, I brought Mama's world a new type of determination.

I'd turned nine that spring. Her drive to protect me hadn't wavered in all those years.

"Mary Beth, get out here, now!" My father's voice ricocheted down the hallway like a serpent locked in on its prey.

"I'm coming, just checking on Amanda."

"I don't know why you do the things you do. It's like you *enjoy* making me feel like this." His words slurred, thick with drink and the poison passed down from his own father's hands.

"I don't enjoy anything of the sort. Why don't you calm down so we can have a nice night? Don't you know what today is?"

He clicked his tongue. "Well, I s'pose you're about to tell me. What is it, Mary Beth, your birthday? 'Cause it sure the hell ain't Christmas."

She reached forward and caressed his arm. He flinched, causing her to recoil in fear.

Easy now, talk him down. You can do this.

"No, it's none of those things. It's our anniversary, darling."

July 2, 1964. A celebration of fifteen years gone to ruin. If she'd known before what she knew today, she'd have listened to her parents when they begged her not to go through with the wedding. Young hearts often blind even the clearest eyes.

They married in a tiny chapel in Eugene, Oregon. Her parents refused to attend, disowning her after the wedding. His father arrived reeking of stale cigarette smoke and day-old bourbon. It should have been enough to make her run.

It wasn't.

Day after day, year after year, she watched the man she fell in love with fade away. By the time I turned six, our money dwindled so low we had no choice but to sell our home in Eugene and move to the outskirts of Stonehaven. And with that move, Mama lost the last few strands of herself she'd been clinging to. Only the softest remnant of her remained.

"'Course I know it's our anniversary. Why you think I brought you that?" He motioned to the near-empty bottle of bootleg whiskey he'd picked up earlier that morning. "That's crystal. Ralphie's wife says that's what you're s'posed to give on the fifteenth anniversary. I paid extra so I could get it from 'em. Once it's empty, it's all yours."

"Well, Ralphie and his wife are mistaken; that bottle's not crystal. It's pretty though, thank you. I can use it for a vase or something."

He scoffed, his gaze darkening further and scorching with fury. His breathing turned primal, almost animalistic when he grabbed the bottle. It met his lips. As the rest of the liquid poured into his body, Mama knew what would come next.

Thank heavens Amanda's napping. Please, God, don't let her wake through this.

He held the bottle upside down to let the last drop hit the floor, the same way he'd done all those times before. His only warning. She knew it well.

"Guess I'm some kind of moron, huh? I don't know the difference between fancy crystal and glass 'cause I didn't come up like you? You think you're better than me? You ain't better than the dirt under my nails."

"I'm leaving you, Mack…"

Four little words. She'd longed to say them for too many years. The sentence fell from her mouth. She couldn't stop it. A brief moment of relief to finally free the thought that weighed her down. But she knew he wouldn't let her go without a fight.

His eyes narrowed. The veins bulged in his neck and forehead. She'd never seen his face this shade of crimson as though all the blood were waiting for his skin to rip apart and spew every ounce of it onto her.

He spat on the floor. The bottle twisted and turned as it fell from his grasp. Too slow. Too deliberate. It thudded against the hardwood, an omen of what would come. Everything came to a stop, all except for my father.

He lunged at her. Thick hands wrapped around her throat in an action so swift, she had no time to react. His grip squeezed tighter while the rage seeped from his pores like sweat. Her lungs searched for air. She fought back the only way she could. She clawed at his wrists. Kicked. Flailed. Begged without words.

And then the fighting stopped. All strength left her. The room dimmed and faded to darkness. For a second she carried a peaceful serenity like nothing she'd ever known.

Please, set her free, Lord. Mama's final prayer before the cold, endless sleep overtook her. She begged the same God who still hadn't delivered, but she knew He would lead me to freedom one day, even if she couldn't be there to see it.

Sometimes prayers are answered in short, but liberty often comes at a painful price. The day should have marked a wedding anniversary, a celebration of love. Instead, it became the catapult for my most haunting memory. Solitude lives in the aftermath of devastation. I questioned everything I believed to be real. If my parents were right, I'd be stranded, forgotten by the world. My best chance at survival only existed if everything they'd ever told me was wrong.

Chapter Two

The day started like any other; my final morning with Mama alive.

I looked at the birds outside the kitchen window. *What would it be like to have wings? To soar through the skies without fear. Without pain. I could be a bird, I bet. I wouldn't even mind eating bugs and worms.*

"Finish your breakfast."

My father leaned against the table to steady himself. He still wobbled even while seated. His breath came out hot and sour, the scent of last night's whiskey racing his words across the table to assault me. Each syllable carried the type of poison only true evil could bring. He glared at me with an unfocused glare. His long, dark lashes shaded equally dark eyes.

I kept eating the oatmeal. Thick and lumpy. Forced one spoonful down. Then another. Swallowing before the blandness had a chance to settle. Without sugar, it tasted like paste, but I knew better than to complain. The feeling of his steel hand on my backside lingered at every meal, reminding me of the time I'd asked if we had any butter for my bread. He accused me of being ungrateful. Mama cried when she saw the purple marks he left on my pale skin.

Mama and I washed our breakfast dishes in silence, afraid to break the rare symphony of quiet. The moment didn't last. She carried a rag toward the table to wipe it down, bumping my father's chair as she reached around him to clean. The brown liquid in his cup splashed and spilled over onto his hand.

"Damn it, Mary Beth. Can't you do anything without harassing me?"

"I'm sorry, I didn't—"

"Of course not. You never *do* anything, ain't that right?"

He turned his focus on me, waiting for my answer. I wished I could disappear.

Mama ushered me toward the hall. "Come along now, Mandy. There are times when adults need to discuss things in private. You know the rules."

Boy, did I. My shoulders slumped as I trudged back to my room, taking care to drag my feet across the wooden floor—a mild act of defiance to a significant flaw in my day. The door loomed ahead like a prison cell waiting to swallow me again. It wasn't fair. They locked me away to stare at the empty walls every time they argued. The sun taunted me, blinding my eyes as it crept across the floor. I did little to hide my annoyance.

"Now you can keep yourself busy, right?" Mama asked, not waiting for an answer. She turned on my TV and left me to sulk.

I stared out through a weathered window at an endless blue sky. What a perfect day for a child to run barefoot in the fields. Instead, I sat trapped inside. Watching the world from behind glass had become my life. There I sat, alone in my dreadful room again.

Pouting was never an option, not out loud anyway. I didn't want to make things harder for Mama, but this time I let her know my suffering. By the look in my eyes. The shortness in my tone. The painful sigh I didn't bother to stifle. Had I known the horror to come, I wouldn't have made Mama feel so guilty throughout the day.

The walls closed in on me, making my pulse race. I stretched out my arms, proving the illusion of a shrinking room false. Three feet remained between each of my hands and either wall of the small bedroom.

Our home had been a schoolhouse for previous generations. Mama wanted to make it feel like a real home for us. She cleaned on her hands and knees, scrubbed the floors, and removed every cobweb. She let me help wipe down the windows with old newspaper and vinegar. Rays of sunshine could finally find their way through the dirt and grime.

But the new light proved her efforts were futile. The walls were stained, evidence of years of neglect written across them like a letter we didn't want to read. And the smell of damp wood lingered regardless of the chemicals she used. This would never feel like a real home. It couldn't.

Still she worked. She made curtains by stitching together old sheets. They'd once been a pattern of pretty flowers. Now they hung limp in the heat, yellowed by my father's tobacco smoke. Faded by the sunlight I dared not touch.

The outside was no better. Our yard was a patchwork display of dirt and high grass, uneven and unkempt. I closed my eyes to imagine it as before. A bright playground with swings and a sliding board. Children once laughed and played there. The fantasy faded, leaving me with nothing but the creaks of an old and sagging floor.

"Tell me your dreams, Amanda," the Unseen pleaded.

"I don't feel like talking."

When he arrived, the rules of my bedroom changed. Nothing was solid. What little sunlight my window permitted became clouded. My walls tightened. This was no longer my space.

His was a whisper from a genderless voice, pouring sentences I could feel more than hear. Decidedly male, as only kindness came from femininity. Like Mama. No, the Unseen was more like my father. Abusive. Controlling. He had no body. No face. An entity without reason, void of colors or shapes, yet I understood his words. His ill intent.

"She's not coming back for you today. I'm all you've got, and I'm bored. Tell me about your dreams."

"I've already told you a hundred times."

"Please, won't you make it a hundred and one? I can help you

bring them to reality if you let me. Besides, what else have we got to do?"

I sighed, relenting. "I want to be free of this place. Free from *him*. Mama and I could have a good life together, like those people we see on TV. We could be safe if we were alone."

My deepest longing. But like the smoke that billowed from our chimney, I knew it only appeared solid from a distance. If she or I ever tried to grab hold, it would spread and fade to nothing.

"And me? You couldn't live without me. I keep you safe. Keep you company when you're all alone. It's always been us together. Getting away from him won't change that."

If I could get away from my father, I could surely find a way to escape the Unseen. His only purpose was to stand between me and the demons hiding in the shadows. My father's demons. But if we escaped him, then we'd escape those dangers too. The Unseen didn't need to know that part.

"Of course. You, me, and Mama."

"Where would we live? Tell me more."

"Fine. I'm not sure how we'd get there, but I know Mama'll find us a way. She'll move us somewhere better. With a garden she's not afraid of tending. And I can play outside every day. I bet it'll be a nice house. The floors won't sag like these do. And she won't have to shove fabric between the cracks in the walls to keep the bugs from coming in."

"We don't mind the bugs so much. But the cold weather hurts sometimes."

I nodded and continued. "My father would never find us there. He'd probably look for a while. But then he'd get drunk again and forget all about us. And we'd be safe from him at last. We wouldn't be afraid anymore."

Talking about my wishes made me feel closer to her. I missed Mama's sweet smile; she didn't share it with me anymore. The Unseen fell silent, leaving me with my thoughts.

My feet kicked back and forth as boredom set in. I blinked. It registered as only seconds. But my eyes opened to find the sun's position in the sky had shifted. Where it lay low in the sky a moment ago, now the light trail rested too high for me to see it through the window.

"What happened?" I whispered to the Unseen, but he ignored my question.

Sometimes he would talk for so long my ears would ring. But other times he remained quiet. I never knew which was worse.

I'd have to figure out how I had gotten to my desk without his help. I looked down at the crayon and the coloring book spread open. I had no memory of sitting down to color, yet my hand ached from gripping the crayon.

I tried to listen for movement in the house, but Mama turned the TV up before she left. The program's chatter acted as white noise while I focused on finishing the picture, rather than worrying about how the crayon ended up in my hand. A lonely world of swirling colors pulled me back into my daze.

I didn't mind playing alone most days, but sometimes the isolation humbled me. I'd made up a world with my sister to fill the silence. Given her a face. Made up stories about our lives. I knew she wasn't real, but the lonelier days were more tolerable with her fabricated company and conversations.

But everything about the Unseen differed from my imaginary sister. I'd built fantasies in which we lived on ships or even in the forest. Whatever I wished to experience, she provided. But the Unseen didn't cooperate with any of my games. Where I'd controlled her, the Unseen tried to control me.

His words came through unsolicited, often ordering me to do bad things. I didn't listen. Not even when what he suggested tempted me. There weren't many things I'd do to risk the possibility of my father's wrath.

"Climb through the window, we want to play outside. They won't know, you don't exist to them today."

"No, *you* don't exist. I'll be the one to get the whooping, and you'll disappear again."

His presence and my inability to manipulate him took the fun out of interacting with my sister's ghost. As if threatened, he called me childish for playing make-believe. I worried he was right—I was nine years old now, after all.

And the Unseen wore me down, refusing to disappear no matter how hard I tried to ignore him. My brain lacked the energy to argue with a manifestation today, so I returned to my coloring book, hoping to find a reasonable distraction.

I pushed the crayon against the paper. It caught beneath my grip hard enough to break in half.

"Dang it."

I saw the pitiful pile of crayons on my desk, all tiny stubs and worn-down pieces. I'd begged my father for a brand-new box. He'd promised to bring home new ones for weeks. But I knew the truth about promises. Like my pile of broken crayons, his words snapped under the smallest pressure.

Did other children have full boxes of sharp, new crayons? The idea seemed unlikely, but what did I know? It'd been so long since I'd laid eyes on a child in real life, I couldn't imagine what went on in their homes.

I did know some things, though. Most children went to school to make friends and learn from teachers. But my days consisted of sitting at the kitchen table with Mama. She did her best to teach me things, often repeating lessons I'd already memorized. I loved learning with her, but I yearned to know more about how other people lived.

Mama tried. I had a real-life best friend in her, except when my father wasn't feeling well. It hadn't always been so often, but these days were now the norm. I longed for neighbors. Friends. Any person to help fill the void and show me how life could be. The idea of normal was more fabricated than a story from one of Mama's books.

One more leaf. I grabbed the last small piece of green, barely long enough to grip between my fingers. Determination filled me to finish the picture before the crayon became too small to use. I shaded the edges, giving it an extra layer of depth. As I worked to complete the final piece, an explosion of glass breaking somewhere in the house caught me off guard and my body shuddered. The crayon slipped out of the line. A perfect picture ruined.

My hands tightened around the page with a type of anger I didn't let myself feel often. I tore it from my book and tossed it in the trash bin. Colorful pictures couldn't brighten my room anyway.

When the entertainment of coloring dried up, I returned to the hostile solitude of my four walls. The TV chatter did little to comfort me as I sat on the edge of the bed to stare through the window; the guard holding me hostage from the world.

My reflection in the thin glass caught my attention. I'd become unrecognizable. Weeks spent trapped indoors bleached my already ivory skin until it appeared almost translucent. My wild mane of mousy brown hair begged to be tamed. Mama couldn't be bothered to help me, so I pushed it behind my ears.

I practiced Mama's smile in the glass, the one she said made people glance over instead of staring too long. It never reached my eyes the way a genuine smile would. No matter how poor, a happy child drew less attention than a sad one. Misery made people uncomfortable; it made them ask questions. My parents couldn't afford questions.

But every attempt was wrong. My lips stretched too wide, my teeth too big. My nose looked like a button in the middle of my small face. I saw nothing close to Mama's delicate features. She barely tried and still held a beauty capable of turning heads. I wanted to be pretty like her. My reflection proved it wasn't meant to be.

A dark, shadowy figure moved behind me. I turned to find my room the same as always, empty. It'd gone again, but the chill persisted, causing prickles on my skin.

Minutes dragged on. I sat still waiting for something or nothing. I never knew what would come. Maybe the figure would return. It'd scoop me up and fly me away to wherever it disappeared to. And I'd go with it. I wouldn't even try to fight. But I knew the truth; nothing and nobody could rescue me from here.

My parents' argument started again. I tiptoed to the television and turned up the volume one notch at a time. The program drowned out most of the tension. Still, parts found their way through the walls. The sound of my father's voice thundered. I could barely hear Roy Orbison crooning from the record player in the front room. The same record she always played when our burdens consumed the air in the house. His songs about love and loss filled the spaces between all the words she couldn't say. When *Crying* came on, Mama's tears fell alongside the lyrics, as if the music had reached into her and pulled the pain free.

Mama's soft footsteps approached my door. She peeked in, letting the familiar scent of the lemon rinse she used on her hair slip through as she stepped forward. I could see the exhaustion in her eyes. And a new purple bruise was blooming on her cheek.

"Can I go outside today?"

I kept my eyes on her hand gripping the door frame and pretended not to notice. The mark spoke volumes. Her argument lost, his point made with fists.

A spot of blood on her shirt caught my attention. As much as I wanted to study her face for the source, I kept my eyes down. She'd warned that if someone wanted me to know their business, they'd say so.

The plate clinked against my desk when she set it down. A peanut butter sandwich with a few broken saltines did little to excite my palate. I could already feel my throat closing off from the combination of dry foods. Still, my stomach grumbled at the sight. Dry or not, at least the hunger pains would go away.

"I'm sorry, Mandy. You'll have to stay inside today. Your father's not feeling well, and we wouldn't want to do anything to upset him more."

Her words carried the warning I knew all too well. I tried to disguise my disappointment.

"Okay, Mama. I didn't know he didn't feel well again. He's getting worse. Why can't he go to a doctor?"

She ignored my question.

"He'll be fine. Will you eat lunch in your room?"

It was worded as a request, but I knew it was a flimsy attempt at making me feel like I had a choice. I could count on one hand how many parts of my life I had a choice in, and eating lunch alone in my room didn't make the list.

"Tell her to let you out. They can't make you stay here. You'll die in this room if you don't fight."

Every piece of me wanted to listen to his demand this time. I could look at Mama and tell her no, I would not eat alone in my room again.

"I'll eat in here," I said quietly.

"Promise me you won't come out no matter what."

"I promise."

I wanted to feel sorry for her and try to understand the things that she drowned in, but my disappointment left me little room to consider her pain.

"You're a good girl. I'll make you a potato casserole for dinner tonight. There's water in the bathroom if you get thirsty, okay? I love you."

"I love you too."

Refusing to look her way, my gaze fixed on the world beyond the glass. Our yard beckoned me, but I knew my toes might never touch its grass again. They'd blessed me with another tragic waste of a beautiful day.

She paused near the door. Her expression hinted she had more to say but chose not to. The mask slipped. For a moment I caught a glimpse of her sorrow. What caused that mournful shadow to fall over her eyes?

Fear gripped me, so I focused on the world outside. Stared at the softer grass that grew beneath the shade of our trees. A gentle breeze urged the leaves to dance about. I could feel its kiss against my skin, tousling my hair and tickling my lashes. My spirit yearned for more. This wasn't the life I should have been given.

It didn't make me feel sad. Not anymore. Instead, I blamed the villain in Mama's world. My father. When he punished her, it trickled down to me.

Her dreams and mine were the same, though I had no way of knowing. At night, when I prayed for freedom or rescue in any form, she lay in her bed echoing my prayer.

I didn't hear the truth in her voice. The devastation she saw coming. She made me a promise—another broken crayon.

"I'll be right back, my dear."

Those were the last words I ever heard her say.

Chapter Three

The minutes dragged on. Uninviting units of time that meant nothing in my world. My attention shifted between the clock and boredom. Every so often, my father's angry voice boomed through the walls, cutting through my thoughts. The desperate sounds of my mother's pleas followed his drunken outbursts. I couldn't understand how they ever resolved anything with words so hateful.

An argument. A disagreement about what, I couldn't say. All I heard were the familiar sounds of his frustration; that terrifying sound between the TV and Mama's tears.

I flopped onto the bed. Out of habit, my gaze shifted to the flickering screen. I had no interest in the figures moving across the television. We had one channel, and it was currently playing a special broadcast. With nothing better to do, I allowed the grainy images to pull me in.

The details were hazy, but the way the suited men moved with purpose told me this was important. A smart-looking man named Johnson sat at a desk. Rows of shiny ink pens sat before him. He used each once, deliberate strokes of ink meeting paper, then passed it off to one of the men beside him. The men's eyes lit up when Johnson placed it in their hands. They held them close as though they were collecting treasures.

I watched him discard the pens. My eyes drifted to the pile of worn-down crayons on my desk. So precious compared to the pens he tossed aside without a second thought.

The men around Mr. Johnson wore fancy suits, with their hair slicked back, handkerchiefs in their pockets. Rich folks. The kind Mama told me not to look at.

But then a change. My back stiffened as the scene on TV caught my attention. A Black man stood among the rows of white men. I'd never seen anything like it before. Mr. Johnson gave him one of the pens and reached forward to shake his hand.

I couldn't believe my eyes. It sounded like somebody referred to the man as a king. I didn't know kings could be Black. I leaned in closer, paying special attention to the program.

Within the crowd, I realized several Black people were in attendance, including two women in dresses and hats who stepped forward to receive a pen from Mr. Johnson. He shook their hands too.

I didn't understand it, but I knew it differed from what my parents told me. Whites didn't stand in crowds with Blacks, and they certainly didn't shake hands with each other on national television.

The program ended. What did it mean? I recalled Mama saying Black folks were different from us. She never gave me a reason why. Most of the time, what Mama told me made sense, but this had been a topic I'd never been able to grasp. How could I believe there were certain people in the world not meant to mingle with others? If they weren't fit to experience life the same way as everyone else, then what chance did I have of ever fitting in?

I knew Mama never meant to lie, but she hadn't witnessed what I'd seen. Maybe the world wasn't the one she thought it was either.

It wasn't the first contradiction I'd noticed while watching the programs on TV, although it may have been the most glaring. The shows on my tiny television sometimes confused me, but I'd never taken the gift for granted. It'd been brought home by my father, after all.

A garbage find he picked up from the side of the road during one of his solo trips back from town. Although it didn't work initially, he put in some effort to repair it and had it running within hours. There were few things my father couldn't do when sober, even with a bum leg. But finding him with a clear enough head to complete anything meaningful had become a rare occasion.

"He used to be good, didn't he?"

The Unseen asked the same question I often asked myself. I didn't like it when he stole thoughts from my head, though thinking of those better days did pull me from the here and now.

"He did. He even let me come outside to help him fix that big pole so the TV would pick up our channel."

"I bet that was a good day. How did he make it work?"

I closed my eyes, pushing myself back in time. "He attached a metal rod to the outside of our house. Then he pushed that thick wire through the wall and attached it to the TV. It didn't make sense to me, but he insisted it would bring us programs from the air. He was right, too; I had shows on my television when he finished."

"It's too bad he's so sick all the time. Do you think he'll ever get better?"

I shrugged my shoulders. No use going over all of the what-ifs again.

The news came on, boring stories about people and places I'd never know. I closed my eyes, choosing to sleep away the slow minutes before Mama would come to wake me once dinner was ready. I drifted off thinking of potato casserole. I could almost taste it.

When I woke up, the house had an unsettling calm that I couldn't shake.

"Are you scared?"

"I'm not scared."

A lie between confidants. But he knew me better. My stomach tightened from the fear of not knowing. Why hadn't Mama woken me up?

"She left you, they both did. But not me, I'm still here. I'll always be."

"Shh. That's a lie. Mama would never leave me alone."

My lips didn't move. I knew I'd said the words aloud. I tried to speak again. This time, my mouth moved, but no sound came out. A hand brushed against my shoulder, leaving a cold spot on my skin. Not my sister's touch. This was that other thing that came when I was alone. I didn't jump this time; I already knew nobody was there. At least nobody I could see.

The Unseen refused to explain why I had these episodes, insisting I'd made up the stories of ghosts or demons. And I could never tell Mama, not after the horrific expression she gave me when I tried to talk to her about the Unseen. She looked at me the same way she looked at my father.

I remembered it clearly. The contorted expression on her face perfectly matched the fear in her voice. "Never speak to him again," she demanded. She'd never been so stern with me. So harsh.

I brushed off the memory and strained to hear movement in the house. My ear pressed against the walls of my room, but still I heard nothing. Turning the volume down on the television didn't help, so I sat near the door to listen for any hint of sound. After several minutes, I decided they must have gone to sleep.

My worry threatened to overtake me. It's nothing—a misunderstanding on my part. I tiptoed to the bathroom to brush my teeth. Quiet. Careful. My father would be angry if he heard me moving around. Then the fighting would start all over.

No sounds escaped their bedroom as I readied myself, a small victory on my part. I'd ask Mama in the morning why she didn't wake me for dinner. Maybe she tried, but I was too tired to get up. She never skipped a meal. Not even when we had nothing more than bread. Had she broken a promise for the first time?

I didn't know I was about to have the last peaceful sleep I'd find for many nights to follow.

The morning light filtered into my room, waking me to an unusual quiet. Mama always got me up, but not today. I sat on my bed and waited for her to come. I couldn't leave my room without the threat of upsetting my father resting on my shoulders.

Hours passed. My stomach growled, jolting me away from my thoughts. A stillness in the house created a quiet too stubborn to stray.

By this time of day, the sounds of my parents' footsteps and distant chatter usually greeted me through the thin layer of my bedroom wall. Even the birds sensed a dreadfulness in the air. I turned on the television to drown out the absence of sound.

My day was spent the same as the day before. Watch TV. Color. Stare out the window. Mama never came. I reached for the doorknob. It was almost in my grasp. Fear got the best of me, and I backed down. I expected the Unseen to push me to go out there, or worse yet, accuse me of being small. But his words had not found me.

There were no sounds of my mother or father using the restroom adjoining our two bedrooms. I kept my hearing on high alert, expecting running water or the toilet flushing. All of these reassurances fell absent throughout the afternoon. I looked out the window again to ensure they hadn't gone somewhere. Our truck sat parked next to the front porch.

And then the Unseen's voice filled my senses. I knew he'd return to taunt me.

"They're not here, Amanda. They're gone now, you know I'm right."

I rolled my eyes, unwilling to play this game today. "That's impossible, our truck hasn't moved."

"Trust me, they left. I'm all you got. Go on out there and see for yourself."

I turned the TV volume up to drown out his words and wished for some way to eliminate him from my life.

As the day turned into night, I did the only thing I knew to do and went to bed. It made no sense that Mama hadn't come back, even though she told me she would. I knew she'd wake me up the next day like always. Things would go back to normal then.

But I woke up alone.

I'd have to investigate. After dressing and brushing my teeth, I sat at the foot of my bed and stared at the bedroom door daring me to play its game. I didn't want to go out there. Even my young mind knew everything was wrong.

I put on a brave face and walked across the room to slowly turn the knob on the door. My eyes went toward their bedroom first. Empty. The blankets were neatly made on the bed, the same as any other day. My hope to catch them sleeping, now a forgotten wish I couldn't remember making.

Turning to face the front of the house, I found no bravery in the deep breath of air I gulped. My body inched closer to the front room. I crept down the hallway while avoiding every creaky floorboard.

A faint humming. Occasional crackling. A rhythmic whir. Unfamiliar noises broke up the eerie silence. I tried to pinpoint the source of the sound.

"Go back to your bedroom," the Unseen ordered.

He'd sent me through the door. Why tell me to turn back now?

An icy shiver coursed through me, my body's warning to stop. I paused, ears straining. Only the whirring could be heard. My inner voice screamed at me to stop as the Unseen cried out again. I shook my head. The whirring grew louder. The sound was suffocating.

Six more steps to turn the corner. Now three, two—one.

The sunlight hit the floorboards in a strange way. Everything inside the house was holding its breath. The air had weight. Something sacred had been broken.

The scene unfolded before me. My worst nightmare in the light of day. I found myself paralyzed by terror. There, on the hard surface of our sagging floor, lay my mother's body. Her chestnut hair fanned out in disarray, a soft contrast to her broken and lifeless frame. Her body sprawled before me in a position no human could comfortably lie in.

Unblinking eyes. Mouth agape. She'd died in a scream I never heard. The moments before her last breath clung to every detail. I searched for the injury that caused her death. Besides the bruise on her cheek and some new marks on her neck, I saw nothing severe enough to end her life.

No blood. No shattered bones. Only her still body remained. And that incessant whirring.

A scream clawed its way up my throat. I forced it back, knowing what my father would do if he heard. My teeth clamped down hard on my lip—a gut reaction to keep myself from crying out. I tasted blood. Tried to swallow before I gagged.

I wanted to close my eyes. To look away. But I couldn't move.

No, Mama! Get up, please! I begged in silence while willing her eyes to blink or her chest to rise.

An unforgiving emptiness filled the room.

Please God, don't take her away from me.

If Mama lay here, then where did my father hide? What would he do if he found out I came out of my room? I wanted to run, but the terror wrapped around my body, rendering my limbs useless.

Chapter Four

His breath escaped him. One big whoosh of air as though he'd been holding it for hours. He stared through me with two blank and hollow eyes. They pierced through me like a madman's. What had he done? Why?

"Say something, you imbecile," the Unseen shouted. His words exploded in my head. But I couldn't speak.

"You shouldn't have come out here."

My father's voice, but more distant. It growled from the back of his throat like a beast. The sound warned of his impending attack.

"You never do as you're told."

And then I saw it. He moved ever so gently in his chair, causing the morning sun to hit the metal of his gun at the right angle. It gleamed across my vision, igniting a new type of fear in me. He killed Mama; he'd kill me next.

I gulped for air. "I'm sorry, Daddy."

"You're sorry? You're *sorry?* Standing over your mother's dead body and that's all you have to say for yourself?"

He sprang from his chair. His hand folded around my arm before I could even flinch at his movement. His wet pants brushed against me, overwhelming with the sharp tang of urine. Had he not left the chair in all that time, releasing his body fluids all over himself? I hadn't heard him in the bathroom; there'd been no movement at all.

"Please, I'll go back to my room. I won't come out again, I promise."

As though I were weightless, he shoved me down toward my

mother. My face was so close to hers, I could taste the aura of death seeping through her skin. Her once warm cheeks and flawless complexion were now a bitter shade of solemn gray. The familiar aroma of her citrusy hair went missing as she lay like a wilted bouquet across our rickety floor.

"It's because of you she's gone. You caused this, always with your whinin' and beggin'. She'd have stayed here forever without your constant complaints. You hear me? She's dead because of *you*."

I whimpered, clinging to a strand of Mama's hair.

"And I ain't mean to kill her. I only needed her to know that I could if I wanted. Do you know I could? I could kill you right now, burn both your bodies in the yard, and nobody'd be the wiser."

He aimed his gun down at me, pulling back the hammer. There was no escaping him. I willed my eyes to shut. They refused to provide me with the blind oblivion I begged for.

"Well, do you? Answer me!"

My throat closed tight, but I pushed the words through anyway. "Yes. I know you could."

He reached down, yanking me up by my hair and held me in the air. My feet swayed above the floor. I saw the faces of demons hiding in his eyes.

"Please, Daddy."

My voice came out low. Unrecognizable even to me. I didn't know if I said it out loud. I may have only thought it. The whirring grew louder. All other sounds dissolved into the incessant hum. I let it take me somewhere far away.

"You're nothing but a bitch, same as your mother, same as her mother, too. Ain't no cure for that either."

He pressed his free hand against his face, the gun grazing his cheek. My feet continued to dangle inches above the ground.

"Open your mouth."

I was locked by fear. My teeth clamped together so tightly that my jaw ached.

He grew louder. Angrier.

"I said open your mouth, or I'll open it for you. You ain't gonna like it if I do it."

My mouth opened, only a crack. Without warning, he shoved the nose of the gun between my lips. The hard metal smashed against my teeth and gums until he'd pushed it all the way to the back of my throat.

"Maybe I'll paint your pretty Mama red with your blood. You two always whisperin' and sneakin' around, making plans to leave me. Cover her with your insides, then you two'd get just what you was askin' for, wouldn't ya?"

I knew not to cry. I'd be dead before the first tear fell. My head throbbed as little strands of hair broke away from my scalp while he held me there.

"'Course, that'd be too easy. Be just like giving you your way. Maybe I'll blow my own brains out, then you can see what it really means to be alone. Yeah, I just might…"

His hand opened, letting me drop to the ground. The gun scraped across my teeth as he released me, making a sickening pop as it exited my mouth. He laughed as I lay there, too afraid to react. The sound he made came out so foreign, so vile, I shivered in the suffocating room.

"Get up."

I did as he instructed, but he lifted his foot, kicking me hard in my lower back. The pain dropped me to my knees.

"I said get up."

I stood again, inching away from him. He reached forward and pulled me so close to him our noses almost touched. His hot breath soured in my nostrils.

"Go into your room, and don't come out again until one of us is dead. Ya hear?"

"Yes, sir."

Another hard shove toward the hallway. Walking, when my

legs begged to run. I dropped onto my bedroom floor and folded my arms around my knees.

"Tell me what to do," I whispered to the Unseen. Silence met me.

I sat like that for hours until I heard the front door slam. The truck's engine turned over. Tires crunched across the gravel.

Minutes passed. I struggled to inhale the air in my bedroom. It was thick. Hot. Every bit of oxygen available became stifling. I needed to get out, but I couldn't face Mama again, so I paced across my floor instead.

"*The window…*" The Unseen reminded me.

The lock wouldn't budge. Years of rain had swollen the wood, trapping it tight. I pushed hard, trying to make it click open like I'd seen my father do so easily. My small fingers were no match for the rusted metal.

"*Smash the glass and get out of here!*" he screamed through my frantic being, but I knew better than to listen.

Maybe I can use something to knock it loose. I thought as I scanned my bedroom and bathroom for anything strong enough to strike it free. My eyes landed on Mama's hairbrush resting on the sink.

"Yes, perfect!"

My hand went over my mouth as soon as the sound escaped. Reality hit; there was nobody to hear me. The only person in the house was Mama. Or what was left of her.

I rushed to the window. Pressed the brush against the lock and hammered it over and over. A dull ache spread through my wrist. The weight of each failed hit came heavier than the last. I couldn't stop. Not now. I gave one final blow and the lock shifted. Only a bit, but enough to reignite my hope. I pounded it until it finally turned.

I dropped the brush and used my last ounce of strength to shove the window open. A critical detail hit me before climbing through—I'd need a way to get back in.

My desk stool was at the perfect height to help me climb back inside later. I tossed it out onto the grass.

I stared ahead. My eyes took in everything and nothing all at once. Our property could have been peaceful. It could have been the home Mama was so desperate to provide. But peace is elusive when you're living in hell.

I shook away my thoughts of then and tried to focus on the here and now.

A distant rumble caught my ear. A car barreled down the highway straight toward our house.

"*Stop them, get their attention,*" the Unseen demanded. This time, I listened. I started toward the road, ready to wave my arms, to yell for them to stop.

As they got closer, the driver glanced my way. All I could offer was a weak smile. A halfhearted wave. They nodded and kept driving. I stood there and watched the car until it became a tiny speck. Then a tear. Only one, but it carried the whole world down my cheek.

Cars rarely passed our house. I'd missed my only chance at escaping him.

I walked to the porch. The roof shaded my body, but the pain shaded my soul. My mother lay inches away on the other side of the door. A thought that carried as much terror as it did comfort. My face rested against the wood.

"I'm sorry, Mama. I'm sorry for everything."

The words were pointless now. An angry realization stirred inside of me, one I'd never felt before. He'd stolen my precious mother. The source of everything beautiful in my life was gone.

"*It's time to go. He's going to catch you. Walk away.*"

"There's nowhere to go. I'm alone."

"*He'll kill you when he comes home. He's going to shoot you right in the mouth.*"

"I want to die. Then at least I'll be with Mama."

I stood up and brushed the dirt from my bottom before climbing back through my bedroom window. My arms were too short to reach the stool, so I left it. What did it matter if he found out I'd climbed through? I'd be dead soon anyway.

The day moved along, welcoming the loneliness of night. Hints of moonlight shone through my open curtains. For a while, I could hear the distant sounds of fireworks from the Independence Day celebration. Even that came to an end. The return of silence engulfed me.

I heard the truck's tires speeding across the driveway. He was back and driving too fast. I don't think he even tried to slow down.

BOOM! The front end of the truck smashed into the corner of the porch, shaking the house to its foundation. He opened the door and rolled out onto the grass below. I watched him chug the last bit of whiskey from the bottle before he got up. He tossed it into the cab, now empty, and slammed the door shut. And then he staggered into the house.

I knew I hadn't meant it earlier; I didn't want to die, even if dying meant being with Mama again.

"I'm scared."

"You should be."

He came inside. I strained my ears to hear his steps moving throughout the house. Into the kitchen, opening the fridge, popping the top off a beer bottle, back to the front room. The squeaking of his urine-filled chair as his body heaved into it. An hour later came a sound so musical it actually made me smile, even if only for a second; he was snoring.

I'd be alright for the night. By morning he'd come for me. I needed a way out. A plan. But I had to see him. To look at him in his most vulnerable state.

"He's gonna wake up and shoot you. Go back to your room."

But I couldn't turn back. One small lamp illuminated the front room. The gun on the stand next to him dared me to come closer.

"Pick it up. Kill him like he killed Mama, like he intends to do to you. Just aim and shoot."

I lifted the gun in my hands. I remembered to be careful not to touch the trigger. It was heavier than I remembered. The solid, cold metal against my sweaty palms did nothing to make me feel stronger.

Mama's voice swirled through my head. *"Don't tell your father I taught you how to use his gun. I hope you never need to, but remember what I showed you, remember how it feels when you fire it. And keep your hands steady."*

I set it back down. My shoulders slumped in defeat.

"Go back to your room. Nothing more you can do now."

My hands didn't tremble anymore as I changed into my pajamas. I knew I could do it if I needed to, Mama had taught me how to save myself. I wanted to go lie next to her, but instead I climbed beneath the covers and closed my eyes to mimic sleep.

The clock on the wall showed a quarter after four. I'd blocked out the minutes that passed following the sound I'd heard less than an hour before. A single gunshot. The end of my nightmare. There'd been a choice all along as to who would die, but that fate hadn't landed on me.

Then the house filled with an eerie calm. There were no more sounds. No footsteps. No snoring. Nothing.

Could he really be dead? I threw the covers off and made my way back to the front room.

A gruesome scene. His body rested in the old chair, his head slumped forward until it looked as though it might fall clean off his body. Blood leaked from his temple onto his lap and the armrest. Spread out in a crimson splatter, it stained the wall beside him. His gun lay only inches from his feet.

The whirring continued, but now I could allow myself to locate the source. Mama's old record player. It continued to spin over the empty edge of her album.

I yanked the cord from the outlet. Held it in my hand. So foreign. My eyes stayed on the album until it slowed to a stop. Only silence. A painful mirror to what life had been and what it had become. Quiet. Lonely. But now it was permanent.

What a mess to be left behind. Mama would've cried to see the state of her home.

I had to fix it for her. A new determination surged through me as I made my way to the hall closet and pulled out two sheets, a bucket, rags, and cleaner. My steps didn't hesitate. I forced myself to be bigger. Braver.

My eyes avoided the front room as I turned into the kitchen. If I looked in there first, I might lose my nerve altogether. This had to be done for Mama.

With a bucket full of water and cleaner, and Mama's kitchen gloves tucked under my arm, I carried everything to where their bodies lay.

I attended to my father first, choosing the darker sheet to cover him. Draping it over his rigid body, I made sure to leave no part of him exposed. The gun looked up at me. Smiling. Full of malice. The sight of it sent a chill through me.

I swallowed my anger and nudged it under his chair with my foot.

Next, I turned to Mama. My soul resisted the idea of simply covering her and leaving. Minutes passed while I searched her face, hoping to find some kind of closure. But there was nothing more than her lifeless eyes. They had once been bright blue, hiding secrets and a hint of mischief. Now they were dull. Drained of life. Fading to gray.

"I love you," I tried to close her eyes one last time. My fingers brushed against her icy skin and my hand jerked back in shock. A few slow breaths. A moment to find my strength before trying again. This time I kept my hand steady. With her eyes shut, I could almost convince myself she might be at peace.

My fingers over the bruise on her cheek. Along the outline of her hair. Over those beautiful locks of brown and amber. The only piece of her I could hold onto forever. I parted her hair and snipped a small section from the back. A keepsake of what used to be.

Covering her body wasn't easy. Especially her face. My fingers met my lips to catch the last kiss I would ever give to Mama. I pressed it to her cold forehead before covering her face.

"I'm sorry," I whispered one last time in hopes she could hear me somehow. Maybe she could. Maybe in all of this darkness, a little of her light still lingered here.

My eyes were dry. The sting of earlier tears faded as I stood before the wreckage my father left. His final gift of misery. But his legacy of pain would be erased.

A long breath escaped me. I'd cleaned worse messes, but with Mama's help. None of those left this hollow aching in my chest.

Scrubbing the blood-stained wall and floor below made my arms go limp from the strain and rinsing the rag over and over. Scrub and rinse. Scrub and rinse. I refilled the bucket five times. Eventually the water dripping from my rags came out clear.

It was done. Our house was restored to its former clean-but-not-clean-looking state. The moon hung low in the sky when I finished. Soon it would trade places with the sun. What a vicious cycle to be left to face alone.

I wanted to stay. To sit by Mama's remains until death came to find me too. But my body trembled from exhaustion. Two days without food didn't even matter anymore.

My feet dragged across the floor on my way to the bathroom, this time out of sheer exhaustion. The sting of hot water did little in the way of reviving me. I scrubbed my body harder than I had scrubbed the bloodstains. When the skin on my arms became raw, I eased up. It did nothing to take away the filth. That type of grime rested in the unreachable places deep beneath my skin.

The house was calm when I came out of the bathroom. Too calm. The polluted air held an evil presence lingering like a shadow out of sight. Relentlessness, it gripped me, twisting my stomach into knots. My body released an involuntary shiver. My empty stomach begged to vomit.

I peeled back the covers and climbed beneath them. Pulled the blanket up and over my head. The lower portion of my back carried the remnant of his footprint. I rolled onto my side to relieve the pressure. The bed offered a false promise of comfort—a soft cocoon couldn't shield me from the horror I'd been dealt. A horror I'd been forced to face alone.

My eyelids fell. The light of an unjust world turned dark. For a moment I welcomed it. As my body drifted, the escape of sleep pulled me into the false reality of a simplistic life I'd taken for granted days before. The tightness released from my limbs until reality settled in my bones.

"I'm afraid of the dark. Will you stay with me?" I whispered to the Unseen.

"You'll never be alone as long as you've got me."

Chapter Five

Did I sleep? The sun sat high in the sky. A clear indication of mid-morning. I'd remained still through much of the sunrise, un-blinking. A dreamless slumber snuck in and stole my consciousness before daylight fully formed.

The memory of the previous twenty-four hours suffocated me until every breath came out tighter than the last. My chest ached. The burden of constant straining made my head hurt. I sat up and slid my body from beneath the covers, letting my tired legs dangle over the edge of the bed. My door towered over me. The wooden frame curled like a smirk. It dared me to open it. To face what waited beyond. To mock me with its stillness.

I stared into nothing. Every memory I'd ever had of my mother played on a reel at full speed behind my eyes. If I hadn't gone to sleep that day, if I'd been bigger, less afraid.

With a shake of my head, all those lingering notions of what I could or could not have done differently dissolved. I remembered her words, *"Things are how they are, Mandy. We can't complain about every little thing we find unfair, not when so many people have it worse. Be grateful for what we do have."*

What remained to be grateful for? It didn't matter if I lived because Mama died. She was gone forever. Maybe I should have let my father kill me too.

"Chin up, Mandy. Things aren't so bad and nobody likes a pouting child, especially not your father," I recalled her gentle warning, the things she said to placate me. Surely she wouldn't have told me to

stop pouting now. Or would she?

I dressed and brushed my hair. A pointless ritual, but I needed to feel some sort of normalcy, so I did it anyway. My hand reached for the doorknob.

"Here goes nothing."

A stench like rotting meat left in the sun surrounded me. I gagged. Spat. An unforgiving foulness coated my throat and stuck to the back of my tongue. The air from the hall swooshed in through the open door, filling my bedroom faster than the wrath of the river's flood.

I slammed it shut with such force that the framed picture of my family came crashing down off the wall. Glass sprayed in every direction as my body gagged and coughed in an attempt to relieve itself from the taste and smell of death. I tied a towel over my face and quickly opened the bedroom window. There were no options left for me. I had to go.

As if I had any idea what to pack. I sifted through my things, curious about what someone like me would need. Each item felt heavier than the last as I filled a paper bag with socks, a nightgown, and my crayons. Every piece of my normalcy fell from my hands and into another life.

I could still carry the bag by its handles when I finished packing, but my belongings almost reached the top. Mama's lock of hair was secured by a piece of shoelace I'd cut from an old pair of shoes, placing it near the bottom of the bag so it wouldn't fall out unnoticed.

I approached my open window, but took a second to look back at my bedroom. Resting on the floor beneath the shards of glass, I saw the picture of the one thing I needed most—my family. I ran back to retrieve it and crawled through the window.

"*Burn it down.*" The Unseen's words surrounded me. I closed my eyes, wishing for the bravery to do as he ordered.

"I can't. I could never destroy Mama's body."

"*Remember what she said. Ashes to ashes. She wouldn't want her body to rot in that house with your father's.*"

"I don't even have a way to light a fire. But I couldn't do it, even if I did."

I'd never admit it, but the idea of destroying the walls my father used to imprison me inspired a thrilling kind of pleasure. Except for Mama's remains, not an item in the house reminded me of anything good. The house was tainted. All memories of pain. Of neglect. Of lonely tears.

My steps paused at the end of the driveway. Turning once more to take in the final image of all I'd ever known. I saw them standing there, Mama's fingers entwined with my sister's. They smiled and waved goodbye, forcing me to abandon the charade for good. My sister had always been a dream, and that's all I had left of Mama now too.

The silence closed in on me. Feeling small and uncertain, knowing both left and right would take me to town, I tried to remember which way would lead me to people the fastest.

I spun in a circle with closed eyes, pointing my hand and counting to five. When I stopped spinning, my eyes opened to find an unwelcome visitor; the shadow figure. It taunted me. I turned my head to follow its smoky path across the yard. Was this a demon? Would they follow me away from hell or remain here confined by the barrier of our cursed yard?

The sound of a bird's song pulled me back into the moment. I had to remember what Mama said. The shadow was nothing. Only my eyes playing tricks on me. But what if she was wrong?

"Make them stay, Mama, bring me an angel instead."

I walked away from our property determined to find help. It didn't take long for my determination to wane. My legs were tired. My feet were throbbing.

My shoes rubbed against my heels until raw skin burned from each scrape. When I looked down, I noticed the blood soaking through my socks which caused them to stick to my blistered feet. Every step turned into a slow torture.

I paused, wincing from the pain. When I looked up again,

everything changed. The ditch I'd been carefully avoiding stretched wide into an endless canyon, my feet teetering on the thin piece of shoulder separating me from the roadway and certain death. I'd taken my shoes off at some point, though the memory of doing so lay absent in my mind.

How far had I walked in my blood-stained socks?

I lifted my foot to see the bottom of the fabric caked with dirt. A chill shot through me. When I dropped my foot, the canyon cinched closed. The ditch previously resting there was swallowed up, as if it had never been there at all. My hair whipped across my face in the wind. I could sense the terror that lay ahead. All was silent except for a haunting melody of indistinct whispers.

Why was this happening to me?

I pulled myself back to reality, but every part of my body matched the hurt in my heart. Hunger became a thing of the past as dehydration set in.

Unshed tears threatened to drop from my lashes. I would not cry.

"You went the wrong way; you should have gone left. You're gonna die on this road, all because you didn't know the way."

"Please leave me alone. I'm gonna find somebody to help me sooner or later."

"You should have stayed with Mama."

Maybe he had a point, but I refused to give up. We'd driven on this road; I knew it would eventually lead to town. My eyes caught a hint of relief in the distance. A tiny house far off the main road offered some much-needed encouragement.

"Yes, another house!"

My excitement caused my feet to pick up speed. Every other door I'd knocked on had been met with silence. Maybe this was the place I'd find a savior.

The first knock landed lightly on the wood. After waiting a minute, I decided to knock a little harder. Silence.

I sat down on the porch, leaning my head over on my bag. I couldn't go any further, there was nothing left to carry me.

"Now you're gonna die here, when you could have laid down with Mama. The birds'll eat your eyes right from your head."

"And if they do, then at least a piece of me will be free to fly with them."

I only partially meant it. Laying next to Mama while I waited to be with her after life sure did beat dying alone on a stranger's porch. Maybe I could make it back. The only way to find out was to get up and try. But something stopped me from walking away. A strong urge to try knocking on the door one more time nagged at me. The driveway was empty, the house was quiet. Still, the urge to knock again surged through me like it was my right.

My hand met the wood. Heavy. Loud. Demanding the skies above to hear my presence.

And my effort was met with the glorious sound my ears had begged for. Someone was coming, I could hear feet shuffling through the windows. I bit down on my cheek. It did nothing to steady my nerves.

"Who's there?" an older man called out.

"Umm—I'm Amanda. I need help, my parents died."

I blurted out the words that should have never been spoken aloud.

I studied him. An older man with the wonder of a child hiding in his eyes. His ruffled white hair matched an equally white beard. He stood hunched. I was sure he wouldn't be much taller even if he were standing more upright.

"Well, Amanda, my name's Pop. I guess you'd better come inside and sit a spell and explain yourself a little better, huh?" he suggested while opening the door wide enough for me to pass through.

I looked back over my shoulder in the direction I came from. Mama always told me not to talk to strangers. I knew she'd be upset if I went inside the man's house.

He could only be one of two things, an angel Mama led me to for protection, or a demon my father sent to punish me for leaving. I had no way of knowing, and few other options, so I took a deep breath and nodded before following him inside.

Please, Mama, keep me safe.

For a moment, I smelled the faint scent of lemon. It dissolved as quickly as it came.

"You can sit right there on the couch. Would you like some water?"

"Yes, Mr. Pop. Thank you."

"Just Pop'll do. Wait right here."

I tried to hide my surprise at how orderly he kept his house. The neglected exterior presented a stark contrast to the inside. I couldn't have imagined the warmth waiting behind the walls when standing on the saggy porch. Wood polish shone across his furniture like he'd only stopped cleaning to come answer the door. My shoulders relaxed at the thought of him working hard to keep a tidy home. The same as Mama did.

Pop's walls were alive with paintings. Each one pulled me away from this world and into the space of the piece. Soft pastels in one, dark, brooding hues in another. They told their own stories apart, but together they shared a thread I couldn't quite grasp.

The largest painting caught my eye, a little girl on a swing set with a rickety farmhouse in the background. A delicate smile contrasted with the shadow in her eyes. Her smile dropped for a moment. Genuine emotions snuck through. Even after she froze back to stillness, a piece of her loneliness stayed with me. I knew her, though I didn't know how.

Pop moved a coaster in front of me on the coffee table to set the glass of water on. "Here you are. Let's talk about how you ended up here on my porch. You couldn't have come all the way from town."

I took a sip. The cool water soothed my dry throat. "We live in the country. My father doesn't like people much."

"And your parents passed on? What happened?"

Mama's warning lingered. A locked door in my mind I wasn't allowed to open.

"I'm not supposed to talk about them."

An expression flashed over his face that I couldn't quite place. Sorrow? Understanding? God, I prayed it wasn't judgment.

"I can't help you if I don't know what's happened. A child inside a man's house alone, well, there better be a good reason for that."

Would he make me leave if I told him the truth? That walk stole the only strength I had. I decided to stick to the necessary details. Mama never liked a liar, but she said sometimes we had to make exceptions.

"I think my father killed my mother. Then he killed himself too."

I went headfirst into the story, insisting they'd died on the same night. My version for Pop came out short; I found my mother, then my father, packed my things, and left. None of the rest mattered anyway.

I waited for him to speak as he absorbed everything I told him.

"I can't pretend to understand what you've been through. Getting help for you today is impossible. I don't have one of those fancy telephones or a car to take you anywhere, but Miss Sally'll be here in a week or so. She'll know what to do."

"Miss Sally?"

"She brings me food and supplies every couple of weeks. She'll help us figure things out."

"Does that mean I can stay?" My trembling voice revealed the desperation I'd tried to conceal.

"Yes, Amanda, you can stay for now. There's only one bedroom. You're small, I think the couch'll be alright."

I rushed to hug him the way Mama taught me to hug my father. I knew if I did, he'd see I'd be a good girl, a child deserving of this second chance. He tensed at my embrace, pulling back instantly. That's when he noticed the bloody socks on my feet.

"Looks like we need the first aid kit. Sit tight."

I pulled back as he reached for my foot. His eyes grew wide at my reaction. What was wrong with me? He was trying to help me and I'd made him feel bad. I wouldn't do that again.

The antiseptic stung like fire, so I bit my lip to stay silent as he worked to mend my wounds. His shaky hands were surprisingly gentle. I noticed the special care he took in cleaning around the sore spots. It had to be a sign this was where Mama wanted me to be.

"Does that feel better?"

I nodded. "Thank you."

"Good. Now, let me show you around the house."

His home was a small space with a cozy simplicity I found welcoming. When we reached the back hallway, he opened a bureau.

"You can put your belongings in one of these drawers. I like to keep things in order."

I pulled out my clothes to place them in the drawer. His eyes lit up at the sight of my crayons and coloring book.

"Should these go in the drawer too?"

"Well, I had no idea we had an artist in the house! No, no, art doesn't belong with clothes. Come on, I've got a treat for you."

He turned to walk back to the front room. The moment of privacy allowed me to put my family picture and Mama's locket of hair in the drawer with my clothes. I kissed my finger and touched it to Mama's face before shutting the drawer.

I followed Pop to the closet nearest the front door, expecting to see coats and boots, but this closet held nothing of the sort. He opened it to reveal stacks of bins, all identified by the neat labels he'd placed on the front of each box.

One by one, he pulled out containers of paint and brushes. He stood on the tips of his toes to pull down a pad of thick paper from the top shelf. "These were my Mona's. She was an artist. Passed on over a decade ago, but her legacy's here in the paintings you see around the house."

"I don't know how to paint."

He smiled. "You'll learn. Here, keep your crayons in this bin. We'll label it with your name."

As I wrote my name, he retrieved an easel from the bedroom. "This belonged to Mona. It'll make painting easier. Let's set it up on the back porch."

We carried everything outside, where he told me stories about his wife. His words about her brightened the shadows on his face, making him appear much younger than before.

"Do I just dip the brush in the container?"

"Sure, or use a piece of cardboard as a palette. I brought you a cup of water to rinse between colors. There you are, all set up. What about lunch? Would you like a sandwich?"

"Oh yes, please! I mean, yes, sir, I'll have a sandwich if you don't mind sharing."

"It'll be nice to have some company. Sometimes I sit out here to eat, but it's usually alone."

My shoulders sagged the moment the screen door closed and a breath I didn't know I was holding escaped. The first full exhale following the moment I'd found my mother on the front room floor. That might have been a lifetime ago. Every second since I'd found her lost its form.

This didn't feel right. I shouldn't have been sitting in the sunshine painting a picture. Not when everything in the world around me had been dissolved. Guilt consumed me for accepting this distraction from the truth of my life. But it was what Pop wanted me to do, so I pushed down my emotions and turned back to the blank paper.

I decided to start with the simple shape of a heart, but the paint oozed down when I pulled the brush from the red container. Thick and haunting, like my father's blood spreading across the floor. It took away my breath. My body froze for a time.

"They're dead because of you; you were too small. You shouldn't have been such a baby."

"Stop it. Pop'll make me leave if he hears us talking."

I dropped the brush into the cup of water and put the lid back on the red paint. My instinct to throw the little jar as hard as possible in the yard nagged at me. I knew throwing Mona's paint wouldn't be nice, so I placed it carefully back into the bin.

When my hands stopped shaking, I chose some different colors. Trees were my favorite, and I was confident in drawing them, so I chose shades of green and brown.

Once I'd finished making the outline, Pop returned with the sandwiches. He squinted his eyes with playful mischief.

"I can see it clearly. An airplane soaring through the sky."

The smallest giggle escaped my lips. Immediate feelings of regret washed over me. I blinked them away and told Pop in my most serious tone, "No, it's not an airplane. It's a tree."

He pulled a chair out at the little patio table for me and set a plate down. "Oh, right. Yes of course, how silly of me."

Our conversation drifted between bites, his chuckle a low hum providing comfort in the silence between words. I caught myself smiling back without thinking.

I found him, Mama, the angel you sent.

His footsteps became familiar in the quiet house. A shuffle here, a creak there. Soon every small movement fell into place, as if we'd been doing this for years instead of hours. It couldn't be this simple. To be so comfortable in the presence of a stranger, even if he was an angel. Nothing in my life was ever simple.

The sunlight faded. He got up from his chair and turned to me. "How about some dinner? I don't have much, but what I have is all yours, child."

"Sure, do you have any eggs? We could have some scrambled eggs and toast, and I even know how to make it."

His smile warmed me. "As a matter of fact, I do. Follow me, we'll make it together."

I gathered the ingredients from the fridge, and Pop found a

skillet and mixing bowl. He slid a chair up to the counter, allowing me to break a few into the bowl. After I'd whisked them enough, he dumped them into the hot skillet while I worked on our toast.

My limbs grew heavy after dinner, and my eyelids followed suit. Pop looked as tired as I felt. I retrieved my nightgown from the bureau, letting the soft fabric bunch between my fingers. But I hesitated. This wasn't like home where I could simply change when I needed. This was someone else's home.

"Can I change my clothes in your restroom?"

The question came out smaller than I meant. It felt like I had asked him for permission to breathe.

"Of course, dear. You don't have to ask. For all intents and purposes, this is your home for now." His reassuring tone relaxed my fearful tension.

"Okay, Pop."

I came out of the restroom to find he'd already made up the couch. I clung to my dirty clothes. What was I supposed to do next?

"You can drop those in the basket next to the washing machine. Have you got any other clean clothes to wear in the morning?"

I nodded.

"We'll put them in the wash tomorrow. I don't think I have anything that'll fit you. We never had children, Mona and I."

His voice trailed off. For a second, I saw it in his eyes. A glimmer of sadness. A reflection of myself.

"Let's get you off to bed, it's late for a young lady such as yourself."

"Thank you for making my bed. I'll get it all cleaned up first thing tomorrow."

He needed to know I wouldn't burden him with extra chores. That I was big enough to tidy my own messes.

"Goodnight, dear. You'll be safe here." His quiet promise lingered in the air.

"Goodnight. I'll see you in the morning."

Chapter Six

My fingers tightened around the doorknob. I tried twisting. Yanking. The skin on my palm began to tear away. Each failed tug sent a jolt of frustration down my spine. Every attempt led nowhere.

Mama's voice called out again. This time it was more frantic.

"Mandy, where are you? Please help me!"

The door refused to open, no matter how hard I pulled.

"I'm trying. Please, hold on!" I screamed.

Tiny fists swung toward the door, disjointed and sluggish. Every hit barely thudded against the wood, like trying to punch underwater. My limbs were useless. It was as if I had been glued to the floor, making any attempt to move futile.

I pleaded with my legs. They refused to obey the panic coursing through me. I stumbled. Each step became more difficult than the last. The air itself thickened—trapping me in place. I struggled to push on.

The bedroom window drifted further as I dragged myself to it. It wouldn't open, so I used my stool to smash the panels out of my way. The risk of getting cut by the small shards of glass left behind wasn't even a concern. I inspected my body once I made it through the opening. Not a single scratch.

I saw my parents through the front room window. Oblivious. Almost peaceful. They looked the same as they always did. Her hands rested in her lap while she stared ahead into nothing. His head tilted back against his chair in the usual way he rested after dinner. The sight of them was familiar but wrong, so terribly wrong.

The room dimmed, but they didn't flinch. Darkness curled

around them, and still, not a single glance toward the door. Mere minutes passed following my mother's panicked voice screaming my name. It didn't make sense.

I slammed my fists against the glass. Nothing. Neither of them looked up. Smoke crept in slowly at first, thin like a thread, curling at their feet. Then it poured in. Gray. Suffocating. Swallowing the room whole in one greedy breath.

Still, they sat motionless.

"Mama, you have to get out of there!" Each word tore through the back of my throat. The sound of my voice became wild and broken, like my vocal cords were being scraped raw. I screamed in hopes the sound would reach them. "Help, someone help me!"

Nobody could hear me. Within seconds, the entire room smoldered. Everything in its wake became clouded. Engulfed. I couldn't see them anymore. I wailed in a way I hadn't done in years.

"Shhh. It's okay, child." A voice whispered through the dark. "I'm here, Amanda. It's gonna be alright."

I jolted awake. My breath paused in my throat. Still shaking from the dream. I needed a second to remember where I was.

"I'm sorry I woke you up. It was just a dumb old dream, you can go back to bed now."

"Nonsense. How about I fix us both a cup of hot chocolate? And I'll stay close by until you fall back asleep, alright?"

Relief filled me when he offered to stay. The dream frightened me in the way little children worry about the boogeyman. It wasn't real. Still, the image lingered in my mind.

Pop spoke about the things he liked doing when he was my age. Our childhoods differed more than I could have ever imagined. It was baffling to think that not all children lived a life like mine.

I tried hard to stay awake. But a belly full of hot cocoa made my eyes fight to keep from closing. Pop's stories were so different from anything I knew. Better than any book or TV show. I couldn't wait to hear what else he had to say.

Sleep came back. This time it was quiet and dreamless. By morning, the light snuck in through the curtain. I rubbed my eyes, reality hitting hard. Yes, my parents were still dead. Yes, a curious old man, possibly an angel, perhaps a demon, had taken me in. I groaned at the realization.

I looked at the front door, finding it slightly ajar, which struck me as odd. I watched Pop shut it tight and lock it before we went to bed. What if a terrible thing happened to him while I slept? He could have gone outside and fallen, or worse, somebody could have come inside and taken him away. I threw the covers off, ran over to the door, and pulled it open.

Nobody was around. I walked to his bedroom and called his name. Nothing. My pulse kicked hard. I stole a peek inside. His bed was made, the room empty. I didn't bother with shoes, but instead just ran through the front door in my nightgown and bare feet.

"He's dead. Don't look for the body. Get your things. Get away from here."

"He's here somewhere, I gotta find him. Pop? POP, where are you?"

I stepped off the porch. Looked left and right in a panic. Nothing but an empty yard met me. This couldn't be happening. Not again.

But then I spotted him. He stepped out of the barn with a large box in his arms. My breath spilled out in shaky spurts as my legs carried me to meet him halfway.

"Well, good morning, little lady," he said before taking notice of my tear-stained cheeks.

My voice caught. I didn't want him to find out I'd been crying. But my trembling hands and quick sniffles betrayed me.

He set the box on the ground at our feet.

"What's the matter, dear?"

I buried my face into the side of his shirt. "I couldn't find you, so I tried calling your name and looked all over. I'm sorry I got so afraid."

Pop's hands rested on my shoulders, his touch gentle but grounding. His eyes locked onto mine.

"Nothin's gonna happen to me. I might be old, but I'm tough, okay?"

He said it softly, as if his voice alone could keep my nerves from breaking. I still shook as he wiped the tears off my cheeks like they didn't scare him. Like they meant nothing at all.

Once he saw I'd settled down a little, he picked up the box again and nodded for me to come on.

"I didn't mean to cry. It was a little scary when I couldn't find you, is all. I won't do it again. I promise."

I said it the way I knew a grown-up would. Like I could handle things. Like I wouldn't cause trouble.

He stopped walking.

"Let's not make promises we can't keep."

"I'll try real hard. You'll see. My parents already taught me how bad crying is. So you don't have to worry about—"

Pop's face softened when he looked at me. His brow pulled in like he could feel it too.

I opened my mouth to try to convince him further. He lifted his hand before I could get any more words out.

"There's nothing wrong with crying. You feel what you feel. Let it all out."

The words hit something deep. Like a blanket I didn't know I needed.

"Now, I don't know everything your parents taught you, but try to remember, they were them, but I'm not them, I'm Pop. When it comes to me, you can laugh or cry or sing or shout. I'm gonna be happy to be there for it either way."

I studied his face for a moment. There was no way to tell if he meant it or not. Could I honestly cry or feel whatever came up? The idea of such a thought filled me with more questions than I knew how to ask. The more I spoke to Pop, the more he seemed like an odd man. But maybe I was the odd one, too used to hiding everything.

I shook the thought away.

"What do you think's in the box?"

He set it down in front of his chair, pulled out an old pocket knife, and started slicing through the tape.

"Well, a long time ago, Mona's niece used to come stay with us for a couple of weeks every summer. I know Mona put the clothes she had here in a box and asked me to haul them off to the barn. I believe this is that box. Let's see here."

The tape tore loudly in the quiet room as Pop's knife cut through it like paper. I leaned in as he pulled the plastic back, allowing a treasure trove of bright, colorful dresses to spill out..

I gasped at the sight. Let my fingers run across the fabric.

"Wowser! They're so soft. And the colors; I've never seen anything so beautiful. And I can borrow them? You don't mind?"

"They're yours to keep. Some of them. All of them. Whatever you like, my dear."

My hands hovered over the edge of the box. The beating in my chest still hammered from before. I swallowed hard. He was here. He was fine. I was fine. My fingers brushed over the soft fabric as a foreign feeling stirred inside me. If only Mama could see this moment. She'd know I'd be okay.

"These are the prettiest dresses I've ever seen."

I could hardly believe they were mine. The first hint of a whole new world of color and softness I didn't know existed.

"Why don't we make two piles? One for the clothes you want to keep and the other for the clothes you don't. How's that sound?"

"Oh sure, sure." I inspected every piece before deciding which pile to put them in. When we were finished, I had a large stack of dresses, more than double the ones I didn't think would fit me.

"Well, how about that? Let's go ahead and take these into the washroom so we can get them clean for you. I think we're gonna have to make space for your clothes in another drawer or two."

I followed him. Paid close attention as he loaded the clothes into the washing machine. The rhythm of his actions stayed steady, like second nature to him.

"Could you teach me how to do it?"

My voice turned shy again. Maybe children my age knew more than I did. I'd never seen a machine like this before; it was so clean and new. This one looked nothing like the old rusted one back home.

"Of course, it's not too difficult." He replied before showing me how to measure the soap and which buttons to press to get it started. "When the timer goes off, I'll show you how to work the dryer too."

Back at our old place, the washer sat in the kitchen. We didn't have a dryer, so everything went out back on the line. When it rained too much and the cold made the clothes stiff, my father hung a cord in the hallway. We made do by letting them dry there.

"Thank you, Pop. I appreciate you teaching me how to use your machines. And for the clothes too. I've never had such pretty things to wear."

"I'm glad I thought about this box. Those clothes have been waiting a long time for someone to come and take them out of hiding." He pushed the knob to start the washer.

An idea came to me as I thought about the clothes. "Do you think we can have a fashion show later? I could try on all the new dresses. Oh, and you can wear that fancy hat by the door."

A curious mix of nervousness bubbled up as I imagined the fun we could have. For a moment, the essence of a child peeked through. The steel bars caging my innocence bent ever so slightly.

Pop's lips curved into a soft smile. I caught his eyes twinkling as if I'd just suggested the most delightful idea. "A fashion show, huh? Now, that sounds like a fine time. I reckon I'll have to dust off that old hat just for the occasion."

I offered him my best practiced smile.

"Come along. I'll show you how to get the shower going and then make us a nice pot of oatmeal." He ushered me out of the washroom.

I followed him, curious what he could gain by being so welcoming. His patience and attention differed from my father's. Even Mama rarely had time for playing games or make-believe. Did people really live carefree and happy all day long? The question rattled my knowledge of reality.

Could he be a good person? I certainly *hoped* he was everything he seemed. But the fear of not knowing worried me. I tried not to think about it. To be grateful for the moment of peace I'd found. These types of moments never lasted long.

Chapter Seven

Standing beneath the steady stream of hot water, I let myself be small again. It hadn't been easy hiding who I was from Pop. The little girl who couldn't make sense of a world flipped upside down threatened to slip through at every turn.

I turned the hot water higher, hoping the steam would alleviate the ache. My eyes clamped shut to keep the tears from falling. To stop myself from remembering. But the memories came anyway. Each tear mixed with the water already running down my face.

I cried for my mother, and for the man my father used to be. I could almost see him again. Not the one who yelled. Not the one who brought terror. There used to be another man living inside his body. A man who held me close long ago.

His voice echoed across my memory. It had been soft once as he sang lullabies I'd long forgotten. Years passed. I'd been clinging to the hope that one day he'd return. In his death, all hope died too.

After my shower, I got dressed and inspected my face. Little evidence remained of the crying mess I'd been moments before. The bruise on my back pulsed when I bent over. Purple and green. Ugly. I stood slowly, letting the pain settle before I grabbed the rest of my clothes and got on with the morning.

I pulled out my comb to undo the tangles in my hair. Mama's job. It took only seconds for me to get it caught. I struggled to get it out. There was no choice but to go ask Pop for help.

Pop's hands were a little shaky. With a furrowed brow, his movements remained slow as he worked to free the knot.

"We'll get this, you'll see."

His soft voice remained calm. Reassuring even. Each careful tug was like a tiny act of kindness. As he worked, I realized how much care he put into untangling it. The same as he'd done with the bandages on my feet.

He spoke up once he'd conquered the stubborn comb. "Don't worry too much about your hair. Let's have our oatmeal before it gets cold and afterwards I'll get you one of Mona's brushes. That'll work much better than your little comb."

I watched him prepare his breakfast in awe. He drizzled honey over the bowl. A healthy scoop of butter. A handful of blueberries. I followed his routine of mixing the sweetness into the bland mush. With the first bite, a surprising burst of flavor met my taste buds. I learned by the second spoonful how good oatmeal could actually be.

We worked together on my hair after breakfast, then ventured out back so I could paint while Pop sat in his rocker. The clothes were done before lunch, but we ate first.

Then came the fashion show. I stepped out of the bathroom feeling like I might be almost pretty. Bright colors sashayed around me. I gave it a little strut, just for fun. The soft fabric of the dress created a cheerful whirlwind around me.

Pop helped me tie the bow in the back extra tight, not noticing my body tensing as the ribbon pressed against the remnants of my father's abuse. I'd keep my promise to Mama, nobody would ever find out about the things he'd done to me; then they wouldn't know how bad I'd been before.

I ignored the pain in my back, shaking away the thoughts threatening to spoil our day, and gave my best attempt at a curtsy. Wobbling and clumsy, Pop's smile beamed at my effort.

"Well, don't you look as pretty as a picture!"

His eyes sparkled. I laughed, a little shy, a little proud.

"You look real smart in that hat, Pop."

He grinned at the compliment I offered him. The feeling left me warm. This sweet old man was a stranger, and I was the plague. Maybe he wouldn't notice if I kept him smiling.

"This here's a Polaroid." He held out the boxy thing slung over his shoulder. I looked at it as though it were some kind of magical machine. He pushed a button. A soft whir filled the room, then a square popped out of the bottom. Bit by bit, the picture showed itself.

"That's neat-o!"

"Let's go out and find some sunshine."

Pop had this cheerful glint in his eye. No grown-up had ever been so happy to play with me. Not even Mama.

"Yes, let's go." I grabbed his hand to walk together. He jerked it back for a second, but relaxed and held firmly to mine as well.

The sun basked warm across our faces as we posed and laughed, the camera clicking with every silly face we made. I twirled to let the dress flare out around me. Pop lifted his arms like a ballerina and stuck the landing. We doubled over laughing, barely breathing as we waited for the photos to show.

He gave me an empty photo book when we went back inside. "Here you are, dear. Why don't you pick one of those pictures for me to keep, and you can put the rest inside the album?"

I clapped my hands. "Oh, thank you. I've never had one of these before. Mama had one, I think. Would it be alright if I put my picture of my parents in here too?"

"Well, of course. That's your book; you can put in whatever you like. I'm gonna see about a snack for us. You can show me how you decided to arrange the photos when you're finished."

He shuffled into the kitchen, and I got to work. I slipped each photo beneath the plastic cover, pausing at the last page. Gently, I pulled out the picture of my family. My fingers brushed over it to trace the familiar faces. I took a deep breath and placed it at the end of the album. My family, too personal a memory to share.

I closed the cover, alone with my thoughts. The house had fallen too quiet, like it was holding its breath, waiting. The Unseen came again, slithering through the silence.

"He's afraid of you, you know. That's why he doesn't hug you. Why he doesn't want to hold your hand. He knows what you are— a bad little girl. You made your parents die."

"He's not afraid of me," I insisted in a low whisper. "Angels aren't afraid of anything."

"Except evil. You pushed him to it, Amanda. You never smiled the right way. You complained. And you kept talking to me, even when they both told you not to. Even when he belted you and made you sleep outside. You talked to me the whole time."

"But I was afraid. I'm scared of the dark."

"You weren't afraid, you were evil. She got hit when she snuck you back in."

"Please stop."

Angry tears brimmed in my eyes. I couldn't let them fall. Couldn't let Pop see them. He'd know then I was bad.

"How many times did he hurt her because of you? How many?"

"I said stop!"

My hands balled into fists of rage. What did this *thing* know anyway? He didn't even have a face. And if I were truly evil, why would Mama have sent me to find an angel?

Forcing the tears to dissolve, I wrestled with the notion of whether I deserved to be here or not. This place held a sort of magic, the kind I couldn't see but knew existed. Magic I hadn't earned. The differences between then and now were stark. Did Mama die because of me? Was it my fault?

Pop called me into the dining room, unaware of the battle twisting inside me. He pulled me out of the bad thoughts. Told stories, sweet ones, and I let him.

We sat out on the porch after we ate, the sun a form of therapy against my skin. I sat on the edge of the porch to see if I could get my whole body into its rays.

"Go on and explore. There's more to see than an old man reading last week's news."

At first, I lingered close to the porch. An invisible boundary lay just a few feet away. It dared me to cross. Coaxed me further from the house and closer to nature. I looked over my shoulder, expecting him to call me back. But he only smiled from his chair and waved me on. I accepted that I could keep going. My feet hesitated, but the pull of the vast open space proved too strong to resist.

Every day turned into an adventure right there in Pop's yard. With so much to take in, it became a learning process for Pop and me alike.

But I stayed cautious. I slid chairs in silently so as not to let them scrape the floor. When I walked, I stayed on the balls of my feet. My steps barely made a sound. The lessons from home were always there beneath the surface of my every move.

I smiled when I didn't feel like it. Pop's face brightened three shades when I did. My politeness became my armor, a shield to protect myself in this new place. Any mess I made, I attended to right away. Pop usually didn't even know there had been any mess at all. I prayed he would let me stay, and I kept myself cautious not to become a burden under his watch.

I'd catch Pop looking at me from the corner of his eye sometimes. He wore a thoughtful expression but never said much in those moments. I didn't understand what lived in the way he looked at me. I feared he would see through all the careful smiles and quiet steps. It made me wonder what his thoughts were. Did he know how hard I tried to be big for him?

He sat down beside me on the porch one quiet morning, staring at the trees while trying to gather his thoughts. His voice came out soft. Hesitant. It struck me as odd. The Pop I'd grown to know was neither of those things. But he'd been thinking about these words for a long time.

"Amanda, you're a good girl. I see how hard you try to be more than that. To be cautious. Quiet. Always so careful not to make any sound."

He paused. The lines on his face deepened. I didn't know where his statements were headed. Not knowing made me fear what could come next. It didn't make sense to feel so nervous. So far, everything he said was right. I'd been doing well.

"It's okay to be a child. To feel excited and make noise. You don't allow yourself to laugh often. When you do, you hush yourself at once. I don't want that for you, dear."

"I'm sorry, Pop."

I meant it, but the words didn't sit right. I'd learned early on to always apologize first, one of the things Mama taught me to keep my father calm.

Over the years, it became an unconscious reflex, like breathing. But Pop wasn't like my father. Guilt twisted in my chest.

"No ma'am, there'll be none of that. You don't need to apologize so often. It's okay to just be and not feel sorry for it. I want you to have a real shot at being a little girl while you still have a chance; it's been a long time coming. You understand what I'm saying?"

I nodded, but the words were edged in uncertainty. Could it really be so simple? Just let go? What if I made too much noise or said the wrong thing? What if being happy made me lose everything again?

He stood up and gestured for me to stand too. "Let's start with baby steps. Our first order of business is to see who can get to the front door and back the fastest. Here are the ground rules: you gotta run directly through the house, and you gotta make as much noise as possible."

A small giggle slipped out. My hand covered my mouth to block the sound at once. An instinct I couldn't control.

"Oh yes, and one more important rule, you gotta set your laughter free. It's not fair to keep such a pleasant sound all to yourself." He moved his body into an awkward racing stance. "Alright. On your marks, get set, GO!"

I took off like lightning. Feet pounding the floor, faster with every step. As if something inside me had finally broken loose. The house woke up to laughter like it had never heard before.

Pop's steps trailed behind me, the sound of his joy making me run faster. I passed him in the kitchen. We were both breathless from the rush of it all. His joy rolled through the house, chasing mine.

I stood there trying to catch my breath. My cheeks were wet again, but it didn't feel the same. I brushed my fingers against my skin, pulling my hand away to find fresh tears glistening in the sunlight. Panic and confusion set in. I was happy, so it didn't seem right for me to cry. These were a different kind of tears, though. Instead of leaving me empty inside, they'd crept up from somewhere deep within me, bringing out emotions I never knew existed.

My eyes closed, letting the tears drop as I made a secret wish. *Please let all my tomorrows be filled with tears like this.*

But wishes were cousins to promises, and just as easy to break.

Chapter Eight

Birds sang their morning songs while perched on the branches of Pop's trees. The leaves moved with the breeze, soft and steady. Mother Nature rustled the world awake.

This is gonna be a good day.

A positive thought on my tenth day at Pop's. He hadn't gotten out of bed yet.

I put my blankets in the hallway closet and turned to the bureau. The sight of my dresses folded neatly made me smile as brightly as the morning Pop gave them to me. I picked a simple one and moved into the bathroom.

The same wide eyes looked back at me through the mirror. This girl in the reflection had seen and experienced more than my old self. Even my hair held a shimmer that hadn't been there before. It caught a glint of the morning light. Amber, warm. Maybe it was only an illusion, but I liked to think Mama put it there. Her way of saying she still saw me.

When I was ready, I tiptoed to the kitchen, hoping to fix breakfast before he came in. Pop had few rules, but one he took seriously, I never touched the stove unless he stood nearby. I knew I could pull something together without making trouble.

Peanut butter, honey, and a bit of cinnamon—this would be yummy. I grabbed a small mixing bowl and dropped a couple slices of bread into the toaster.

The soft shuffle of his slippers on the floorboards carried across the house. My spirits lifted as each creak came closer to the kitchen. I needed this perfect; warm toast, peanut butter still melting. He stirred into the room right as I finished setting the last plate.

"Well, what's all this?"

I set down two cups and went to the fridge to get the juice.

"I made us breakfast. Don't worry; I didn't go near the stove, just like you said."

He sat and picked up the juice to pour into our glasses. "How very thoughtful of you. I can't remember the last time someone made me breakfast. And this looks delicious too."

Content with his reaction, I took a bite of the toast, which tasted even better than I had predicted. My pride from a job well done made every bite much more enjoyable.

We finished eating at the same time. As usual, I stood up to gather the dishes, but he stopped me.

"That's alright, Little Chef. You let me tend to the dishes this time. It's a fair trade for such a lovely meal."

Out to the back porch after breakfast; a nice routine I'd come to expect. I looked out at the yard while imagining it as it must have been before I arrived. Quiet. Empty. Had he always sat here watching the same sun climb into the sky?

"Did you come out here in the mornings before I showed up, Pop?"

"I did, but not every day. Sometimes I didn't come outside until after dinner when the sun had already gone down. Other times, I stayed inside all day. Sitting outside alone didn't give me much pleasure, not much different than sitting inside alone anyway."

"Were you bored a lot back then?"

The memory of my boredom from sitting in my old room crept into my thoughts. I wondered if Pop might have been as lonely as I'd been at my old house.

"I wouldn't say bored. More restless. I guess I didn't have much to look forward to. I thought about going home a lot."

I didn't know what he meant by going home. I nodded

anyway.

"I look forward to sitting on the back porch with you when I wake up."

He smiled. "Me too, dear. Me too."

When we'd had enough of sitting, Pop went back inside. I stayed on the porch to work on a new painting.

My ears perked up when I heard a woman's laughter spilling through the screen door.

Barefoot, I hurried in. My steps smacked against the floor as I ran.

In the front room, I froze. A woman stood with Pop. She turned to offer me a slight smile, but it never reached her eyes. Not quite as old as Pop, the lines on her face suggested she could be older than Mama. Her stare stayed fixed on me, like I'd invaded her spotlight.

"Hello, you must be Amanda." She bent down over me the way she would a toddler. "My name is Miss Sally. I've been talking with Pop, and he's explained the ordeal you've gone through. I'm here to help, okay?"

I nodded.

Her smile stretched too wide. She looked like those heavyset TV women with round hips and pearl necklaces. The ones who sipped tea with their pinkies out. But she didn't move like them. She was too stiff, almost out of place. Tightly curled salt-and-pepper hair framed a face caked with makeup. Mama would have scoffed to see the amount of rouge on her cheeks. I didn't know what to expect when Pop talked about Miss Sally, but I knew this didn't match what I'd imagined.

"Do you think she knows where her house is?" she asked Pop as if I weren't standing right there.

"Well, she knows which direction—" Pop began to answer, but I cut in.

"I know how to get to my house. You go that way and it's on that road." I pointed to the left.

"What's your last name? Do you know your parents' names,

hun?"

Her voice dripped with too much sweetness, like syrup stuck to your teeth. Every word made my skin crawl. Her fake smile stayed plastered on her face, doing little to lessen my mistrust of her.

"It's Hollings. My whole name is Amanda Lee Hollings. My mother's name is Mary Beth. I don't know my father's first name, but Mama always called him Mack. I know that wasn't his real name." I hid behind Pop's arm to ease my embarrassment.

He spoke in a soothing tone. "We'll figure it out, don't you worry none."

"They've got a telephone down at the feed mill. Why don't you throw on some shoes and we'll head over there?"

I went to grab my shoes, but her words rooted me in place.

"We'll have the police officer come out to talk with Amanda. I'm sure he'll need her too—"

I interrupted her before she could finish. The word "police" sent icy shivers down my spine. "No! No, we can't call them! Please don't let her! They'll take me away, I know they will. Mama said—"

My voice came out sharp and panicked. I darted toward Pop and clutched his arm, knowing it offered the only safety in the world.

Miss Sally's eyes went wide from my sudden outburst. Pop bent down and opened his arms to wrap around me as I buried my face in his shirt.

"Now, sweetheart, nobody's gonna take you away. I won't let them. Listen, we'll go with Miss Sally to make the call and come right back here. If you're afraid, I'll stay with you the whole time the policeman is here."

It hadn't occurred to me that the police could help people. My father always warned me not to talk to them. I knew if they ever showed up at our house, they were there to hurt us in some way.

"Okay, we can call them. They won't take me away?"

"Cross my heart," he promised. Miss Sally shot him a sharp glance, but he paid her no mind.

I finished putting on my shoes while Pop helped Miss Sally bring in the groceries from her car. They put the refrigerated items away and left the rest on the counter. It wasn't like Pop to leave things undone. I didn't like the new feeling of urgency when Miss Sally arrived. What if he'd been counting down the days until he could rid himself of me? What if the Unseen was right and he knew I was bad?

The adults ushered me into the car. Pop kept busy talking while Miss Sally went inside to make the call. Something shifted in him. Barely, but I saw it. The calm slipped a little, and no matter what I told myself, I couldn't shake the dread that settled in.

Miss Sally came back outside within minutes. "Alright, the officer I spoke to said he's leaving now. He'll meet us here and follow us back toward your house, Amanda."

I couldn't speak. Her words were too nonchalant. Too carefree for such a dreary situation. She had no idea what I was going through.

"Now, are you positive you know how to get to your house?"

Her eyes squinted with skepticism. She didn't trust me, and I sure didn't trust her.

I shut my eyes. Tried to see the road again. Left or right? Nothing came clear, like trying to grab smoke. My head spun. Everything blurred. The more I reached for the memory, the more it ran from me. Panic crept up high in my chest. I couldn't get a full breath. What if I never found the way back?

The sting of tears burned behind my eyes. I wrapped my arms around myself to try to hold it together, but the pressure building inside me became too much. My hands shook. I wanted to hide from everything —Miss Sally's questions, the threat of the police, the entire world.

This wasn't the way things were supposed to be. I only wanted Mama to come into my bedroom and wake me for dinner. She said she'd be right back. I ached for this awful dream to end. This wasn't my life. My life had four walls, one window, sagging floors, and wilted curtains. My life had Mama.

"I don't know. I could have shown you the way from Pop's

house."

Pop took my hand into his. "Hey, it's okay. We can go back to my place and start there. Don't you worry."

The officer arrived a few minutes later and followed us to Pop's. He asked me questions I didn't know how to answer. I did my best to give him the information he needed while he took notes of what I said. True to his word, Pop remained right by my side.

He perked up when I mentioned our home used to be a schoolhouse. "I know exactly what property you're talking about. You walked all the way from there?"

"Yes, sir, that's right. It was a long way, and my shoes made my feet bleed a little, so I took them off."

"Well, that's nearly four miles away!"

The number meant nothing to me. Four miles could have been four steps for all I knew. The pity in his eyes shone through his shock. I only shrugged in response. My feet hadn't hurt in days, and I could barely remember the walk now.

He shut the notepad and stood. "Alright. I think I've got enough. Amanda, you're a brave little girl. You've been a big help."

Pop stood up also. "So, what happens now? Do you need us to ride with you to the property?"

"No sir, I know the way. I'll radio the station to send the coroner and someone from the crime scene department. We'll take care of every-thing. A social worker will be by sometime this afternoon. Sit tight until then, alright?"

Pop's jaw tightened briefly as he turned toward the officer. He forced the corners of his mouth into a smile. I saw him trying to hold something back. I didn't know what, but it was there.

"Yessir. We'll keep an eye out. I appreciate your help."

A chill filled the air as Pop's eyes met Miss Sally's in a silent conversation for the people in the know.

"Pop's lying to you. So is Miss Sally. Look at their faces, they're keeping things from you."

"Please stop," I whispered. "Pop wouldn't lie, he's the angel Mama sent to keep me safe."

"How do you know? He could still be the demon; demons are good at tricking humans."

"Then maybe you're the demon…"

Chapter Nine

Miss Sally stayed after the officer left, parking herself at the kitchen table to talk to Pop. I needed her to go, to leave Pop and me alone so we could continue our adventure without her prying eyes.

"Would you mind hanging around until the social worker shows up to speak to Amanda?" he asked in a worried voice.

"Of course, anything you need. I've got the whole day free. Bobbie's gone to one of her friends' houses for a sleepover."

Her voice curled like cream gone sour. Too sweet. Too fake. It made the inside of my stomach turn. I shifted where I stood, itching to cover my ears but too proud to let her see.

I wondered if Bobbie might be her daughter. The possibility of her having a child brought a prickling sense of unease; mothers were soft and patient. This woman was anything but. If she had a daughter, maybe, just maybe, I could meet her. Would she want to play with me? Would she smile and mean it? I used to imagine what it'd be like to have a real friend. Someone who stayed. Someone who didn't make fun of me or disappear when things got hard.

The prospect was always out of reach.

Their conversation moved on without me, their voices floating past like I wasn't even there.

I turned to Pop. "Can I go outside to play?"

He gave me a look. Not stern, but careful. "Stay close, alright?"

"I will, I promise," I said. And I meant it.

"They're coming to take you away today." The Unseen sang

the words, an evil tune intent on breaking my spirit. *"They're coming to take you away..."*

I shook away the sound of my faceless tormentor and focused on my exploration. It took everything I had to block the voice out, but I did. Not long after, a sleek black town car turned onto the drive, tires crunching the gravel like they owned it.

Another cop pulled up behind.

The door opened slowly. A woman stepped out. She didn't look around, just headed for the porch. Her every step was sharp and sure, like she already knew the answers to questions nobody had asked.

She kept her back intensely straight. Each calculated step matched the speed and distance of the one before. She walked like Gort. That robot from Mama's old movie, the one who marched out like he had orders from the sky. Her arms barely moved. Her legs were stiff like she was made of metal. Like nothing soft ever touched her.

I pressed my back against the tree behind me. The bark bit into my skin, but I stayed there anyway. Watched her. Watched the way her feet hammered the ground.

My pulse thudded in time with each step.

Seemingly invisible, I studied her as she waited to be greeted at the door. A serious-looking woman, with dark hair slicked straight back into a bun. Not one piece dared to fall out of place. Her ankle-length skirt and full-button blouse were a combination of bland monotones. I wondered if she'd ever touched her bare feet to wet grass. A betting person would wager she hadn't.

Pop opened the door and invited her into the house. A few minutes later, he called for me to come inside.

My feet dragged in the dirt as I looked toward the barn and then the woods. I heard the Unseen again, urging me to run and hide. But Pop's voice rang louder than the one inside my head, and I knew I had to listen. Each step felt heavier as the earth tried to pull me away from whatever fate waited in the house.

"Hello, Amanda," she said, lips tight like she'd bitten a lemon and never recovered. "I'm Mrs. Blithe. I'd like to have a few minutes to speak with you privately. Let's sit in the dining room."

She gestured like it was a command, not a question.

I looked at Pop. He gave me the slightest nod, the kind that said "I'm right here." So I went.

Her questions were straightforward, carried by a hardened voice and strict demeanor. In a world of endless colors, she existed in a void of solid blacks and whites.

I told her as much of the truth as necessary when she went down her list. Every second stretched like hours. My hands fidgeted in my lap first, then twisted the hem of my dress until it wrinkled. I answered everything she asked, hoping with each word it would be the last. The clock hands turned slowly and grew louder, making it nearly impossible to hear Mrs. Blithe's voice.

She asked about everything from being home-schooled by Mama to how often we went to the grocery store before she moved on to the more uncomfortable topics.

"Did your father ever touch you in any way?"

"Sometimes, I guess so. I got whoopings when I was smaller, but haven't bent the rules in quite a while."

A half-truth. He hadn't given me a traditional whooping in years, but the times he'd shaken me or slapped me across the face remained burnt images inside my mind. Even with the abuse I'd experienced, what she said next still caught me off guard.

"No, Amanda, I mean did he ever touch you like a man would touch a woman? Do you remember any times he put his hands on your private areas? Or did he ask you to put your hands on his?"

I found myself appalled. In no reality could I imagine a father doing those things with his daughter.

"Absolutely not! That's disgusting!"

"I'm sorry, young lady, I have to ask these things. Now what about your mother? Did she ever touch—"

I stopped her before she could say the words. "My mother was an angel."

My fist came down hard on the table. The sound cracked through the room. Heat flushed through me, burning up my throat, my chest, my face.

I didn't mean to cry, but I did.

I saw Mama in my mind. Her fingers combed through my hair. Her arms wrapped around me, humming that low tune only I ever heard.

And then gone. Just gone. How dare she accuse her like this?

I stood up.

"Sit down, Amanda. I'm not finished with my questions."

"I don't want to talk to you anymore," I snapped. "I want to go outside and paint a picture. Pop, please let me go outside."

That last part came out quiet, not because I was afraid, but because it was safer in the silence.

He came around the corner as Mrs. Blithe grabbed my arm. Hard and fast, as if I were her property.

"Now you will sit here and answer the questions you are being asked."

"Hey now, there's no need to grab her like that." Pop demanded.

My last bit of control snapped. The sight of her fingers digging into my arm sent me spiraling, my mind pulling me back to that day. To my father's hand yanking me up by my hair. And Mama lying there. I saw her body again. Still. Cold. Eyes open, but not seeing. Mouth frozen in the middle of goodbye. And her voice, clearer now than ever, still circling my head.

"I'll be right back, my dear."

"Let go of me. I don't want to talk to you. Leave me alone."

I dropped to the floor, unwilling to hold myself up anymore. Folded in. Wrapped my arms around my knees and buried my face. My hands flew to my ears, pressing hard. The noise wouldn't stop. Not the sound of the chaos inside the house, the noise trapped inside my head.

The screaming. The promises. The hatred in my father's voice. The gunshot. If I'd only woken sooner, been bigger for Mama.

Hot tears streamed down my cheeks, soaking into the soft fabric of my dress. Everything blurred together. The room spun until only fear wrapped around me. I couldn't find air. I thought I saw Pop crying, but my eyes were too cloudy to make out anything real. The sound of Mama's pleas blared through my memory. I shut my eyes tight and rocked myself, praying for a savior.

The Unseen echoed through my mind, loud and unforgiving. *"I told you to hide; you should have run. You never listen, and now you'll never get away. They'll take you from Pop, they'll lock you away forever. You'll die alone, like Mama."*

"Leave me alone, leave me alone, leave me alone—" I kept saying it, even as my voice broke into pieces. "I don't want to die alone," I whispered.

The rocking slowed. My head slumped sideways, too foggy to hold up.

Pop came to my defense, standing in the space between the social worker and me.

She began piling her papers back into her bag. "We won't be able to finish this meeting at this time. This child is incorrigible. The hostility she has displayed is direct evidence that she needs an intense psychiatric evaluation."

Miss Sally spoke up. "What does that mean? You'll have to bring a doctor out to meet with her?"

Mrs. Blithe walked to the front door and waved to the officer waiting in his car. "She will meet with a doctor when we get her settled at the facility. They'll complete her intake and add her to the schedule."

"Now you wait one second! You're not taking her anywhere. Amanda is to stay with me, I gave her my word."

Pop's voice came out loud and unshakable, a force demanding to be heard. I watched his whole body grow taller until he appeared to tower over everyone else. His hands clenched into fists at his sides as the usual warmth in his eyes disappeared. A cold fury showed through his expression, determination masking the softness I'd grown so used to. I'd never seen him look like this before, not even for a second.

The officer stepped forward. Intent on de-escalating the already chaotic scene. He spoke calmly in an attempt to reason with Pop.

"We'll have to take her with us, sir. Now that doesn't mean you don't have the right to file a grievance. You're more than welcome to follow us to the facility. There'll be someone there who can hear your argument and present it to the courts."

As though it could ever be so simple.

I could barely speak. "Please… don't let them take me." It came out small—the voice of a girl who'd seen so much and still wasn't ready to go.

I hadn't heard that voice in so long, like a locked-away piece of me had escaped into the open. And I was desperate to stay.

"Let's do what they say, okay? I'll get everything straightened out." He looked at Sally. "Do you mind driving me into town?"

"Of course. I told you before, I've got the whole day. Whatever you need to do."

"I'm scared, Pop."

My voice trembled as Mrs. Blithe's hand guided me toward the door. I clung to his eyes, searching for a promise he couldn't make. Each step carried me further from my angel.

The car door shut with a hollow thunk. The seat swallowed me. I pressed my forehead to the glass. Tried to breathe. Tried to see Pop's porch through the blur. I'd been a fool to believe I could ever be free.

Chapter Ten

I watched the world fly by from the backseat of Mrs. Blithe's car. She didn't speak during the drive, but the hum of the car's engine filled the void within the vehicle. Even the voice in my head remained quiet. I welcomed the dull, empty lullaby. For once, the silence shrouded the chaos in my mind.

Country roads slowly turned into the city streets of Stonehaven, replacing trees and wildflowers with houses and businesses. I could see why my father hated being in town; there was no nature, and everything moved too fast. The people rushing to and fro reminded me of leaves when the wind pulled them from the trees during autumn. They dashed along the sidewalks without knowing they were part of a significant scene in my ever-changing life.

They didn't notice me as they went about their day, careless and free, but I saw them. I took note of their normalcy, wondering all the while if I would ever be the same. My muscles tensed until they were as stiff as the iron gate creaking open before us. Its sharp clank echoed across my chest, causing a tightness in my ribs.

"Tualatin Valley Home for Girls," I read the words etched above the entrance.

It didn't look like any home I'd ever known. It looked like something built to hold people in, not welcome them. The building rose from the ground, too big, too gray. Its shadow fell over me like a warning.

Not even the trees wanted to grow too close. The weight of oppressive air flooded in as the car edged forward. I took notice of the building's windows, which were covered with decorative metal embellishments. Under the guise of their stylish design, I could see they were no different than plain bars, intent on keeping what was already inside, in, and everything else out.

If I had to guess what a prison looked like, it wouldn't differ much from what loomed before me.

Mrs. Blithe opened my car door. "Come along, let's get on with it."

She tapped her foot as she waited for me to exit the vehicle. Once I moved out of the way, she closed the door with too much effort. Its sudden slam caused me to jerk. My body jumped, flinching again as her hand settled on my shoulder. Unwelcome and searing. She'd branded me with her touch, a mark I couldn't shake off fast enough.

I looked back to see if Miss Sally's car had pulled in through the gate yet. The driveway behind us remained empty.

She pressed a button on the door and held it until it buzzed. A voice came through the crackling speaker to ask the nature of our visit.

"Good afternoon, it's Diane Blithe. I have a new child with me for intake." She glanced down at me, waiting for something—a smile maybe, or a sign I trusted her. But I didn't give her anything. I stared straight ahead. Didn't blink. Didn't flinch. I kept my eyes on the door.

It clicked as the lock turned. That sound stuck in my ears like a dropped coin on linoleum.

I followed behind Mrs. Blithe, careful still to keep my gaze fixed directly in front of me.

Even without trying to look around at the inside of the building, I could see how much the interior resembled a hospital. I'd only ever been in one once when Mama and I rushed to my father's side after his accident at the lumber yard. Though it was a hazy memory, I remembered it enough to recognize the similarities. I didn't like the eerie feeling that filled me back then, much like how this place made me feel now.

The adults were talking, but I'd become too lost in thought to hear what they were saying. Certainly Pop would be here soon. I knew it wouldn't take him long to straighten this out and bring me back home. By tonight, we'd be sitting on the porch waiting for the crickets to start their song.

Mrs. Blithe turned me over to a nurse before leaving. She didn't give me another glance, and I gave none to her. The nurse she left me with chatted as we went further into the building. Her voice tried to be sweet, tried to settle me. But she wasn't Pop. She wasn't anybody I'd asked for.

"I know this must feel scary," she said, her hands folded like she was praying I'd behave. "But you're in good hands here. We're like a big family. Most of the staff have been here for years."

Years didn't mean trust. Years didn't mean safe. I kept my face still and my arms wrapped tight across my chest.

Her warm words left no trace as they slid over me. I blinked hard to push back the tears pooling behind my eyes. My entire being ached to return to Pop, even more than it ached for the family I'd lost. I had no choice but to revert, to be big again.

The nurse continued talking as we made our way through the home. I listened halfway, but mostly I inspected the area as she gave me the tour.

"This is the cafeteria," she went on. She pointed like she was giving a tour of something nice. "Breakfast is served at seven-thirty, lunch at noon, and dinner's at five."

I didn't ask. I didn't nod. The words formed a knot in my stomach. Like I was a guest in a place I'd never get to leave.

"We all pitch in with the chores. Even the children help to keep the area clean between meals. We've found that if everyone does a little, it adds up to a lot."

"That makes sense. What's that painting up there?"

A wide canvas caught my attention above the windows of the largest wall. It displayed a peaceful field of swaying grass. I could almost feel the kiss of the gentle morning wind causing it to lean to one side. The sun appeared to be coming up, rather than going down, over the old buildings making up the rural community—a fantastic show of time and feeling for a simple still painting.

It stirred my insides, a gentle and undeniable pull. I was overtaken by the feeling that I was standing at the edge of a breeze carrying more than simply air. Memories of places long forgotten came rushing back into my young mind. I'd become so enthralled with the painting that I didn't hear the nurse calling my name.

"Amanda?"

I blinked out of my trance and turned back to her. For a second, my body and mind disappeared from this place and into a reality I'd not yet experienced.

"Thought I lost you for a second."

"I'm sorry, it's just that painting. It's almost as if I've seen it before or something."

"Oh yes. That's a Wells painting, dear. Her art has a way of capturing the viewer and drawing them in. It's of the very property this home sits on. She painted it before they broke ground to build the structure. It's called 'A Brand New Day.'"

"So it's actually the sun coming up then?"

"Yes, I believe so. At least it looks that way. I'd say it's a pretty safe bet the sun is rising. Come along now. Let's get you a change of clothes and settle you into your room."

Unknown to me, an old man with a white beard and a name too important to forget walked into the City Hall building across town.

At first glance, he might have been any other hunched old man shuffling through the halls. But with each step, his stride sharpened and his cane tapped with purpose to show the years had not dulled the fire in his chest.

"I need to speak with Judge Aimson," he insisted to the unsuspecting woman behind the front desk.

The secretary blinked, her fingers freezing on the typewriter keys. An unexpected force behind his words made her throat tighten.

"That's not how it works, sir…" Her words faltered.

He hadn't raised his voice. Not once. But Pop didn't need to. He stood there with his hat in his hand and a look in his eye that could burn holes through stone.

She tried to stand tall behind the desk, but he'd rattled her. You could see it in how she blinked too much and her fingers fussed with the ring on her finger.

He leaned in just a little. Not enough to threaten, just enough to make his point. His jaw was locked tight. His knuckles bleached white against the edge of the counter. His lips pressed flat, like every word he didn't say was still loud enough to hear.

He refused to let his tone assault her, but he needed her to know he was a man who could prove there was fairness left in the world. Still, the truth hung there between them.

They were going to let me come home one way or another. Determination seeped from his pores.

"Pardon my insistence, young lady, but I must speak to him at once. Please tell the judge Pop Wells is here to see him? He'll not leave me in wait, I assure you."

The name Wells caught her attention. Certainly this old man with faded clothing and an unkempt beard couldn't be *that* Mr. Wells. Still, she did as he requested and went to see if the judge would accept the visit. She knew the old man would be let down when she returned. Judge Aimson didn't accept unscheduled drop-ins, but for a select few people.

The judge had always been stern and well-suited for his job. But outside of the courtroom, he was unapproachable. She'd been working the front desk for two years and had yet to overcome her nerves in his presence. Her hand shook as she knocked lightly on the door to his chambers.

"Yes, come in."

"I'm sorry to bother you, sir. There's a man here asking to see you. He says his name's Pop Wells."

The judge's demeanor shifted from annoyance to interest. He rarely let on to any emotions. He was a fair man, but she often wondered if he ever smiled. His face carried no weight from the lines of laughter, though he did have a deep indentation between his eyes from a furrowed brow.

His silent response, a simple nod and a wave of his hand. Her steps slowed as she returned to the front and tried to guess what to tell the old man.

Pop stood taller as the secretary reappeared from behind the judge's door. He ran one hand down the brim of his hat. "Hold tight, my dear," he whispered under his breath. "I'm coming."

Chapter Eleven

The judge came out and invited Pop to speak with him in private.

"To what do I owe the pleasure, Mr. Wells?"

"Just Pop'll do, thank you. I'm here to talk about the scared little girl ripped away from the safety of my home this afternoon. I'm sure you've heard the buzz about town by now."

The judge's expression showed genuine ignorance when he denied any knowledge of what Pop referred to.

Over the next ten minutes, Pop did his best to relay all of the details of what happened with Amanda and her family. When he got to the point of explaining she'd been taken from his home, the judge interrupted.

"Where else would she go, if not the orphanage?"

"I intend to keep the promise I made that I would keep her safe, that she could stay with me. Now, I know I'm getting on in years, but I'm only sixty-two. Many people live well into their seventies. Besides, I'm still as healthy as a horse. Amanda's place is with me, I'm all she's got."

"I commend you for your intentions. Honestly, I do, but it just doesn't suit. She's a child who will grow into a young lady and eventually a woman. She needs space to grow and find herself. You can't expect her to stay living on your couch when she's fifteen or sixteen years old. You've got to understand what they're doing is looking out for her best interest, don't you see?"

"If it's about the space, I'll have a bedroom built for her. I've already told Sally to arrange for a phone line to be installed at the house. I'll do whatever needs to be done to keep Amanda home with me where she belongs, where she wants to be."

"Okay, okay. Listen, you're going to need to get those things started. If you're serious about this, which I believe you are, I'll get a hearing for you scheduled on my docket. It's going to take some time; this isn't an overnight fix."

"When? When can you fit me in?" Pop's heel bounced against the floor, each tap growing sharper. The rhythm of his breath quickened as the judge flipped slowly through his book.

"I have a space available this Friday at nine in the morning. That doesn't leave much time for your attorney to prepare—"

"That'll do. I'll be ready."

Satisfied with the results of their meeting, his steps landed a little lighter as he made his way outside.

He climbed into Miss Sally's car. "Would you mind driving over toward the home? I'm gonna get a room at The Inn. It's close enough to walk over and talk to Amanda, and walkable to my attorney's office too. I'll meet with him in the morning. I'm not goin' home until Amanda's with me."

"Now I understand why you brought the suitcase. You're welcome to stay at my place tonight if you'd like; there's plenty of room. You can stay as long as you need."

Her offer came in vain. She'd long since abandoned any regular routine of cleanliness and knew her house couldn't possibly host guests. The bulk of the housework was done by her daughter, Bobbie, and its current state offered little in the way of hospitality.

"Thanks for the offer, but I'll be alright. I've put you out enough for one day."

They pulled into the front drive of The Inn. The sight of the home's roof in the distance brought a welcome wave of relief, a brief anchor against a current threatening to pull him out to sea.

The moment Amanda stepped into his life, a renewed sense of

purpose stirred deep within him. His once empty days now hummed with meaning. In her laughter and through her tears, he found himself mending too. The aching void he'd ignored for so long slowly faded with every smile she gave him. He had to make this right for her; there would be no rest until she came home.

Miss Sally broke through his thoughts. "I'll wait here to be sure they have a room for you. Give me a wave when you're certain you'll be alright."

There were no issues with the room, so he sent her on her way. After unpacking his belongings and placing his clothes in the drawers, he left to check on Amanda at the home.

His shaky finger pressed and held the buzzer at the front door. "Good afternoon, Mr. Wells here to speak to Margaret Shoemaker, please."

The doors unlocked. He walked inside and followed the old familiar route to the room labeled 'Director.'

The door swung open before his knuckles got close enough to touch it. Margaret stood there, her smile as warm as always. He took notice as her fingers fidgeted at the edge of her blouse; a hint of nervousness betrayed her usual steady presence.

He'd always liked Margaret. When he and Mona first met her twenty-five years prior, they were both drawn to the passion she never feared expressing out loud. Although technically underqualified for her current position at the home, her love for children far outweighed anything taught in a university.

"Well, hello, Pop. It's so lovely to see you." She reached out to warmly shake his hand.

"Good afternoon. I wish I could say I'm happy to be here, but this isn't a social visit, I'm afraid."

"What brings you by? You're here on business then?"

"Not business either. A little girl came in today. Her name is Amanda Hollings and she's nine years old. A social worker by the name of Mrs. Blithe removed her from my care, insisting she needs a psych evaluation. I know there are procedures and rules and whatnot. It's not my intention to get in the way of anything she may or may not need to have done. I'd like it to be known that this little girl is here only temporarily. She will be returning to my care by the end of the week. Any evaluations or other actions you believe she should have done need to be completed by Friday. Understand?"

She sat back in her chair as her eyes flickered with curiosity. A small breath escaped her lips, relieved to find Pop wasn't here to discuss funding.

"I haven't gone through her file yet, but anything you can tell me would help speed things along. If I can get a little background on the girl, I'll share it with the psychiatrist so he knows exactly what to look for during his evaluation." She pulled out a pen and paper to take notes as he gave her the tale of what brought Amanda to the home.

When he finished explaining, she had filled an entire sheet of paper with the most critical points of what he told her.

"I'd like a chance to see her if you think that'd be alright?"

"It might do her good. I'll have her brought to my office at once."

"One more thing I'd like to address before she gets here. That new social worker, Mrs. Blithe, needs to be fired. I would hope whatever job she finds next keeps her far, far away from little children. I didn't build this place to have them ripped away from homes by cold and callous hands. Whether Amanda needed to come or not, it didn't have to be as traumatic an ordeal as she made it into."

"I can assure you if she'd known who you were—"

"Regardless of who I am, her behavior was unacceptable for this type of work. Period."

His tone of authority dissolved at once when the nurse knocked at the door to announce our arrival. In my world, there was only one version of Pop. But he had layers, personalities I would never know.

My fear disappeared. Like a switch had been flipped, only excitement and relief stirred inside of me as soon as I saw him stand from his chair.

He opened his arms and I ran straight into them, squealing as I hugged him tight.

"Pop, you're here! Can we go home now? I don't like this place."

"Hello, dear. Now, I know you want to come home, hopefully you'll be able to soon. I'm sorry I can't take you with me today."

My bottom lip trembled, but the words lay stuck somewhere deep in my throat. The Unseen took advantage of my silence.

"It's too late now, he'll forget about you. He'll leave you here and you'll be alone, just like before. You should have run. You should have run. You should have run."

I flinched as the Unseen tormented me with his chant. The promise of my happily ever after slipped further from my grasp.

"Listen, I'm not going home either. I've rented a room only a block away. First thing in the morning, I'll meet with my attorney and we'll figure this all out. I won't make any more promises I can't guarantee. If everything goes as planned, we should have this sorted out in a couple of days. Do you think you can be brave for that long?"

"I think so. I mean, I know so. I'll be really big, I promise." My lips stretched into the smile I knew he loved. The strength I wanted him to see threatened to fade, but I held tight to my facade of bravery.

"Try to do what they ask you to do. It's alright to feel scared or sad, remember? We've talked about this. You don't have to hide your feelings here any more than you would at home. I do regret this happened, but I'll get it all straightened out. You'll be back home with me before you know it."

The Unseen sneered, his voice drowning out Pop's confidence.

"You're not safe anywhere. They're lying to you. He's lying to you."

My hands shook, but I couldn't let him see. I couldn't let him know how much the Unseen made everything feel so wrong, even when Pop was right in front of me, telling me everything would be alright.

"I'll be okay, it'll be a piece of cake. I love you, Pop."

"I love you too, sweetheart. We make a good team, you and me." He tipped the brim of his hat. Despite everything, a small giggle escaped me.

Sweet Pop, always tucking bits of sunshine into the folds of a gray and gloomy day.

Chapter Twelve

"My name's Amelia."

One of my three roommates spoke up. A small-framed child with bright blue eyes and constant pink lips. She looked out of place; an impossibly delicate thing. Like a porcelain doll trapped within a valley of trolls, I feared she might crack if placed under any pressure at all.

"I'm Amanda."

I answered in a flat voice, almost speaking to myself as I fiddled with the hemmed pocket of the white shirt the nurse had given me. What did one child say to another in an everyday world? Desperately searching for shallower depths, my legs kicked hard to escape the bottomless ocean I'd been dropped into. Did she see me drowning?

She smiled, oblivious to my dysfunction.

The nurses, the girls, and even the beds all merged in an unsettling blur of white. Aside from the different hair colors and heights, we may as well have been part of one big, meaningless machine. Duplicates churned out one by one to keep the monster full.

Everything here terrified me. Matching bleached outfits. Blank stares. Even the smiles plastered on the nurses' faces cast an eerie fog throughout the building.

Two other girls shared the room with Amelia and me, but neither paid me any mind. Had Amelia not chosen to break the silence, I'd have found contentment in staring through the bars beyond the glass.

She rambled on about issues that held no bearing in my world.

"How old are you?" she asked between stories.

"I'm nine and a half. I'll be ten in March."

"Well, I'm already ten. My birthday was last month, June twelfth. I've been here a long time, almost five years. The schoolteacher is nice, but it's been boring since it's summer. Do you like school?"

"I've never been to school before."

One of the other girls stopped reading and looked at me over the pages of her book. She had her long dark hair pulled into a low ponytail resting on one of her shoulders. With dark, brooding eyes, she tossed her hair to the back and laughed. "Great, another dumb, crazy one. You might as well get comfortable here; nobody ever adopts your kind."

"I'm not dumb or crazy. Besides, you haven't been adopted. Maybe you're the dumb one."

My words stung. Anger flashed across her face as she slammed her book closed. When she climbed down from the top bunk, I cowered, realizing right away how much bigger than me she stood.

She charged in my direction, wielding a furious fist. I flinched from the anticipation of the impending blow. The door to our room swung open before she had a chance to make contact.

"Come along. It's time for supper."

The nurse took no notice of the thick scent of drama clouding the air around us. She continued down the hall to round up the rest of the girls.

I took my time leaving the room, distancing myself as much as possible from the angry girl. Amelia waited for me to come out.

"Don't worry about her, she'll forget all about it by the time we're done eating. She's got a short temper but an even shorter memory. You're right though. She really is dumb. And she's *definitely* crazy. That's why she got so worked up back there. The truth hurts sometimes."

A part of me wished the girl had been able to hit me. Maybe the familiar jolt of pain would have brought me back to reality. The past ten days had been a decent distraction, a vacation from what my life had been and would always be; unworthy of belonging in any space, even in my own mind.

I'd been close at Pop's, nearly able to pretend all that had happened was nothing more than a dream. Like the lost memories of my parents before the shadows cast our world into darkness, I pushed down the truth until it didn't control me. But deep down, I knew what I was, even if nobody else figured it out yet.

With my unshakable worries, I followed Amelia around the cafeteria. She didn't expect me to discuss myself too much, which made me even more grateful for her presence. I'd meet with the doctor the following morning for my evaluation and have my life picked apart. I preferred listening to Amelia tell me about what went on in hers.

We finished dinner and cleaned up our trays before working on our kitchen chores. Once we finished, we retired to the common room for social time. Somebody turned the radio on and a rhythm of songs I'd never heard before filled the room. A few of the girls started dancing, but I sat on a couch next to Amelia to watch.

The radio host came on to announce the next song. "Alright now, folks, we've got a hot new track coming. This one's not released yet, but we've been given a sneak peek straight from Motown. Here's *Dancing in the Street* by Martha and the Vandellas!"

Amelia's eyes lit up. "Oh my gosh, they're sharing a secret song with us! Come on, let's dance!"

She grabbed my hand, daring me to stand. The only songs I'd ever heard were the ones Mama played at our old house, and most of those were sad love songs. This one begged me to move and shake. I observed the way the other girls danced and did my best to imitate them. It felt awkward at first, but by the time it ended, I'd laughed so hard my cheeks hurt. For a second, I was human, almost like a normal girl. Perhaps I could manage a few days here after all.

My moment of bravery passed at the intrusive words of a not-so-dear old friend.

"You may as well get used to this. Pop's not coming back for

you. He's gone, Amanda. It's over."

"Stop it," I whispered under my breath. "He'll come back."

"He'll die before they let you out, just like Mama. And his body will rot away alone in that tiny house. He's probably already dead."

"I said stop!"

Amelia stopped dancing, tears welling up in her glassy eyes. "I'm sorry, I thought I was doing a good job. I didn't mean to embarrass you."

"No, you didn't embarrass—"

She turned and ran toward the bathroom as the nurse made her way over to me.

"Is everything okay, Amanda? You look upset."

"Oh, I'm sorry, everything's fine. I was dancing with Amelia and got a little breathless."

I'd become a liar. The line between truth and necessary dishonesty blurred until I couldn't see it any longer. Mama would have been so disappointed in me.

A worried look flashed across her face, but she quickly covered it with a plastic smile. "Okay, dear. Make sure you talk to the doctor in the morning if you're having issues."

"Yes, ma'am."

We retired to our rooms at eight, when we were free to do what we wanted until lights out at nine. Some of the girls read books, others chose to work on art. Amelia and I spent the time gossiping; or rather, I listened as she shared the girls' secrets with me.

"I bet the family who adopts me will be filthy rich. The house will be a mansion and we'll eat caviar for dinner every night," she declared.

Though I'd heard it mentioned on TV, I didn't know what caviar was, and I had no desire to live in a big mansion. My dreams were on a much smaller scale.

"I just hope Pop can adopt me. He'll let me paint pictures on the back porch every day and run in the yard without shoes if I want. It'll be just the two of us, safe and sound."

"Who's Pop?"

"He's the old man who saved me. I had to walk four miles to find him. I thought I might die until I saw his house."

I wanted to tell her about Pop, that he was secretly an angel Mama sent to protect me, but I feared she'd think I made it all up.

Her eyes grew wide with surprise to hear I'd gone on such an adventure. I continued the story, doing everything possible to make it seem more exciting. I left out finding Mama's body and cleaning up my father's brains.

"I'd been left alone at an old schoolhouse for days. There was no phone or anyone to help. When I got too hungry to wait any longer, I picked up my bag of clothes and started walking."

"Oh wow! Did the bag get heavy while you walked?"

"Boy, did it ever. All I had to wear was an old pair of Mary Janes, and they didn't fit right, so I had to take them off. That's when I saw how much my feet were bleeding. I kept walking. I knew I'd find someone who would help me."

"How long did it take you? You must've been so afraid."

Her voice rose with excitement. This may have been the best gossip she'd ever heard. I noticed our other two roommates were staring at me and listening in.

"It took hours. I wasn't afraid of walking, though. It was a lot scarier being alone in the old schoolhouse."

"And that's when you met Pop?"

"Yep, and now he's going to be my family."

There were parts I left out, but I couldn't tell her the whole truth. Some things weren't meant for other kids' ears.

The nurse made her rounds to tell us goodnight and switch off our lights. Once she closed our door, the angry girl from the top bunk whispered to me through the dark.

"Why do you think your family left you at an old abandoned schoolhouse if you're not crazy?"

"I'm awfully tired. Maybe we can talk about this tomorrow."

"Fine, tomorrow then. I'm Linda, by the way."

Satisfied with the possibility of hearing the darker details of my story, she closed her eyes and went to sleep.

I'd been awake for hours when the Unseen slithered into my thoughts. I tried to block him out.

"She's an awful girl and she's out to get you."

I lay still, hoping he'd go away if I didn't react.

"You need to stop her, make her pay for being so ugly to you. The pillow, push it over her face. Nobody'll know what you did."

I clenched my teeth, pressing my fingers into the palms of my hands. Maybe the pain would distract me from his words, from the temptation to listen.

"It's right there, pick it up and do it. She wouldn't be afraid, she wouldn't even hesitate. End her before she ends you."

I covered my ears, which did nothing to drown him out, so I tried forcing my thoughts to extinguish his voice. *Ignore him and think of Pop. Think of leaving this place. Of fresh air and the smell of his cooking.*

I sucked in a breath, held it, held it, held it, until my vision swam. The air burned in my chest. I kept holding it until I thought I might pass out.

Then I exhaled. My body had moved from lying beneath my covers to sitting up, both of my legs dangling over the side of the bed. I found my hands clutching soft fabric. Too tight in my grip. My fingers were sore from the strain.

An eerie silence encompassed the room around me. The Unseen had gone. I didn't remember moving, or even picking up the pillow.

I didn't remember anything.

My stomach lurched as my eyes turned toward the top bunk. What had I done?

Chapter Thirteen

A cough from across the room startled me awake. Morning had arrived. My body lay still, tension creeping into every cell.

Each finger ached from gripping the pillow all night, the ridges from its fabric still etched into my palms.

I hadn't looked, I couldn't.

A rhythmic tune took over my shallow breaths. In, out, in, out; my ominous song, but barely there. I thought that if I didn't move, if I didn't acknowledge the possibility, maybe it wouldn't be real.

But the silence pressed against my ears, a terrible, suffocating sound.

What if she's not breathing?

A shift, a rustle, a creaking from the top bunk. I swallowed hard in anticipation. The forgiving sound of someone turning over in the bed above me met my ears and the tension snapped. I let out a breath so thick that I thought my ribs might collapse inward.

Linda was alive. But I worried next time I might not wake up in time to stop myself.

We filed into the bathroom, toothbrushes and clothes in our arms. Taking turns with the sinks and changing areas, I purposely finished among the last of the girls to leave the bathroom. By the time I dropped my nightclothes in the hamper, the others were already filing out toward the cafeteria. The hallway had gone quiet except for the soft echo of footsteps.

Later, while we were heading toward the common room after chores, a strange sound crept in from the distance. It didn't belong.

Gathering around the windows, we saw them, the quiet morning street filled with a crowd outside the gates surrounding the orphanage. Even through the space and glass separating us, the frustration and determination in their voices echoed across the lawn and into the sanctity of the home.

Their chants were growing louder, which scared many of the other girls. They backed away from the windows, mirroring each other's fearful expressions. I found the scene too curious to look away.

A unity of Blacks and whites, the same as I had witnessed on the television program the night Mama died. Some held signs with slogans I didn't fully understand. *"Stop the Hate," "Civil Rights Are Human Rights,"* and *"End Segregation Now,"* were the only ones I could read from where I stood.

These people were passionate. I needed to know more.

The crowd grew louder and more impatient. A nurse yelled for us to go to our rooms.

"Stay away from your windows. We're going on lockdown until we know what's happening outside." She held her voice steady, but the way her hands twitched gave her away. "I know some of you are frightened, but the police have been alerted and are on their way."

I couldn't tell if they were more scared of the lockdown or the world outside the walls.

We went through the corridor, either driven by fear or the opportunity to get a better look at the situation happening outside. As soon as the doors to our bedroom closed, Linda and I went to the window to keep an eye on the scene. Amelia and our other roommate stayed as far from the window as possible.

Several police officers arrived at the scene. They quickly went into action to create a human barricade between the protesters and us. It was unlike anything I'd ever witnessed, even on television. The threat of danger meant little to me, as did the nurses' warning to stay away from the windows. My curiosity lured me to peek through the glass.

A Black woman stepped forward and stood at the front center

of the protesters. The crowd went silent as she lifted a megaphone in front of her to address them. The world paused mid-sentence. I leaned in closer to the window as she started to speak.

"Two weeks ago, President Johnson signed a document granting equality, granting freedom, and granting justice. Not only for us, but for all people. So our sisters and brothers may be welcomed anywhere in this country as equals. To ensure our children receive the same treatment as white children. The time is now for our people to live with the dignity and the respect every human deserves."

The roar of the crowd startled me. Even Linda jumped back when their cheers rang out.

She raised her hand to silence them again before continuing. "We are here today to demand that all people can live in harmony on this beautiful earth as God himself intended. Unite with me, friends. Stand with me in this moment as we shout that we will no longer be trampled on. The color of our skin or the shape of our eyes will not decide our futures. We are not less than. We are worth this fight. And this is the day our voices will be heard."

The crowd raised their fists to the sky, erupting into cheers that made the first one sound like a whisper. Their voices gave birth to an unwavering determination, one that was not willing to back down. Her words gave me chills. Even though I didn't understand their fight, I closed my eyes and wished their dreams would come true.

Linda veered down at the crowd, a hatred burning in her expression so deep it made me inch away. She didn't blink or move a muscle. Her dark-eyed glare reminded me of the look my father wore on his bad days. She'd been afflicted by the same sickness as him, no doubt.

I thought back to the program I watched the day Mama died and knew now what made it so important. The man I'd called Mr. Johnson was no ordinary man. It amazed me to realize I'd seen the president of the United States, even if only on television. The man I'd envied as he wasted all of those precious pens turned out to be the same man responsible for aiding all of these people's dreams. He must be pretty special, just like Pop.

No sooner had I thought his name than I saw him trying desperately to make his way through the crowd. He looked up at the home in a panic. I tried to give him a reassuring wave, but the bars blocked any chance of him noticing my flaring arm.

The crowd tightened, making it even harder for him to get to the front. By the time he reached the police officers, he'd become winded. My chest filled with worry as the Unseen's threat of Pop dying draped like a wet cloth across my mind.

"Who are you waving at?" Linda asked.

Without shifting my eyes from the window, I replied quickly, "It's Pop."

At the mention of his name, Amelia found her courage and came closer to the window to see him. Both Linda's and Amelia's eyes lit up with curiosity.

"Pop's out there? Which one is he?"

"He's right there in the front of the crowd talking to the police officers." I tried pointing to him. The girls eventually picked him out standing near the line of police.

I watched him as he continued talking to the officers, his voice lost in the sounds of the protesters. Someone handed him a megaphone. My worry twisted into something sharp. Pop never asked for attention, and now the whole world was listening.

"Ladies and gentlemen, if you'll give me just a moment." Pop stood tall near the center of the crowd. His voice rang out like it belonged there. "My name is Pop Wells, and this place has been in my family since it first stood as an empty field more than twenty-five years ago."

The onlookers quieted. Every head turned toward him like they'd been waiting for someone to finally say something real.

"If you're looking for the person with whom your argument can be made, you've found him."

I gasped as he made his speech, unable to believe my ears. It hit me. He'd introduced himself as Pop Wells; I'd never heard his last name before. The painting in the cafeteria. I remembered what the nurse said when she spoke about the artist; she called it a Wells. The way it appealed to me was so familiar because it reminded me of the artist who painted all of the artwork at Pop's house. Mona. His words were true. The realization of it all made me dizzy.

Pop continued talking, but I missed a lot of what he said. I shook the confusion out of my head and focused back on the crowd outside.

"...and I will hear your argument, but this is not the way. Scaring the little girls inside this home is not an answer to your fight for equality. One victim should not be replaced by another simply because you are on a journey for justice. I ask you, please, go home. Your message has been heard loud and clear. We will have a meeting in a few weeks to discuss how we plan to incorporate this new way of living, not just for the sake of some children, but for the sake of them all. You have my word."

Parts of the crowd broke up, while the others stood their ground. The police held firm to the barricade. I sat on my bed and waited for Pop to come inside to check on me. He'd come all this way; surely he'd take the time to stop in.

The girls eyed me suspiciously. Linda spoke first.

"I guess we're supposed to believe one of the richest people in our town let the girl he wants to adopt get tossed into this place? Into his very own orphanage? You're not just dumb and crazy, but you're also a liar. You're never getting outta here."

Amelia's eyes pleaded for me to set her straight.

I had no words to defend myself, and I couldn't have cared less to do so anyway. It wouldn't be much longer until I'd get to go back to Pop's house, or so I hoped.

When the protesters thinned out, the nurses came around to let us know they were lifting the lockdown. They gathered us up to go back out to the common area, all except me. The nurse held me back, explaining she needed to take me to my appointment with the doctor.

"Good morning, Amanda," the doctor greeted me. "Are you feeling alright after the little issue we had outside?"

The way he phrased the question bothered me. Certainly those people wouldn't have considered their gathering as a little issue. Even as a child, I knew these were far more pressing matters.

"Yes, sir, I'm fine."

"That's great to hear. So let's dive right into it then."

For the next few minutes, he asked me about my family and upbringing. When it came time to talk about the day they died, he kept his questions direct, leaving little room for my mind to wander back there. Most everything could be answered by a simple yes or no.

I stuck to my story of finding both my parents dead at the same time; nobody questioned it.

"How did you come under the care of Mr. Wells?"

"He was the first person to answer their door. I walked for hours, until I thought I might die. If I hadn't found him when I did…"

"I see. And is that something you think about often?"

"Is what?"

"Do you think about dying often?"

I shook my head. "I don't ever think about dying, sir."

"Liar. We talk about it all the time."

The Unseen forced his way into my thoughts. I kept shaking my head, hoping I could break his presence loose by the effort.

I knew I must have looked insane to the doctor, but his expression didn't change as he wrote in his notepad.

"There was an incident at Mr. Well's home. A problem between you and the social worker. Do you know what I'm referring to?"

"Yes, sir. You're talking about Mrs. Blithe." I sank lower in my seat, forcing my eyes to drop to my lap. "That was my fault, sir. But she was hurting me. She grabbed my arm real hard and shook me just like…"

"Just like what?"

"Just like my father used to do to Mama. I didn't mean to get so upset, honest."

He softened at my response, setting his pen and paper on the table to lean over and pat my arm.

"Sometimes the things we live through don't know how to stay in the past." The doctor's voice was quiet but weighted. "They hang on. Make a mess of your thoughts."

He took a slow breath. "But we've got to try and work through them, or they'll end up working through us. While I don't agree with Mrs. Blithe's behavior, your reaction created a just cause for alarm."

I wanted to crawl into myself and hide as I remembered how I'd allowed her touch to consume me. All of it came rushing back. Pop's panicked expression and tear-filled eyes. The shock on Miss Sally's face.

"I don't think I handled it very well. Does that mean I'm broken?"

"No, you aren't broken. You're just trying to figure things out, and that's typical for a child in your situation. Let's move on from this. Are you getting along with the other children here?"

"I'm trying to learn how to be like them."

"What do you mean when you say, 'like them?'"

I didn't want to say "normal," as I had no basis for comparison to know whether they were or not.

The silence dragged as the doctor waited for my response. Each wall inched closer until the room was half its original size. The more I tried to think, the further the answer slipped from me. I rambled instead of answering directly.

"Well, I don't want to be like Linda. She's a nasty girl and she's hateful. But if I could learn to be more like Amelia, maybe I could figure out how to fit in with everybody. She's made my time here easier, always knowing what to say to keep me distracted. Maybe that's what everybody does, they distract themselves."

He started scribbling in his pad again before responding. "I'm sorry, there are so many children between this home and the one for boys. Which one is Amelia?"

"Oh, she's one of my roommates. Blond hair, blue eyes. She reminds me of Pollyanna. Have you seen that movie?"

"No, I'm sorry, I don't think I have."

"Well, it's simply terrific. And Amelia, she looks like the girl in the film. You should try to watch it. Do you have children?"

He smiled, putting down his pen and pad. "No, I don't have any children yet, but I'll keep that in mind about the movie. We've gone through enough for today. I appreciate your honesty; that helps speed things along. The nurse should be waiting to bring you back to your quarters now."

I nodded and stood, legs a little stiff. "Thank you for inspecting me. I hope I did a good job."

"You did just fine," he said with a soft smile. "Don't worry too much about these sorts of things. It's all part of the process."

Mrs. Shoemaker was waiting outside when I stepped into the hallway, her face unreadable. I knew it only meant one thing. Pop was here. I all but soared toward her door, my smile refusing to diminish.

"Hello, dear."

He bent down and opened his arms in wait for my embrace. I rushed forward to hug him.

"Hi, Pop. I saw you outside talking to all those people. You sounded really smart."

"Did you now? Well, I'm sorry if you were scared when the crowd arrived. As soon as I heard the commotion, I hurried to come make sure you and all the other children were alright."

"Don't you worry, I wasn't scared one bit. I hope those people get what they're asking for. I don't think their lives are very fair."

"I do too. There's a lot more to it than I'm sure you understand, but I think you get the basics."

"They said they want to be treated like everyone else," I said. "I think I understand what it's like to want to be free."

He looked at me. His eyes glistened before he blinked the shine away. "Yes," he said. "I suppose you do. Let's make a wish for tomorrow, that you never have to want to be free again."

"Okay, Pop. Can I wish for all the people outside too?"

"I think that's a fine idea."

"And if we both wish for it, then it's sure to come true." I crossed my fingers.

Chapter Fourteen

With each passing minute, my anticipation grew until my bones trembled. I couldn't wait to sleep on Pop's couch again with Mona's art pieces to keep me comfortable through the night.

Amelia's voice buzzed through my ears. Her stories became a constant hum in the background of my hours, and I couldn't have been more grateful for the sound. "And then, the doll broke, and Miss Penny said I had to…"

I nodded when I was supposed to, eyes locked on the ticking clock, wishing it would move faster.

By Friday morning, the ache in my stomach had let up. Not even Linda's scowl could break through my mood. She barked complaints about my shoes being untied, but I only smiled. My thoughts were too focused on Pop coming to care.

I held my chin a little higher while picturing myself back in Pop's kitchen. The smell of cornbread baking and the sound of his steps on the wooden floor filled my senses. I'd go home today, I knew it.

"What are you so cheery about?" Linda asked.

Typically, I would have ignored her, but I decided to take the bait instead. "It's court day. Pop's gonna get me after breakfast so I can talk to a judge. This is my last day here."

She rolled her eyes. "Oh, right, I forgot you're still living in a fantasy world. That old man doesn't want you in his house. You're damaged goods, same as the rest of us. You'll see."

"It's sad you see yourself that way. Just because something's been damaged doesn't mean it stays that way. I know that, and I'm dumb. And crazy."

The crimson in her cheeks traveled down to her neck as her fists balled so tight I thought her knuckles might split.

"Even if Pop did plan on taking you, he won't want you once the doctor tells him you're nuts."

Her words were like stones in my gut, but I stood firm. I'd not allow her to see the sting, biting my lip and focusing on the way the morning light hit the window instead. Memories stirred within me of the days when I could only look at the sunshine, but never touch it. Those days were over. Pop would come and sit me right back where I belonged.

Unless he didn't.

Maybe I'd convinced myself he wanted me because I wanted him. What if he knew about the Unseen? What if Linda was right, and he didn't come for me?

Linda's tongue lashed out, venom dripping from every word. Intent on poisoning me with her voice, her speech stung as my newfound fear embedded itself into my thoughts.

The nurse called us to breakfast. In an attempt to get away from Linda, one miscalculated step paired my soft shoulder with the unforgiving door jamb. The cracking sound it made caused Linda's mouth to slam shut, eyes wide as she waited for me to yell or cry out.

I inhaled a breath deep enough to rupture my lungs. She waited for the sound, but when I exhaled, only laughter came out. Tears fell from my eyes and I didn't bother to wipe them. I couldn't stop laughing, even when I tried.

She wanted crazy, and I showed her my best imitation of what I thought crazy might look like. She pushed past me and ran from the room. Mission accomplished.

The throbbing in my shoulder did little to take me away from my small victory, but it did wonders for the splinter of insecurity she pushed beneath my skin. I knew I had to be big again, so I shrugged off the pain and walked to the cafeteria.

Mrs. Shoemaker came to get me as soon as I finished eating. Curious eyes fell upon me, and a whisper of gossip ensued as she whisked me away before we'd even begun our chores.

"Good morning, Amanda. I've got an outfit waiting in my office for you to change into before we leave for court. Pop dropped it off this morning."

"Do you know when he's gonna be here to pick me up?"

"He won't be, I'm driving you to the courthouse along with one of our social workers. We should be—"

"Oh no, not Mrs. Blithe. She hates me."

"No, it's not Mrs. Blithe. Don't worry, just get yourself changed and I'll be right here when you're finished. We're leaving in fifteen minutes, alright?"

"Yes, Mrs. Shoemaker."

She pulled the door shut, allowing me to get dressed.

"He won't be picking you up. He won't be there waiting for you either. You're too much trouble for such an old man. Better you accept it now while you're alone, this way nobody'll see you cry."

"You don't know that. He sent me clothes. Why would he go through the trouble?"

"Why wouldn't he be here to get you? He said he would."

I wasn't sure anymore. Maybe he did, perhaps I made it up. I tried to replay the words in my head, but they all ran together now, one big tangled mess.

Mrs. Shoemaker knocked at the door, forcing me to abandon the conundrum and put on a brave face.

I dropped my voice. "Leave me alone. I'm trying to think and you're making it worse."

Silence, at last.

We made our way outside, meeting the social worker in the parking lot. My eyes went wide when I saw her car. With its round top and short ends, it resembled a regular car that somebody had tried to squish into a bright yellow ball.

Mrs. Shoemaker opened the door and pulled a lever to fold the front seat forward. I seized up.

"What is this thing?"

"It's a Beetle. Have you never seen a VW Bug before?"

I shook my head and took a step forward to climb in. My knees touched the back of the front seat when she pushed it upright again. The seat stuck to my legs. Hot. Tight. Locked in. My chest tightened. What if I couldn't get out?

The thudding in my chest pounded louder with every turn toward the courthouse. I kept my hands flat against my dress so no one would see how bad they were shaking. Every nerve in my body tingled with electricity from the unknown. The women up front didn't notice, they were too busy talking about the weather.

We pulled into a parking space, my body sprang from the back as soon as the seat flipped forward. The sound of my skin unsticking from the hot material made me queasy. A demon of a car; I couldn't get out fast enough.

Mrs. Shoemaker and the social worker stood on either side of me like bodyguards once we entered the building. I scanned the room for a familiar face once we made it inside.

"Where's Pop?"

"Oh, I'm sure he's around here somewhere, probably in an office nearby with his attorney."

"I hope so."

A door across the courtroom opened, and Pop stepped through with freshly combed hair and a confident smile on his face. I saw him standing there and all the weight in my chest finally let go. He winked, and I grinned before I could stop myself. My fingers relaxed for the first time all day.

He followed behind a younger man with determined eyes and jet-black hair. His shoes shone like mirrors. I could tell he was somebody important. I figured he had to be Pop's attorney.

The courtroom became a sea of adults dressed in formal attire, including Pop. He'd trimmed his beard and tamed his wild hair. I decided he looked handsome in his nice clothes.

He gave me a quick nod from across the room and took a seat next to the attorney. A few minutes later, the judge entered.

"All Rise! The Washington County Court, with the Honorable Judge Aimson presiding, is now in session."

Everybody around me stood up when the bailiff announced the judge's presence. I did the same. "Please be seated and come to order."

I didn't have any idea what going to court meant when Pop talked about it. Trying my best to behave and keep still proved difficult while battling the ball of nervous energy threatening to explode at any second. I squirmed in my seat, my legs swinging back and forth as the judge droned on about other people's cases. My eyes glazed over, but I forced myself to sit up straight.

Pop's attorney stood to speak to the judge first. "Good morning, Your Honor. I'm representing Mr. Wells in his petition for guardianship over one, Amanda Hollings. I have here with me all of the required documentation to appease this court's required burden of proof."

The bailiff stepped forward and received the stack of paperwork the attorney offered him, and walked it to the judge.

"I do applaud the work you've put into compiling this information in such a short amount of time. However, I don't see a release for the claim of guardianship from any relatives."

"It's my understanding Miss Hollings doesn't have any known living family."

My back ached from sitting so rigidly, but I refused to slouch. I kept my hands clenched in my lap and my ears strained to catch every word.

"Let the record state that the petitioner has fulfilled all document requirements. At this time, I would like to speak to her current guardian of care. Mrs. Shoemaker, if you could please step forward."

She stood and walked to the podium at the front of the court. "Yes, Your Honor?"

"Thank you for your presence this morning. Mrs Shoemaker, is it your opinion that Miss Hollings would benefit more under the care of Mr. Wells than at the Tualatin Valley Home for Girls?"

"Indeed, it is."

"And you can attest all necessary evaluations, both medically and physically, have been observed to show Miss Hollings is not a danger to herself or others?"

"Yes, Your Honor. Physically, she is a healthy little girl. Her psychological evaluation was completed yesterday. It is the doctor's opinion that her reaction to the trauma falls within the normal degree for a child faced with these special circumstances. He recommends she continue with psychiatric care and treatment as her psychiatrist sees fit."

"When you use the phrase 'normal degree,' are you taking into account the manner in which Miss Hollings found her parents and all she endured before? I need to be sure you're not insinuating her outburst against Ms. Blithe could be part of a bigger pattern."

"No, Your Honor." Mrs. Shoemaker's heels clicked against the floor as she spoke. The voice she used differed from the one she used at the home, her words cutting cleanly through the room. "She has been observed both with and without her knowledge, and I have written statements from two different nurses who've spent time with her during her stay at the home. All sources agree she is a healthy little girl still grieving the horrific loss of her parents. It's believed the incident that brought her into our care was the reaction of an already distraught child, mishandled by the social worker assigned to her case. Mrs. Blithe has been reported for previous grievances and has since been relieved of her position within our facility."

"Have you any other words before you're excused?"

"No, sir. I want to thank the court for letting me speak on this child's behalf."

"Mr. Wells, please approach the bench."

Pop stood up and moved to the podium. "Thank you, Your

Honor."

"Mr. Wells, you've petitioned this court to be the sole guardian of Amanda Hollings. Is that correct?"

Pop stood tall, his face lined with determination. He nodded slowly when the judge asked the question, keeping his hands on the podium as if steadying himself. "Yes, sir, that's right."

"I commend your eagerness to open your life and home to this child, that in itself is a notable act." He paused to find the paper he needed to reference for Pop. "Are you aware of what it will take to ensure this child continues to grow into a responsible adult?"

"I believe so, Your Honor."

The judge's words washed over me. I leaned in closer. He praised Pop the way he would a hero, the kind from the books I'd read.

"I'd like to go over the requirements for guardianship to satisfy the court. Any child placed with a guardian by this court shall be enrolled full-time in the public school available within their respective county. A provision for both mental and physical health care must be in place and upheld by the adult with whom said child is placed. Living arrangements should include a bedroom inhabited by not more than three same-gendered children. Access to emergency care must be available to a reasonable degree. All petitioners for guardianship must provide evidence of their ability to support the child's financial needs before placement. Mr. Wells, do you understand these requirements as they have been relayed to you?"

"Yes, sir, I understand and have completed each one. I've been in contact with the local elementary school. We have scheduled an assessment for proper grade placement for next Tuesday. She will begin care with both a psychiatrist and my family doctor by the end of this month. In the stack of papers my attorney handed you, you'll find all of my financial records."

As Pop spoke, the aching pull of gravity lifted. He sounded so sure, like there wasn't a single thing on this earth that could keep him from walking out with me. I clenched my fists to hide the joy and bit my lip to keep from grinning too big.

He paused in his response while the judge looked through the papers to verify he had the information. He continued when the judge nodded.

"Also in those papers, you'll find the deed to a two-bedroom house bought yesterday afternoon. Amanda will have her own bedroom as well as plenty of room to grow within the walls of her new home. I've purchased a car and there's a working telephone line, in case of emergencies."

Judge Aimson's eyebrows shot up, his lips parting in surprise as he flipped through the papers. He glanced at Pop, reevaluating the man before him.

"Mr. Wells, it seems you've done your part. That leaves us with the word of a child. You may have a seat. Good morning, Miss Hollings, would you be so kind as to come forward?"

With buckling knees and shaky legs, I took my time to stand. All eyes were focused on me now. I tried willing them to look away, but each pair followed my steps to the front of the court.

"*You're going to choke. You'll probably die right here in front of all these people,*" the unseen warned.

I shook the words away while trying to get my feet to move forward. Alone. Mama always spoke for me, my father made decisions for me, and Pop sheltered me. Here I had no shield, no protection from the strangers' eyes.

What if I said something wrong? What if I made him wish he had never come? I wasn't big enough anymore, and right then, I wasn't sure I ever had been.

Chapter Fifteen

My palms were slick with sweat as the judge's eyes bore into me. I lifted my chin like Pop and tried to ignore the knot in my stomach.

"Good morning, Your Highness."

He nearly laughed but stopped himself just in time.

"Good morning, young lady. This'll be easier if you can tell me where you'd like to be and why. Think you can do that for me?"

My toes wiggled inside my shoes, a trick I'd learned to reroute pain or fear without anyone noticing. My lips pulled into the smile I'd practiced for so many years. By sheer will, I managed to stand upright. Every cell in my body was filled with the determination not to let anyone see my fear.

"Well, I don't know where I want to be for sure."

My nervousness grew heavier. I looked over my shoulder at Pop sitting in his nice clothes, his expression now one of confusion.

"When they took me away to the orphanage, they took me away from what Pop told me would be my home. But then he moved to a new house, and I don't know where it is. So even if I don't know the place, I know the person I want to be with, and I just want to be wherever Pop is."

"Very well said, Amanda. May I ask what it is that makes you want to be where Pop is?"

"Because Pop makes me feel safe. He teaches me stuff and doesn't get mad when I mess it up. If I have a nightmare, he brings cocoa and tells me stories. He stays till I stop being afraid."

My voice cracked. My throat tightened, chest shaking. I tried not to cry, but one tear slipped out, then another. Before I knew it, they were falling fast, dotting the edge of the podium. "And because Pop told me it's okay to cry if I need to, and he told me I'm allowed to be small sometimes too. Nobody's ever told me it was okay to do those things before."

"Do you need a moment, Miss Hollings?" the judge asked when my voice cracked.

I shook my head and continued talking. "Pop's house might have been old, but the inside stayed filled with warmth. The kind that wraps around you like a safe blanket. Pop's like that, too. He doesn't wear fancy clothes or worry about a neat appearance, but he has a love in his heart that makes the world feel less scary. He protects me. I love him and I want him to keep me because he's my family now."

I looked at my feet to keep myself from making eye contact with anyone. Mama's sharp voice echoed in my mind. *"Just smile, Mandy. No one wants to see a crying child."*

The tears wouldn't stop, and my mouth refused to turn upward. I'd blown it the way Linda said I would. What was wrong with me?

"Thank you, Miss Hollings. You may return to your seat now."

"You failed. Grow up, Amanda. You're not a baby anymore."

I only had myself to blame. The Unseen's hollow words echoed through my head. I knew he was right. How I wished he was wrong, but I'd blown it. I kept my head down on the way back to my seat, eyes focused on the scuffed-up floor. My cheeks burned. I didn't dare look at Pop, too afraid to see his disappointment.

The judge straightened the papers in front of him, stacked them clean, and moved them aside.

"I want to thank you all for your time and effort in helping this court reach a decision. Under the time restraints, I know that was no easy feat. As all requirements have been fulfilled, this court will support the petition brought forth by Mr. Wells. Guardianship of Amanda

Hollings is hereby granted in full."

His words hung in the air for a moment, and then it hit me all at once. Guardianship granted. The storm lifted. Before I knew it, my body jumped up from the bench. A wide grin spread across my face, and I looked at Pop. He wore a smile as bright as mine.

Pop wrapped his arm around my shoulders and steered me toward the back door. My smile stretched so wide it made my face hurt. I didn't care. I saw Amelia sitting in the back row, watching. She raised her hand in a small wave. I waved back, excitement bubbling up inside me. She could see now Linda didn't know anything, and I wasn't a liar.

"Who are you waving at?" Pop whispered, his voice light, but his eyes flickered briefly in the direction I waved.

"It's my friend, Amelia, we shared a room at the home. Are you getting a new family too?"

A few heads turned at our exchange, and Pop gave my hand a gentle squeeze. "We're not supposed to talk in the courtroom, dear. Let's get going." He kept his tone soft, but unreadable thoughts hid deep in his voice.

Amelia placed a finger over her lips, a playful smile on her face to show she already knew the rules. I smiled at her and gave one last wave, then followed Pop out of the room.

We walked down the courthouse steps hand in hand. Sunlight warmed my skin.

"You ready to see our new house?"

"Yes, sir. Let's go."

"Look at this here." He pulled a strap from the side of my car door and placed it over my lap before attaching it to a clasp on the opposite side. "This is called a three-point seat belt. These were invented a few years ago. The salesman said that soon all cars will have them. They're a little scratchy, but he said the belt could save our lives if something happened."

I ran my fingers over the rough material, still getting

accustomed to its feel.

"It's really neat, Pop."

"Mhmm," he replied before closing my door and getting into the driver's seat.

We left town using the same route Mrs. Blithe used to bring me in. I watched again as all the houses and businesses turned back into trees and wildflowers. Relief filled me when I realized Pop's new house was still in the country. I wouldn't have complained either way.

He pulled the car onto a long driveway lined with large Red Maple trees. Their delicate leaves swayed in the summer breeze. Each mesmerizing shadow they cast danced across the car's hood as sunlight slipped through their cracks and spaces. A kaleidoscope of red and burgundy spun above; a natural beauty like I'd never seen. For a moment, my awe became more important than my breath.

"The trees, Pop." It was the only thing I could think to say.

At the end of the driveway, a small cottage waited for us. It looked like it had been expecting me. When we went in, a large stone fireplace sat in the corner of the front room aching for the cold of winter to welcome its flames. My mind drifted, imagining how much fun it would be to help Pop gather wood so we could burn it while enjoying his famous hot cocoa. I'd never craved cold weather until then.

"Your bedroom is right through here," he said as he led me through a doorway on the right side of the front room. "Mine's the one on the other side. What do you think?"

"It's amazing. This is the best house in the whole world. There's so much space."

"It does feel bigger. It's not much bigger than the other house, but the ceiling is higher, and there are no hallways, which adds up to a lot of room to move around."

He gave me a tour of the rest of the house's interior before we went out the back door to see what was waiting outside. There in the backyard, I saw the one thing I always wished to have, but had accepted I never would. My very own swing set.

Everything inside me rushed up at once. A jolt ran through my chest so hard I could feel it in my throat. I didn't know what to do with it.

"I'm so happy," I shouted to the sky as my arms stretched out to heaven.

I didn't know where the words were meant to go. Maybe they were meant to reassure Mama I'd be alright. It could have been a bold display of defiance against every rule and punishment my father had forced upon me. Despite what he'd done in his life, I'd found happiness after his death.

All that mattered to me now was Pop's reaction to my outburst. His genuine laughter, the sound infectious, became the only thing I craved during the happy times. The joy had always been there, waiting for this moment to bring us together. I held onto it gingerly, fearing it too would slip through my tiny grasp.

Chapter Sixteen

The new house gifted us with a maze of possibilities. Carefully labeled boxes waited to be unpacked, every item begging to claim a place in our new home.

The fresh paint mingled with the earthy tang of cardboard in the air. Each box we emptied held the promise of a new chapter for Pop and me to navigate together.

I let out a low whistle as my eyes drifted over the fortress of boxes.

"Looks like we brought a whole world with us."

"Sixty-two years of it. We'd better get started, huh? You go ahead and unpack your things, and then we'll work on tackling this mountain together."

I nodded and ran into my bedroom, fighting the urge to skip. One large box waited for me. I pulled open the flap to find a trinket waiting atop my clothes. It sparkled as I turned it over in my hands. I hurried out to the front room, the gift held tight in my fist.

"Thank you so much for hiding a present in my things." I wrapped my arms around his neck to offer him all I had, a hug. "Umm… what is it, though?"

He turned the small rotating hinge on the side of the locket, causing it to flip open.

"It's a keepsake pendant. We'll have to get you fitted for a chain later. I thought it might be a safe place to keep your mother's lock of hair. You could wear it on days you miss her the most, or every day, or hang it somewhere in your room. Whatever you like."

Every box opened to a trove of treasures, revealing fragments of Pop's life. As I peeled back the tissue paper, he stayed close by. His eyes sparkled as he told me the story behind each little trinket. I hadn't lived those memories, but the way he spoke, I could almost see them.

"Do you want me to unwrap the paintings, Pop?"

He smiled from his perch on the stool. "Sure, I think that'll be alright. You know what would help? You could find the places where they ought to go."

"Really? You'd let me choose?"

"Absolutely. This is your house too. You should have a say in how it's decorated."

Unwrapping each painting carefully, I paused and gauged the mood of the room. To make sense of the task, I categorized Mona's paintings by size and type. The bare walls called to me, each waiting for its perfect match.

Working methodically, I held the art against different walls before placing it on the floor below where it would hang. By the time I finished, Pop had completely unpacked the front room and moved on to the dining room.

"I'm done." Pride flooded into my voice. "I think I did a good job."

He rose from his stool. "Well, let's have a look. Perfect timing too, I could use a break."

We started in the dining room, then moved on to the kitchen, and finally to his bedroom. I trailed behind him, my nerves causing me to fidget all the while. What if he didn't like my arrangement or if he wanted one of the animal paintings I'd placed on my bedroom floor? Would he think me selfish for taking them all? But he nodded at each choice with a smile.

"This is interesting," he said after inspecting the front room. "I like your system. It's more organized than the one I had at the old house."

"How did you decide?"

"Well, we didn't really put much thought into it," he said with a laugh. "Whenever Mona finished a painting, we just hung it wherever the wall looked empty. It was chaotic, but she loved it. The way the room lit up when she smiled—you and she would've gotten along famously."

"Oh, I think so too. You talk about her so much, I feel like I know her."

Pop's gaze lingered on the biggest painting, the little girl on a swing. I'd admired it from the first second in his old house. The way her carefree afternoon caught in the brushstrokes, with a subtle hint of so much more embedded in her eyes.

He picked it up gently, a soft smile tugging at his lips.

"This one's special. It meant the world to Mona."

"I like it too. Sometimes back at the old house I talked to her. She talked to me too."

Pop's brow furrowed slightly, but he said nothing. "This is called *'Once Upon a Little Girl.'* It's Mona as a child."

"She's smiling, but her eyes are sad. That's why I like it. I used to smile when Mama told me to, even if I was really sad inside."

"You're not wrong. Mona carried a lot of pain with her. It's the burden of a life filled with tragedy. Her father died in the First World War when she was eight. Then her brother got sick, and after months of hope and heartbreak, he passed too. By the time she turned twelve, her mother was diagnosed with cancer. She died before Mona's thirteenth birthday."

"What happened to her after that?"

"Her uncle took her and her sister to an orphanage. But her sister ran off to marry her boyfriend, leaving Mona to figure things out on her own. She poured her pain into this painting. I think it might have been her way of reclaiming the childhood she lost. The farmhouse in the background was their old place. She said it was a castle to her."

I studied the painting anew, imagining the layers of emotion in each brushstroke.

"Did she always paint when she was sad?"

"She painted to release whatever churned inside her. That's why I gave you art supplies when you showed up. I hoped it'd help."

"It did, but I felt a little guilty because I enjoyed it. Is that why this painting is your favorite?"

"No. That's why it mattered to Mona, but my love for it stems from different reasons. The first time I saw this painting, it hung in the window of a gallery. I'd passed there every day on my walk home from work and never been inside. But this painting pulled me through the door. And what I found was the most beautiful girl I'd ever seen. I had to meet her."

"It was Mona?"

He nodded. "She'd just started at the gallery, and they already loved her work. For me though, I knew I'd found the woman I wanted to grow old with. I asked her to dinner several times, but she kept saying no."

"Why?"

"She didn't think her clothes were good enough. Her work uniform was what she considered the nicest thing she owned, and she worried people would judge her."

"How did you get her to say yes?"

"I told her I didn't care about her clothes. All I wanted was to spend time with her. I had to think of an offer so lovely, she couldn't say no. So I packed a dinner basket, and stood outside with it. When she came out, I dropped to one knee and pleaded for her to have dinner with me. I told her I might never eat again if she wouldn't join me for a picnic at the park."

"You did that? Right in front of everyone?"

His eyes lit up. "I did. She gave me the same shocked look you're giving me now. But it worked, and that picnic turned into one of the best evenings of my life. We sat on the blanket for hours, talking and laughing until the sun went down. Afterward, she asked me to walk her back to Main Street. She lived in an apartment above one of the cafes near the gallery. She hugged me tight and asked if we could eat together again."

Love could look different from what I'd seen growing up. A surprise revelation. The warmth in his voice, the twinkle in his eyes; it differed from the fleeting moments of love I remembered between my parents.

I knew they'd cared for each other once, but those memories were hazy. I hoped my father loved Mama back then the way Pop loved Mona, the way she deserved.

We continued to hang paintings in the front room, chatting as we worked. Eventually, the conversation turned to the orphanage. Though I'd only been there a few days, I shared stories about spending time with Amelia and how mean Linda had been.

"Mona's painting is hanging in the cafeteria. I didn't know it was hers at first, but I figured it out when I heard you say your last name to the people outside the home."

"Well, it's nice to hear they've still got it up. It's a beautiful piece."

"I thought so too. Is it true? Did you and Mona really build the home?"

"Yes, that's right. It's getting late. Why don't we move into the kitchen? I'll tell you all about it while we figure out dinner."

At the word "dinner," my stomach growled.

"Sounds good to me."

We settled on buttered noodles and baked chicken. As the kitchen filled with the aroma of roasting meat, Pop shared stories about the orphanage.

"Mona and I realized early on we had a shared passion for helping others. On our own, caring for ourselves proved difficult at times. But when we came together, well, there weren't many things we couldn't get done as a team."

"You two must have been pretty special together."

"Indeed we were."

Pop paused to baste the chicken; the savory smell made my mouth water.

"My father taught me to invest half my earnings and save the rest after my bills were paid. When the stock market crashed in 1929, Mona and I weren't in too bad of shape."

"Mama used to talk about those days. She said the whole country was depressed."

"I think you're talking about the Great Depression."

My eyes lit up at the familiar phrase. "Yes, that's what she called it. She said her family struggled when she was a little girl because of it."

"Those were tough times. Mona and I'd been married a few years by then, and we'd saved enough to buy our house outright. The crash wiped out much of our investments, but we were luckier than most. We couldn't stand sitting comfortably while others had so little, so we started a food pantry. People needed a place to find help where nobody asked them questions. A way to fill in the gaps, and still hold onto their dignity. Wouldn't you know, other people heard about our pantry and started bringing food, clothes, and all sorts of necessities to share as well."

"I bet it helped a lot of people."

I remembered my parents bringing home boxes of food or clothes. I couldn't help but wonder if they'd gotten those things from his pantry. Maybe Pop had been caring for us all along. Little prickles appeared on my arms at the idea of it. I shook away the thought and put my attention back on what he was saying.

"…and I'll never forget when the first donation came. An older couple who heard about the pantry through church brought a bag of clothes and some food from their own cabinets. Their kindness spoke louder than words."

"Did things get better after that?"

"It took time. But as the stock market started to recover, Mona and I dreamed bigger. In 1939, we built the Tualatin Valley Home for

Girls, the same year World War II began. We found therapy in focusing on such an important project amid all the turmoil."

Pop pulled the chicken from the oven. I set the table while he carved the meat, continuing the story.

"We started planning a boys' home the same year, but didn't begin construction until 1941. The United States started deploying its soldiers into the war, and more children found their way through the doors of our orphanages. We wanted them to find safe, loving places with people who cared."

"Didn't you think Black children deserved those things too?"

His face reddened. "I'm ashamed to admit it hadn't occurred to me. Back then, I rarely encountered any. The world was different in those days."

"What about now? Do you think about them now?"

He met my gaze, his tone earnest. "I do. It's long overdue for things to change. Now, let's eat and get our rooms in order before bed."

"Okay. Thanks for sharing so much with me, Pop."

He didn't realize how deep my gratitude ran. Not only for his stories, but for his home. For his kindness. For the pieces of himself he gave so freely. I learned a valuable truth. The world needed change, even if I had to be the one to initiate it. I didn't know how, but I knew one day I'd be strong enough to be the change in someone's life, the way Pop and Mona had been for so many.

Chapter Seventeen

Soft droplets kissed the windowpane on the day of my parents' funeral. The sound of their melody was a welcome distraction in the stillness of the early morning. I pulled back the curtain to watch as the rain gathered on the glass, its heaviness beneath an overcast sky mirrored the dolor that sat deep in my chest. Mother Earth grieved with me while I prepared myself to say goodbye, though I still wasn't ready.

The need to feel the rain pulled me outside. I slipped on my robe and stepped through the back door. My bare feet sank into the grass. The cool rain soaked into my skin.

Back then, the rain would've meant being called back into my room, back to being invisible. But here, I had permission to stay. No walls, no eyes watching. Each drop fell on me like a quiet promise, the kind of liberty I only dreamed of before. The price of my freedom had not been lost upon me, a fact that glared into my soul on this day of farewells.

It wasn't only my parents I would be saying goodbye to, but everything I'd ever known. A new life formed around me, and with it came new people and new experiences. But my grief overshadowed each minute. My fear sharpened to a point that stabbed through my fragile mind at all times. For now, Pop's presence eased my pain. What about when I went off to school? I would walk alone.

"I'll be there, Amanda. I told you this already."

Not today. I didn't want to hear from the Unseen today, yet here he was, ruining the only moment of calm I'd allowed myself.

"I can't *do* this right now, can't talk to you. Please, please go. I don't need you anymore."

"You're wrong. You need me because you've always needed me, and you always will. I'm the one who saved you, I'm the one who gave you the courage to—"

"Just go!"

The command came out louder than I'd intended, and my hand flew over my mouth. If Pop found out about the Unseen, if he knew the truth, he'd send me away. Even Mama knew the Unseen was bad; that's why she demanded I not talk to him. But I couldn't help it. Sometimes the things he said were right; I needed him to survive.

I heard Pop calling my name from inside the house, pulling me from my thoughts.

"Here I am," I called back as I walked through the back door.

"Good morning, my dear. Have you already eaten breakfast?"

"I'm not hungry. I think I'll take a shower and get ready for the cemetery if that's okay with you?"

"Yes, of course."

My shower lasted longer than usual. Once the water turned cool, I stepped out and wrapped myself in a towel, wiping the mirror to stare at the foggy shape looking back.

Behind the blur, I saw a glimpse of my mother watching me. The tears I'd been fighting to hold back all morning escaped from my eyes in an instant.

"Mama." My hushed voice echoed through the still room. Her face waited in the fog, like she needed me to say more. I pressed my palm against the glass to find it as cold as her skin on the day I found her body.

I drew a breath and reached for my green pants; the color of fresh earth after a storm. The black dress I had picked out the night before still hung there, but it didn't feel right. I wanted to show hope, not sorrow. My hands shook while I buttoned my cream shirt. I stepped back to see how it looked. My image was still partially distorted, but I could see I'd made the right choice in colors.

"I don't think this rain will be letting up anytime soon. We're supposed to be at the cemetery in half an hour, but maybe I should call and tell them we're gonna wait a while to see if the storm passes," Pop suggested when I came out of my room.

"Do we have to wait? I don't mind the rain."

"Well, if you're okay with it, I am too. Let's get a move on. It might take us longer in this weather."

I hurried to the car and slid in fast so he wouldn't be stuck standing in the rain.

"Thank you for doing this for my parents."

"Of course, but I'm doing this for *you*. One day, there'll be things you need to say to them, and this way you'll have a place you can go to do that."

The somber space of the cemetery came into view, shadows clinging to the wet grass. A dark gray tent stood over the plot, its fabric flapping gently in the wind. Two wooden boxes sat beside each other. Too small. Too quiet. The air smelled like wet dirt. A hole waited in the ground, wide open, ready to swallow what remained. What was left of what had been.

The pastor waited in silence as I looked over the scene. A thin barrier of wood separated my life from their death. He led us in prayer and allowed me to spend a while at the gravesite as Pop held tight to my hand. When the time came, the workers stepped forward and lowered the boxes into the hole. I dropped in two envelopes, a painting I'd made for Mama, and a note to my father. I turned my head when they sprinkled the first shovel of dirt into the hole, unable to bear the symbolism.

"I'm ready to go home now."

He turned on the radio as soon as we got settled in the car. I found myself drawn to the distraction of music. Pop stayed gentle with me the rest of the day. By the next afternoon, the goodbye started to settle in.

The house exhaled by Monday night, the stillness lifting as normalcy crept back into the corners. Pop's silly jokes stole away some of the aching embedded inside me. I laughed. It wasn't enough to lift the sadness, but it quieted it somewhat.

Early Tuesday morning, I heard Pop banging around in the kitchen. I crawled out of bed to see what he was up to.

"Morning, dear. Sorry if I woke you. I've turned this whole kitchen upside down looking for my little cast-iron skillet. I can't seem to find it."

"Hmm. I think I know where it is. When we were putting everything away, I remember seeing it down here with the lids."

I opened the cabinet and pulled it out from the back.

"Perfect, thank you. I'm gonna make us some cornbread. It comes out extra crispy if I bake it in one of these cast irons. After breakfast, we'll get ready to head over to the school. Miss Sally'll pick us up around nine o'clock."

"You don't want to drive to town in your new car?"

"I don't care much for driving anymore. It's good to have in case of an emergency, or if Miss Sally's not around, but I don't plan to use it much. It'll probably still be near new by the time you're ready for a car. We'll get our money's worth out of it either way."

"I'm gonna pick out a nice outfit to wear. Mind if I hop in the shower? If I do it now, my hair'll have enough time to dry before Miss Sally gets here."

Pop's expression grew serious as his gaze locked with mine. "Listen here. If you'd like a snack or need to use the restroom, please feel free to do so. No need to ask."

His words were soft, but his eyes were sharp—like he was pushing me toward something I hadn't seen yet. I knew that look. He wanted me to understand something.

"Okay, I'll try and remember." I smiled up at him. "My pinky promises."

We locked our smallest fingers together to seal the pact, and I went to find an outfit suitable for going to town.

By the time I finished dressing and brushing the tangles from my hair, Pop called out to me for breakfast. I opened the bathroom door, and the mouthwatering scent of bacon lulled me into the kitchen.

I poured us both a glass of cold milk to accompany our bacon and cornbread. Careful not to get anything on my dress, I finished every bite on my plate.

"Well, you must've been hungry. I've never seen you eat so much. Now don't touch those pans, they're still hot."

I picked up our dishes to carry them to the sink.

"It's easy to eat fast when it tastes this good."

"You're too comfortable. Don't forget what you are, though. Damaged goods, just like Linda said. Pop's gonna see through your act sooner or later."

My smile faded. Had my back not been toward Pop, he'd have seen my happy moment dissolve. Like a bubble floating weightless in the wind, my psyche proved to be equally fragile and easy to burst. I didn't argue that he was wrong about me, that I'd hidden nothing from Pop. I knew my defense would be filled with lies, and the Unseen knew better. There were too many layers, too many pieces of myself still locked away.

I'd begun to relax during my time with Pop. Without realizing it, my mind calmed, almost too much so. He made it easy to let my guard down, although I tried to keep it up most of the time. But on mornings like this, parts of my armor crumbled, leaving me wide open for disaster.

The Unseen found those moments to torment my thoughts, though I did my best to ignore him. I often wondered how Pop would react if he caught me talking to him. Or worse yet, doing anything wrong at all. Would his punishment be physical like my father's had been? No matter how hard I tried to do things correctly, missteps always found their way into my world.

Chapter Eighteen

A moment of carelessness. A slight distraction to weaken my facade of perfection. That's all it took for the spell to break and the *real* me to peek through. I'd done so well, tried so hard not to be a problem. But I'd always be what I'd always been, and no amount of pretending could change the truth.

Pop usually poured bacon grease into a coffee can he kept under the sink. After the dishes, I bent down to grab it, but my hands were still wet from the soapy water. The can slipped from my grasp. In slow motion, it tumbled round and round before crashing to the ground in an explosion of old grease.

"Oh no!" The words flew from my lips as quickly as the grease from the can. I watched in horror as it splashed onto my legs, my dress, the floor—all of it covered in a slick, oily mess. Pop rushed over, his eyes wide. A wound from long ago reopened. I flinched as the all-too-familiar fear of reprimand settled in my chest. The air crystallized between us, my eyes filling with the unknown terror of what I'd just done.

"Run away now or you'll pay for what you did," the Unseen cautioned from somewhere deep inside me. But my legs were planted in place.

I drifted away.

"What have you done, Amanda Leigh!" my father's voice bellowed. So close to my face as he shook me, I could feel the spittle and taste his whiskey.

"Please, Daddy. I didn't mean to. It just slipped."

I paused, silent and stiff. Milk dripped from the counter and pooled on the floor. His fingers dug into my arms.

"You're hurting me," I said, just above a whisper.

"I'm hurting you? I've barely touched you. Now stop your whinin' or I'll give you a *real* reason to cry."

I sniffled. It happened too quickly for me to stop it.

"I said knock it off!" he roared, slamming my head against the counter with such force I lost control of my bladder. Warm urine slid down my legs.

"I'm sorry, Daddy."

He sneered. "Pissing on the floor. Typical bitch. Get down there and clean that up, and the milk too."

He shoved me to the ground and stood over me, waiting for me to do what he wanted.

"I don't have a rag."

"Use your clothes. Lay down and soak up your mess, you nasty little girl."

Without hesitating, I rolled around in the milk and urine, hoping my thin dress would absorb everything and this could be done. Maybe he'd leave me be afterward.

"Now give me your underwear."

His words shocked me. Why would he want my wet underwear? But I did as he instructed out of fear of what he'd do if I refused.

I did my best to cover myself as I took them off, before handing them to him. He spread them across my face, wrapping the leg openings around my ears to hold them tight, and shoved me toward the wall.

"Don't you move one muscle or there'll be hell to pay."

He'd have left me there all night if Mama hadn't come inside to get a pair of scissors for her garden. She took one look at me and removed the wet fabric from my face.

"Go shower, sweetheart. And don't come out of your room until I say. Got it?"

Yes, ma'am, I said, and hurried to my bedroom.

Next time I saw Mama, her arm was in a makeshift sling and her jaw was bruised. She never tended to her garden again without me.

What felt like hours lost in memory turned out to be only seconds. And there was Pop, gentle yet fierce. His hands turned soft, almost like silk, as he steadied me.

"Don't move. The floor's slippery, and I don't want you to fall. Let me grab a couple of towels."

The hands of time started ticking again. I tried to respond, but my throat closed off, denying any sound to escape. I could only nod.

Towels overflowed both arms when he returned. Certainly he didn't intend to clean the mess I'd made with his nice towels. He handed me one to wipe my legs and dress off while he cleaned the floor around me.

"I'm sorry. I didn't mean to drop it. I was trying to help. I ruined everything."

I couldn't meet his eyes while I braced for his anger. For the familiar sting of a necessary punishment.

The first tear fell, breaking my flimsy illusion of strength. I tried to keep control.

Pop's hands rested lightly on my shoulders, and again I flinched. The old memories surged up. My father's rough grip. The way he'd shake me and scream out what a terrible child I'd been. But Pop's touch remained gentle.

"Hey, now. It's alright. Accidents happen to the best of us. We'll have this cleaned up before you know it."

"Okay. Please don't be mad, Pop. I won't let it happen again," I whimpered.

He pulled a clean rag from the drawer and wiped my cheeks.

"It'd take a lot more than this to make me mad. Come on now, let's clean you up. No point crying over spilled grease."

"Okay." I looked down at my dress, the grease stains spreading like ink.

The fabric clung to my legs, damp and destroyed—or so it

seemed. "My dress. Do you think it's done for?"

"Well, it just so happens I know exactly how to get grease out of clothes. You go find another outfit to wear and wash your legs with soap and water. I'll take care of the rest, okay?"

"Alright, I'll go find a new outfit."

I kept my head down as I walked into my bedroom to search for new clothes.

What a dumb thing to do. I chastised myself silently, feeling terrible over the mistake and even worse when I couldn't think of any way to make it up to him.

By the time I washed the grease from my legs and redressed myself, Miss Sally had arrived. I came out of the bathroom slowly, still embarrassed about the mess I'd made and curious if Pop had told her what happened.

"Well, don't you look cute as a button in your little dress," Miss Sally marveled when I entered the front room.

"Thank you. Do you want me to put this in the regular clothes hamper, Pop?"

"You can put it right on top of the washing machine, and I'll have a look at it this afternoon."

I headed toward the washroom.

"Oh, what happened to her dress? She didn't stain it, did she?" Her eyes squinted in accusation, making her round cheeks look even puffier. She kept her tone sugary, but I could feel the judgment tangled in her words. I hung my head lower as I walked by.

"Oh no, nothing like that. It's a little big, so we're gonna see if I can add a stitch or two to make it fit better."

Was this a necessary lie? Would Mama have covered for me as well? Maybe to my father, but only because she knew what he'd do if he found out about the mess I'd made. But why did Pop lie to Miss Sally?

The grease disaster became a distant memory as we climbed into the car. Still, my stomach tightened again with nerves. The thought of meeting the lady at the school made my palms sweat and my throat dry up. I could already feel her curious eyes on me. She'd seek out my ignorance faster than Mama'd smelled the whiskey on my father's breath.

Pop and Miss Sally chatted during the drive. I spent the time trying to ignore the Unseen's irrational warnings and hold on to a shred of bravery.

"Bobbie's looking forward to school starting back up in a couple of weeks. She's been going on and on about how bored she is all the time. As if I'm supposed to entertain her somehow."

"Well, it's nice to hear she's excited about school. No matter the reason, having a child who shows interest in going is a blessing, I'd say."

"That's true. You know, I told her we could go shopping for some new clothes and supplies sometime this week. I've been waiting for my payment from the main office, but I think I've got enough to get her a few items. If you'd like, we could take the girls together tomorrow morning. Bobbie knows the little shops over in Hillsboro like she designed the layout. She's got an appointment in a couple of hours, or we could go today. Speaking of which, I'm cutting it a bit close on time this morning."

Miss Sally's tone took on a subtle shift, almost too smooth. It reminded me of Mama, the way her voice would drop when she tried to sweet-talk my father. I glanced at Pop and wondered if he noticed the difference, but his face remained steady. I couldn't imagine why Miss Sally would care whether we joined her and Bobbie for school shopping.

"What a fine idea, Sally. We can go in the morning and grab lunch afterward. It's been a long time since I've been to Hillsboro. If you wanna leave us at the school, you can go tend to your errands and meet us back here in two hours."

She dropped us near the front sidewalk. My hands trembled as we passed through the entrance. Before I could hide them, Pop's hand slipped around mine. His grip acted as a warm and calming comfort. When he gave my palm a gentle squeeze, the shaking quieted.

The empty halls of the school sent a shudder of unease down my spine. My whole life I'd longed for friendship, and I knew this place would offer me my first real chance of finding it. But what if the other kids found me unworthy of friendship? Would they think I'd fallen too far behind them to catch up? Insecurities danced through my mind, creating a rhythm to every scenario I could imagine. In all of them, I remained alone.

"They'll never accept you here. You're no good. You know it, and so does Pop. He's only sticking with you now because he made a promise before he found out. He doesn't really want you; even Linda could see that."

I tried to ignore him, but his words mirrored the truth I had buried deep inside.

Our steps echoed as we walked toward the door marked *'Office.'* I hid behind Pop when we got closer.

"Don't worry, dear. I'll be right beside you the whole time. You're a bright girl. They'll see it right away."

Pop's presence acted as my security; his faith was my strength. He overpowered the hold the Unseen tried to keep on me, shattering its chains with a simple smile or touch. I believed in him, knowing he would always keep me safe and protected.

I raised my head high, squaring my shoulders the same way I'd seen Pop do so many times. Together, we stepped through the door.

Chapter Nineteen

"Good morning, you must be Mr. Wells." A tall woman with dark, wavy hair smiled as we reached the front desk. Her voice was welcoming. "And you must be Amanda. I'm Ms. Donaldson. We spoke on the phone. It's so nice to meet you both."

"Good morning. We appreciate your help arranging this on such short notice," Pop replied.

"If you'll follow me, we can begin with Amanda's placement testing. Are you ready?"

I took a seat next to Pop at a big desk opposite Ms. Donaldson. "Yes, ma'am, I think so."

"Great. We will be going over the four main subjects: Math, Social Studies, Science, and English. It's nothing to stress about. If we encounter something too advanced, we'll move on. Let's begin."

She opened the math folder first, allowing my nerves to fade a bit. Math had always been more like putting the pieces of a puzzle together, especially when Mama explained it. Each number clicked into place, and with every problem, my confidence grew.

After flipping through all the pages, she said it was time to move on. I thought I'd done okay, but she didn't say what my scores were.

"Want to pick which subject we do next?"

"How about Science?" I asked.

"Alright, Science it is."

Like with math, I flew through the questions. Every answer made me feel lighter, the nerves slowly melting away.

"You're doing very well, Amanda. What would you like to try

next?"

"Hmm. I know English is going to be a little tougher, but I do like the subject. Social Studies is my least favorite. Maybe I should get it over with."

"That makes perfect sense."

She pulled out the next folder and offered a gentle smile similar to the one Mama wore when I'd done well in my lessons. I hoped her expression stemmed from the same cause.

"This is a real school. All you know is what Mama knew. She's smiling because she's nice, but she feels sorry for you—the poor orphaned girl, too dumb for her own grade."

I squeezed my eyes shut, wishing him away. Hellbent on stealing my confidence, he continued.

"And Pop's gonna know you're a dud, then he'll find out you're a phony too. They're gonna lock you away, and nobody's gonna even care. But you'll still have me."

I struggled more as we went through the social studies pages. The Unseen rattled my brain, and I'd always found trouble in the subject. Mama hadn't been a fan of it, but she tried to explain a lot of it to me.

I took a moment to breathe, to step back and put myself in a different space and time. Mama was there, sitting at the table, the quiet hum of her music in the background. I thought about the news reports I used to watch on my tiny television and knew I had the information, I only needed to pull it out. I exhaled and continued working through each question. The answers came naturally then, like a forgotten lesson rising to the surface.

"Good job answering those. I know social studies can be rather dry. That leaves us with my favorite subject, English."

Ms. Donaldson's eyes moved across my paper, her lips curling into a small smile each time she turned to the next page. The way she nodded and scribbled little notes hinted I'd done a good job. A small flower of pride bloomed inside my chest.

We moved on to grammar, which allowed me to write out my

answers in my own words.

"Your handwriting is lovely."

She traced her finger over the neat lines of my work. Her tone carried the genuine admiration of a person who'd come across a rare find.

"Thank you. Mama said the way my writing looks is as important as the words I've written."

"I suppose she had a good point. Even the most beautiful stories would be lost if they were unable to be read."

Pop leaned forward, not disguising the note of anticipation in his voice. "What's your take on her placement? Does it line up with her age?"

Ms. Donaldson shook her head slightly, almost in disbelief. "Amanda excelled in every subject. She's beyond what we typically see, so much so that it's difficult to even compare her to a specific grade level."

"What does that mean exactly? We can still get her enrolled for the new school year, can't we?"

"Mr. Wells, her knowledge is far beyond the elementary level. If I had to estimate, I'd say she's already in the mid-seventh-grade range. She's a very gifted little girl."

"Wait, I can't go to this school?"

"No, you can. This simply means you may find yourself rather bored during many of the lessons. Boredom from knowing too much can be as damaging as boredom from knowing too little. Children tend to have their attention wander when they aren't learning from the environment they're in. That often leads to behavioral issues, withdrawal from peers, and other social discrepancies."

"I doubt very much this school would have any issues with Amanda's behavior," Pop argued. "What would you recommend for her?"

"Ultimately, the decision is yours. If she were to enter this school, I'd write a formal recommendation for her to begin at a sixth-grade level. Her age places her in fourth grade, but I urge you to consider how much time she'd lose by reviewing material she has already mastered. Mr. Wells, what would you say of her maturity level? She presents herself in a very sophisticated manner for a child her age."

"Yes, she's a little more independent than a lot of children tend to be. Without getting into too many details, she's spent a lot of time with adults and has very few childish traits as a result."

"I see. What would you think about taking her to the middle school for placement testing? She may benefit more by being challenged, but the children will be a bit older."

"That would be a discussion for her and me to have. This is her life we're working out; she should have a higher vote on where she goes than either of us."

"Gifted? You really tricked them today. They don't see it yet, don't understand that the only gift you'll bring is misery. Look what you did to your parents. And if you go to middle school with older kids and smarter teachers, they're gonna see through you the first day."

I clenched my fists in my lap, determined not to let the Unseen ruin this moment for me.

He continued despite my efforts to tune him out. But there was truth there simmering beneath the surface. I tried not to look too closely, tried not to hear the reality of his words.

"Tell them, Amanda. Make them understand you're not special. You're just a girl whose mother had nothing better to do than teach. You might understand the math, but you'll never make it in this world."

I shook away the taunting and spoke over his voice.

"I wouldn't like that very much. I don't need any time to think about it, I'd like to come to this school. It's okay if I start in sixth grade if you think that's best."

"What do you think, Mr. Wells?"

"That's fine," Pop said with a nod, as if he'd already decided.

"I'll get my formal recommendation written up and submitted to the district for approval. Then her registration will be complete, and she can begin with the rest of the students on the first day. Let me grab a supply list so you can get what she'll need in the meantime."

The classroom door swung open. A tall, skinny boy with messy hair leaned in. "Hey, everything okay?"

Suspicion filled his eyes as they landed on Pop, only softening when he noticed me sitting at Pop's side. "I'm sorry, I heard a man's voice and just wanted to make sure—."

"No worries, son. Actually, why don't you come in and say hello, Buster? This is Amanda Hollings. She's new to the school and will be in your grade. I'll see if I can get her into your class as well. Would you be so kind as to give her a little tour? That is, of course, if you don't mind, Mr. Wells."

"Not at all, go ahead, Amanda. I'm sure it'll be easier to have a look around without a school full of other children racing about."

Buster held out his hand with a grin, a hint of playfulness in his eyes.

"Nice to meet you. Buster Donaldson, at your service." His hand took mine, firm and filled with excited energy. The air around him buzzed as though he couldn't wait to get moving.

I returned a clumsy attempt at a natural handshake. "Nice to meet you too."

He bounced on the balls of his feet as we walked. He could barely stay still. His words tumbled out rapidly as he pointed out each classroom rattling off the names of teachers and sharing which had been his favorites and the ones who handed out the toughest homework. He showed me the cafeteria, which doubled as a gymnasium, and tripled, as he put it, as an auditorium.

Every so often, he removed a quarter from his pocket and flipped it in the air before returning it. I wanted to ask him why, but I kept quiet instead. My first experience in a boy's company proved one part uncertain and two parts embarrassing.

Outside, the sun warmed the pavement as Buster gestured to the playground with sweeping enthusiasm.

"The girls play hopscotch over there. You ever played? Or jump rope? They're always jumping on that part of the yard."

My fingers fumbled with the lace on my dress as I glanced down. "I've never done either of those things."

"Really? It's easy. I can teach you, I just need to find a rock to mark the squares."

"Sure, you can show me how to play. What about using the quarter you were flipping earlier?"

"No, I wouldn't want to risk losing it. It's special, my mom gave it to me. It's my safety quarter."

"What's a safety quarter?"

"You know, if I ever get into a jam and need help. It's more than enough to make a couple of phone calls."

I tried to act like everything he said made perfect sense. In someone else's world, it probably would. But in mine, I didn't even know two people to call for help. Even if I did, I'd never used a phone before.

His eyes sparkled as he searched for a rock, his eagerness contagious. The smile he wore beamed even brighter as he ran across the sidewalk and picked up a pebble.

"Okay, here's what we do, the first player tosses the rock to land in one of these squares. They hop through the boxes, one foot up in the first box, then one foot in each box of the second row, and so on. Whichever box the rock lands in, you have to skip over. You go all the way to the end and once you're there, you turn around and hop back across, stopping only to pick up the rock from the square it was in. We go until either one of us has lost our balance or has successfully gotten the rock onto all of the squares of the grid."

"I think I get most of what you're saying."

I only halfway understood, but I couldn't let him know that.

"Normally, I'd have you go first since you're a lady and all. But I think maybe I should, so you can see what I mean."

I nodded.

Buster hopped across the squares, his feet moving with practiced ease as I watched closely. My steps were tentative at first on my turn. The rhythm of the game soon pulled me in, and I found myself laughing along with him. It may have been a silly game, but each jump felt lighter than the last, and soon I'd forgotten some of my insecurities.

By the time we finished, I was breathless and carefree. My chest heaved, but not from worry this time. Playing the game made the world feel a little less daunting. As much as I'd have loved to continue playing, I knew we needed to get back to the adults. Surely Pop wondered why we had been gone so long.

"We should go back to the classroom. Miss Sally's gonna be here to pick us up soon."

"Okay, let's head out. But who's Miss Sally?"

"She's a friend of Pop's. She normally picks us up when we need to be somewhere. Pop doesn't like driving much."

"Oh, I see. Well, what do you think about the school? Is it better than your last one?"

An innocent question, but I worried about how to answer. Reflecting on Linda's reaction when I said I'd never been to school before made me approach questions with caution.

Rather than lie, I only answered halfway. "I like the school. It's big though, remembering where everything is might be hard."

"Don't worry about it. My mom's trying to get us in the same class. Meet me by the front entrance on the first day, and I'll make sure you don't get lost."

"Thank you, Buster. That's kind of you. Are you sure it's no trouble?"

"Cross my heart. I'll wait there until I see you, no sweat."

As we rounded the corner, Pop and Ms. Donaldson were standing close with their heads bent together, their voices barely above a low murmur. Their posture made my steps slow. Pop's back faced us, his hands tucked into his pockets as he was nodding at whatever Ms.

Donaldson whispered. She looked up as we came closer. Her eyes widened for just a second before she smiled. Her demeanor changed, too abrupt for it to be innocent. Curiosity nagged at me as I questioned what they were discussing. Like a scab I needed to scrape away, but I worried how much the answer would make me bleed.

Pop straightened when he heard our footsteps, his face slipping into a grin that never quite reached his eyes. "Oh, there you are."

He kept his tone light, but unusually bright. We'd stumbled into a conversation we shouldn't have overheard. Ms. Donaldson adjusted her glasses, her polite smile now firmly in place, but her gaze flickered to Pop before settling on me.

"Well, what did you think?" Pop asked.

My smile stretched wide and genuine. "I think it's perfect. Buster even showed me how to play hopscotch, so I'll be ready to show the other kids I know how."

"I'm happy to hear it. We'd better get going, Miss Sally's probably waiting for us out front by now."

The ride home from the school found me in an opposing spirit to the one I'd had on the ride to town. I thought about Buster and the game we played. For the first time in my life, I felt a hint of normalcy. No worries or creeping shadows at the edges of my mind. Only laughter, sunshine, and hopscotch. A strange feeling, but I wanted to hold onto it, even if I couldn't explain why.

The little bars around my heart bent slightly. Without notice, the winds of freedom crept into the empty room where nothing else lived. I didn't notice the change, but still it came to heal my body, one cell at a time.

Chapter Twenty

As promised, Miss Sally arrived the following morning to take us into town. Pop opened the back door for me to climb into the car.

"Good morning, ladies," Pop announced when he got seated.

"It's a lovely day today," Miss Sally responded. "Amanda, this is my daughter Bobbie."

"Nice to meet you," I said.

Heat crept up my neck. I pressed my hands against my lap, hoping she wouldn't notice the nervous tremble in my fingers.

A couple of years older than me, she had the same round face as Miss Sally. Her bright eyes lingered for a moment too long, hinting that she hid heavier emotions behind them. She kept her straight, strawberry blond hair in a sharp cut right above her shoulders.

"You'll never be that confident, that put-together. Look at her, she's normal."

I shook my head, a quick motion to try and quiet the voice taunting me from within.

"You too. My mother's told me so much about you." She pulled a small silver mirror case from her pocket, then applied lip gloss. "I hope you're as stoked as I am about getting some new threads."

"Threads?"

"You know, pants, shirts, skirts."

"Oh, of course. Yes, I'm excited too."

The outfit she wore reminded me of what I'd seen older children wear on television. Her button-up shirt, with a Peter Pan collar, was tucked into a sharp mini-skirt. Even her scarf matched, tied like a ribbon across her hair.

I glanced down at my lace-trimmed dress covered in pink flowers. It was like I'd been dressed for a tea party I didn't ask to attend. Suddenly I'd grown insecure over the clothes I adored so much. Bobbie looked like she'd walked out of a magazine. I tugged at the ruffles and tried to push down the doubt building in my chest.

"How do you like living with Pop?"

"I love it there. Pop's wonderful, I wouldn't wanna be with anyone else."

"Not even with your parents? I mean, if they were alive, of course—"

"Barbara Lynn! What in the world is the matter with you?" Miss Sally shouted from the front seat.

"What? I wasn't being harsh, Mother. It was only a question. I'm sorry, Amanda. Honest. I don't know why I even asked you that."

"It's alright. I don't want to talk about my parents, though."

"Of course not. What grade are you gonna be in when school starts back up?"

"I'll be in sixth, but I don't know anybody. Well, I did meet a boy who offered to help me get around the school."

"Wow! Sixth grade? You're so tiny, I would have thought you were much younger."

"Ms. Donaldson did my placement tests and said I should start at sixth grade, but I should really be going into fourth. I'm nine and a half."

"Oh, that makes more sense. Well, you must be pretty smart to be skipping all the way to sixth grade. Ms. Donaldson's over there now? She was my school counselor in fifth grade, but she left the summer before I went to sixth. I always wondered where she went. I liked her."

"You sure did see enough of her when you were causing trouble for your teachers," Miss Sally cut in with a sour tone.

Bobbie rolled her eyes. "Don't listen to her; she gets bent outta shape over every little thing. You want me to help you pick out some clothes like what the other kids are wearing? I love shopping."

"I'd really like that. I'm not sure what I'm doing when it comes to picking out clothes. I've never gone shopping for new stuff before."

I left out the part where all the clothes I'd had in the past were donated or bought second-hand. The only things I'd ever had new were my socks and undergarments, and even those I'd kept until the holes made them unwearable.

"Can you turn the radio up? I love this song," Bobbie pleaded when the faint sound of the Beach Boys singing *I Get Around* played through the speakers.

Miss Sally scoffed, reaching forward to turn the radio off.

"Nonsense, it's an inappropriate song for you, and it's way too old for Amanda."

Bobbie pouted for a second before we continued chatting amongst ourselves. Pop and Miss Sally had their own conversation in the front. Bobbie grinned, all innocence on the surface. But her eyes gave her away. There was a spark in them like she was waiting for her moment to break loose and run.

I found it thrilling, as if she had a secret adventure tucked beneath the surface, waiting to be unleashed.

The drive went by too quickly. Soon enough, we found a spot to park outside the shops lining the main road in town. Pop opened the car door for me. I'd never seen so many stores lined up in a row. The wind tugged at their awnings. For a second, anything was possible.

Each one called me in with promises of wonder. The brightly colored signs. The clinking of glasses from nearby cafes. I could have been walking through a scene from a dream. The town loomed around me. Too perfect. Too far removed from the quiet corners of my past. I almost pinched myself, half-expecting to wake up.

Pop set his hand on my shoulder. I looked up. His eyes had that warm crinkle they always got.

"This'll be fun," he said, bending close. "If it's too much, give me a wink. That's our signal."

"Okay, thank you."

Bobbie took my hand and pulled me into the store. "Come on! You're gonna love this, going through all the clothes is unreal."

I didn't understand a lot of the words she used, but I agreed with the last one, even if she'd meant it some other way.

Her fingers darted through the clothing racks like they knew every stitch. Without hesitation, she plucked out different blouses and skirts, her eyes gleaming as she piled hangers into my arms. She made her way over to the pants and shorts section. Choosing a pair of capri pants she thought appropriate, she held them up against me to check the length.

"Perfect."

She stopped to pull her mirror from her handbag and reapply her lip gloss.

My arms struggled to hold the massive pile of clothes she had loaded on them. "This is an awful lot of stuff."

"Oh, don't worry, these are to take back and try on. After we decide which ones we like, the shopkeeper will put everything we don't want away."

She spoke with a knowledge I hoped I'd grow into one day. I'd never even imagined a person like Bobbie could exist.

"It seems unfair to the shopkeeper. Don't they get annoyed having to keep putting stuff back all day long?" I glanced at the growing pile of clothes in my arms and winced. My stomach tightened at the thought of the shopkeeper sighing as she returned everything to the rack.

"Not at all. That's called job security, my friend."

Heat crept up my neck, spreading across my cheeks. *Friend.* The word lingered in the air, light and casual for Bobbie. I tied a pretend ribbon around the moment and tucked it somewhere safe.

"Let's go find something the girls at school'll wish they'd picked first."

"Now remember, Bobbie, we're low on cash until the main

office pays me," Miss Sally called out, causing Bobbie to blush.

"Let her get what she needs, Sally. I'll pay for it. Clothes mean a lot to young ladies," Pop offered.

I remembered the story he told me about Mona and understood his reasoning. I gave him a knowing glance, which he returned with a smile. The motive behind Miss Sally's invitation for us to come along might have been for this moment, but I pushed the idea aside and focused my attention back on Bobbie.

Again, we went through all of the racks until my arms were full enough to satisfy her. In the dressing room, she picked through the clothes she'd gathered for me while placing them in corresponding outfits.

"Okay, now's the fun part. You go into your stall, and I'll go into mine, and we'll come out when we're both dressed and grade each other's outfits. Are you ready?"

"I think so."

I changed quickly, afraid of leaving Bobbie to wait for me. "I'm ready to come out now,"

"Just a second, I'm almost done."

I waited for her to tell me she was ready so we could exit our curtains at the same time.

"You look beautiful, Amanda. Okay, lay it on me. What do you think of this one?"

She made a full circle, allowing me to see her outfit from every angle.

"I like the colors you picked. The shirt matches your eyes."

She donned a pair of bright white capri pants with an electric blue blouse. The shirt had tiny silver and white shapes printed across it.

I stepped closer to the mirror and caught sight of the girl staring back at me.

The pleated skirt and deep wine-red blouse belonged to someone more confident, more sure of herself. For a moment, I stared at a stranger. I didn't deserve to be in these clothes or even in this store.

"You're an imposter, they're all gonna know."

I cringed at the words being whispered inside my head, but I knew they held a certain amount of truth. Why did the Unseen always have to make me feel so much worse?

Bobbie looked at me confused. "What's wrong? You don't like the outfit?"

How was I supposed to explain without sounding like a loon? My chest tightened, but I offered her the kind of smile I'd practiced and worn before. Thin and forced.

"No, I like it alright. I think it surprised me." I managed to let out a laugh, wondering if she could hear the dishonesty. Shaking away my insecurities, I changed the subject. "So, what's my grade for this one? Is it a keeper?"

She clapped her hands. "Definitely a keeper. And my grade?"

"I give yours a perfect score, all the girls are gonna wish they had that outfit for sure!"

We continued trying on the different clothes she picked for us until we'd gone through everything, settling on three outfits each. Pop paid for our items and put the bags into the boot of Miss Sally's car.

"Three outfits?" Pop said, feigning disbelief. "We can't have that. No way those will last the whole school year. So, where's the next stop, ladies?" His eyes sparkled with mischief as he looked between us.

Shocked to learn we were getting more things, I looked to Bobbie for guidance.

"Can we go to the Fashion Bar down the street? There's always a good sale there."

We repeated the same routine as the last store. This time, we ended up with four outfits each, as well as shoes and some hair accessories.

"There's one more store we might be able to find some good

stuff in, it's down the block. Is that okay?"

She gave her head a slight tilt and blinked slowly, like she knew how to work the room. The kind of face no grown-up ever says no to.

"I think that'll work," Pop said. "Afterward, we'll need to head to Weil's to pick up school supplies and other things you ladies might need."

By the end of our shopping adventure downtown, I had ten outfits and four extra interchangeable shirts. I'd gotten a nice pair of shoes, but Pop insisted I get at least one other pair. At Weil's, we were able to find every item on the list of supplies that Ms. Donaldson provided. Pop approved my second pair of shoes and sent us on our own to gather socks and undergarments.

Bobbie pulled out her mirror and reapplied her lip gloss. The urge to ask her about it had grown too strong, I couldn't hold back my curiosity any longer.

"What a pretty mirror. Why do you put that stuff on your lips so often?"

Closing the lid to her gloss before dropping it and the mirror back in her handbag, she paused. "Well, my mother gave me the mirror last Christmas. And she insists I keep my lips shiny. She won't let me use real makeup yet, but she thinks the gloss shows everyone I'm putting effort into my appearance."

"Why would she want you to do that?"

"It's just the way she is, you know, a real mirror warmer. I couldn't care less, but if looking fresh keeps her off my back, then I don't mind a little lip gloss and dressing like a square."

"Oh. Mama never got around to talking to me about any of those things before she…" I couldn't say the word, but Bobbie knew.

"You want me to show you how to put lip gloss on? I doubt Pop'll mind."

I nodded and held her small mirror while she applied the gloss.

"Okay, now rub your lips together, like this."

"It feels sticky. I don't know if I could get used to wearing this stuff every day."

"Sure you could. It just takes a little time. You'll see. I think we have everything we need. Let's go find the adults."

She gave me a wink, returned by my shy smile. Studying Bobbie had been the treat of the day, so I pushed on in hopes I could make it a little longer without embarrassing myself or Pop. I wondered if I would ever be as put-together as Bobbie. A perfect girl, with a perfect life.

Chapter Twenty-One

Guilt continued to pick at my mind with every new item we purchased. A day fit for royalty, but I was nothing of the sort. I didn't know how to blend in anymore, so I studied Bobbie harder. If she caught my eyes lingering, I couldn't tell. There was a kindness to her that I couldn't understand. To all of them, really. Even Miss Sally, who still eyed me with unease when she thought I wasn't looking.

We all piled back into Miss Sally's car, and Pop said exactly what my stomach thought. "Boy, am I hungry! What do you say we go feed these little girls and call it a day, huh?"

Miss Sally agreed. "You want to go to the Apple Cafe? Been a while since I've gone there."

"Sure, that'll be a good spot."

The restaurant offered a whole new experience for me. The sound of plates tapping and chatter around us made my palms sweat. I watched Bobbie and copied what she did, still not sure how to act in a place like this.

The waitress smiled as she handed us menus. My hands trembled. I looked around to see if anyone could tell I was lost. Bobbie offered me a knowing grin.

"When she comes back, she's gonna ask what you want to drink first. I always pick a Coke float," she said in a quiet voice.

"What's a Coke float?"

"It's a regular Coke with a scoop of ice cream in it. The flavor is the tops! If you've never had one, you should try it."

When the waitress came back to take our drink order, I asked for a Coke float like I'd been doing it all my life. Bobbie gave my hand a secret squeeze and ordered one for herself as well.

We made small talk while we waited. My curious eyes inspected the people at the neighboring tables, all laughing and carrying on the same way we were. I knew I blended in, but the Unseen picked at me—unrelenting even as we ate. His voice grew loud in my mind, so loud I missed whatever joke Pop made that left the rest of the table in stitches. I forced a laugh because they laughed, but I had no clue as to what could have been so funny.

After lunch, Miss Sally asked if we needed to go anywhere else. I remembered the signal Pop had given me, so I gave him a wink when no one else was looking.

"We're good for today. I'm a little worn out now, so I think we ought to head home."

When we pulled up to the house, Pop asked if they wanted to come in. Bobbie jumped out of the car like she'd been waiting for the invitation.

"It's so nice, Pop!" she exclaimed after taking a quick tour. "I like how high the ceiling is, and the beams and the big, pretty fire-place. It's like we're standing in a fairytale."

"Do you wanna see the backyard?" I asked, barely containing a grin as I led Bobbie toward the door.

"Sure, let's go look."

Worried she may be too old to enjoy my swing set, I paused. The answer came the second she saw it.

"Do you wanna go swing for a minute before my mother says we have to go?"

"I'd love to," I said, grinning through my words.

"My Golden Birthday's coming up in August. You wanna come to my party?" she asked as she pushed off to get her swing moving.

"What's a Golden Birthday?"

"I'll be turning thirteen and my birthday is August thirteenth. It's whatever day your birthday falls on when you turn the same number.

My mom said since I'll be a teenager, I might be allowed to have a coed party this time."

"I don't know if Pop would let me go. I'll have to ask him and let you know."

"Well, if you decide you're coming, you can invite a friend or two. So you don't feel so nervous with only mine being there."

"Well, I don't have any friends—"

She cut me off mid-sentence. "You'll make some, you'll see. Besides, I'm your friend. No matter what happens, you know you've got at least one."

"Thank you for being my friend, Bobbie. I wondered if you'd like me. I'm happy you do."

The back door swung open, and Miss Sally stuck her head outside. "C'mon, Bobbie, it's time to go."

"What's not to like?" she said with a grin. "Alright, we're outta here. I'll see you again soon."

Guilt nipped at me, but the idea of all the unfamiliar faces at her party kept me silent. One day, I hoped the thought of joining a group of children in celebration would give me excitement. As it was now, the idea of such an occasion terrified me.

I stayed on the swing set for a while after she left, thinking about the morning. Each day I slipped further into a new skin. My reflection would catch in a window, or I'd hear my own voice and wonder if I even knew this growing, changing girl.

There were moments when my new life was haunted by emotions I couldn't push away. Blame. Guilt. The steady belief that I could have saved my mother if I'd been stronger. But Pop's steady hand on my shoulder and familiar words pulled me back. Like an anchor, he kept me from drifting too far from shore.

At times, the Unseen's harsh reminders of who I'd been and what I'd done slithered through the cracks of my armor, causing me to question if I was weaker than I'd convinced myself. On those days, Pop could always sense my burdens. He tried his best to keep me grounded in the reality of my new life; it wasn't always an easy task. We discussed these issues at great length before my first appointment with my psychiatrist.

"You'll like the doctor, he's a gentle and patient man," he assured me in the way he always did.

"Will I have to go in by myself?"

The thought of being alone with the doctor hovered in my mind like a thin layer of fog. One part relief, one part unease. I hadn't quite figured out how to deal with strangers, but then again, there were things I needed the doctor to help me fix, things I didn't want to share with Pop. As hard as he worked to keep me busy with his company, I worried if he recognized the loneliness that consumed me.

"I'm going to have a word alone with him when we get there, and then we'll call you in. I'll only stay until you feel comfortable, but then I'll need to go. The therapy will help you more if you can talk to him alone. Do you think you can handle that?"

"Yes, sir, I'll be alright."

The doctor smiled and invited us in. An older man wearing a smile similar to Pop's. He had short white hair combed neatly to the side. I could see where it thinned, a significant contrast to Pop's full head of wild hair. They were familiar with each other. I realized then Pop had known him for some time, a trusted friend I would try my best to trust too.

He reached out his hand to shake mine. "Well, good morning. You must be Amanda." His smile reached all the way to his eyes and cured a fraction of my nervousness. "I'm Dr. Beall. It's a pleasure to meet you."

"Good morning, Dr. Beall."

"Would you mind sitting here while Pop and I go over a few things? We'll be back in just a few minutes."

I tried not to listen after they closed themselves inside his office, but their voices carried through the wall beside me.

"…and you know how I feel about medication. We can get her

through this without it; she's a resilient child." I heard Pop say in a hushed tone.

"These issues aren't calling into question her resilience; this is bigger. I don't think you understand."

"I'm not budging on this. I will not have her safety put at risk because she's different. I've spoken to the guidance counselor at her school, and she assured me she'd discuss everything with Amanda's teachers. She's gonna be fine. There's already a large network of people looking out for her. Your job is to counsel, that's all she needs."

"If you're sure this is what you think is best."

"Don't tell them about me, they won't understand."

Not now, not when I already had the task of trying to act normal.

I kept my voice low, too quiet for anyone else to hear, even through the walls. "I don't think you have a purpose other than making me feel bad. Please go. Leave me alone, I've got enough trouble without you butting in all the time."

"Don't tell the doctor about me or you'll be sorry. Pop already knows you're different, he said so himself."

I hesitated. What if the doctor could help me quiet this voice for good? The idea tugged at me in a soft yet dangerous way.

A part of me worried that he might look at me like I was crazy. He would tell Pop, the one person who still believed I could be normal.

This time, I knew I had to listen. If I didn't understand the Unseen's purpose, how could anybody else?

I sat up straight in my seat as Pop pulled the door open and called for me. He stayed with us for a few moments until I gave him a wink, our secret signal. After he left, I answered the doctor's questions as thoroughly as possible, never revealing my lifelong, invisible companion.

The sinking feeling I'd been dragging around finally lifted some. A hint of sunlight cutting through after days of gray. I started to look forward to my weekly visits with him. Almost like visiting an old friend. But this friend didn't judge me or expect anything in return. My time with the doctor cured a shred of my loneliness in ways I couldn't have imagined.

By the time summer ended, only a shadow of the old me remained. The little girl with fear in my eyes and sorrow in the places I never showed was now a whisper of the memory of who I'd been. But the whisper lingered, like a shadow in the corners of my mind, shaping each new version of me. Deep down, I knew no matter how much I grew, the pain from my parents and the mistakes I'd made would follow me. Until I faced it all head-on, it would always weigh me down.

Chapter Twenty-Two

"Are you ready to go?" Pop called from the front room.

I opened my backpack once more to inspect the supplies we'd placed inside the day prior. Everything sat in order as it had been the two other times I'd checked. I kept opening and closing the flap of my bag, as though something inside could help. The excitement I'd carried for weeks had turned into a knot I couldn't untangle.

There were kids waiting to meet me, Pop had said so for weeks. But what if he were wrong? What if I went, and everyone turned away, and nobody wanted to be my friend?

"I'm coming."

"I'm gonna drive you to school today in the new car. Miss Sally has a busy day, and I have an important business meeting at City Hall this morning."

I remembered what he told the crowd on the day of the protest.

"Are you gonna tell all those people from the crowd that all children will be allowed to stay at the orphanage? No matter the color of their skin?"

Pop's gaze drifted to the window, his fingers tapping lightly against the table. The silence stretched, thick with his worry and unspoken doubts.

"This isn't an easy topic, and no matter what, somebody's gonna walk away angry with my decision. In answer to your question, yes, I'm changing the policies at both orphanages. While I can't simply open the door and make the changes happen overnight, I'm gonna make it clear no child will be turned away from those homes again."

"You think it'll be scary for the first Black children when they come and stay at the home?"

"Indeed, I do." His voice dropped. The weight behind each word revealed the burden he carried when considering the future of the children and the home. "I've gone over the emotional toll it may have on them, and the best solution I've come up with is to employ some Black folk at each of the homes. Again, it's gonna make a lot of people angry, but I see no other way. My thought is if the children get used to seeing Black adults every day, the shock won't be as much when the first new children arrive."

"I bet that'll help them feel more comfortable when they show up too."

"You are wise beyond your years. Alright, young lady, I think it's time we get going."

We got into the car, and he paused before turning the key. "You look lovely this morning, very grown up."

"Thank you."

My smile came without effort this time. Unfamiliar yet natural, reminding me of feelings I hadn't experienced in ages.

Pop's voice filled the car with light chatter, sharing stories to pass the time. His voice barely registered, but the steady hum of it acted as a rope holding me steady while my mind raced.

"Okay, you've got your lunch, and you should have everything you need for class in your backpack. You want me to walk you inside?"

I thought about Buster's promise to meet me near the front entrance. I didn't want to do this alone, but I took the risk and decided to go ahead. My heart filled with the hope he'd stick to his word.

"I think I can manage."

"I'll be here waiting when you get out of school."

I exited the car, and reality set in. There were children everywhere. Some much younger, walking hand in hand with their parents. Others around my age and older walked alone or in groups of two or three.

I watched the other kids, noting the easy way they laughed with each other and their confident strides. Hoping my stiff steps wouldn't betray my feelings of alienation, I mirrored their childlike gestures.

My feet followed the path the other students took toward the double doors at the front of the school. I didn't see Buster anywhere. In a panic, my chest tightened. The noise came from everywhere at once. Voices, footsteps, and lockers slamming. I couldn't find my breath.

I turned and smacked straight into somebody. My lunchbox hit the floor with a loud clatter.

"I'm sorry," I said, scrambling to grab it, but instead hitting my head against his elbow.

Relief washed over me when my eyes made contact with Buster's.

"It's alright, I'm fine. Are you hurt?"

I shook my head while he picked up my lunchbox.

"I tried calling your name," he said. "But this place gets loud. Figured you didn't hear."

"Thank you for helping me find my class."

"It's no problem at all. We can drop your stuff in the room and go outside till the bell rings, if you want. My mom said you got into Mrs. Daly's class, same as me."

We looked for my name on each of the desks. When we located mine, I hung my backpack on the back of the chair and set my lunchbox on my seat.

Buster pointed to the basket below. "We usually put our lunches under there."

"Thank you." I blushed, feeling separated from this world again.

He moved like he belonged there. I kept my head down and followed, hoping no one noticed me.

"We can sit on the bench. Unless you wanna try and get into a game with the other girls."

"No, I'd rather sit."

"My mom says you're super smart. She said you could have gone to middle school if you'd wanted. I'd do anything to get through school faster. As soon as I graduate, I'm taking the first train to San Francisco for a nice, long vacation."

"I'm already so much younger than everyone in sixth grade. I didn't wanna be with kids even older," I explained. "What's in San Francisco?"

His eyes lit up as he spoke, gesturing his hands wildly as if painting the scene before him. I liked watching him; he was so animated and brimming with excitement about everything.

"The Golden Gate Bridge, the cable cars, the music in the streets! It's all so alive there. The smell of the food from the restaurants moves down the sidewalks before you even step inside. You can feel the city's heartbeat, you know? My mom and I went down there to meet with some of her old friends last summer. It's all I've thought about since."

I smiled, grateful to share in his happy memory.

"So, you said you're much younger than everyone in sixth grade. How old are you?"

"I'm nine and a half. I'll be ten on March eighteenth. I guess I'm supposed to be in fourth grade, but your mom said I'd be wasting time if I started there."

"Started? What grade were you in before?"

I didn't mean to slip. It just came out.

I was still trying to think of an answer when the bell saved me. I'd never appreciated the sound of a bell until then.

"We should go. I hear Mrs. Daly doesn't play when it comes to being late," he said.

I'd pictured school much more neat and orderly. The kids would sit in rows, marching in single-file lines like at the orphanage. I thought of children raising their hands to ask questions, just as I had seen them do on television.

This was not that. The sounds of the classroom made my head hurt. When the bell rang for recess, the hallway exploded. The noise hit me so hard it made me flinch. Laughter bounced off the walls, feet shuffled without rhythm. It all blurred together until my stomach ached from the constant movement and noise.

"Is it always so busy? There hasn't been a quiet second all day," I said as we headed to lunch.

In the middle of the noise, a voice cut through. It came soft at first, then sharper, and called out my name. I turned, but no one was there. Still, it pressed on, curling around my ears like breath against my skin. *"Amanda. Amanda."* I swallowed hard, but it stayed with me, threading through the noise, separate yet impossible to ignore.

"It's not always like this." Buster's voice cut into my delusion. "Usually, the first few days, the teachers check out the students. Kind of see who fits where. By next week, everything will calm down. Line leaders and hall monitors will be assigned. It'll feel a lot more organized then."

"I hope so."

A couple of boys came and joined us at the table with a nervous-looking girl trailing behind.

"Hey, Donaldson. Who's your friend?" A tall boy with shaggy blond hair and thick glasses nudged Buster.

"This is Amanda. She's new."

"I'm David," he added, sticking out his hand.

The room shrank with every new face. The air pulled me away from my body until I couldn't remember how to breathe.

My practiced smile stretched across my face, but my jaw ached under nervous pressure. Their laughter circled me, a blaring buzz causing my head to pound.

"They can see your smile isn't real. Do what Mama said, relax and breathe. Don't mess this up, or you'll be walking around this school alone."

I sat at the lunch table in a bubble of awkward silence, smiling only when necessary. The edges of my cheeks tightened from the effort. And then came the forced laughter, a wave to push me further from the moment. My mind was miles away from the table. When the bell finally rang, I let out the breath I'd been holding. The rest of the day slipped by like I was watching it happen to someone else.

One moment, we were walking to class, and the next, I stood on the sidewalk looking for Pop. He waved at me from the parking lot. I told Buster goodbye before heading toward the car, wondering all the while if I'd done anything embarrassing without knowing it.

"Well? How did you like your first day?"

I smiled up at him while I put on my seatbelt. "It was good, but school is a whole lot louder than I expected. I can't wait to go home and change into play clothes so I can paint and enjoy some peace and quiet."

When we got home, I ran inside to change out of my nice clothes, and Pop had a seat in his chair in the front room. By the time I'd finished dressing, he had his shoes off and the newspaper spread open in front of him.

"How did your meeting go today?"

"No better or worse than I expected. Some people were upset by the news, but the majority were content by the time we ended. More than half of the staff from both facilities were on the side of right. I hadn't expected such a welcoming bunch."

"I'm sorry some people got upset with you."

"That's normal, child. You can never make everyone happy, it's an impossible task. You do your best to stick to what you believe is right."

"Okay, I will."

I let him know I'd be out back painting and made my way outside with the container of art supplies.

The sounds of nature calmed me, but I yearned for a friend to share my days with. Pop stayed nearby to laugh and keep me company, but I craved the friendship of a child, somebody to swing on the swing set with me or trade stories of our secret thoughts.

While I painted, my eyes kept drifting to the empty swings. The chains moved like someone had just stepped off.

My brush slowed from the ache of the quiet all around me. They kept moving, begging me to warm their seats, but with no one to share in the fun, the magic of its pull faded.

"You're never gonna be happy. You whine when it's noisy, whine when it's quiet. You begged Mama to let you outside, and you're outside now. And still you complain. He was right about you, always carrying on and complaining. No wonder he drank so much."

My visits from the Unseen stretched further apart. But I found myself craving him at times, even when he made me feel bad. Anything was better than being alone. I closed my eyes and pleaded for him to come back. To be kind. But he refused to speak again. My mind lay as empty as the canvas in front of me.

Rather than beg an entity I couldn't control, I poured myself into the art I'd been working on—an image showing a world of my making. One with noise I could turn down and faces that didn't laugh without me. A world where Mama didn't leave. Where swings never sat empty.

If I could figure out how to paint a person, maybe Mama would smile down from Heaven and bring them to life.

Chapter Twenty-Three

I'd been painting for a while when I heard a dog barking. I set my brush down and stepped off the porch to take a closer look.

A golden retriever bounded through the empty lot next door. His tongue lolled out like he was grinning. He came straight for me.

"Duke!" someone called in the distance. He paused, but not for long.

"C'mere, Duke. Good dog." I patted my legs.

He came close enough for me to loop my arms around his neck. "I've got you, boy."

I almost caught him, but he slipped loose and knocked me flat on my backside. His tail whipped around as he licked my face like I was already his. I giggled at his warm, slobbery enthusiasm.

The woman whistled again, but Duke planted himself beside me. I looked for anything to fashion a leash out of, my eyes landing on a piece of scrap cord hanging on a hook. The back door swung open as I secured the makeshift collar.

"What's going on out here?" Pop called.

"The neighbor's dog got loose, but I caught him. Can I take him back home?"

"He seems friendly enough, but you've got to be careful with dogs. You never know their temperament."

The woman's whistle rang out again. Pop nodded toward the sound.

"Go ahead and walk him home, but straight there and back, understand?"

"Yes, sir."

Excitement bubbled through me as I led Duke across the yard. Pop trusted me with this responsibility, and I didn't want to let him down.

Duke, however, was a handful. The cord slipped through my grasp, the friction of it sliding over my delicate skin until it burned. I stopped in the field to tie it to my shorts.

"Amanda, Amanda." Harsh and raspy whispers on the breeze made me pause. The demon once living inside my father found me. I dropped low and held onto Duke, convincing myself he could protect me. His tail wagged, and he licked my cheek. I shook all over.

Please make it stop, Mama. I sent out a silent prayer, hoping it would find its way to her somehow.

The wind blew again, marrying my senses with the faint scent of whiskey and venom. The fields appeared empty, but I knew better. My father was here somewhere, watching me, waiting for the perfect chance to strike.

With shaking limbs and a deep-rooted fear, I stood up to run. My legs refused to follow orders. With each step I attempted, my feet sank deeper into the earth until my calves were completely buried. The smoky black outline of the shadow figure strolled past, close enough to touch me.

"I knew you'd come," I whispered in defeat, turning my head to follow its path. It disappeared each time my eyes tried to focus. Flashes on my right, then my left. It continued to evade my direct line of sight. A cold presence closed in on my back. Its hand reached out to take hold of my body and drag me into its realm.

It would take me away from Pop. From my new life. From everything Mama died for me to have. And then I'd go to Hell, where my father waited.

Icy fingers grazed over my skin. I lunged forward, falling face-first into the dirt. When I opened my eyes, it was gone. My legs were free. Duke wagged his tail like he was proud of himself. I stood up and brushed off the dirt clinging to my clothes. And then we ran.

Duke dragged me up the steps of the neighbor's porch. I could hardly catch my breath.

I had no time to knock when the door swung open. Duke bolted inside, pulling me along with him.

"I'm so sorry, I didn't mean to barge in."

A petite Black woman with a concerned expression crouched to help untie the cord.

"It's no bother, Duke can be a lot without my daughter 'round to keep him in line."

As she worked, I noticed a family portrait on the mantle. "Is that her in the picture?"

"Yes, that's my Patricia."

"And the boy's your son?" I asked, pointing to the older boy beside her.

"Mm-hmm. He's back in Georgia now, where we're from." Her smile buckled, only for a second, but I noticed the shift.

"She looks about my age."

I couldn't tear my gaze from the girl's bright smile and braided pigtails. A little girl living right next door, the possibility of a friend.

"I'd say that's about right." Her voice quieted a little, inner thoughts escaping through the barrier she'd placed herself within.

There were things to know here, things my young mind couldn't comprehend. I pressed on about the girl.

"Maybe she could come over to play sometime. I've got a swing set."

"I'm sorry, honey, but that's just not possible. You should head on home. Run along, don't wanna worry anybody."

"Yes, ma'am. Thank you. My name's Amanda."

"Nice to meet you, Amanda. I'm Mrs. Taylor. Please let your parents know Duke won't be coming around your yard again."

I hesitated, wanting to ask more about Patricia, but Mrs. Taylor guided me toward the door. I left with the questions still buzzing in my mind. Even though she'd said no, my desire to meet the girl seeped through my skin and into the air around me.

I'd forgotten all about the dangerous entities lurking in the distance as I kicked a pebble down the side of the road, contemplating ways to meet the girl.

Back home, I told Pop about the Taylors over grilled cheese and tomato soup. My words came out fast between bites, excitement overflowing from my mouth. The sound of someone knocking cut me off mid-sentence.

I jumped up, but Pop stopped me, taking a moment to glance through the window.

"Look, they've brought Patricia with them!" I squealed.

Pop studied the trio on the porch for a moment. A grimness flashed in his expression as he reached forward to open the door. I noticed the way his body turned rigid until he forced it to relax. Did it bother him that they were Black? It hadn't occurred to me to mention it. I stood behind him, considering the conundrum as he opened the door.

"Good afternoon. I'm Pop Wells, you must be the Taylors."

"Yes, sir. My name's Henry, and this here's my wife, Sissy. Now, I wanna apologize for Duke. He gets real excited when he escapes. We've been trying to train him not to go runnin' off to any of the neighbors yards."

"Just Pop'll do," he replied, extending his arm for a handshake.

Mr. Taylor looked at his hand as if he were unsure what to do with it, glancing sideways at his wife before meeting Pop's grasp with his own.

"No harm done. Amanda says he's just a big sweetheart. Would you like to come inside? We've got some fresh lemonade in the re-frigerator."

Again, they exchanged looks of confusion before Mr. Taylor replied. "You want us to come inside? Your home? Us?"

"Unless you'd rather we stood here in the heat..."

Mr. Taylor looked at his wife, and she gave him a slight nod, and they stepped in through the front door with Patricia in tow.

"Please have a seat. Amanda, would you go into the kitchen and fix everyone a nice glass of lemonade?"

Patricia and I didn't move a muscle until her father smiled. "That's awfully generous, Mr. Wells—I mean Pop. Thank you."

We hurried into the kitchen while the adults made small talk. "Do you want lemonade?"

She shook her head.

"Me either," I said as I pulled down three tall glasses.

"Do you all invite Black folk into your home often?"

"We don't really invite anyone over at all."

"Hmm, interesting," she replied.

I placed the drinks onto a serving tray and carried them back to the front room with Patricia following behind.

"Thank you, dear," Mrs. Taylor said with a tight smile.

Patricia tugged at her overall strap and shifted from one foot to the other. She glanced toward Pop as if waiting for a signal to either stay or flee.

"Is it all right if we go out back to play in the yard? I wanna show her my swing set."

Mr. and Mrs. Taylor shared another uncomfortable glance, confusion etched in their faces. Their eyes shifted between Pop and me as though they were trying to figure out our angle. I considered that they might feel unwelcome, or perhaps as out of place as I did. Though for them, it came from somewhere deeper beneath the surface of every word and gesture. It wasn't the same as my usual nervousness; theirs was much older.

Mrs. Taylor opened her mouth to respond, but Pop's voice cut through her hesitation. "Sure, that's okay." Patricia grinned like they'd handed her the moon. We bolted out the back door.

"What grade are you in?" I asked her as we swayed back and forth on the swings.

"I started fifth today. What about you?"

"I'm in sixth. I go to Willamette Park Elementary."

"Oh, not me. I go to the school they send all the Black kids to. It's pretty far. Back in Georgia, Mama let us walk. I don't think I'm gonna like riding the bus all the time."

"Pop's driving me the first few days, but I'll ride the bus next week. Too bad we aren't in the same school, we could ride together."

"Yeah," she replied shortly.

"I've never been to Georgia or even out of Oregon. Do you like it here?"

"It's different. I've made some friends, though, so summer was alright."

As the minutes slipped by, Patricia's shoulders began to relax. Her laughter came out easier as she shared stories about her friends and the games they played. It didn't sound much different from the ones the girls played at my school. Her voice steadied, words flowing like we'd known each other forever. I found I enjoyed listening to her perspective on the world. She was different, like me, which gave me comfort in spending time with her.

"I'd better go inside and check in with my parents. We've been out here for a while now."

I jumped off the swing and followed her through the back door. The adults were still talking when we came in. Pop's voice came out low with a hint of pleading in his tone.

"She just needs a little time to adjust, that's all. I'm sure once she feels stable, these issues will dissolve on their own."

The back door clanged behind me, causing a direct shift in their topic of conversation.

"He's talking about you, about YOUR business. And with strangers no less. The Taylors won't let their daughter come around you. You're no good for her. You're no good for anybody."

Patricia looked at me, unable to hide the pity in her eyes. She hadn't heard the Unseen's words, she couldn't have. But she'd heard

Pop's loud and clear, and now she knew the truth; I could never be her friend.

We stepped silently into the front room, and the adults turned their attention toward me. I gasped to see their faces. Their judging eyes had grown wider, too wide to be natural. Mr. Taylor's mouth contorted into an evil grin, exposing blackened teeth and tongue. It lashed out, smacking against the glass of lemonade in his hand.

Mrs. Taylor began to shrivel, her tiny frame becoming even smaller as her skin shrank tighter and tighter until it clung to nothing but bones—her flesh disappearing beneath the strain.

And Pop's eyes, those happy eyes crinkling at the corners, continued to grow until all I saw of his face were two black hollows staring intently into my soul.

They became characters. Like the ones from my father's stories when he was drunk and trying to scare me straight.

I stepped backward, my feet stumbling against Patricia's, and I fell. When I looked up, she stood unmoved as if her body were nothing more than a fog I'd fallen through.

Pop's voice came through distant, and then Mrs. Taylor's. Muffled at first, but becoming clearer. And I found myself standing next to Patricia. Hadn't I fallen? When did I get up?

I shook my head, trying to clear away whatever darkness lingered there. A blink. A breath. A sound too solid to be imagined. Reality slowly came back into focus.

"...here? At your house?" Mrs. Taylor asked. "And you're saying *you're* gonna cook for *us*?"

Her words came out with long pauses, revealing her curiosity and doubt. I didn't need to hear the whole conversation to catch the strain behind it.

"That's right, ma'am. I'm glad to have finally met the folks next door. Besides, it would be a nice opportunity for me to gain a little insight into the changes we're making at the orphanages. But it wouldn't be a complete waste of time for you, I'm actually an excellent cook, and modest too."

"You can't expect me to believe you're serious, Mr. Wells."

"Pop," he corrected her.

"Right. Pop. Now you gotta know this is a very unusual invitation. Not only have we never been invited into a white person's home before, but they surely ain't offered to cook us a meal."

"Now, Sissy. Where are your manners?" Mr. Taylor chastised.

"It's alright, this isn't the norm for what we're used to. But with all due respect, the world we've been brought up in is fading. Soon it'll be nothing but a memory. A story of the old days parents and grandparents will tell. By the time Amanda's my age, she'll be living amongst people of all colors. Who knows, maybe it'll be the norm by the time she's *your* age."

"One can only hope," Mrs. Taylor said.

"So how about it? Dinner at my place on Friday, say around six o'clock?"

They looked at each other as if in a silent discussion before Mr. Taylor reached out his hand to shake Pop's. "Yes, sir. We'll see you at six on Friday. Sissy and I will bring dessert."

And so it was set, a real-life dinner party like nothing I'd ever experienced before. I hoped they would bring Patricia too, and prove to the Unseen he was wrong about me. I could be good for somebody if I tried harder.

"Don't get too comfortable. Remember why you're here. He'll get rid of you when he finds out the truth. You don't deserve this life or new friends. All you'll get is all you've got. Me."

Chapter Twenty-Four

The week inched by. Every passing second bled into hours. The Unseen grew insistent, their constant warnings crowding my concentration at all hours of the day and night. I kept thinking about dinner with the Taylors, but the Unseen's voice bounced around in my skull louder than ever.

No matter the poison he spat, I wouldn't allow him to break my spirit.

On Friday, I stood in the school bathroom, alone with my reflection and the voice I couldn't shake. I held the sink tight and whispered, "They're coming tonight. Patricia will be with them." Saying it aloud was supposed to make it true.

A soft creaking noise came from somewhere across the room. My attention snapped toward the sound, but when I turned back to the mirror, my head hadn't moved.

A chill slid down my back like ice water. I stepped away, but the girl in the mirror stayed still. Her head was turned, eyes locked on something I couldn't see. My fingers trembled as I reached up to touch my face.

"What's happening? Help me somebody, please."

The bathroom walls closed in. A shadow slithered up behind me, stretching long and thin across the tiles. My legs gave out. I dropped down and covered my head, praying that would help. Is this when it happens? Will they take me with them this time?

"Please stop," I begged the Unseen.

"It's not me. This is something else entirely. I've always been

your friend. I'm what keeps it from getting too close. I'm what protects you."

I knew he wasn't lying. He'd been with me through every second. Every secret. Every jagged, aching moment. But I needed a real friend to experience life with, not a voice intent on hiding my true self from the world.

The bathroom door swung open. I jumped up as Mrs. Daly appeared in the doorway. "What's the holdup?"

"I'm sorry, my shoelace had a tangle. I've fixed it now."

"Come along then, it's not proper for children to dawdle in the restroom."

I nodded, glancing once more at the mirror. My reflection stood there, perfectly in sync, as if it had never left. But I knew better.

It had.

And next time it might not come back.

For the rest of the day, I ignored the Unseen until he eventually fell silent. When the bell rang to dismiss us, I flew to Pop's car, words spilling from my mouth faster than I could control. My hands danced in the air as I relived the better parts of my day, excitement overflowing from me like a shaken pop bottle.

Pop chuckled, glancing sideways as he gripped the wheel. "Slow down. You'll wear yourself out before we even get home."

I paused long enough to catch my breath. "I'm just looking forward to our dinner guests tonight. What if they don't show? Mrs. Taylor didn't seem too thrilled at the idea."

"They'll come," Pop reassured me, adjusting his hat. "It's not because she wasn't interested. Mrs. Taylor said she's never had dinner with white folks before. Same as you've never shared a meal with your neighbors. She's probably as nervous as you are."

When we got home, my feet wouldn't keep still, tapping out an anxious rhythm on the hardwood floor as I moved from the kitchen to the front room.

I paced the house until Pop noticed. "Why don't you go out

back and paint a picture for our guests? It'd be a nice gesture."

I grabbed my art supplies and headed to the back porch. The blank canvas dared me to begin. I thought of Mona's sunrise, bright and hopeful, and started sketching the empty lot next to our house. In half an hour, I'd outlined trees, a field, and the sun, bringing the scene to life with a splendor of colors. The trees stretched high under a sky of puffy clouds, with sunlight spilling warmth across the field.

But it looked incomplete. I picked up my pencil and, hesitating, marked a spot for a figure. Mixing new colors, I painted her blurry shape, pigtail braids, overalls, and a white shirt. The image appeared clear yet indistinct. Patricia came to life on the canvas, the friend I'd always dreamed of, someone to share my secrets with.

Pop came out to check on me as I rinsed my brushes, now that I had finished the picture. I gestured to the canvas. "It's not as nice as Mona's art, but I think the Taylors will like it."

He studied the piece, his hands unusually still. "It's beautiful. Will you tell me about it?"

I glanced back at the golden-lit field. "It's inspired by Mona's painting at the orphanage. Patricia is a new beginning, maybe even a friend. Growing up, I spent so much time alone, always dreaming someone would step out of the woods and rescue me. She's blurry like the people I see in my dreams. And I don't know how to paint people well."

"If that isn't the most elegant explanation. What will you call it?"

"I think I'd like to call it *'On a Summer's Daydream.'*"

"Perfect. Don't forget to sign it."

I signed the corner and packed up my supplies, then went in to wash up. Time dragged until we finally heard a soft knock at the door. Pop opened it, beaming. "Good evening, Taylors!"

"Apologies for being late," Mr. Taylor said with a smile, nodding toward his wife. "One of us took forever picking out clothes."

"Oh, don't worry about it." Pop smiled big and kind, his eyes crinkling as he took the dish from Mrs. Taylor's shaky hands.

"It's peach cobbler. My mama's recipe," she said, nearly dropping it as she passed it to him.

I'd been holding my breath for too long. But when the Taylors separated, I saw Patricia standing behind them. They'd brought her along. Relief washed over me.

Dinner passed with light chatter. The adults continued their conversation while I cleared the plates. Patricia followed me to the kitchen, both of us quiet as we strained to hear what they said.

"You're not uncomfortable having Black folk at your dinner table? I gotta be honest, this has been an awkward night for me."

He paused like he always did when he wanted to get it right. "I get why you feel that way, but I want to ease your mind, Mrs. Taylor —"

"Sissy," she corrected. "And my husband is Henry. If we're gonna be on a first-name basis, it goes all the way around."

Pop took a moment before responding. "Sissy, I understand. But I shared meals with Black people throughout my childhood. My mother passed when I was young, and my father employed cooks and maids, some Black and some white. When dinnertime came, everyone sat at the same table. So, no, I don't feel any way except pleased you came, and excited to try your cobbler."

My chest warmed at how gentle Pop was.

"Think it's okay if we go out back?" Patricia asked in a whisper.

I smiled, excited for the chance to show her the painting.

"Can we go out to the back porch, Pop?"

"Of course, dear. Stay close, it's getting dark out there."

My throat tightened when I picked up the picture and handed it to her. "I made this for you and your parents. It's not perfect, I'm just learning how to paint."

Patricia studied the art, her brow furrowing slightly. "Why did you do this?"

"I've never had friends before, but I wished for one all my life, so I made you something. Thought it might help us be friends."

"I didn't think you'd even like me. We're so… different. But the painting is nice. My parents'll be happy to take it."

"You wanna go inside and see if they're ready to have some cobbler? I've been thinking about it since your mother handed it to Pop. It looks delicious."

"Yes, let's go."

The adults were still at the table, deep in conversation.

"It seems like you've thought this through," Mr. Taylor said.

"And Black folk are gonna earn the same pay as whites?" Mrs. Taylor asked.

Pop's hands tightened on the edge of the table as he leaned forward. "It doesn't seem right to pay less. All I care about is making sure all of the children are as comfortable as possible during the transition. That's the foundation these orphanages were built on."

Mrs. Taylor's eyes widened, her grin breaking through before she slapped the table with an open palm. The sharp sound echoed through the room. "Sign me up!" she exclaimed, leaning forward in anticipation. "Money like that would change our lives."

"Now, I need you to be realistic. This job isn't for the faint of heart. Some people won't be thrilled to see a Black person walk through the door. My director, Margaret Shoemaker, has done her best to hire kind people, but a few bad apples always find their way in. Amanda and I had our own unfortunate experience with a bad seed recently."

Her tone turned sharp with determination. "I'm not faint of heart. If the job's available, I'd like to apply. If you're hiring for the boys' home, Henry'll apply too."

Henry blinked, surprised. "I will?" he asked, his voice rising slightly.

"Of course you will. If this man is serious about paying Black folk the same as whites, why wouldn't we try? I'm tired of us working ourselves half to death and still only making scraps."

"Well, the lady's spoken. I guess we're in," Henry said with a chuckle.

"Now, this is not why I asked you to come to dinner. I wanted to share my thoughts and get your opinions. I could never see this through the eyes of a Colored person any more than you could see it through mine. I'd hate for you to think I lured you here with my famous meatloaf as a bribe to get you to work in my orphanages. But if you're serious…"

"We are," Mrs. Taylor assured him. "Just let us know when and where to interview. But Pop, try not to call us Colored. While I'm sure you mean no harm, the word feels offensive to me. I'm Black, you're white. No reason to use any other language than that."

Pop looked at her, startled. "I didn't know, and I appreciate you telling me."

She nodded. "Thank you. Now let's have some cobbler, I think we're all long past ready for a treat."

I washed Mrs. Taylor's casserole dish so she could take it home clean. As they gathered their things to leave, I went out back to get the painting from the porch. Patricia followed, stopping me briefly.

"I'm sorry if I acted strangely when I first saw your painting. I do love it. Nobody's ever done anything like this for me before." She waited a second, then pulled me into a hug. "If we're gonna be best friends, you gotta call me Patty. Only my parents and teachers call me Patricia."

"Neat, like Patty Duke. That'll be easy to remember. I love that show."

She smiled as I carried the painting inside to show her parents, hoping they'd enjoy it as much as Patty had.

We stepped through the back door to find the adults talking in low voices. I couldn't hear much, but I knew their words weren't meant for us. Pop looked tense, the lines around his mouth drawn tight. The Taylors glanced at each other, sharing some silent thoughts I couldn't read. My chest tightened. Were they talking about me and Patty? The worry of it pulled at the fragile pieces of my core.

My subtle cough cut through whatever they weren't saying out loud. I gripped the canvas, a knot curling in my stomach. I glanced at Patty, unsure.

"I… I made a painting for you guys."

"Show them, they're gonna love it," she said, doing her best to reassure me.

The room went still. Even my swallow sounded out loud against the walls. I handed the painting to Mrs. Taylor. She lifted a hand to her mouth as she took the painting. Her eyes shimmered. She blinked fast, but one tear still slipped down her cheek.

Mr. Taylor's voice broke up the silence. "What a fine-looking painting. We'll cherish this, won't we, Sissy?"

She blinked away the remaining tears she hadn't let fall. "Yes, it was so thoughtful of you to make this. You're a talented little girl."

"Are you sure you like it? I didn't mean to make you cry."

Mrs. Taylor's fingers traced the edge of the canvas. She smiled. "I cried at the sentiment. This means so much to us, Amanda. Thank you."

The moment caved under a crushing tension I hadn't anticipated. When they stood to leave, my shoulders sagged in relief. An evening of splendor had turned into a tightness in my chest. I needed quiet.

The following week, Mrs. Shoemaker met with the Taylors and offered them both jobs. Mrs. Taylor started in the kitchen at the girls' home, while Mr. Taylor became the maintenance worker at the boys' home.

They came to our place often for Friday night dinners, and sometimes we would go to theirs. After the new year, the Taylors had relatives move in with them. Mr. and Mrs. Taylor looked forward to coming over for Friday night dinners even more once their house filled up. Pop told me they probably welcomed the break from all the extra family.

Patty and I grew close as time went by. We made it a ritual to meet halfway between our houses after school almost every day. Most Fridays, we had sleepovers at my place, sharing stories and playing games together. Our bond grew thicker than blood, stronger than the world refusing to see us.

Everything I'd ever hoped for inched closer to my grasp. Time had finally found its place in my world, and so had routine. Pop and I enjoyed lunch with Miss Sally and Bobbie on Sundays. Buster met me at the front of the school every morning, sometimes riding the bus home with me to share in my playtime with Patty. But Pop and the Taylors kept me steady—a strange little team of grown-ups patching my scars in ways I didn't fully see yet.

The shadows stayed hidden, just out of sight, but I knew they hadn't gone far. Words from the Unseen faded slowly into the background, their endless chatter replaced by the voices of real-life people in my world. I could learn to be like them, to be normal. The demons had gone, leaving me in the hands of angels.

At least that's what I told myself.

Chapter Twenty-Five

Time moved to its own beat until four years had passed in a blur. Now thirteen, during the summer before my sophomore year of high school, the age gap between my classmates and me became a new type of void. While they were learning to drive, I was trying to find someone who could explain what was causing me to bleed.

Thinking about asking my friends made my stomach twist. My throat tightened imagining their reactions, curious if they still saw me as a baby. I didn't want to be the girl who didn't know what every other girl already figured out, so I kept my mouth shut and went to find Mrs. Taylor. With fingers crossed, I hoped she could steer me in the right direction.

She sent me on my way with a pep talk and a paper bag full of supplies. It hit me like a punch to the gut to realize I couldn't run to Pop for everything. The idea never crossed my mind before, but now it loomed over me. As much as I loved him, there were things he couldn't fix, things he didn't even know how to talk about. I'd figured this one out without Pop's guidance, but what other issues would I have to face alone?

My worries weren't so different from my friends, but my troubled past haunted me in ways I knew no one around me understood. I craved normalcy from within, to feel like I belonged in the same world as my friends. I was still an imposter. Would I ever get past my ghosts to join in their smiles and laughter? I wanted to enjoy every day of summer, not only the days these buried things allowed me.

As it did every year, July came in a fury, bringing the fourth anniversary of my parents' death. The sun blared through my window, so I hid myself beneath the protection of my blankets, squeezing my eyes shut to wish the world away. But the world doesn't stop for one tragic memory, one sad little girl.

The phone's wail reached into the dim recesses of my retreat, pulling me out to face the morning.

"Hello." My tired voice croaked out the greeting with little enthusiasm.

"Hey, uh, it's Buster. You feelin' alright?"

"Oh, yeah. Sorry, I just woke up." My face cringed at the dishonesty, but I couldn't tell him I'd been wallowing in a pity party for one beneath a fortress of blankets.

"I didn't mean to wake you, just thought I'd see if you wanted to come see the fireworks with me on Thursday?"

The Fourth of July had always been a huge celebration in our city, but for me, it held little magic. The year before had been the worst. Nobody noticed as my body tightened, my eyes flinching as each explosion rang out. I'd kept my composure as long and as well as I could, ignoring the memory of the blast from my father's gun. I needed an excuse, another lie to tell a friend.

"I promised Pop I'd stay in on the fourth this year. I guess there's been a lot of delinquents running about, causing all sorts of trouble. He worries too much, you know how he is."

The sigh he tried to conceal made its way across the phone line. "I see, yeah, he does worry a lot. Well, what about Saturday? My mom's gonna take me driving after my paper route, but we could pick you up afterward. Maybe we can hit the matinee, think they're playing The Odd Couple."

"Sounds great. I get my allowance on Friday, so we can go get a milkshake after if you want."

"Perfect. See you Saturday."

"Bye, Buster."

Now I only needed a way to fix my mind before then.

Saturday came, and I still didn't have a clear head. I tried to smile and act nonchalant, but my shaky ruse wouldn't fool Buster. He asked if I wanted to talk about it, all the while expecting me to brush it off as nothing like usual. This time, I couldn't push it down.

I hadn't meant to unload it all, but the years of anger and confusion spilled out without pause. I held back almost nothing. My voice cracked as I told him about my mother and the way she looked when I found her. And the things my father did to torment us along the way. A century of grief unraveled from my shoulders. A weight I'd carried for too long. I finished talking. My body was drained, but my core had become lighter somehow.

Buster sat quietly, staring off at nothing. He gave a slight nod, his jaw tight, as he tried to keep something inside.

"Amanda, I'm so sorry. If you'd have chosen to walk the other way…" He didn't have to say more. I knew he understood.

His words stuck with me long after our conversation. I couldn't stop thinking about what would have happened if I'd knocked on someone else's door. What kind of life would I have then? The thought sent a shiver down my spine. It could have all been so different, but I would've been none the wiser. Knowing what I could've missed made it worse somehow, not better.

When Buster's mother dropped me off at home late Saturday afternoon, I was still feeling down. I needed the comfort of a sister. I needed to see Patty.

"Is it all right if I go to the Taylors for a while?" I asked Pop while drying the last of our dinner dishes.

"I think that'll be alright. You want me to walk you over?"

"Thanks, but I can manage. Don't forget to take your medicine," I said, handing him a glass of water as I passed by to leave. "Love you."

"Love you too, dear."

Even in the summer heat, a cold shiver followed me across the field. I picked up speed, that old feeling creeping in; the sense that someone was watching. By the time I reached their steps, I'd broken out into a sweat, my trophies of fear now dampening the hair at the nape of my neck.

I knocked once, Mr. Taylor opened the door, and invited me in.

"Hey kiddo, you alright?"

I bent over, catching my breath, feeling silly for rushing in like that. "Think I scared myself. Patty around?"

"She might be in the back room. You can check."

I headed down the hall, slow and careful. One soft knock, but no one answered. I eased the door open enough to look inside. The room used to be bursting with color and clothes everywhere. Now it looked hollow, like someone had cleared the life out of it.

I hesitated in the doorway, knowing that everything was wrong. What happened to Patty's room? The posters, the soft blue blanket draped over the bed, the pile of clothes always in the corner; gone. A flat gray bedspread stretched smooth across the bed. The walls stood blank, except for one picture I didn't recognize. The usual freshness of the room lay absent in the stale, old air. It was as if the room had been waiting too long for someone to come back.

I stepped inside, slow and careful, my breath coming quicker with each step. I crossed to the closet and swung the door open. Empty. No clothes. No shoes. No trace of Patty at all.

A cobweb in the corner of the closet caught my attention, the glaring eyes of its spider dared me to come closer—to enter the portal I knew without question would drag me to Hell, to my father.

The floor beneath me shifted, or maybe it was the sound of my legs threatening to give out.

"Patty?" my voice cracked.

Mrs. Taylor's footsteps barely made a sound against the hardwood. "Amanda?"

I turned and swallowed hard.

"Where's Patty?" My own voice startled me, too sharp and

filled with a desperate pleading for Patty to appear. I pointed at the closet. "Where are her clothes?"

She paused, her face unreadable, then softened in the way she did when she thought I needed handling. "She's spending the night at a friend's."

"But Mr. Taylor, he said—"

"Henry didn't know, I just got back from droppin' her off."

Her words wobbled as though she were speaking through water. I clenched my eyes shut, willing myself to hear her right, to believe her. I'd seen things incorrectly before, but never been caught in the middle of a private battle between reality and delusion. She'd seen my paranoia, seen me succumb to the tricks my mind played. I had to get out of this, to show her I was normal so that she wouldn't take Patty away from me. If I opened my eyes, it would all be back the way it was supposed to be.

I inhaled, exhaled.

When I looked again, there it was. The blue blanket. The posters. The smell of Patty's perfume hanging in the air.

Heat flooded my face. "I—" I backed toward the door, ready to leave before she could say anything else.

Mrs. Taylor reached for my arm, her touch gentle and reassuring. "Sit with me for a minute?"

I wanted to run, but the calm pleading in her voice made me stay. I sat on the bed, keeping my eyes down as she settled beside me.

"You've been off this week," she said after a long pause. "I know why."

I picked at a loose thread on my skirt, my throat too tight to answer.

"It's only been four years, I know the wounds are still fresh, child. Time has a way of moving along. Weeks and months can sometimes feel like days. But for the pain, time doesn't move so fast, does it?"

I shook my head, leaning over on her shoulder.

"She loved you, you know? She'd be so proud of you. And I know I could never—" She stopped, then tried again. "I'm not her. I know that. But I'm still here, and I always will be."

My eyes stung, and I looked away. Mrs. Taylor had been there through every scraped knee, every lost battle with my temper, every long, aching night when missing Mama felt like a sickness intent on killing me. She'd been stepping into the space Mama left behind for years, quietly filling those empty shoes. And I hadn't seen it until now.

I gave a small nod, unable to find my voice.

She smiled and tucked a piece of hair behind my ear. "Come on, let's go hunt down something sweet. I think we both need it."

I let her pull me to my feet, the weight in my chest a little lighter. She hugged me tight before I left, a vast embrace from the arms of a dainty woman. The warmth spread across my skin like the first note of a familiar lullaby. An illusion of safety warmed me for a time. But my moments, good or bad, were never meant to last.

I began my walk home unguarded. But the hot summer air carried a scent meant to stop me in my tracks. Whiskey and smoke. Thin as a whisper on the wind, it curled through the air, coating my skin and covering my tongue. My stomach twisted. I hadn't smelled it in years, not since back then.

I turned sharply to scan the quiet field. Only the rustle of leaves and the distant echo of laughter from someone's backyard. My fingers curled into my palms.

It's nothing.

But my legs carried me faster, my body refusing to believe the lie my mind wanted to see. The past couldn't creep back through an open window, or seep into my skin like the evening heat. I'd left it behind years ago.

Hadn't I?

By the time I reached the porch, I was sweating and my body was quivering. I stopped and tried to calm down. It was just nerves. Shadows of a shaky evening creeping in to haunt me.

Still, I hesitated at the door. Something moved in the distance. Then a deep chuckle, low and cruel. Threatening me from somewhere beyond my vision.

My father's laugh.

I flung the door open and slammed it behind me. Every breath came rough and ragged.

There was nothing. No one. Only the silence of our cottage. But the walls were too tight, the air too thick. I shoved off the door and bolted to my room, hands still shaking.

It was a struggle to convince myself I was remembering things wrong, that it was all in my head. But under the blankets, every creak sounded sharp. Something waited in the dark that I couldn't see.

I folded myself into sleep and prayed for the lie to end.

Chapter Twenty-Six

I woke up with a purpose. The night found me tangled in an endless web of memories, but by morning, I'd found clarity. I would prove my father was gone entirely and without a trace. Whatever doubts haunted me from the darkest corners of my mind were mine to conquer. Not his. Not anymore.

The smell of coffee drifted in, filling the house the way it always did. Steady and familiar, not like my father's. He drank his black and burnt, bitter enough to curl the tongue. Pop enjoyed his lighter, softened with a touch of sugar, offering a welcoming sweetness.

I took a slow breath. Yes, things were different now, and I would prove it.

Pop was already waiting at the table when I came out of my bedroom, the Sunday paper unfolded in front of him.

"Looks like they're closing down North Bridge High School. Been a long time coming, I'd say."

I nearly stepped out of my socks as I rushed forward to see the article in the paper.

"North Bridge is closing? But that's the high school Patty's supposed to go to. Oh my gosh, do you think this means she'll have to switch to my school?"

A realization of sorts flashed across Pop's face, but I couldn't decipher the meaning. He looked through me, a far off expression in his eyes.

"I don't know, sweetheart. Let's get some breakfast, huh?"

I barely tasted a bite, washed up quickly, and bolted out the door. I had to see if the Taylors knew.

"What do you think this all means?"

Patty smiled. "If I can talk them into it, I'll switch to your school. We can ride the bus together and everything. But wait, would you want me to sit with you?"

"Are you kidding? You're my best friend, obviously I'd wanna sit with you."

Her smile softened. "Thanks, Amanda. You're mine too."

We talked on her porch a while longer before I headed home to see if Pop needed help with lunch.

When he announced he was teaching me his secret cornbread recipe, I blinked. "Wait, really?"

As we cooked, we laughed like two teenagers gossiping. Pop had a way of turning even the simplest moments into adventures. When the timer dinged, he supervised as I carefully removed the cornbread from the oven.

"Perfection in a skillet!" he declared, beaming. "Look at those golden brown edges."

Every good thing in my life, I blamed on Pop. We'd come so far from the damaged little girl and reclusive old man we once were, healing each other in ways I never thought possible.

I'd gotten through most of the day without letting the events from the night prior spoil my spirits. Instead, I held strong to the possibility of Patty joining me at school soon. But those hopes were shattered when I caught the sound of Pop's and Mrs. Taylor's whispers in the front room.

She turned her head, guilt buried in her big brown eyes.

"What's going on?" I asked, already half sure of what she would say.

"We know you were hoping we'd let Patty come to your school next year. But Henry and I aren't ready to let her risk her safety at a school meant for whites. She'll go to school in Albina with my sister's kids."

"But that's half an hour away! There'll be more Black kids at my school now that North Bridge—"

"Have you ever heard of the Little Rock Nine?" Mrs. Taylor set her eyes on me, intent on making me understand. "Nine children. Guards all over the school. Angry crowds. People throwing things at them and worse while the staff just turned their backs."

I remembered hearing the story in government class, but the teacher kept the details vague. I'd gathered enough to know that the children involved were treated horribly by the other students. And even some of the adults.

"That was then, though," I insisted. "Times are different, our city is different. It's not like we're in the South."

She sighed. "You speak like it's been a hundred years when it's barely been a decade. Some doors just aren't open yet, whether you and I want them to be or not. My prayers will be with the Black children that *do* end up in you school. I hope somebody looks out for them, my guess is they're in for a long road."

She didn't need to say more, and neither I. The case had been made and abandoned. Patty would be devastated to find out, if she didn't already know.

Summer ended. Pop drove me to school on the first day like always. I couldn't help feeling a little sour, knowing all too well that Patty could have been in the car riding with me.

When I crossed the parking lot, Buster waved at me from the front of the school. I put on a brave face and ran to meet him, noticing a Black girl standing awkwardly on the sidewalk. Her hands trembled when she adjusted her worn book strap as though she was caught between the decision of whether to stay or run.

"She looks lost," I said to Buster. "Should we help her?"

He agreed, and we approached her. "I'm Amanda, and this is Buster. Do you need help finding your class?"

Buster offered his hand, but she hesitated, flashing a confused look at the introduction.

"I'm Marie. I appreciate the offer," she paused, eyeing us both. "As long as this isn't some kind of trick, I'd very much like the help."

"No tricks. What's your first class?" I asked, keeping my tone calm, the way Pop always did.

She handed me her schedule. "Math, I think."

"Oh, great, I had this teacher last year." I turned the paper toward Buster. "You ready?"

Marie didn't look convinced, but she nodded anyway. We walked inside as if it were just another Monday. But this day was different. The chatter around us began to quiet, until the deafening sounds of teenagers' voices gave way to the hushed silence of whispers.

Her back straightened, her head held high. I stepped in closer to her, intent on using my small frame as a shield if necessary. But Buster knew what to do. He rolled his eyes for theatrics. "Oh no, a Black person. Whatever will I do?"

He placed the back of his hand over his forehead, feigning the possibility of fainting. I giggled, and Marie's tense shoulders relaxed as she offered a slight smile.

My stomach knotted as we walked to her first class. We were walking too fast. I wanted to keep her safe from a danger I couldn't see, but feared anyway.

Buster must have sensed my worry. "She'll be alright. Change is rough, but somebody's gotta push it through."

"If you need us, we're right here when the bell rings," I told her.

She gave a tiny nod and slipped inside.

And we were there. Every bell. Every hallway. Just like we promised, but at lunch, she lingered inside until she saw us waiting.

"Everything okay?" I asked.

Her hands shook. Eyes wet but not letting go. "There's this girl in my class, mean as a snake. She kept fanning her face, acting like I stink. Do I smell bad?"

"Not at all. Some people are mean just to be mean."

The cafeteria buzzed with its usual chaos. We found space at the table that Buster and I used the year before. David's sister, Sarah, stood nearby, unsure whether she should sit or not.

"I have math with you," she stammered to Marie, taking a seat next to her.

"Oh, yeah. You're one row over from me," Marie replied, grateful for the kindness.

I smiled at the idea of a friend, not for myself, but for Sarah. She'd always been kind, but terribly shy. I crossed my fingers, hoping for a friendship to build between the two.

"Where's David?" Buster looked around the cafeteria.

Sarah kept her eyes low, fiddling with the corner of her tray. "He said he's sitting with some other kids today." Her voice barely made it out.

Buster smirked as his eyes found David across the room. Then he shrugged, like it didn't matter one bit.

"His loss," he muttered before turning back to his sandwich as if nothing had changed.

I looked around the cafeteria and saw that there were a few other Black students, which relieved me to find that Marie didn't have to feel like an absolute anomaly. My gaze stopped upon a familiar face. Linda. Her eyes cut across the room like a sharp blade full of malice, lips curling into a sneer. With narrowed eyes, she looked like she could set the table on fire with her stare.

I tried to look away before our glances made contact; but it was too late, she knew I had seen her. She came over to our table with a smirk.

Marie's fingers tightened around her tray. A shallow breath escaped her as she glanced nervously around the table, her eyes wide with unease.

"Eww, something smells awful!" She fanned her hand in front of her face. "Figures you'd be sitting here with that nasty girl at your table. You're probably the reason the old man tossed all of *their kind* into the home with us purebreds. Gross."

You ignorant little twerp, I thought to myself. I didn't take the time to point out she'd referred to herself as a dog. Reflecting on what Marie said when she came out of her classroom, I should have known the story of the girl harassing her had Linda written all over it.

"Leave us alone. Go find someone else to terrorize, you're not welcome here."

"You don't own this table, Amanda. You think because a rich man took you in, you're somehow above the rest of us. Well, I hate to be the one to break it to you, but you're not. You're still an orphan, a nobody. You're trashier than the Negroes wandering around this *white kids'* school!"

Heat surged through my veins. My eyes narrowed until Linda's smug face became the center of my vision. My chair scraped against the floor as I shot to my feet with my hands balled into fists at my sides. "I'm only going to tell you one more time, walk away."

She leaned forward until her face almost touched mine. "Make me," she said through clenched teeth as she reached her hand up and yanked hard on the back of Marie's ponytail.

"Ouch!" Marie yelped as her head was pulled backward.

For a second, Marie was gone. Patty sat there instead, wide-eyed and afraid. Her hair pulled back just the same. Mrs. Taylor was right not to let her come here; the realization only angered me more. I didn't think before I swung.

I hit the center of her face with a closed fist, hard. The sound dropped out, replaced by a high, mean ringing.

My vision tunneled, narrowing to nothing until the world folded in on itself. The air around me thickened, pressing in, warping, shifting —then nothing. A gap. A severed thread.

When the noise returned, Linda was on the floor, holding her face. My hand pulsed as if it weren't mine. I couldn't even remember the moment it happened.

My aching knuckles were the only proof I had to believe that I'd struck another person.

A high-pitched wail erupted from Linda louder than a siren. It pierced through the steady chaos of the cafeteria. All eyes turned to us. Her hands flew to her nose as blood seeped between her fingers. The thick shade of red threatened me with its truth. Buster hurried to give her a napkin to catch it before it spilled over onto her clothes. The teachers rushed over to our table.

Without knowing what happened, they carted Linda off to the nurse's office like a victim, while Marie and I were taken to the principal's office as the villains. They made me call Pop, and she called her parents. Nobody came to question us until the adults arrived. We all sat down in front of the principal to give our side of the events.

"It appears your story differs greatly from what Linda said happened. I have to admit, she's the one with the bloody nose. I'd be hard-pressed to believe she's the one lying. But with these," he paused to look at Marie and her parents, "*special* circumstances, I'll have to dig a little further into the matter before making my decision on where the punishment should lie. As for today, you will go home with your parents and do not return to school until you are informed to do so. Am I clear?"

"Yes, sir," Marie and I said at the same time.

Pop ushered me from the building to the car. Tears blurred my vision as my chest tightened and the guilt twisted my insides. I wiped my eyes, but new tears formed in their place. My knuckles still throbbed, a sickening reminder of what I'd done.

"I'm sorry, Pop. I don't know what came over me. She yanked Marie's hair, and I just swung. I didn't mean it. I swear."

"Don't worry. I have no doubt that you believed you were on the side of right when you defended your friend. We'll have to work on that some more. There will always be a bully. As long as there's ignorance, there will always be a force to fight against. Let's work on using our minds and words. Once things turn violent, the argument has already been lost. Do you understand?"

"I do."

He leaned forward and turned the radio on as we coasted down the country road back to our house. The soft melody of *People Got to Be Free* filled the car. Hopeful lyrics clashing against the storm raging inside me, a storm I didn't know how to contain. But I had Pop, and with him, I could solve almost anything.

How would we rid my body of the demons my father left behind? Pieces of him still lived inside me, buried deep within the girl I kept trying to become. I told myself I was nothing like him, that I'd scrubbed his influence from my bones, but there he rested, waiting. He lived in my clenched fists before my mind could catch up, in the way my anger swallowed reason when I should have walked away. My father's fire still burned in me, and no matter how hard I fought it, I'd proven as much when I hit Linda.

Pop brought me out of the dark place I'd let my past drag me back into. He always knew how to show me the way, to calm the waters of every impending storm. I found shelter there, safety beneath the wings of my angel.

Looking back, I should have seen the stillness in the air. The world held its breath in wait for a change my eyes were too blinded to see. When the destruction came, it arrived without a sound. All at once, my universe snapped back into focus. I'd been close to feeling normal, to blending in. But the world, as with me, was never as it appeared.

Chapter Twenty-Seven

Pop understood without words how ashamed I felt over what I'd done. I'd never been in real trouble before, not at school or at home, and the guilt dug into me. But with him, I could breathe easier, my shame was a little softer.

At the close of the school day, the principal called to share the statements from the other children who witnessed what happened in the cafeteria. Four agreed that Marie and I were telling the truth, while only one gave a conflicting story. In that version, they claimed Marie punched Linda.

We were cleared to reenter school the next day.

News spread about the fight. People whispered as we walked past, but that was the worst of it. Linda came back and didn't so much as glance our way.

I caught a look at her face—eyes dark and puffy, with bruises under both. I shifted in my seat, hands tingling, the memory sharp and ugly.

Buster's friend David refused to speak to him after the first day. He took Linda's side and cast hateful glances our way whenever he could. Buster pretended it didn't bother him, but I knew deep down how much it hurt to lose somebody he'd known his whole life.

Sarah and Marie found themselves in a fast friendship, dividing the once-close bond between brother and sister. The divide didn't stop there. As skin colors merged in our school and in the community, the sneers and whispered words of hatred separated our once peaceful city. Now there were two sides—those accepting of change, and those unwilling to bend.

It took months, but the initial shock of seeing Black students around school died down from a daily avoidance to a rare sideways glance. When springtime came, it was more common to find Black children occupying the spaces where once only white ones had sat.

Patty and I started to relax more on Saturdays when Bobbie picked us up to go to Hillsboro for a treat at Don's—though I still saw the unease in strangers' faces every time I leaned in to speak to Patty. The side eyes. The whispers. It was impossible not to notice the way people stared.

Bobbie glanced over her shoulder at some teenage boy snickering behind his hand, then turned full around and gave him a look that could've sliced through glass. "Find something better to do," she snapped.

The boy moved on, only glancing back once as he whispered to his friend. I wished I could do that; defend my best friend so easily. We were lucky to have someone like Bobbie on our side.

I couldn't make sense of it. It wasn't unusual to see Black people in any of the places we frequented. When it came to Patty, they still whispered, giving hateful glances everywhere we went. Mrs. Taylor said it wasn't really Patty that bothered them; we simply didn't fit into their idea of what was normal.

We refused to let anyone discourage us from enjoying our time together. Buster sometimes joined us. He'd saunter in, flipping his quarter in the air and flashing his carefree grin. His smile lit up the whole room as he sat in his chair, leaning back like he owned the place. Within moments, the four of us would be laughing together. Nothing outside Don's Ice Cream Parlor could touch us. And then the strangers' judgment no longer bothered me so much.

Early one Saturday morning, I headed to Patty's so we could get ready to go together. We sat on the front room floor as Mrs. Taylor worked on crocheting. Her hands slowed, the needle suspended mid-air as her brows furrowed. She bit her lip, trying to piece together whatever had been tugging at her mind for a while.

Patty shared the same expression as her mother. I tried to cut the edge.

"What's on your mind, Patricia?" I said, knowing full well she hated when I called her that.

"Girl, stop." She playfully slapped my arm. "I was thinking how different everything is now. I mean, before I met you, I wouldn't have dreamed I'd be sitting with some skinny white girl, fooling around with my hair and makeup. And I certainly wouldn't be waiting for a ride to town to go out for ice cream with y'all. I don't know, I feel kind of free, you know?"

I nodded.

"I bet if we were still living in Georgia, I wouldn't feel this way. There weren't as many," she paused while trying to find the word. "*Open-minded* people there."

"What was it like living in the South?"

Mrs. Taylor stopped rocking as we turned to her for help in answering.

"It was fine as long as Black folk kept to Black folk's business and stayed out of white folk's way. We loved livin' there. The weather was nice, and the kids had all sorts of cousins to play with. It didn't affect us much, so long as everyone stuck to the rules."

"Is that why you all were so nervous after Duke ran into my yard? You looked absolutely horrified, and it made me feel awful."

"Yes, it's why we made a point to come over and apologize. We've seen what happens firsthand when folks like us don't keep to ourselves. My boy didn't listen, and it caused us a world of pain."

I was stunned by this mention of her son. Often, I'd wonder where he was, careful to tread lightly when asking Patty. The only answers she ever gave me were so vague, I began to wonder if he existed at all. She'd never even told me his name.

"I don't know much about your son. Patty doesn't talk about him."

"Well, I do. His name's Marcus and he's twenty. He's still in Georgia."

"Why didn't he come to Oregon with your family? He couldn't have been much older than fifteen or sixteen when you moved here, right?"

"I wanna tell you about my son, to tell you everything. I do. But it's… a lot."

"You can talk to me."

She looked down. "My boy's in jail. He took a liking to this girl, this *white* girl. Her name's Denise, and she liked him too. When I found out, I warned him to stay away from her. Told him talking to a white girl would bring him nothing but trouble. He didn't want to hear it, though. And then Denise fell pregnant with Marcus's baby. She told her parents. Pleaded for them to understand. But what she'd done was unforgivable in their eyes. As soon as her brother found out, he gathered a couple of buddies, and they came after him and Patricia."

A sharp breath escaped me as I imagined what they must have gone through. My fingers curled tighter around the makeup brush, waiting for her to continue.

"What did they do?"

"Three boys attacked them one night when they were walking home from the corner store. He told his sister to run, and she tried to…"

She paused, her eyes filled with the pain of words her mouth didn't want to set free.

"They roughed him up pretty good, but he fought back. Just because it was three on one didn't mean you couldn't tell he'd been there. Those boys didn't expect Marcus to pack a punch as hard as he did. He knocked one boy out cold, but the other two took him down. Hit him over the head with a metal rod. Those two boys took off to try and chase down Patricia, leaving their friend and my boy for dead on the road."

"Oh my gosh, how awful! I don't understand why Marcus is in

jail if they attacked him?"

"Well, someone saw the fight and called the police. When they showed up, the boys went to the hospital to get checked out. In the end, it was Marcus in handcuffs. The police all but applauded those white boys for the beating they gave my son. And everything else they did after, too. Rich white boys don't have any law in the South."

"How's that even possible? A person is allowed to defend themselves, aren't they?"

"Sure, as long as that person's skin looks like yours and not ours. Look, things were different there. Everyone in town knew Marcus and Denise had been foolin' around. Nobody liked it, not the whites and not the Blacks either. Marcus and Denise both knew the risks, but love makes people reckless sometimes. Now Marcus has missed the last of his teen years as well as the first part of his daughter's life. And poor Denise, her parents disowned her completely when she refused to give the child away. And the real victim of it all—"

Her lips parted to finish the sentence, but the words never came. A deep sigh escaped her instead as her eyes clouded with thoughts she didn't dare share.

"Where did Denise go after her parents kicked her out?"

"She and my granddaughter went to live with Henry's sister and her kids. I tried to get her to come with us to Oregon, to get away from the danger in the South. But she refused to leave without Marcus, so she's been there ever since he got locked up. Henry and I have been working nonstop to get him out of jail so he can finally hug his little girl. We're working with the NAACP. The pastor at our old church sent a letter to the LDF. That may be Marcus's last hope."

"I hope they can prove he's innocent and get him out. It's not fair what happened to him."

"No, it isn't, but a lot ain't fair. We're ready for change, for true freedom. It's time for everyone else to catch up."

Unwanted but insistent memories I'd buried deep began to surface. The familiar taste of suffocating fear clung to me again. What

I'd experienced wasn't the same as what the Taylors went through, but we'd all been given a raw deal. I knew as well as they did that the situations life lent weren't always fair.

Patty gave me a little grin, like she was trying to pull us out of the heaviness. "I'm just glad we're here. Right now. That's enough. And even happier to share this reality with you."

The sound of Bobbie honking the horn out front pulled us from the moment. We jumped up to meet her, doing our best to put the dreariness behind us for the day.

"You mind stopping by my place? I need to let Pop know we're heading into town now."

She shook her head. "No problem."

I rushed into the house to find Pop sitting in his chair, reading the paper. He took a moment to stand, offering me a big hug once he'd gained his bearings.

"You girls have a good time this afternoon, alright? Tell Buster I said hello."

"I will, don't worry. I love you."

"I love you too, dear."

Bobbie parked the car in the lot next to Don's when she saw that there were no empty spots in front of the building. We waited, but Buster didn't show up, so we finished our ice cream and walked down Main Street to look at the shops.

"Look at all of these cute summer dresses." Patty pointed at the display. "I wish my mama would let me wear stuff like that. She still thinks I'm a tomboy." She looked down at her faded overalls and white t-shirt, and frowned.

I admired the soft fabric before flipping over the tag. My jaw dropped. "How is this on sale?" I whispered, eyes widening at the ridiculous numbers.

"I've got a whole pile of clothes if you wanna look through," Bobbie said.

"Would we ever." I clapped once, excited.

"Let's swing by my place first. Then I'll get you home. I've got a date tonight. We're gonna go to the Hill Theatre and watch a scary movie. You know what that means."

I laughed too, even though I didn't get the joke. We grabbed the clothes and hit the road. Pop's car wasn't in our driveway.

"Weird," I said.

"What?"

"Pop's not here. He doesn't drive anywhere unless it's super important. Otherwise, he calls your mom to pick him up."

"He couldn't have called her for a ride today." She tapped the steering wheel pointedly. "This one's our only car. You want me to come inside and wait with you?"

"It's alright, Patty's here, maybe he needed something from the store. You go ahead and get ready for your date."

Her fingers clutched the wheel. She didn't say anything, but her eyes were loud. *You sure?* I waved her off with a smile, watching her pull away.

I went inside and scanned the room. Everything looked to be in order, but somehow still off. I searched for anything out of place, but there were no scattered papers, no half-drunk cup of coffee, no sign at all of where he could have gone.

Patty stayed with me for a while, but I knew her mother would worry, so I sent her home as well.

An hour passed, and my chest grew heavier with worry. I walked into the kitchen to get a drink, retrieving a note that'd fallen on the floor.

Dear Amanda,

I wasn't feeling well, so I went into town for a quick check-up. Dinner is at six. Please remember to feed yourself if I'm not home by then. There's leftover turkey in the refrigerator.

They'll have me in great shape in no time. I'll be right back, my dear.

Love, Pop

My chest seized up until I couldn't breathe. I re-read the last sentence again. The exact phrase I'd played over in my head for years glared back at me in warning. My eyes shut to force the tears to dissolve before I even thought about opening them again.

It's just a coincidence, I told myself, my fingers tightening around the paper. I'd laugh about it later with Pop and tell him how my imagination got the best of me and how silly I'd been.

I drifted to the front room, drawn to his chair. The leather was worn and warm under my fingertips. I sank into it, feeling the faint indent of his presence, as if he were still here. But the comfort he'd always offered couldn't reach me this time, not when it was him I was so afraid of losing.

Chapter Twenty-Eight

The clock ticked more slowly than reality. My pulse raced ahead, refusing to follow. It knew something I didn't. The sound of the sluggish seconds was matched only by my labored breaths. Six forty-five and still no word. My fingers tingled as I gripped the armrest, forcing myself to stay put. Fear gnawed at my mind. Certain fifteen minutes had passed, I glanced at the clock again. Six forty-nine.

"Four minutes." I rolled my eyes.

My body needed to move. I doubted the radio would provide its usual gift of distraction, but I turned it on anyway and went to the kitchen to make a turkey sandwich. When Pop came home, his first question would be if I'd eaten.

I pulled a knife from the kitchen drawer, noticing how the sheen of it caught the light. Its sharp glint sent a ripple of memories through my mind. In an instant, I wasn't in the kitchen anymore.

Mama's trembling voice rose to begging. The air filled with the smell of whiskey and sweat as a shadow loomed. His arm raised to expose his threat. A knife. His grip tightened. Knuckles paled. Mama backed away with her hands in the air, her eyes locked on the blade. She opened her mouth, but nothing came out.

He laughed. "Look at you. As pathetic as you always been. Whatcha so scared of, Mary Beth? You know I ain't gonna kill you, might carve up that pretty face a bit, though. That'd be somethin', now wouldn't it?"

Static on the radio yanked me back. When I looked down, the sandwich lay in shreds on my plate. I didn't even remember making it, let alone tearing it apart. Sighing, I dumped it in the garbage and washed the dish.

There was no strength to waste battling my father's ghost. I needed to focus on who mattered now—Pop.

Tires on gravel. For a second, I let myself hope. Then I saw Miss Sally, and my spirits dropped to the floor.

"Amanda, come with me at once! Pop's in the hospital and he's asking for you."

I didn't even close the front door before I leapt down the porch steps, taking them two by two.

"What happened? He left a note saying he wasn't feeling well."

"The doctors think he had a heart attack. I'm his medical contact, so they called me. It took time to get to the hospital since Bobbie had the car dropping you off."

"Why didn't you call me? I could have ridden with Bobbie back to your house."

"If he wanted someone to call you, he would've told someone to. It's not my job to play secretary. Besides, Bobbie was already on her way home when the hospital called."

"But you just said you had to wait because she was dropping me off."

Her teeth clenched, cheeks reddening to the point I could see it through her thick layer of rouge. "Don't you smart your mouth off at me, I won't tolerate it. Every minute is precious in these situations, and because of *you*, I lost several waiting to get to Pop."

I cringed at her words, her tone dripping with blame. Miss Sally always found someone to fault. If her food wasn't perfect, she'd accuse the waitress of tampering with her order. If her house was messy, blame Bobbie. And now, somehow I'd caused her delay in getting to Pop sooner.

"But he's gonna be okay, isn't he?"

"All I know is he got sick. He was having trouble breathing, so he drove himself to the hospital. The chest pain didn't start until he got there. Then he asked for you. I came to get you right away."

Before she could put the car in park, I'd already sprung from it and ran through the entrance.

"I'm looking for Pop Wells," I told the first nurse I saw. "He came in a few hours ago, possibly a heart attack."

"Yes, dear. Come along, I'll show you to his room."

I nodded and followed her. I thought maybe I'd see him sitting up, cracking a joke, but he was sleeping. His hair was messier than usual. It didn't even look like him.

He'd become so thin. The white sheets clung to the outline of his small frame. An IV dripped into his vein, and wires covered his chest. Below his nose, an oxygen hose pushed clean air into his body.

I rushed to his bedside to take his hand in mine. The same hands that were once capable of moving mountains now felt small and fragile. The nurse walked in with Miss Sally.

"How long has he been sleeping?"

"Oh, honey," the nurse said. Miss Sally looked at me with pity that mirrored the nurse's. "I was just explaining to Sally that he took a turn for the worse after she left. Another heart attack, I'm afraid. He's in a coma. The doctors say he's not strong enough to pull through this time. I hate being the one to tell you, Mr. Wells was such a loved man."

Was. The word hit like a blow to the head. As if I weren't sitting right there holding Pop's warm hand, a clear sign of life. He still had a pulse. Strong. Steady. That meant something.

"You don't get to talk like he's already gone. You don't know. Nobody does."

"Amanda—" Miss Sally began.

"No. Don't tell me he won't be alright. He wouldn't leave me like this. He wouldn't leave me alone." I turned to Pop. Desperation cracked through my voice. "Please. If you can hear me, squeeze my hand. Wake up. I need you. I can't—"

My words crumbled. Aching sobs clawed their way up my throat. I looked to the nurse for reassurance. Her brimming tears and trembling mouth gave her away. She knew. No amount of begging would change it. By the end of the day, Pop would be gone. I'd be alone again.

I stayed by his side for hours. My fingertips rested against his pulse, clinging to each beat like the rhythm could anchor him here.

Thump-thump, thump-thump. Fast and steady. It stayed the same.

Another hour passed. The nurse returned to check his vitals. "His blood pressure's dropping. I don't think it'll be much longer now." She left to inform the doctor.

A soft, exhausted sigh escaped his lips; a sound too fragile to give hope. I held my breath, willing the next one to be stronger.

His chest stilled. Mine did too, fear stealing my air.

Thump-thump……….thump-thump.

His pulse began to slow. I stared at him, using every inch of my being to will him back to life. "Please, Pop. Please don't leave me." I whispered.

Thump-thump………………thump-thump.

"I'm sorry," Miss Sally offered when she saw the undammed river of tears flowing down my cheeks.

I ransacked my mind, begging for a solution—some trick. Some prayer. Anything to pull him back.

Thump-thump…………………………thump-thump.

Even slower now. My fingers struggled to feel the beats. What began with the strength of an eagle's wing now faded into the silence of a moth's.

Thump-thump……………………………………thump.

Nothing remained. It had been three minutes since his chest lifted to receive the sweet breath of life. At ten forty-three p.m., the doctor called the time of death.

I kept holding his hand. Wouldn't let go. Not until it went cold.

Stiff. That's when I knew. Wishing wouldn't fix it. He was gone.

Nothing made sense anymore. Pop was my guardian, my *angel*. Angels didn't die.

Miss Sally stood in the hallway, filling out forms and chatting with the staff. She hadn't a care in sight, which filled me with anger, but I pushed it down.

"I'll be in the car," I muttered.

She barely looked up.

I shut the door and leaned back. Pop's smile at breakfast. His hands on my handlebars. The way I never had to worry when he was around. He was in everything I loved, everything I knew. I lowered my head to try to hide from the night.

By the time Miss Sally made her way out to the car, I had fought off the persistent urge to cry.

"*There's no use crying over spilled grease.*" I heard him say.

We drove in silence until the car pulled into my driveway. "I'll wait here while you grab an overnight bag. We'll sort things out in the morning."

Intent on staying, I looked at her in despair. "Don't make me leave tonight. I've already lost what makes this house a home. I'll lock the doors and stay inside until you come back tomorrow. Miss Sally, please."

She shrugged, indifferent. "If you want to stay, fine by me. I don't know what to do with you yet anyway."

I nodded and walked inside without saying goodbye. If I spoke another word, the fragile strength holding me together would shatter.

The sound of the radio startled me when I entered, as though time in our home stood still in my absence. I switched it off and stood in the front room, staring at Mona's paintings. My gaze traced the flowing colors, the emotions in each piece covering me like a shroud. Her art held pieces of Pop and a sense of home. With every brushstroke, she captured the purest forms of love.

Remembering the story Pop told about the night Mona died, I

went to his bedroom for his old record player. He'd listened to Billie Holiday the whole night, explaining that her sad lyrics and heart-rending voice quieted the deafening sorrow in his mind.

I chose the first album I saw and wrapped a blanket around myself, sitting on the floor next to the player. The record was a single. *I'll Be Seeing You* on side A and *He's Funny That Way* on side B.

The piano's opening notes filled the room. Before the first verse ended, tears welled in my eyes.

Her voice carried my anguish, each note melting me into the music. I played the song over and over, whispering the words through tears until fourteen years of sadness began to escape me.

Before flipping the record, I decided to get my photo album. I turned the pages slowly, reliving the adventures Pop and I shared. When *He's Funny That Way* began to play, I listened carefully. The first song perfectly matched my broken soul. Maybe the second would offer the same bittersweet comfort.

As the second song played, I knew Pop had guided my hand to this album, to the one record in the stack filled with lyrics that expressed my feelings. Everything Pop ever told me had been right. These emotions were a stark contrast to when I'd lost my parents. The hurting existed then as it did now, but in a different way.

A slow smile tugged at my lips as I found the picture of him from our fashion show. Pop, his ballerina pose so outlandish, I could almost hear his bright and carefree laugh echoing through the room.

I peeled the picture from the book and held it close to my chest.

A sudden lightness filled me. Without thinking, I climbed to my feet and swayed around the room, the memory of him urging me to move. For a moment, I could feel him there twirling beside me.

When the song ended, I stood still as the familiar sound of a songless record player filled the space between my breaths. I remembered Mama. The look on her face as she said those final words to me, the same ones Pop had written. The cursed line to say goodbye without knowing it meant forever.

I climbed into Pop's old leather chair and let my body welcome a restless sleep. I woke as sunlight crept into the morning sky. No confusion remained, only Pop's memory. I needed a friend. Knowing Patty would be having breakfast with relatives before church, I dialed Buster's line. He picked up on the third ring.

"Hello?"

"Buster…"

"What's the matter?"

"It's Pop." My words caught in my throat.

"I'm on my way. Are you at home?"

"Mhmm." I stopped myself from crying out, using the tricks I'd learned as a child.

I sat waiting on the porch when he parked his car and rushed across the yard to me. His embrace was my lifeline. I leaned into his warmth, borrowing the strength I could no longer find.

"What happened?"

I could only whisper. If I spoke any louder, I'd shatter. "His heart. He's gone"

"Oh, Mandy. I'm so sorry."

Nobody had called me Mandy since before my mother died. I hugged him tighter. We sat on the front porch swing. It creaked beneath us. My head found his shoulder. His hands rested in his lap, still and sure. A moment shared between friends, innocent and necessary.

Then we heard a car's engine coming down the driveway.

I lifted my head, curious. Miss Sally's car stopped just outside the canopy of trees. She got out and paused, her eyes lingering on Buster. A faint line tightened across her mouth, sending a shiver down my spine.

"Good morning, Miss Sally," I said.

"Don't you good morning me, young lady!" she snapped. "What is this boy doing here? Is that why you refused to come to my house last night? You wanted to play grown-up with your boyfriend?"

Her eyes burned with accusations. I shrank beneath her glare.

"Wait just one second," Buster said. "I've been here fifteen minutes and haven't set foot inside. I have respect for Pop, and I know the rules."

"The rules of a dead man?" she scoffed. "I doubt a young man like you cares about much other than the company of a loose girl!"

"You don't get to twist this. Not today." Hurt and shock tangled in my chest, but I held my ground.

"Buster, leave. I'll speak to your mother later. Amanda, go inside and pack a bag. We're leaving for my house in five minutes."

I met Buster's eyes, a silent exchange passing between us. His face tightened, caught between staying by my side and respecting Miss Sally's order. His wordless goodbye carried an apology. I watched him drive away as she pushed past me into the house. When he was out of sight, I followed her inside.

She went to Pop's bedroom and began rifling through his belongings. I stopped in the doorway, watching her frantic search.

"What are you looking for?"

"Go get your bag ready. Now."

"Well, I might know where it is if you'd just tell me—"

"I said go!"

The shock of her outrage numbed me. I moved on autopilot, my body falling back into an obedience I thought I'd left behind.

When she came out of Pop's bedroom, her hands were empty. We headed to the car without a word.

She stopped me from getting out of the car when we got to her house. Not knowing what I'd done to anger her, my old shield lifted around me.

"We need to be clear before you walk in there. I knew what you were the minute we met. You may have fooled the old man, but you're not fooling me."

I opened my mouth to protest, but she cut me off.

Her fist came down on the dashboard in a fury. "Do not interrupt me. As I was saying, my daughter will not be poisoned by your ways. She's a child of morals, and I won't let your influence change her. You may stay friends with Bobbie, but know I'm watching your every move. You're in my home only because of the love and respect I had for Pop. He wanted you with me if anything happened, and I'll honor his wishes. However, I won't let you forget that you're here because of my generosity. Don't make me regret it."

Her words landed hard enough to leave a sting. She got out, didn't wait, just waved me on. I grabbed my bags, but every step toward that porch felt like walking off a cliff.

Chapter Twenty-Nine

In my haste, I'd forgotten to bring a dress for Pop's funeral the following morning. I bit my lip, glancing at Miss Sally's closed door. The thought of asking her for anything made my stomach twist, so I sought out Bobbie instead.

"I only brought school clothes. There's no way your mother'll take me back to my house to grab a dress for tomorrow."

"Don't worry, I'll run you out there to get an outfit," she insisted.

She went to talk to Miss Sally, their voices carried across the house like wind.

"No. She can wear something of yours. She's trying to get back out there to be alone with that boy. Or to be with those *Black* people. Either way, she's not leaving my sight until we get through the funeral and the reading of the will."

Her hate for the Taylors stained each word as they shot from her lips like bullets aimed to kill. How could Pop leave me with a woman so wrapped in judgment? Did he ever see the truth in anyone? This was no Godly woman. She was bitter, cruel, and the embodiment of everything he worked so hard to protect me from becoming.

I knew Pop, knew the depths of his heart. In all of our years together, he'd never witnessed the pieces of myself I kept hidden. He chose to remain blind to the darkness in others, never even realizing the worst parts of me. I'd not have changed his outlook, even if I knew all along that his miscalculation would land me in the arms of evil.

"Isn't this just like you, Mother?" Bobbie's words dripped with accusation. "Pop's body has barely had time to cool, and all you can see are dollar signs. The same way it was with my father."

"Don't you speak about him, young lady!"

The sound of a slap immediately brought me to my feet.

Bobbie started to cry. "Stop, please, I'm sorry."

The second slap stole my breath.

"Two hours. That's all it took for her to turn you against me. Go through your closet and find her a dress. If you want to cry about your face, go cry to Amanda. It's her fault you got hit anyway."

Bobbie's cheek was bright red when she returned to the room, a lingering mark displaying the force of her mother's angry hand.

I shifted my eyes down to avoid looking directly at her, remembering Mama's warning.

"Sorry," Bobbie shrugged. "We'll have to see if anything of mine fits you."

She pulled out three dresses and handed them to me.

I settled on a deep navy blue prairie dress with ruffles on the sleeves and a thin white lace trim. It reminded me of the dresses Pop had given me when I first arrived at his house.

"I have to get outta here. My mom won't let you come with me. I need a smoke and some fresh air."

"It's okay. I get it."

She stayed gone for the rest of the day, creeping through the door after dark. Miss Sally had already retired to her room by then, and I'd changed into my nightclothes.

We talked at the table for a few minutes before I excused myself to lie down. This time, I didn't struggle. Instead used sleep as an escape from reality. Once again, my world teetered on its axis.

The sound of Miss Sally grumbling in the kitchen the next morning forced my eyes open. "What's going on?" I asked Bobbie when I saw she was awake as well.

"She hates her life, that's what," she scoffed.

"What's not to hate?"

We took turns showering and getting dressed. Bobbie helped me with my hair, a reminder of the times we shared when we were younger.

"Thank you, Bobbie. Do I look alright?"

"Beautiful as always."

We arrived at the cemetery early. My shoes sank into the grass as we walked to his grave. I longed to take mine off, to ground myself to the earth and to the reality of this moment.

He lay motionless in his casket. His normal, unkempt hair was combed neatly, not a strand out of place. Someone had also trimmed his wild beard. He wore a suit, and I couldn't help but wonder if he'd have preferred to wear his normal t-shirt, suspenders, and flannel.

The man who lay before me may have *looked* like Pop, but the angel I knew and loved no longer existed. I urged myself to be big, grateful I still knew how.

When the guests started to arrive, the Taylors' seats beside me remained cold and empty. I glanced back once more as the pastor began speaking, finally seeing them sitting together in the last row.

"Herbert 'Pop' Wells was a beacon of hope," he began. "His legacy is strong and will not soon be forgotten. As we take this time to say goodbye, let us honor him by continuing his mission. Take the time to check on your neighbors. Say hello to strangers on the street. Laugh often and childlike. And above all else, love without bounds."

My mind drifted. A breeze brushed against my cheek. The familiar scent of freshly turned earth filled my senses. Everything blurred. The pastor's voice. The people around me. The world became a distant hum. They blended with the wind until all was lost through my filter of reality.

For a moment, we were back on his porch. He rocked gently in his chair. I did my best to bring life to an empty canvas.

"What's on your mind, dear?"

His eyes crinkled with warmth. I opened my mouth to answer. To tell him I couldn't do this alone. But the scene faded.

"If you would, please bow your heads with me to pray."

The world snapped back into focus. My hands were clenched in my lap, the grass damp beneath me. I bowed my head, though I hadn't heard a single word the pastor said.

Miss Sally told me to stand near Pop's casket. A line of people stopped to offer me their condolences. I nodded to each one. They paused to press my hand and look at me with sympathetic eyes. Each kind word dropped into me like a coin in a bank I didn't know I was holding.

But Pop's presence carried me through the day.

As the last person walked away, I took my turn to say goodbye. Standing there, I poured out every word through my thoughts instead of my voice, feeling them settle somewhere deep within.

I kissed my fingertips and brushed them against his cold forehead, gently tousling his neatly combed hair and giving him back a bit of himself. Before me lay my savior, a tiny old man with ruffled white hair and a beard to match.

"I'll be seeing you." I said goodbye to Pop for the last time.

"He looks better with his hair like that," Buster's voice broke through my quiet thoughts. "There's the Pop we remember. Are you okay? I've been worried sick about you since the day on your porch."

"I'm fine. Thanks for coming, it helped knowing you were nearby."

"I wouldn't have missed it."

We made our way over to where his mother chatted with the Taylors. I thanked them for coming as well, grateful to see their familiar faces.

Out of the corner of my eye, I caught Miss Sally stiffen as I talked to Patty. She couldn't see the hate wrapped so tightly around her; she'd never realize her own ignorance.

And then they were gone, leaving us standing in an empty graveyard, fresh dirt now covering the man who'd taught me how to laugh. I smiled up to the sky, knowing he looked down at me, watching over me as only a true angel could do. But my smile was cut short by the harshness of Miss Sally's voice.

"Let's go, girls. Can't keep the attorney waiting."

We walked into the office and took a seat in the waiting area while Miss Sally alerted the receptionist of our arrival. A look of confusion washed over her face when the woman behind the desk announced I'd be going in for my meeting first.

"What do you mean first? Aren't we going in together? When Bobbie's father died, we went in at the same time."

"Well, you're not her parent or legal guardian as of now. Amanda isn't tied to you by any official means, and neither are her finances," she replied in an even tone. "Come along, Amanda."

I followed her into the office to find the man with jet-black hair from the courtroom all those years before.

"Good morning, dear. We haven't been formally introduced. My name's Mr. Graham, and I represented Pop's legal interests. Now I'll be representing yours."

I reached out and shook his hand. "Good morning, Mr. Graham, I'm Amanda Hollings."

"You sure have grown up to be an amazing young woman. Pop lived a humble life, but for you, he was extremely proud. I'm very sorry for your loss."

"Thank you. I miss him terribly."

"As I'm sure you will for a long time." His eyes locked on mine, and in them, I could see his certainty. He may have been Pop's attorney, but for many years, he had also been his friend.

"Are you ready to begin?"

I nodded.

"He created all of the parts of his will through formal paper-work, except when it came to yours. I have the documents necessary for the legalities, but he drafted this letter for you several years ago. If you'd like to read it on your own, you may, or I can read it to you."

I reached for the letter, fighting against the tightness already gathering in my throat. The familiar tremor in Pop's handwriting threatened to shatter the fragile control I held on my composure. "Thank you, I'd like to read it myself."

Pop's voice threaded through my thoughts, clear and warm. His essence surrounded me. As if he were right there beside me, holding my hand like he'd done so many times before. I was safe for the moment with his strength coursing through me.

My Dearest Amanda,

If you're reading these words, then I've gone home to be with Mona. I'm sorry I couldn't stay longer. I hope you can find comfort in the people who love you, as well as peace from within your own heart.

You've come a long way, dear. No longer are you little; you are now as big as you always strived to be. Please take a moment here and there to remember it's still okay to be small. Smile into the sunrise. Laugh when it suits you. And don't ever be afraid to stand your ground. You've always been strong in that way, never change.

If I could, I'd give you the world. I don't have much, but what I have is yours. Take care of Mona's paintings. They mean more to you than anyone else left on Earth. Keep the ones you love the most, donate or sell the others. No sense in carrying them around as you find your way.

I've left the house to the Taylors. We made it a home, but I fear my passing may have tainted the walls. They'll love it and care for it as it becomes their own. This decision did not come lightly.

There's plenty of money in your trust to create your home when you've chosen where to plant your roots. Don't worry about where you will live, now or ever.

Should you choose to go to college, art school, or travel the world, you won't be burdened by a lack of funds. If you haven't already, when you turn eighteen, you'll have complete control over the choices in your finances and life.

I've had discussions with Miss Sally, as well as with the Taylors regarding who would oversee your care should I pass on before you come of age. Everyone agreed they wouldn't hesitate to take you in. We decided Miss Sally's home would be the best placement. She'll watch over you and provide for you through the money in your trust. Don't hesitate to ask for the things you need, as well as the things you want. The money spent on those items is already yours.

I've left instructions for you to have the opportunity to remove anything from our home that you'd like to keep. You'll have a storage building for your belongings, which you can add to or take away from as you please.

This is a lot for anyone to take in. It's okay if you feel overwhelmed. Remember, those are normal emotions. Take a breath. Lean on the people who have been put in place to help you through this.

I'm proud of you. You're going to be alright.
All My Love,
Pop

A single tear clinging to my lashes slipped free when I blinked. It landed on Pop's words, leaving a faint stain in its wake.

"I'm sorry," I said as I tried to dry the paper.

"It's okay. And you can hold on to that letter, he wrote it for you. Everything in it has already been dictated in the file." He offered me a small smile edged with a hint of sadness. "It doesn't make sense now. Even the hardest things happen for a reason. One day you'll look back and see. All of this pain wasn't for nothing."

He handed me a business card with his number. "Hold on to this. Should you need me for anything at all, you call me right away."

My tears slowed, leaving a faint ache as I tried to gather myself.

"Yes, sir, I will."

I caught a glimpse of heat in Miss Sally's eyes when I walked out, but I shifted my gaze, turning from her as she made her way into Mr. Graham's office.

Bobbie squeezed my hand. "Are you okay? You look like

you've seen a ghost."

"Pop left me a letter. I could hear his voice when I read it. It was almost like he was there with me."

"Sometimes I feel like my dad's with me. His presence is so thick at times, I can smell his aftershave."

I'd often wondered about how her father died and why she rarely spoke of him. It never felt right to ask. Now, though, might have been the only proper time, if ever there would be one.

"What happened to him? You don't have to answer if it's still too painful, but if you want to talk about it, I'm here."

"He died when I was seven. For Christmas the year before, he built me a dollhouse. It was beautiful. The doors opened and closed, and there were even working light fixtures. My mother said he worked on it for months. Then he started getting headaches. They were so awful. He had to lie in bed with the shades drawn for hours."

She paused. Her fingers fiddled with the clasp of her handheld mirror. Open and close. Open and close. I could tell she was deep in thought.

"That must have been awful for him. I'm sure it was hard for you to understand what he was going through. What caused the headaches?"

"No one knew at first. He saw doctor after doctor. They tried everything money could buy. After the headaches, he changed. He'd scream out curse words or go into full panic, convinced somebody was coming to harm us. His fits caused the doctors to believe he was a danger, both to himself and to my mother and me. They took him away to some hospital in Portland to try to help him recover, but it was too late. We visited him a couple of times before he shut down completely. He died two weeks after my seventh birthday."

"Oh Bobbie, I'm so sorry you had to lose him in such a way."

"That's not the worst of it. By the time anyone realized what was killing him, he was too far gone."

"What was it?"

She sighed, her eyes falling on the overcast sky outside the window. "Turned out, the paint he used on my dollhouse was loaded with lead. He'd shut himself in his workshop for hours, breathing it in. All the time he spent making that beautiful house for me was poisoning his body. He just wanted it to be perfect, ya know? My mother never says it, but I know she resents me for what happened. I think that's why I let her treat me the way she does. A part of me blames myself as well. This dark cloud has been hovering over me ever since we lost him."

"You can't blame yourself for what happened. You were just a little girl."

She shrugged, her gaze fixed still on the view outside. I held back any words and let the silence settle between us.

Miss Sally returned with a pale face and angry scowl. She moved in silence, without looking at either of us. We followed her to the car, the quiet never breaking during the ride back to her house.

She didn't say a word. But whatever she decided that day would follow me for years to come. And she was far worse than any shadow I'd ever fought by myself.

Chapter Thirty

In the weeks following Pop's funeral, a tightness crept into my chest that only eased with the distraction of school. At night and on weekends, I found myself enveloped in the airless fog of loss. When summer began, there was little to occupy my shifting thoughts.

"Do you wanna come to the creek with me today?" Bobbie pleaded.

"I don't think your mom will let me go. She hates me. I'll hang around here and wait for Patty to come over."

She rolled her eyes. "Please. I'm her own daughter, and she acts like she hates me too. It's not us she hates, it's herself. She thought Pop was gonna leave her a lot more money than he did."

"Do you know what he left her?"

"No. She wouldn't tell me even if I asked. But as far back as I can remember, she always said Pop was gonna take care of us. My father left a lot of money behind when he died, we're cool. When I turn eighteen in August, I'm supposed to get what he left for me."

"What are you gonna do with the money?"

She thought for a second. "The first thing I'm doing is buying a car. I'm barely allowed to touch ours without her making it some huge deal. She's so lame. Speaking of lame, you're not gonna make me go swimming by myself today, right? My mother has a friend picking her up in a little while, and they'll be gone most of the day. We'll take off as soon as she leaves and only stay at the creek for a couple of hours. She won't even know you're gone."

"That sounds awfully mischievous, Bobbie."

"Nah, if she finds out, we can tell her we assumed she wouldn't care if you came along. It'll be easier to ask for forgiveness later than to ask for permission now. C'mon, live a little."

I couldn't resist her pouting mouth and pleading eyes.

"Fine, I'll go if we can bring Patty. You're sure we'll make it back before your mother does?"

"When she goes shopping with her friend, it's an all-day affair. You have nothing to worry about. Now get changed and I'll call the Taylors to see if Patty can come. Do you wanna ask Buster if he wants to come with us?"

"Sure, I'll give him a call once she leaves."

I heard the front door open and close loudly, signaling Miss Sally had gone. After watching her friend's car back out of the driveway, I ran down the stairs to call Buster.

"He said he'll come with us," I yelled up to Bobbie after hanging up the phone. "I told him we'd be there in about half an hour after we get Patty."

She came down the stairs with a full beach bag, tossed it on the floor, and pulled out her compact mirror to fix her lip gloss.

"My graduation is next weekend, and I need to catch some rays. I wanna look great when I get my diploma."

"You look amazing no matter what you do."

We made sandwiches and stuck four bottles of Coke in the bag, piling everything into the trunk. I breathed clear and easy from my lungs for the first time in forever. My fingers drummed against the car door as I looked out the window, the taste of freedom circling all around me.

The trees of my old driveway arched overhead, filtering soft light onto the car hood. I stepped back into a memory. Beautiful and haunting. My palm pressed against the window to reach for the familiarity of all that I'd lost.

Patty waited for us on the front porch. She grinned, waving as we parked the car. Mrs. Taylor stepped through the front door to follow Patty down the steps.

"Good morning, girls."

"Good morning, Mrs. Taylor," we replied in unison.

"What time will y'all be back? We've got some plans later on today."

"Shouldn't be much later than three o'clock," Bobbie replied.

"And your mother knows where you're going?"

Bobbie answered before my eyes revealed any deceit. Her hand reached over and landed on my thigh to give me a quick squeeze, silencing my confession.

"Yes, ma'am. She knows I'm driving out to the creek. She said it's okay."

"Alright, you girls have fun. We'll see you in a few hours."

"You lied to Mrs. Taylor!" I exclaimed when we pulled back onto the road.

"I didn't lie. I told her my mother knows where I'm going, and she does. I never said she knew *you* were coming, too."

She wasn't wrong, but I knew we were being dishonest. I shook away the thought and focused on my friends instead.

We drove toward Buster's house with the windows down, belting out Bob Dylan songs at the top of our lungs. Our voices rang out loud and off-key. Nothing else mattered but the lyrics.

The serenade didn't end after Buster climbed into the car; if anything, it only grew in excitement and volume.

As soon as we parked, Bobbie hopped out. "Last one in the water's the rotten egg!" she squealed before she started running.

We girls took off behind her, each of us pulling off the clothing covering our swimsuits as we ran. We hit the water with a splash, too quickly to realize it was freezing cold. Shock tore a squeal from our lips as we stumbled deeper, our skin prickling under the bite of the icy water.

Buster lingered by the car, his grin widening as he watched us splash about in shock, desperate to claw our way back to the bank. His laughter rumbled over the sound of our chattering teeth.

He dropped the bags and let out a full belly laugh at our expense. "I guess sometimes it pays to be the rotten egg."

We hurried to find our towels and wrapped them tightly around ourselves. I shivered as I looked at Buster in his dry clothes. "It's not bad. You should go ahead and jump in. I bet you'll feel refreshed when you get out."

"No thanks. I think I'll sit right here and have one of these sandwiches instead."

"That's odd. I just heard you say you were an egg. You sound more like a chicken," Bobbie quipped.

"Well, bock-bock, Bobbie," he replied with his hands on his hips and a grin on his face.

We spent the next few hours enjoying the sunshine. I relaxed. My body relaxed, pushing away sharp splinters of grief through my sun-baked skin. But the sun dipped lower. I found myself glancing around, trying to etch every second into my mind. These few precious moments needed to be saved, stashed away for a time when I'd need the warmth of this day. I wasn't ready to leave when we loaded into the car. The comfort of laughter. The warmth of the sun. I needed these things to help heal me.

My head was still spinning from the joy I'd found in the simple company of friends. We dropped off Buster and Patty and headed back to Bobbie's house. The combination of the sun and excitement had been exhausting, leaving me tired but happy. My head rested against the window, reliving the day in quiet smiles.

Everything changed the moment we pulled the car into the driveway. Miss Sally burst from the house, her fists tight and eyes narrowing as she stormed across the driveway.

"You girls get out of that car this instant. And just where have you been all day?"

Bobbie tried to rationalize with her mother. "You said it was all right for us to go swimming at the creek."

"I did no such thing," she hissed. "You asked if *you* could go with some of your friends. You absolutely did not ask if Amanda could come along. I've been worried sick. I almost called the police!"

I bowed my head in embarrassment. She'd caught me. I knew it was wrong. "I'm sorry. I shouldn't have gone."

My breath hitched as she barreled toward me. I took a nervous step back. The hairs on my arms prickled as I remembered other angry hands. Would she slap me the way she had Bobbie? Would she shake me as my father had done?

She grabbed hold of my arm and tried dragging me across the porch toward the front door. But I pulled back. She'd burnt me with her touch. I didn't push her; I knew I couldn't have. Still, she flew hard against one of the porch columns before falling dramatically to the ground. Her printed dress flew up around her frumpy body, exposing her undergarments. I blushed upon seeing them and looked away.

"Oh my lord," she wailed. "That girl knocked me down, she *pushed* me."

Bobbie hadn't seen what happened as she made her way up the stairs with the beach bag in her hands. She dropped the bag and rushed over to help Miss Sally to her feet while sneaking me a puzzled glance.

I wasn't sure whether I should help. Maybe I should have run away. She threw her arms above her head and cried out as I got closer. "Don't you come near me. Bobbie, don't let that insane girl hurt me."

I stopped dead in my tracks. "I'm sorry, Miss Sally. I didn't mean to."

Now back on her feet, her eyes narrowed on mine. "Sure you didn't mean to. You never mean to do any of the things you do, and yet I still landed on the ground."

Her words struck a nerve I thought had long gone quiet. They sounded like him. Sharp, mean, and full of an ugliness I didn't care to recall. My fingers curled into my palms. My body remembered, even when I tried to forget. He used to say those things about me, his voice low and bitter. My mother tried to shield me from it. Tried to make us shrink, to disappear into the silence of the walls, away from where he could harm us. But he always found us. The same way his words still found me, no matter how deeply I buried them.

I blinked hard, forcing the memory back into the dark, but his demon still slithered through Miss Sally's voice. It clung to her words, twisting them around me like barbed wire. They cut deep, forcing their way through my skin, running rampant through my veins. She was still talking, still throwing blame like stones, but all I could hear was him. I focused on her hands, the sharp movements of her mouth. Anything to remind myself where I was.

"…and the money to keep my life afloat, money I *earned*, that I deserved. All you do is show up and everyone around you turns to shit, while you come out smelling like roses."

"Miss Sally, please. I honestly don't mean to make so much trouble for you."

"Do not interrupt me, young lady," she screamed. "Don't forget I was there the day the social worker came, and you attacked her when all she was trying to do was talk to you. The poor woman. She lost her job because of you. And the little girl at the school you punched in the face. She was an orphan, for crying out loud. The very type of person Pop and Mona dedicated their lives to helping. Do you know her foster family almost sent her back to the home after you blamed her for everything? You are a vile little girl, Amanda. And your poor mother —"

"You leave my mother out of this," I said through clenched teeth.

Her calculated smile stretched wide, never reaching her dead eyes. "I'm trying to help you. I wish you could see how hard I'm trying."

Her voice turned sweet. Rehearsed lines used to watch me squirm. I knew it was fake. "You think I don't know you're going through a lot? You've been through more than most girls your age. Believe me, Amanda, I know. But what Pop did when he got you didn't help you, always sweeping your transgressions beneath the rug.

Cocooning you from reality, shielding you from the truth. Pretending you're a normal child rather than a—"

"Mother." Bobbie stepped forward, placing herself between her mother and me. Her voice became low and stern, giving Miss Sally reason to pause.

Her mouth curved into a thin, tight line. Cold eyes locked on me, almost demanding me to cower beneath her. "You have to learn that your actions have consequences, and I guess today's as good a day as any."

She walked into the house with Bobbie and me close behind. Not knowing what to do, I followed Bobbie's lead and sat on the couch with my hands folded in my lap while Miss Sally continued into the kitchen.

"Is she going to paddle me?" I whispered to Bobbie.

She shrugged as we listened to see if we could piece together what Miss Sally was doing. After thirty seconds of rustling paper, we heard her pick up the telephone and start talking.

"She's calling the police," Bobbie mouthed without so much as a whisper.

Chapter Thirty-One

The sound of my doom arrived in the form of a patrol car's brakes squealing in the driveway. I flinched when the car door slammed, a quick flash of numbness spreading through my shaky fingers. Each hollow knock on the door echoed inside me.

Miss Sally opened the front door and motioned for the officer to come inside.

"Afternoon, ma'am. My name's Officer Jenkins. We received a call about an assault?"

"Good afternoon, Officer. Yes, that's correct, please come in." She feigned an injured voice.

As much as I forced myself not to cry, I could see she was fighting to do the opposite. Her eyes filled with unshed tears as she sobbed into the officer's sympathetic ear.

By the time she finished telling her side, I questioned myself if maybe I *had* accidentally pushed her. Her story was convincing. He took me outside to the porch to hear my side of the events.

The officer's gaze flicked over me, his voice steady but edged with doubt as he listened. He preferred Miss Sally's version. An older woman opens her home to a damaged and troubled teen girl, and gets assaulted when trying to dole out a warranted punishment. Why would this sweet and selfless woman make up such a story? What was there to gain?

We walked back inside, where Bobbie and Miss Sally sat waiting.

"Emotions have been high today for everyone. I can take Miss

Hollings downtown to the Juvenile Center to allow everyone a chance to cool off. But it's Saturday. She won't be able to stand before the judge until Monday morning at the earliest."

"I don't want her to have to go through anything like that. She's been through enough, the poor dear. It's not really a criminal issue. It's more mental. She needs help, not jail."

Miss Sally cast a tearful look my way, pressing a hand to her chest as if her pain was genuine. "I think we'll be alright to get by until Monday, when I can contact a psychiatrist to have her evaluated. There's a doctor in town, whom I've known since grade school I'm certain will make room for her in their schedule."

"If you're sure, I'll put these notes in the back of my folder and let you try to handle it as you see fit. You do seem to have this child's best interest in mind." He turned his attention to me. "Young lady, I hope you realize the sacrifices this woman has been making for you to have a better chance at life. She's giving you a break tonight and I'm allowing her to make that decision. This will not happen again. If there's a next time, you'll see yourself in handcuffs. Do you understand?"

My head stayed bowed, the words barely escaping my lips as I nodded. His eyes were like daggers stabbing through me. "Yes, sir."

"Alright, I'll keep what happened here today between us for now." He handed a card to Miss Sally. "Here's my information if you need me again."

"Thank you, officer. I do hope I'm making the right decision."

Once the officer was gone, she turned to me. "You're welcome."

"Thank you, Miss Sally. I really am sorry."

"Indeed," she replied. "Go to your room and get changed. Stay there for the rest of the night. I'll bring your dinner when it's ready."

I wanted to scream. To spit that thank you back in her face. But I nodded and turned toward the stairs like a good girl.

"Yes, ma'am." I tiptoed up the stairs, afraid the mere sound of my footsteps would set her off again.

Mona's paintings, once bright spots on the walls, now seemed to hover above me with silent judgment. My room became a gray tomb, dull and dreary beneath the pain of my reality.

The sun spilled across the bright and inviting lawn, teasing me with a world I could only touch in memory. Patty snuck over often when Miss Sally went to town, and Bobbie brought me letters from Buster every chance she could. I wrote my responses in the late-night hours to avoid being caught by Miss Sally.

Life moved on without me; only a few people noticed. I missed everything that summer, catching only fragments of the war and the distant news that men had set foot on the moon. I remained invisible to the world. Forgotten in time.

I started therapy again. Weekly at first, then tapering down to every other week. The office smelled like peppermint and printer ink. She had one of those fake calm voices that made you feel crazier from sitting there. I took the pills she gave me. I didn't ask questions.

My morning medication lingered well into nighttime. Sleep wouldn't find me. Each minute stretched long with my eyes refusing to close. I let my thoughts wander in the silence as the clock ticked louder with each rotation.

I was sure Miss Sally would start letting me come out of my bedroom when the new school year began. She couldn't keep me grounded forever. As the end of summer neared, the thought of returning to school left me both excited and anxious. I'd begun to accept what Miss Sally and my psychiatrist knew to be true, I wasn't like the other children.

Bobbie snuck into my room to spend time with me most nights after Miss Sally went to bed. She told me how strained their relationship had become. What began as borderline dysfunction elevated to outright abuse. Bobbie had reached her limit with her mother's accusatory remarks and angry slaps.

"The money's all gone. She spent everything my father left me, and now I have nothing for myself. I was going to buy a car and go to

California to live with my aunt. She's my father's favorite sister. My mother's always tried to keep her from my life."

My fingers pulled at a loose string on my blanket. "What were you going to do in California?" The idea of escape sounded almost magical.

"Well, my aunt owns this beautiful vineyard north of San Francisco. They make wine and have a fancy restaurant. People come from all over to sample her selections. She wants me to work there with her and eventually run it one day. She's talked about it for months." Her voice filled with real pain. "Now I can't even afford a car to get there. It was my only escape. I'm trapped."

The medication I'd been taking caused my thoughts to float in and out like clouds. I fought my way through the thick fog. The gears turned slowly as I tried to piece together a workable plan.

"I've got it, I think I can help you."

"How? You can't even leave the bedroom without my mother having an aneurysm."

"I have a car. Nobody's using it; it's just wasting away in my storage unit in Stonehaven. I've got the key to the gate, and the key to the car is above the sun visor. I watched them put it there when we were bringing everything from my old house. You could take it."

"I can't. It doesn't seem right to take something Pop left behind for you."

I gave a half-smile, but there was no joy in it. "Let's be honest, your mother isn't about to let me drive it anytime soon. So it's supposed to sit there until I'm eighteen? That seems like an awful waste. You're one of my best friends, and I want you to be happy. You've been trapped here with her for long enough. This is your chance to get away."

"I appreciate what you're trying to do. It'll never work. The car is in Pop's name. Or yours. Or the attorney's. I'm not sure how it works, but I know it's not in *my* name. Plus, there's money for gas. I have enough cash to get myself to the California border, and then what? I'd be stuck sitting on the side of the road in someone else's car. It wouldn't be long before the police dragged me and the car right back here to Hillsboro."

"Listen, there's a lockbox in the storage with cash inside. It was Pop's. I think your mother was looking for it the day after Pop died. I put it in the storage because I didn't trust her not to steal it. Your birthday's in two weeks, and after that, nobody can stop you from leaving. There's no reason for anyone to find out you took the car. Mr. Graham and I are the only ones with keys to the storage. I'll call him and let him know I'm giving you the car, and write him a hand-signed letter to file as well. When you're ready, go and take as much cash as you need. Load your stuff into the car and drop the gate and lockbox keys off to Mr. Graham on your way out of town. Okay?"

She sat in silence while considering the plan I'd detailed before her. Finally, she spoke. "Are you sure you think that's what I should do? What about you? You'd be stuck here all alone with my mother," she warned.

"School starts the week after your birthday. I'll throw myself into my studies like I've always done. Once you get out of here, don't look back. I'll come find you when I can."

She thanked me and hugged me tightly as we heard the sound of Miss Sally's car pulling up.

"I'll talk to you later when she's not around," she said as she exited my bedroom before Miss Sally caught her talking to me.

Bobbie left the day after her birthday. Miss Sally believed she was going to sleep over at a friend's house, but I knew the real reason why she'd packed so many clothes. My hands trembled as I tucked the keys and letter into her bag. A silent birthday wish echoed in my mind.

She hugged me extra tight. We knew it would be a long time before we had the chance to do so again. I watched her from my bedroom window. She cast one last glance at the house, her eyes lingering before climbing into her girlfriend's car. Our eyes met, she kissed her hand, and raised it up to me. I kissed mine and placed it on the glass.

My only ally was gone, leaving me to battle Miss Sally alone.

I'd known she was ready to run from the first day I met her. Until now, though, I never understood why. A strange calm washed over me, a quiet satisfaction knowing she'd slipped the net.

Bobbie had found her freedom. Now I just had to figure out how to get to mine.

Chapter Thirty-Two

The same night Bobbie left, the insomnia became unbearable. My sheets twisted around my legs like vines as I shifted for the hundredth time. The buzzing in my mind proved too loud for rest. I tiptoed to the closet and pulled out my container of art supplies.

An old familiar voice filled the space around me. his words invading my trance. *"Two down and two to go. What will you do? Patty and Buster are gonna leave you, just like Pop and Bobbie."*

I tried to ignore him, but the words kept coming until I couldn't take it any longer.

"Leave me be," I said, no longer the child he'd tormented before. "It's all in my head. You're not real. You can't hurt me anymore."

Shadows stretched long across my bedroom walls. Twisting. Creeping. Alive in his realm, he threatened the sanctity of mine. My pulse pounded against my ribs, each breath coming fast as the air in the room thickened. The Unseen slithered closer. He vibrated through my bones and into every fiber of my existence.

"You think you're big now? Think you've beaten me? You can shout all you want, but I live in the silence. I live in the cracks of your mind. And I'm never leaving."

The room pulsed, the walls shrinking against me. My chest burned. My throat locked. The whispers of the Unseen threaded through me, poisoned needles stabbing deeper with every threat. My father's voice, Miss Sally's accusations, all of them layering over one another until I couldn't tell who was speaking or who was real. My breath became lost somewhere beneath it all, drowning under the weight of his words.

"You will never be free."

The dark spaces spread through the corners of my mind. They clawed toward me. I dug my fingers into my scalp as I squeezed my eyes shut. *It's not real. It's not real. It's not real.*

But the Unseen only laughed.

"Think it all you want, it won't change a damn thing."

I kept my eyes closed, refusing to allow him to come to life in my world. A silhouette appeared behind my eyes. Grainy and distorted, like an old photograph left too long in the sun. It flickered in and out, becoming. A shape without edges. A face without features. Yet I knew he stared at me. Watching. Waiting.

The suffocating darkness around him thickened, bleeding into something almost tangible. His grainy image sharpened, revealing deep caverns where eyes should have been, pulling me further into their open grave. My stomach churned. My body screamed to run, to wake up, but I couldn't move.

The Unseen grinned. I couldn't see his mouth, but I felt it stretching wide in amusement.

"That's it," he crooned as he slithered through my skull. *"Now you see who you're dealing with."*

Hours passed in a blur of reality and delusion, but when it ended, my canvas sat in front of me. Thick paint dripped down onto my legs and the floor below. Four people sat on a bank, four sloppy depictions of my friends and me. And in the distance, hidden beneath the shade of trees, stood the shadow of who I knew could only be the Unseen. Who did this? Certainly, it couldn't have been me.

I pushed it away, causing the canvas and easel to crash to the ground. My door swung open, Miss Sally's hate-filled eyes blocking my only exit, my only escape.

"What are you doing up at this hour?"

"I couldn't sleep."

She clicked her tongue. "You've been doing this a lot. I hear you shuffling around all night, keeping me awake. I think you do it on purpose to punish me."

"I'm not, I swear. It's my medicine, it won't let my brain slow down."

"I figured. I'll call the doctor, see about adjusting your dose or adding a sedative so you'll sleep."

I didn't want more pills, but arguing wouldn't help, so I nodded.

A few hours later, after she left the house, I tiptoed downstairs for a drink, fearing the walls might tattle if I made a sound. I stared out the window at the freedom waiting outside. As if sensing my need for company, Patty crept through the back gate. I waved her in.

"Am I glad to see you. Miss Sally gone?"

"Mhmm. She left a little while ago, but she won't be gone long."

"Did Bobbie get on the road?"

I was surprised she knew Bobbie's plan when she'd said she wasn't telling anyone except her ride and me. "I think so. She left yesterday. If all went well, she's probably in California by now."

"Wow. I hope she made it, but I worry about you being here with Miss Sally alone."

My breath came sharper than I intended. "I'll be okay. I've got you and Buster. Everything will go back to normal when school starts."

"Girl, you're the only one I know who counts down to summer ending. Always been that way since I met you."

We talked for a while. I longed to tell her about the Unseen, about everything plaguing my brain. But she worried too much; I wouldn't add to the load. She stayed until we heard Miss Sally's car in the driveway.

Patty sat upright. "She's back, I'd better go."

"Thanks for checking on me." We hugged before she slipped

out the back door, and I rushed upstairs.

Miss Sally came in with toast and water. "Here." She handed me pills. "The doctor wants to switch your medication. Take these pills and eat the toast, or you'll be sick."

She watched me swallow them before leaving me to eat alone. Silence settled over the small room. I hummed a melody, trying to fill the emptiness with echoes of Bobbie's old records. I prayed she made it to California.

My hands began to tingle. I shook them, but blurry traces of fingers spread across my vision. The walls leaned in and out, alive and breathing. I stumbled through a tilted room toward the bed and let it pull me down into darkness.

When I woke, shapes blurred together. Colors were all either too sharp or too dim. Morning had slipped into dusk as time spiraled out of reach.

How long was I out?

My legs buckled, every step like dragging chains as I staggered to the door and turned the handle. It wouldn't budge.

"Hey!" I exclaimed, trying again. The door remained stuck. Raising my arm felt like pushing through syrup, and each knock landed with a dull thud.

I turned to scan the room. My vision blurred, a cloudy halo distorting everything around me. The furniture was all there, but my paintings and photographs were gone.

I went to the window and caught my reflection. A stranger stared back at me. Her hair was cropped short and jagged, hacked in the dark by trembling hands. My fingers traced the uneven edges, panic rising.

Keys jingled outside the door. Miss Sally entered, her expression unreadable. "Well, good, you're up."

"What have you done to me? My hair? My paintings and photographs? Where are my things?"

Her mouth tightened, a faint twitch at the corner of her eyes.

"We've been through this. You can't keep blaming everyone for what you've done to yourself. Bobbie left, pushing you into a psychotic break. You took scissors to your bedroom walls, destroying all of your belongings. And then you turned them on yourself, hacking off all your beautiful hair. I called your psychiatrist. She sedated you, and we removed anything that triggered your episodes. Your paintings, photographs, and even Mona's art. All of it."

I didn't remember the scissors. I didn't remember destroying anything. But maybe that's what she wanted.

"It doesn't make sense. When Bobbie left—"

She cut me off. "Things happen. I know you miss her. I know you miss Pop. But the Lord gives us challenges to strengthen us. You need to find a way to cope."

"You've locked me in my room."

"At your doctor's advice. It's been a lot, looking after you, but I promised Pop I'd take care of you, and that's what I'm doing."

Something sharp twisted in my stomach. "How long have I been like this?"

"Over five months. We've had this same conversation a dozen times. Your doctor isn't optimistic, but I won't give up on you."

"Five months?" My voice slurred, more to myself than to her. "What date is it?"

"January twenty-fifth."

"1970? I've lost half a year?" My heart raced. "What about school? And Patty? Buster? Didn't they come to check on me?"

"They did," she said, her tone sharpening. "Your doctor advised against exposing you to anything upsetting. Those friends of yours are triggers. You get agitated when they're mentioned, especially Bobbie. She left, but sometimes, tragedy is for the best. Now, let's get you to the restroom, and then you can eat and take your medication."

"Okay, Miss Sally," I murmured, misty thoughts slipping through my fingers.

She helped me to the bathroom and then back into bed. I took the pills. Forced a few bites of the sandwich until my stomach churned. I pushed it away.

"It's a shame to see you like this. I feel so helpless knowing you're in so much pain."

Her gaze lingered, as if expecting me to apologize. I stayed silent, unwilling to give her the satisfaction.

She sat in the chair next to the desk and whispered my name, testing if I'd fallen asleep. I stayed still.

She rose, gathered the plate, and left the room. The clink of the lock slid into place as she secured the door behind her.

I sat up and stumbled to the window, desperation growing with every step. Screws bolted into the frame mocked my need for freedom. Scanning the room for anything to remove them, I found nothing.

The medicine was kicking in; I knew time was running out. On my desk sat a cup once filled with pens, now reduced to holding crayons. A simple reminder of familiarity sent shivers down my spine.

I had an idea. Before the medication completely removed me from reality, I picked up a crayon and opened the desk drawer. I realized I'd had this idea previously. Scribbled inside, beneath blank papers, I'd written dates. *Sept. 17, 1969, Oct. 11, 1969, Dec. 21, 1969,* and finally, I included today's date, *Jan. 25, 1970.* I didn't know why, but it was reassuring to know I'd thought to do this before, as if previous versions of myself were communicating with the present one.

A fog engulfed me as I staggered back to the bed. I lay down, trying to make sense of it all. Had I finally lost my mind, or was Miss Sally poisoning me with some cruel voodoo?

Maybe I was insane, but I'd never apologize for feeling pain. I ached for my mother, weak and insecure. For my father, frozen in death, haunted by regret. And for Pop, who cherished me and tried to make me whole again in the little time we had. I wanted them all.

The tears came freely. No medication could cure my sorrow, but I took it anyway to keep Miss Sally happy. Like it or not, there was no escaping her.

Sleep claimed me, pulling me into its empty depths. Most days, the medication trapped me in a haze where time slipped by without regard. Miss Sally would wash me, drag me to the restroom, force me to eat, and give me more pills before the last dose even faded. On days she found me alert, she upped the dose, leaving me helpless and unaware.

More than two years passed by unnoticed. In November, a faint tapping at my window pulled me from my sleep. I steadied myself on the edge of the bed. The room spun. Again came the tapping.

I drew back the curtain to see Buster on the porch roof, his face pressed to the glass. He gestured to the window, his eyes desperate. I pointed to the screws to show him I couldn't open it.

Miss Sally's car was gone. My body relaxed from a flicker of relief. Buster spoke to me through the glass.

"I don't know what she's done to you. I've tried to get someone to listen to me. They all insist you're crazy. But it's not true. I know you, Mandy. She's doing this to you—her and that idiot doctor."

"I'm okay. Don't worry,"

My words slurred. The world spun around me, incoherent and off-balance. I must have looked awful to him. I didn't care, I needed to hear his voice.

"I'm always gonna worry, my dear. You're my best friend. I've come by so many times, sometimes I'd catch a glimpse of you lying there through a crack in the curtains. I know you're not okay."

A flicker of anger filled my mind, knowing Miss Sally's cruelty wasn't just mine to bear. Her wrath was reaching everyone I loved.

"I'll worry even more now since I have to go away. At least here I can stand outside your window. I've begged Miss Sally to let me see you."

"You're going away? What about school?"

He looked at me apologetically. "I graduated this past May."

Life continued without me on the other side of the glass. I should have been there beside him in my cap and gown, taking part in all the firsts; dressing up for formals, learning to drive, and a chance at a first kiss. All the milestones of my teenage years had slipped away, stolen by blurred together days. I wanted to scream or cry, but the medication made it so that even speaking became a chore.

"Where are you going, Buster?"

"I've been drafted. I'm heading out for Vietnam early next week. November twenty-third."

My head was so foggy that I found it difficult to think rationally. There was something inside my mind begging to be addressed, but I couldn't get to it easily. I stayed silent while trying to take control of my brain.

It hit me at last. "Buster, they can't draft you. You're an only son," I cried out in desperation.

"That's what we thought too. My mom went with me to speak to the draft board after my number was pulled. It turns out it's only a rumor. I don't qualify for deferment."

"I see." Despite the fog of medication, the ache found its way through. "Oh, Buster, what if I never see you again? I can't lose you, too. Can't we run away to Canada? You could bust me out of here. We could leave tonight."

"I wish we could, Mandy, I really do. We'd be fugitives, and you deserve a real life. One without running."

I knew he was right. I put my hand on the window, and he placed his against it from the other side. "You'll come back?"

"There's nothing that could stop me."

He reached into his pocket. The quarter he'd carried since I'd known him glinted in the sun. Its face, now worn by fret and time, captured the sunlight as he placed it on the window ledge.

"Your safety quarter, what are you doing?"

"I'm leaving it here, a piece of me to watch over you while I'm away."

"You can't possibly leave it behind; it means so much to you."

"It's just a coin. My real treasure is sitting right in front of me. Besides, I can't make calls from where I'm going. Open your curtain when you think of me, as long as it's still sitting here, you'll know I'm thinking of you too."

"Okay."

My mind cleared. Whether it was determination or the shock of seeing Buster, something deep within helped pull me into the reality of this moment. I didn't want him to go, but I'd been reduced to a caged bird with no way to save myself, let alone my friend.

"I'd better go. I'm not sure when Miss Sally'll be home, and I'd hate to cause you more trouble. You'll be eighteen in less than a year and a half, and my deployment will go by in no time. Don't worry. I'll be right back, my dear."

I couldn't breathe after hearing those words. I knew what they meant. His figure blurred at the edges. Another ghost slipping from my life.

I crossed the room and opened the drawer, my hand moving instinctively to remember this moment the only way I knew how. *There's a coin in the window. Vietnam took him away.*

Chapter Thirty-Three

More than a year passed following the day I saw Buster outside my bedroom window. Every time I opened the desk drawer, my hand hovered over the words I wrote when he left. Even in the silence, I heard echoes of his laugh, each memory pressing against me, never letting me forget.

As time went by, I found that my system adjusted to the dose Miss Sally gave me. My fingers obeyed again. The thoughts I formed held steady, finally mine to keep. Doing my best to feign oblivion made her believe the pills were keeping me medicated enough not to be a problem.

But she was a peculiar woman when she didn't know I was paying attention. She mumbled to herself, her lips moving rapidly, as if spilling secrets meant only for her shadow. Her gaze darted around the room, watching walls that watched her back. I wondered if she knew how crazy she truly was.

Word found its way to her about Buster being drafted. She began talking about him often. Careless. Never putting any effort into disguising her true feelings.

"The boy was cursed the moment he set foot into your life, you know. His poor mother, too. Of course, Ms. Donaldson is a strong and willful woman; she's proven so time and time again. Still, it'll be a shame if he doesn't make it out of the war alive. She'll go insane, I've seen it happen. It's no good for a mother to lose her only child. Trust me, I'd know."

She paused to study me, taking a moment to reassure herself

that I was still in a state of oblivion.

"When I lost my sweet Bobbie, I thought I'd lose my mind too. I'll never forget how awful it was to open her bedroom door and find her compact mirror smashed to pieces on the floor. She'd gone and left me all alone, but I think you already knew that. Hell, it was probably your fault she ran off. At least she left me a note to say goodbye."

And now I knew why she came rushing into my room the morning after Bobbie left. She already knew Bobbie had gone, and yet she didn't say a word.

"I don't know why you pushed me into this corner where I have no choice but to keep you like this. You're an unruly child; you always have been. Perhaps that's what caused your parents to fight so often."

The accusation stung, sinking into my skin. My jaw tightened as her words echoed, as if she had reached into the past and placed their pain at my feet. I saw red from her words, but I remained still.

"I'm the one who stayed when everyone else left you. I've cared for you, fed you, kept you healthy. Every time you've broken down, I've been the one to put you back together. Now I'm doin' this for your own good. You don't fare well, Amanda, not when people leave you."

Even through the lingering haze, I saw the difference. Death took, but they hadn't left willingly. Miss Sally stood there with her clear eyes, blind to the truth she so freely twisted. What could she possibly gain besides the satisfaction of my pain by making me believe I was crazy? There was something here I was missing, or maybe I was too drugged to see.

She took me to bathe and then back to the bedroom. It was time for her to give me my medicine, but for some reason she didn't. I waited on my bed for her to return.

The longer I lay, the more my head cleared. It was the most sober I'd been in years. She never came back, so I went to sleep. In the morning, she didn't show up again. Maybe she died. Could I have been so lucky?

Late afternoon came, and the sun dropped low behind the

neighboring houses. The sound of Miss Sally's footsteps pulled me from my daydream. Her lips were tight, her words hesitant. Unshed tears shimmered in her eyes, but she blinked them away quickly, pressing her mouth into a line as if to stop anything fragile from escaping. She'd not let a single tear destroy her ridiculously made-up face.

I refused to move, to get up and face her. Maybe she'd forgotten all about the pills. I could be sober enough to run by tomorrow if I did this right.

"Amanda," she hollered. "I have something to talk to you about. You need to sit up and pay attention."

My spine straightened, curiosity flickering beneath the charge in her tone as I waited.

"I've just read the newspaper. I don't want to tell you this, but I have to. He'd want me to make sure you know."

"Who? Know what?" The words tumbled from my mouth, fighting to stay trapped on my tongue.

Her hand struck me, sharp and sudden. The sting spread as a dull ring echoed in my ears. I touched my face, feeling the heat seep into my fingertips.

"Something happened. You need to listen." Her voice dropped to a near whisper, and a strange urgency settled around us.

"I'm listening, Sally,"

"That's *Miss* Sally, young lady," she demanded. "I was reading through the paper when I came across the names of local soldiers reported as lost to the war. Buster's name was on the list. He's dead. I'm so sorry to have to be the one to tell you such awful news. Here, I've cut out the article."

She held out the square of paper in front of me. I stared at it, my eyes straining to catch the letters and stitch them together. Spc. Charles "Buster" Donaldson. His name was solid, while the rest blurred and slipped past my focus. I felt nothing but an empty space where sorrow belonged.

I should have cried, should have been broken inside. But the words sat there, mocking me. *"I'll be right back, my dear."* An empty phrase, painted with a promise no one could keep. I let out a brittle laugh. The sound hung in the silence like a cruel joke.

She slipped her hand into her pocket, pulling out the small pills with practiced care. Her eyes never left me. "Here, take your medicine. You need it." The edges of the pills grated on my throat as I swallowed, the bitter taste lingering while her gaze followed me.

The clink of the lock made me flinch, but the sound of her footsteps retreating settled my nerves. Bobbie's old record player sat beckoning me from the floor of my closet. I pulled it out and dusted off the cover before retrieving the box of albums. Certain the band I was looking for was somewhere in the stack, I thumbed through each one slowly.

I could only half-recognize the covers, but my hands knew the album I was searching for and guided me to the one I needed. I placed it on the turntable and set the needle within the grooves.

As the record spun, the haunting lyrics wrapped around me, dragging me deeper. I mouthed the words, "Hello darkness, my old friend," feeling each syllable slip and blend, the room swaying as if caught in the song's spell.

The music played on, my mind falling further and further into the realm of delirium. For once, I didn't fight it. I'd given up trying to prove to the world I could be like everybody else when all along I'd known the truth—there'd be no normal life for me.

Mama appeared. Her figure flickered like candlelight swaying to the music's slow rhythm. Her hair flowed around her, twisting into gentle waves of smoke. I reached out, my hands slicing through her form, causing the light to scatter like glitter beneath my touch.

I pulled back my hand and stared at it, curious as to what magic hid within my grasp.

And then I saw my father crouching low across the room. He watched her with a fixed stare. His unblinking eyes held the same expression of violence forever etched into my mind. Blood seeped from the dark wound on his temple. A crimson trail rolled down to the floor into a pool below him. A wave of nausea hit me, but I couldn't look away.

I had to protect her, he'd strike at any moment. I tried to stand and move to where I blocked his view, but my legs were not my own.

I dragged myself toward him, fingers clawing against the floor. No fear remained between us. My hand reached out to hover by his face.

"You did this, Amanda. You killed your mother. Woulda been better off without you, she'd still be mine."

"That's not true. You took her away, you ruined my entire life."

His voice took on a threatening growl, the one he used when the whiskey took over. I didn't care this time. If this were real, let him kill me. I wanted to die.

"You killed her, you killed my wife."

"I didn't kill her, Daddy, I only killed *you*."

I'd never said the words aloud, never acknowledged the truth of what the Unseen made me do. But it'd always been there. The memory of when I held the gun in my hands. The explosion that threatened to deafen my ears as the shot rang out. The way his body slumped, he fell forward as all life poured from the side of his head and dripped down the wall beside his chair.

I'd ended him then, ended his threats and saved myself. He couldn't hurt me anymore. Not with his hands. Not with his words. He was nothing.

As the realization took hold, his image slowly vanished. He turned into dust beneath my fingers.

I looked back to see that Mama had also gone. Glancing around the empty room, a strange calm settled over me. The walls stilled, as if finally freed from their secrets. The shadows held no more ghosts, only the quiet sound of my breath, steady and alone.

Silent tears traced down my cheeks. Buster's laughter echoed across my mind, the familiar sound grounding me back to reality. He'd been a constant from day one, his life deeply woven into my world.

The music continued in a distant hum, while his voice filled the air around me. Every song was his, every note a reminder he was no longer there.

With all of my flaws, he loved me. Though he'd never said the words, I'd known for quite some time. Every moment I shared, every secret, every dream, I did so because there was no other way to express my feelings without admitting the truth. I loved him too. He would never hear the words my softest places longed to say.

"I love you, Buster."

I sank to the floor beside the bed. My cheek pressed against the chilly wood. An unbroken chain of sorrow and tears fell from my eyes. Dampening my hair, drowning my skin. I welcomed the release.

Like a forgotten stone in an empty forest, I lay still. I'd been lost to the world, the silence as vast as the distance between me and everyone else.

A deep, relentless sleep crept over me, dragging me under as the medication took hold. If reality had been present, I'd have seen Miss Sally watching me from the crack of the bedroom door. Her lips twisted into a crooked smile as satisfaction glinted in her eyes. She held the camera steady, each click capturing me in the depths of my despair. She'd found the key she needed to end all the suffering that my simple presence had embedded into her world.

Chapter Thirty-Four

A crushing stupor clung to my mind, obscuring the edges of memory and fantasy. Images drifted in and out, refusing to solidify into anything real. I thought I remembered Miss Sally crying the night before. Perhaps it was an illusion I'd created to feel less alone. She wouldn't have shed a single tear for Buster, not a real one anyway.

She'd be coming in soon. Every time my mind began to clear, she came again with the pills. I was nothing more than a living dead, as if I'd stepped off the screen of a George Romero film.

"Good morning." She breezed through the door with a smile so out of place it prickled my skin. I eyed her suspiciously.

"Good morning, Miss Sally."

I struggled to sit up on the bed. When had I moved from the floor?

She pulled the curtains back. The sudden burst of light stabbed through my throbbing head. I squinted, my hands raising in a defensive pose to ward it off.

"I hope you're able to find some peace with what happened. Poor Buster. This war has stolen the lives of too many of our young men. But maybe the rumors of it ending soon are true, it's gone on long enough."

When I spoke, my words were slurred, my voice hoarse. "I don't want to talk about him."

"That's a shame, dear. Even though he's gone, talking about him helps keep his spirit alive." She looked at me pitifully.

"What do you care?"

"You've caught me. It's not Buster I'm concerned with, it's you. I know how fragile you can be when somebody you care for dies. You've made so much progress over the past few months. I guess I'm trying to help you get it all out so the depression doesn't weigh you back down."

"I'm fine."

Yesterday's medication lingered, causing trouble with my ability to focus.

"Well, you might say you're fine. Heck, you might even believe you are right now. But these things have a way of festering. It's January eighteenth, exactly two months until your birthday. I wanna make sure when you cross the threshold into adulthood, you're in the best possible shape mentally."

"Okay."

"Speaking of which," she pulled the pills from her pocket. "Here's your medication. Take those and I'll grab your breakfast."

I put the pills in my mouth and took a big gulp of water as Miss Sally observed. Satisfied with my compliance, she left me to wallow in the harshness of the morning light.

As soon as she left, I spit out the pills I had stashed in my cheek and stumbled across the room to drop them down the heat vent. They made a light tapping sound as they bounced through the ductwork. I prayed Miss Sally didn't hear.

Still groggy, but my head would eventually clear. A flicker of resolve broke through my delirium. I had to find a way out. A plan was already spinning in Miss Sally's mind. I needed a better one so I could save myself.

Scanning the room, I took a silent inventory of everything in sight. No wire hangers or any item I could use to try to remove the screws holding my window shut. My art supplies were gone, as were all my other possessions. In their place were pillows and blankets. There were no clothes hanging from the rod any longer. On the floor of the closet, only Bobbie's record player, albums, and a bag of her old stuffed animals remained.

There wasn't much to choose from, so I would have to be more creative.

The sound of her steps neared my bedroom. I tiptoed back across the room and sat on the bed with my shoulders slumped and my head rolled limply to one side.

She came through the door carrying a plate of buttered toast. "Here, let's have a few bites of this before you doze off. I know how sleepy your medicine makes you."

A twisted satisfaction drove her to tear apart every scrap of freedom Pop had left me. Yet for some reason, she let me live. What hadn't occurred to me was that my well-being was of no significance to her. The only thing driving her to keep me somewhat healthy was knowing I was worth more alive than dead. Each time she fed or washed me, her hands lingered a second too long, as if I were no more than a fragile link to the fortune she craved.

I pretended to fall asleep after clumsily eating a few bites. She stood and watched me for a long time before she left again. When the coast was clear, I walked across the bedroom back to where the vent was on the floor. Remembering the sound the pills made when I dropped inside reminded me of one crucial detail, sound traveled through these things.

I lay on the floor with my face against the metal grate and waited. The rigid vent pushed into my cheekbone, but still I lay in wait.

A faint murmur drifted through the vent—a low hum slowly sharpening into Miss Sally's voice, tinged with urgency. My breathing slowed to keep the sound from overshadowing what she was saying. Her voice rose to a shout.

"I need you here at once. We can't discuss this over the telephone. Never know who's listening."

She was on a phone call. I wished I could hear what the person on the other end was saying.

"You want your share of the money? You need to come now. A lot has happened and I'd feel more comfortable explaining it in person. I saw what went on with the Watergate scandal, the same as everyone else."

She slammed down the telephone receiver. The sound reverberated loudly through the ducts, as if I were standing only feet away. In a sense, I suppose I was right next to her, only vertically.

I sat up and rubbed the tender spot on my cheek. My reflection in the window revealed the outline from the vent was set perfectly into my skin. I rubbed the area until my entire cheek turned red, hoping maybe she'd think I'd fallen if she saw the mark.

The sound of gravel stirred as an unfamiliar car pulled into the driveway and parked. My pulse quickened. Every nerve tingled with the urge to dart to the window, but I forced myself to stay rooted until the sensation subsided. Slow and careful, I peeked through the corner of the curtain while keeping myself out of view of whoever waited outside.

My body filled with a quiet moment of vindication when I saw my psychiatrist getting out of the car. It should have been evident from the start when Miss Sally boasted of their lifelong friendship. She'd known all along my sanity was intact, and still she made me question everything, including myself.

They'd planned to destroy me. They almost succeeded.

Quietly, I hurried back over to the vent to try to hear what they were saying.

"It took you long enough to get here," Miss Sally pouted.

"Sally, I was with a client. It's bad enough that I had to stop our session to take your call. You're going to have to stop being so melodramatic. We don't want us to stand out as co-conspirators when this is all over. Now what is it that's got you all worked up?"

"I've got the evidence we need to prove the girl has lost her mind," she squealed. "Last night, I showed her a clipping of her little boyfriend's name in the paper and told her that he died. It's a shame to have resorted to such a dreadful weapon, but it's not like I killed the kid.

She deflated when I told her. I knew somehow showing her that twerp was dead would push her over the edge, and I was right. A couple skipped doses of her medicine made sure she felt the pain of what I was saying. And when she saw his name, that's all it took. She's broken, any judge would agree."

"If you're certain, this means we need to start getting her set up for transfer to the long-term facility. You'll have to keep her cared for until she's of legal age in two months. I trust that won't be an issue?"

"Of course not. Now, you're sure after she's been declared legally insane as an adult, her trust will be opened to me, in full?"

"Stop worrying. I've done this so many times. You just get her safely to her next birthday, and I'll handle the rest. You'll be free of her soon, Sally, with nothing to do but savor your well-earned reward. You deserve everything coming to you."

"We both do."

"I'd like to try another medication, it's called Meprobamate. It can sometimes cause confusion and depression, which will only further our case."

Sally paused. "Wait, is that Miltown?"

"Yes, you've heard of it? I'm surprised, it's not really prescribed much anymore."

"We can't give her Miltown," Sally cut her off. "That's what Mona was taking when she killed herself. Pop swore it's what caused her to lose it, and he had a few doctors agree with him. It's too big a risk. If the girl dies, my fortune dies with her."

I sat up and rubbed my cheek while absorbing everything I'd heard them say. Mona killed herself? Pop lied to me when he said she'd died of cancer like her mother. What else had he been dishonest about? I'd been so naive, so trusting of everyone, but if Pop could lie…

I pushed away my confusion to concentrate on the most significant hurdle staring me down. Only two months remained for me to save myself. I climbed back up on the bed to try to come up with any semblance of a plan.

Her footsteps approached my door, growing louder as she closed in. I stilled, hoping she wouldn't come inside. She unlocked the door and cracked it open to find me lying over with my face turned to the wall. She scoffed and pulled the door closed, relocking it before her footsteps faded again. The sound of her car starting urged me to exhale. I waited until she'd gone before getting out of bed again.

My eyes landed on Bobbie's record player, its worn edges and familiar shape became more than a simple escape through song. This time, it presented the possibility of a way out of this prison.

I slid it out of the closet and flipped it upside down to examine the parts that made up its inner workings. I tugged and twisted each piece, but every part was bolted down.

Carefully tracing all corners of the bedroom, I looked in between my mattresses and beneath the bed. My bedside table drawers were empty, as were the dresser and desk. I found nothing.

I squeezed my hands into fists until my nails bit into my palms as I walked over to the desk to think. The chair wobbled beneath my weight. I paused and eyed it with new interest, catching the fresh glimmer of possibility. One of the L-shaped brackets holding the leg in place was loose.

This might be something.

I knew Miss Sally would be back soon, so I decided to wait until after she'd made her evening rounds. My urge to write one last message compelled me to pick up a crayon. In the sprawling mess of incoherent babble, I wrote simply, *January 18, 1973, I will be free.*

Buster's quarter beckoned to me from the window. Pressing my forehead to the cold glass, I stared at it. Even in death, his presence gave me comfort.

What would it be like if I were somehow able to get outside? I'd have to keep my steps closest to the house. The porch roof was old and should have been replaced a decade ago. The structural integrity of the tin was damaged enough without the added danger of the cold, wet climate. I'd be barefoot, so I knew I'd have to be cautious of popped nails or jagged metal.

Studying my would-be route, I found in my line of vision at least two nails were protruding, but only one piece of jagged metal invaded my path. I'd have to take it slow if I were to get out.

Where would I go? The only clothing in my bedroom was undergarments and nightclothes. Could I bring myself to run away wearing nothing more than a thin gown?

My hands shook. Light-headedness crept in. The spinning room threatened to knock me to the floor. I gripped the edge of the desk to ground myself. Heart racing and hands tingling, oxygen would not find me.

"This is it, you're having a heart attack." The long-absent presence of the Unseen warned. *"You'll die alone, just like everyone else."*

A shiver of fear ran through me, but it faded fast. The thought of rejoining Mama and Pop softened the fear, like a gentle hand releasing my panic. I remembered what Pop said all those years before. *"I thought about going home a lot."* I finally understood. By 'home' he meant to Heaven with Mona. As Pop was home to me, Mona had been home to him. Dying felt less like an end and more like finding my way back to the love in Mama's determination, Pop's quiet strength, and Buster's playful smile.

"Why did you come back?" I asked the Unseen.

"I never left, you just couldn't hear me. But now that you can, let's take that woman down. End her the same way you did your father. She won't be missed."

Could I do it? Was I strong enough to kill Miss Sally?

Chapter Thirty-Five

The door unlocked and swung open. At the sound of her footsteps approaching, I'd positioned myself in a manner to suggest I'd passed out while sitting up. My neck was bent in an intentionally uncomfortable pose.

Her hand clamped around my arm, fingers digging in deep as she gave me a sharp, bruising shake.

"Amanda!"

My eyes fluttered, then drifted half-shut again. I tried to hold my head at an awkward angle, praying the act looked real enough.

"Goodness, girl. I thought you were dead," she let out a sigh of relief.

"Who's dead?"

"Oh, nobody. Come on, let's get you up to use the restroom. I'm not cleaning soiled sheets tonight."

She pulled me up and wrapped her arm around my waist. I half walked while she half dragged me to the bathroom. My body fell limp when she placed me on the toilet. A low growl of impatience. A violent yank at my clothes. The roughness of her hands turned clumsy as she struggled to keep my dead weight from toppling over.

There was joy in seeing her struggle so much to keep me upright. Eventually, she pushed me over to lean on the sink, while she filled the tub with water and complained loudly to herself.

Watching her jaw tighten as she dragged me toward the tub brought a flicker of satisfaction, small but electric. Even limp, I was still making her day harder.

"Two more months, Sally. You can get through this nightmare for that much longer. And I'm leaving this godforsaken town as soon as I get my money."

As usual, the water was scalding. I tensed when she plopped me into the tub. Thankfully, she didn't notice, but instead went to work scrubbing soap over my skin. If she were using a Brillo pad to wash me, I'd not have been surprised.

She poured a cup of water over my head and picked up the bottle of shampoo. Rather than applying it to my hair, she set the bottle back down.

"What in the world happened to your face?"

Her thumb rubbed over the tender spot on my cheek where I'd forced it against the vent. Panic set in. Not knowing how else to distract her, I improvised.

"Mah faceee–" I mumbled as my right hand came out of the water and wiped down over her left eye and cheek.

"Imbecile!" She hurried to the mirror to see what damage my clumsiness caused.

Mascara dripped down her cheeks. Jagged black lines raced toward her snarling mouth. She wiped her face in a fury, causing the mess to smudge further.

Enjoying her misery, I decided to take it a step further. I let my body slide down into the water until my head went under and I began to gurgle.

"Jesus, Amanda." She ran over and pulled me up using my hair.

It hurt like the devil, but it was a blessing in disguise. A grin crept up, restrained only by the threat of laughter spilling out. Seeing Miss Sally caught off guard, mascara smeared and frantic, was sweeter than any escape I could have imagined.

She wrapped her hand around the bottom of my chin and forced me to face her. Again, I didn't allow my eyes to focus but rather stared blankly through her head.

"You're lucky I didn't let you drown, you little moron," she hissed.

After washing my hair and pulling me from the tub in haste, she shoved a new nightgown over my still-wet body. Then it was back to the bedroom. More pills. More anger. Without waiting to be sure I swallowed them, she shoved me onto the bed, glaring at me from above.

"Enjoy a night without dinner. I hope those pills burn your stomach from the inside out." I flinched when the door slammed, but by then she was out of sight.

I let out a silent laugh. Seeing Miss Sally's face streaked with panic and black mascara—pure entertainment. And it cost me nothing. The best part of it all was knowing my quick thinking paid off; she never even looked back at the mark on my cheek.

I waited on the bed for hours until the house had been quiet for some time before tiptoeing over to pick up my desk chair and see about removing the bracket. The screws holding it in place didn't budge when I tried to twist them with my fingernail. Instead, I began pushing and pulling on the opposite end until the screws started to hollow out the wood holding them in place.

It took a long time, but eventually it came loose. Holding the bracket up to the light, I ran my fingers over the rough edge and let the metal bite against my thumb. It was solid and sharp—proof that my patience finally paid off.

"*Kill her. Smash her skull with the leg of the chair. Break the window and slice her throat with the glass. Do something, anything, to save yourself.*" The Unseen became frantic, even more so than the night he'd urged me to kill my father.

"I can't protect myself, I'm too weak. This is the only way."

"*You can, but you won't even try. You'll die here, and nobody will even know.*"

I hummed low in an attempt to drown out the words scorched through my brain. I stopped humming when I heard a light creaking coming from outside my window. A face emerged from the shadows. A spirit? A demon? What lurked in the night? My heart leapt into my throat, blocking my scream. But it wasn't hell's agent. Instead, I found familiar eyes crinkling into a smile.

"Patty?"

Patty's childlike grin glowed softly in the moonlight, as if the night itself had conjured her. Her voice drifted through the glass.

"I'm so happy you're up. Every time I've come, it was too dark to see in. I tried knocking, but I had to keep it quiet so you know who didn't hear. I've missed you."

My hand pressed against hers, the glass cruelly cold. I ached to feel her warmth. To believe she was really here and not an illusion.

"I thought I'd never see you again," I whispered.

"As soon as Buster told me how he climbed on the roof to get to you, I started doing the same every chance I could." Clouds formed in her solemn brown eyes at the mention of his name. "I heard about what happened. I'm real sorry, Amanda."

"Can we talk about something else?"

"Sure thing. What are you doing?"

I showed her the bracket. "I'm trying to loosen the screw enough to remove it so I can get away from here."

"Why not just break the window? I can climb down and get a rock or something if you need me to."

"The panes are so tight, I'd slice myself to bits trying to squeeze through them." I stopped talking when I heard a sound coming from somewhere in the house. "You'd better get going, if she catches you here... But Patty—"

"Yeah?"

"Tell your mom what she's doing to me. She's kept me drugged, scalded my skin, chopped off my hair. Try to get help, please."

"I'll tell her, I'll find help."

I sat still while straining my ears for any sign of movement inside the house. Only silence greeted me, so I went back to work.

Even with all of my strength, the screw didn't budge. My thumb throbbed and my fingers trembled. Exhausted, I stepped my feet further back from the wall and leaned in to gain momentum in my pushing. I slipped. My body slammed against the window, the bracket falling from my grasp as it clanked loudly on the floor.

I was left motionless by the fear of what I knew would come next. There was no doubt she'd heard me. I picked up the bracket and quickly reattached it to the chair by shoving the screws into the now-too-big holes and set it back beneath the desk.

Please don't let the chair fall apart.

Heard her footsteps approached only seconds later. My heart beat so hard, I worried she would hear the sound coming from my chest. She opened the door with conviction as if something told her I was up to no good.

She scoffed when she saw me lying on the ground.

"You can just sleep on the floor like a dog then."

Her words slurred together as the sour stench of wine filled the room. It clung to her like a second skin. She staggered slightly, her eyes glazed and unfocused as she took on the form of a nighttime demon, dulled by her own poison. Knowing she was secretly a drunk would fare well for me, though I didn't know how yet.

She turned off the light, her steps retreating back down the hall. A new flicker of hope came when I realized she hadn't locked the door. The small flame was doused by the harsh click of the lock sliding into place. My heart sank. A single, salty tear burned down my cheek.

"Maybe some other time."

Night after night, I returned to my secret rebellion. Each failure left me emptier, but I couldn't stop. This bracket held the promise of freedom, no matter how faint.

Every morning, I made a tally inside the drawer, a secret calendar counting the days. But every time I cheeked a pill, my pulse spiked. Terror gripped me considering what would happen should she catch me. So far, she hadn't noticed, too blinded by her arrogance.

It was a few nights before Patty returned. Her face fell, shoulders sagging as she whispered, "I tried, Amanda. My mother tried, too, but no one will listen to people like us."

"This town is full of bigots," I spat. "What about Ms. Donaldson?"

Her eyes lit up. "I didn't think about calling her, but I'll do it first thing in the morning. In the meantime, keep trying with the screws."

"I won't give up."

She stayed with me for hours, filling the lonely hole in my being. I listened to her stories. Every word left me thirsty for the opportunity to experience real life with my best friend.

I'd made it through the years of isolation, the drugs she'd forced upon me, the abuse, the insanity, and the nights I sweat through my sheets when my body craved her poison. She wouldn't best me. Not anymore.

Chapter Thirty-Six

The first turn of the screw sent a thrill through me. Patty's eyes lit up. The faint creak of metal ignited a fire deep inside.

I stayed by the window until dawn, each hint of progress another heartbeat closer to escape. The following day was easy to fake oblivion, I was as tired as Miss Sally believed I was drugged.

It took another week, but I'd removed the first screw from the binding wood. Every time she came in, the fear took hold. I was sure she'd notice the screw's empty socket or the slight shift in the window frame. Her eyes skimmed over the room without a second glance. I let out a breath as she left, my prize—the long screw—tucked under a pile of albums like a buried secret.

My day passed more slowly than any others had before. The nagging to start working on getting the window open was loud, like a constant alarm inside my head. Not long after sunset, I noticed headlights sweep across the front of the house.

Miss Sally rarely had visitors. Whatever time of night it was, my only thought was of Patty and her mission to find someone to help me. I hurried to push my face against the vent again to see if I could hear who was coming through the front door.

She was talking a mile a minute, but too far from any vents for her voice to carry well enough for me to make out her words. The sound of the front door closing was followed by the voices getting louder. They must have been moving across the house to the dining room which was directly below my bedroom.

A familiar, clinical tone set my pulse on edge. The psychiatrist was back again. A new horrific thought rushed into my subconscious. *What if she wants to come and check on me? Would she know I'm faking this medicated delirium?*

I lay in the dark, biting back the urge to scream. Every laugh from below crawled through the vents, and each careless clink of glass left me with a seething anger. They drank while I lay imprisoned counting my breaths. Relief washed over me when I heard the front door close and the doctor's car pull away. Sally's footsteps retreated to her bedroom.

Lying the chair on the bed to remove the bracket caused almost no sound at all. After lifting it, I removed the screws holding it in place and set it carefully beside the chair.

As I knelt by the window, the shadows shifted and Patty appeared. A faint smile rested on her face, her eyes focused on mine. Her presence stilled my trembling hands and gave me the strength to keep turning the screw.

"You're so close, Amanda."

The hardest part of the first one was getting it to break free. After it moved once, the rest of the turning came with at least a small amount of ease. With a sturdy stance and a careful hand, I began pushing and praying for the screw to budge. After only a few tries, I lost my footing. As before, my hand slammed into the glass and the sound of the bracket ricocheted across the floor.

Patty's expression mirrored my horror as the crash sliced through the silent night. She ducked down as I rushed to put the chair back together. My fingers grazed the screws, one falling between my bed and the wall.

"Shoot," I whispered.

Frantically, I looked under the bed but didn't see the screw anywhere. I could hear Miss Sally coming. The only choice I had was to lay the chair on the floor along with the bracket and broken leg. I did so quietly and hurried to get into bed. Her steps thundered closer. There was only enough time to ruffle my hair to make it look like I'd been sleeping when she got to the door.

It burst open. Miss Sally's drunken silhouette swayed in the doorway.

"Who's in here?" her words carried scents of wine and rage.

I didn't move a muscle except to display nice and even breaths. Her eyes went to the chair, now lying on the floor.

"Demons!" she screamed. "You've brought demons into my home, Amanda Hollings!"

She bent down to pick up the broken chair before stumbling back out to smash it into pieces against the hallway wall. Her outburst of violence didn't make me flinch. I was ready for the unpredictable tonight. She came back in to grab the broken leg, and with it I heard the bracket scrape across the floor. My last hope had been dissolved.

Staggered back in, I opened my eyes to see her coming at me, harboring a thousand days of vengeance. She was on top of me, hands clamped around my throat. I tried to use my arms to push her off, but she was too heavy. I was too weak. Too small.

My lungs begged for air. A numbing cold crept through my veins, pulling me away. I saw my mother, her face contorted with the same fear gripping me now. As light faded to dark, I found calm.

Patty's fists pounded against the window, her voice a shrill plea in the stormy night. "Stop it!" she cried. Her words went unheard as Miss Sally's grip tightened, raising the furious pounding of my heartbeat. Patty's face was a blur of desperation, but she didn't exist to Miss Sally. Nothing did.

She didn't finish the job as my father had done. Instead, she let go of my throat and climbed off of me, staring from my bedside, my lungs devouring every inch of air available. My eyes watered. I coughed and rubbed my tender throat.

"Next time, I won't let go," she threatened as she staggered back out of my bedroom and slammed the door shut behind her.

I'd have allowed it to be my breaking point if I weren't fully aware of the most important detail. She had once again left the door unlocked.

I lay motionless against the mattress, my limbs unwilling to react. Every instinct screamed to move, but fear pinned me down as Miss Sally's hands had moments ago. The house creaked around me, every sound magnified in the silence.

Patty's soft but firm voice cut through the darkness, "Get up, Amanda. It's now or never."

I threw the blankets off and stepped across the cold wood floor. For a moment, I was nine years old again, terrified of what lay in wait.

Pop's words gave me strength. *"You're as big now as you always strived to be."*

"Stay with me, Pop," I pleaded as I turned the knob. Either I'd make it out or she'd catch me and finish the job. No matter what, this hell would end.

I stepped out into the hallway to tiptoe toward the stairs. Broken pieces of the chair threatened my path as I made my way closer to freedom. My toes touched the first step. Her bedroom door swung open. Loud, angry feet boomed as she rushed toward me.

"Amanda, get back in that bedroom now!" she roared.

She lunged, her fingers grazing my arm. I knew what I had to do, and I knew I needed to do it *quickly.*

"The wood—it's so close. Pick it up, Amanda. Do it now."

I squeezed my eyes shut, paralyzed. It was right there; the perfect weapon of defense. But I couldn't move. For a second, I didn't exist in reality. An eternity passed in pure darkness until I snapped back into the moment, now taking the stairs two at a time.

Patty stood waiting when my feet hit the porch. We ran at full speed out into the night. The only light came from the sporadic lightning crashing through the torrential downpour. The wind howled as if urging us forward. I didn't look back.

"Help!" I called. "Somebody help me!"

Patty joined in, her voice louder and stronger than mine.

Every shout tore at my raw throat. "Help!" I gasped while forcing the word out until my lungs burned. I knew if I stopped, my last hope would wash away with the storm.

Headlights cut through the darkness, slicing through the trees as we pressed ourselves deeper into the shadows. They rode past where we hid, and I noticed the red and blue lights fixed to the top of the car. I emerged from the trees and screamed while waving my arms.

"Come back!" I yelled after them. Lightning crashed again, illuminating my figure once disguised by the dark.

The officer hit his brakes and put the car in reverse. He got out and rushed around to let us into the back seat. I didn't realize who he was until he got back into the car. Officer Jenkins. The same man who'd threatened to lock me up years before when Miss Sally accused me of pushing her down.

"Miss? Are you okay? We had a call about a woman screaming."

"Yes, sir, that was me. I've been held prisoner, and my guardian has been keeping me drugged. You gotta help me, please."

"What's your name?"

"I'm Amanda Hollings, and this is Patricia Taylor."

His eyes swept across the backseat. He did nothing to hide the disapproval on his face.

Another bigot. I thought to myself in anger. I'd never get used to the sideways glances and awkward stares when Patty was around.

It finally clicked in his head why I looked so familiar. His expression changed to one of skepticism. "You've been held prisoner, you say?"

"Yes, please. I need help. Miss Sally's crazy. She's done all sorts of awful things to me. Kept me locked up in my bedroom, forced me to take medicine. She's evil, Officer."

"Where would she have gotten the medication?" he asked, still unconvinced I was anything less than a troublemaker.

"She got them from my therapist, but you don't understand."

"I think I do understand, young lady. Let's go find Sally and hear her side."

"No, please. You can't take me back there. She'll kill me."

I glanced at Patty for help and found her expression more terrified than mine.

He started driving back toward the house. "I've seen this before. You have to try to listen to your elders. She's a nice lady with the best intentions. You might not see it now, but you will one day. She's probably worried sick about you, out in such a dreadful storm."

"Please don't let her take me again."

We pulled into the driveway. He left us sitting in the police car while he went inside. No more than thirty seconds passed when he came running out.

"What did you do to her?" he screamed as he reached for his radio. "I need an ambulance at 229 Southeast Oak Street."

He ran back inside before Patty made a peep. "What happened before you made it out?"

"Nothing. I mean, I don't know. She was chasing me, so I ran out the front door."

But I knew what had come of Miss Sally, and I'd never tell a soul.

A siren approached. The rain poured as I watched the paramedics rush inside.

Everything became a part of the chaos. The rain. The lights. The strangers. A cold sweat broke out across my body. I could barely find a way to catch my breath. My vision spun, colors fading to gray as I leaned into Patty's shoulder. The last thread of my strength slipped away.

"Don't leave me, Patty."

"Shh, don't talk, I'm not going anywhere."

Despite my will to fight it, my eyes rolled back. My body lay limp when the officer returned to the car. Unconscious. Unaware of what would come next.

Chapter Thirty-Seven

The invasion of thick boots rushing through puddles pulled me back into reality, making my head spin and my stomach churn.

"Miss Hollings, can you hear me?" a man's voice called out as a flashlight swept across my eyes. "I think she's coming out of it."

"What happened?" I tried to sit up. A tight pressure across my chest held me down. I was helpless—trapped.

"Go ahead and load her up. She'll need to be evaluated," the man said as the emergency lights flashed red and blue against the misty rain.

Patty's voice pierced through the commotion. Her delicate fingers slid through mine, and I was safe again.

"They're taking you to the hospital."

The colors pulsed in dizzying bursts. My eyes fought against my will to keep them open. Each blink dragged me closer to darkness.

The weight of exhaustion threatened to drown me in its depths. As my eyes closed, my body dissolved against the hands of strangers.

When we arrived, staff members were already waiting. The paramedics pulled my stretcher from the ambulance and wheeled me inside. Nurses took my vitals and started an IV, their curiosity only partially veiled.

A doctor stood over me. He inspected my limbs while the nurses continued working.

"Hello, Miss Hollings. I'm Dr. Laydon. Looks like you've had a rough night, young lady."

I opened my mouth to ask for Patty, but the door burst open. A police officer strode in, flashing his badge smugly. "I'm Officer Jenkins, and I need a moment alone with the suspect."

The doctor straightened, not willing to back down.

"You'll get your moment after I ensure the *patient* is stable."

"I'm investigating a crime. You're currently hindering that investigation. Either step aside, or I'll call my Sergeant to make you comply. If that happens, you might face charges."

Dr. Laydon placed his body between mine and the officer's. "Then call your Sergeant. No one speaks to my patient until I confirm she's physically and mentally able. Be careful the door doesn't hit you on the way out."

He stormed through the door. One of the nurses did her best to stifle a laugh. The doctor shot her a sharp glance of reprimand, making her cheeks turn pink. His face softened when he turned back to me.

"Miss Hollings, your muscles aren't responding properly. Have you experienced this before?"

"I don't think so."

He tapped my knee with a rubber hammer. My leg barely twitched, deepening his frown.

"You're suffering from atrophy. You're malnourished and extremely underdeveloped. I'm going to order some bloodwork to check your electrolytes and liver function."

He nodded to a nurse while she gathered supplies for the test.

"Tell me a little bit about your diet?"

"I eat what Miss Sally gives me. Sometimes toast or a sandwich. Other times, some fruit or maybe a piece of chicken. She gives me whatever she has extra, I think."

"And who is Miss Sally?" His eyes narrowed.

"She's my guardian. I've lived with her since my adoptive parent, Pop Wells, passed away." My voice dropped to a whisper. "She locked me in a room, drugged me until I couldn't tell if my thoughts were real or not. She wanted me broken for Pop's money. But I stopped swallowing the pills and threw them down the vent when she wasn't looking. Once the drugs wore off, my head cleared. She wasn't medicating me because I'm crazy. She was trying to *make* me that way."

His eyes widened as he processed my words. "Pop Wells was your adoptive father? My family knew him well. I think I met you at his funeral. I'm gonna look into this. For now, don't say a word to the police when they come back. Okay?"

I nodded.

"Good. I'll let the staff know to keep a close eye on you. My shift's nearly over. I'll do what I can to help make you comfortable before I leave."

"Thank you. Do you know where Patty went? She's the girl who rode in the ambulance with me."

His brow furrowed. An expression of curiosity I didn't recognize flashed across his eyes.

"I'm not sure. I can ask around and see if anyone's seen her."

The noise of the hospital should have comforted me. It should have made me feel less alone. But the silence in my room overpowered the sounds in the halls. I needed Patty.

My door swung open again, and Officer Jenkins strode in. He squared his shoulders, a sharp look on his face.

"Evening, Miss Hollings. I trust you're more coherent since you've had time to calm down." He flipped open his notepad. "Sally's on her way to surgery now. She may not pull through. If she doesn't make it, you'll likely face murder charges. You're young. I want to help you through this, but you'll need to tell me exactly what happened tonight."

Dr. Laydon's warning echoed in my mind.

"I… I don't remember."

His expression darkened. "You were a chatterbox in the car, but now you can't remember? You're lying."

"I don't remember." Exhaustion tugged at me. I allowed my eyelids to close him out of sight.

"Miss Hollings, I know you're not sleeping. We can do this all night if you'd like."

After a few more probing questions, a nurse came in to check my vitals. She caught the frustration on the officer's face and pushed herself into the small space between the bed and him.

"Medical Team, two; Officer Jenkins, zero."

I did not allow anyone to see my reaction to the Unseen's observation, but my heart wore a long-awaited grin.

"I'm sorry, Officer. I can't let you stay while the patient rests. Doctor's orders."

"I'm fine right here," he huffed.

The nurse's tone sharpened further. She moved to the door and held it open. "I didn't ask how you were. Doctor's orders are clear. Out."

He stormed out again, his heave of angry frustration echoing down the hall.

The nurse leaned close, speaking in a whisper, "Goodnight. I won't let anyone bother you again."

"Thank you. Goodnight."

A moment later, the door creaked open. I made out Patty's familiar face in the dim light as she peeked through. Bright eyes. Gentle smile. Her presence warmed the sterile room.

"Come on in, Patty. I'm awake."

"I wanted to give them space to work on you. The doctor just came and said you were asking for me, though. I called my mom. She said she'll come by as soon as possible. I can stay tonight if you want me to?"

"I'd like that." I scooted over on the bed. "Come on, you can sleep up here."

"The bed's not very big. Are you sure you'll be comfortable?"

I patted beside me on the thin mattress, smiling. "Look, I'm half my old size, and you're as small as ever. We'll fit."

She climbed in, clasping my hand, my head resting on her shoulder.

I couldn't quiet my thoughts. Even with Patty beside me and extra blankets, a chill seeped into my bones. My teeth chattered, waking me each time I drifted off.

Nurses came and went throughout the night. Between the bustle of the hospital staff and unfamiliar sounds, I couldn't find real rest. I woke up feeling more tired than I had the night before.

Patty tapped my shoulder as sunlight whispered through the window pane. "I have to go. I'll be back when my mom comes to see you."

A new doctor arrived before breakfast, introducing himself as a psychiatrist.

"Good morning, Miss Hollings. How are you feeling today?"

"I'm okay, just a little cold."

His gaze lingered on my frail arms, lifting one in gentle demonstration. "No wonder you're cold. I'm here to discuss the ordeal you've been through and what impact the experience has had on your mental state. You think that would be alright?"

I sat up higher in the bed, a new type of nervousness enveloping me. Despite my fear of his probing, I agreed to play along.

The questions began with Miss Sally, but at some point there was a gentle shift. A less inquisitive person may not have wondered the purpose, but I'd spent my life questioning everyone and everything. It struck me as odd that he wanted to know so many details about my personal life *before* going to Miss Sally's. What my hobbies had been. How I'd gotten along in school. And he lingered on the topic of my friends; who they were, what they enjoyed, how often I saw and spoke to them.

I answered everything, but couldn't shake the feeling that there were other answers he was trying to find without my knowledge. My hands finally unclenched the sheet when he announced he'd reached the end of his examination.

But he said he'd be coming back to check on me daily.

"The nurses should be bringing the breakfast trays around shortly. Take your time eating. I wouldn't want you upsetting your stomach on top of everything else," he warned as he stood to leave.

"Okay, I'll try and get something down. My stomach already doesn't feel so great this morning."

I wasn't hungry. My body had adjusted to so little in Miss Sally's care, it'd been ages since the last time I'd even craved food. I'd escaped the monster. For the second time in my short life, I'd managed to free myself from a demon on earth. How much more evil would I have to face in my life? My thoughts were cut short as the nurse brought in the breakfast tray.

"Here we are," she said, sliding the table into place and helping me sit up. "Take your time. I'll be back shortly to take the tray."

"Thank you."

What most would consider a normal meal swelled before me like a feast. I picked up the toast first. Its edges crumbled in my grasp as I took a small bite. It caught in my throat before I could force myself to swallow. I peeled back the cover of the apple juice, using the liquid to push the bread into my body. When I tried the sausage, my stomach churned. I set it down, covering the tray as if the act alone could settle my queasiness.

As I repositioned myself, the door swung open. My attorney stepped in.

"Mr. Graham. I'm so relieved to see you."

Lines creased his face as he hurried to my bedside. Worry and guilt. Embarrassment. Concern. I knew those expressions well. He tried to conceal his emotions, but his face betrayed his efforts.

"I'm so sorry. I can't believe what you've been through. Dr. Laydon called me late last night. Are you okay?"

I looked down, twisting my fingers. "No… no, I'm not. They're saying that I hurt Miss Sally. Do you know if she's alright? Did she make it through surgery?"

"Shh, it's okay, sweetie. She'll heal just fine. You have nothing to worry about. Officers are at her house now. I'll go there after this to see what they find. I feel awful for letting this happen to you. When I came to check on you, I demanded to speak with your psychiatrist. She and Sally were very convincing about your diagnosis."

"You came to check on me?"

"I did. The story they told seemed plausible. With everything you'd already been through, and then losing Pop so suddenly, the ingredients for a breakdown were certainly there. When I visited, you just stared off into nothing. The psychiatrist said you'd locked yourself away from reality. I was so blind. I even thanked Sally for sacrificing so much to take care of you."

"You couldn't have known. Even if you questioned it, Miss Sally would've convinced you I was crazy. She fooled everyone."

"I should have come more often. Time slips away. I kept putting it off and convincing myself you were in good hands. All sorry excuses, I know."

I gave his hand a gentle squeeze. It wasn't his fault. The only person I could blame was Miss Sally. And maybe myself.

"I'm free now. I'm gonna be okay."

Relief softened his expression. "Yes, I suppose you are. Have you spoken to the police?"

I shook my head. "Dr. Laydon told me not to. When the officer came last night, I said I was tired and pretended to sleep. He tried to threaten me, but I kept my eyes closed until a nurse chased him off."

"Good. Please refrain from speaking to them without my presence. Tell me everything Sally did to you?"

"It started the day Bobbie left..." I whispered, feeling the weight of each word.

For the next hour, I detailed everything I could remember about Miss Sally's abuse. Mr. Graham's pencil flew across the notepad while I spoke. When I finished, my throat was raw, and his pad was filled with dense notes. Slumping back against the pillows, I let exhaustion settle over me.

"This helps a lot. There's evidence here that the police can use.

I'll let them know what to look for. You did well, Amanda. Really well."

"Okay. Oh, and Mr. Graham?"

He paused on his way to the door. "Yes?"

"Can you help me get a hold of Bobbie?"

"I have her address and phone number. She gave it to me before she left. Should I tell her what happened?"

"Yes, please. Thank you for everything."

"Don't thank me yet. Let's get you better first, okay?"

"Deal." I forced a smile as he left.

Lunch proved equally as painful as breakfast. The nurse frowned when she took my tray away. I'd only eaten three bites. As the door closed behind her, a flood of relief washed over me. Mrs. Taylor's familiar voice traveled down the hallway, followed by a light tap on the door.

"Come in."

I rushed to try to smooth my hair before she saw me. Pointless.

She swept into the room. The enormous energy I needed emanated from her small frame. Her presence replaced the stale air with warmth. I expected Patty to trail behind, but she came alone.

"I've been so worried, Amanda. That Sally refused to let us see you. Every time we tried to visit, she swore you were too fragile. She even called me a trigger! Can you believe it? When I tried to speak to your doctor, she just repeated everything Sally said."

I found comfort in her voice, even when I wondered if she'd take a moment to breathe. I listened intently as she recounted her attempts to raise concerns. It didn't surprise me to hear nobody had taken her seriously, rather, it angered me even more.

I reached for her hand. Hers were soft and gentle against my dry and cracked skin.

"I'm so sorry. I can't imagine how hard that must've been."

"Oh no. Don't you go feeling sorry for me. I let you down. And so did everybody else. My heart knew something was wrong, child. My heart knew…"

"Where's Patty? She said she was coming back with you."

Her hand tensed in mine. Eyes shifting. There was something here she wasn't telling me.

"Oh, well, she may be by shortly. It's been a hectic morning. But when Mr. Graham called to say you were in the hospital, I rushed right over."

I hesitated. Patty told me last night she called her mother. Was she lying then, or was Mrs. Taylor lying to me now? Did she truly have permission to stay with me last night? It had never been like Patty to defy her mother. But then again, I hadn't known Patty in years.

Letting the uncertainty go, I told her the story of everything Miss Sally did to me. She listened without interrupting, though I was sure much of it Patty had already shared.

"I think I need a break from this town. Maybe even the whole state," I said when I finished. "Once I'm feeling better, I'd like to go to San Francisco. Patty and I could take the train. Would you let her come with me?"

A pained expression took over her face, and I considered she worried about the cost of such a trip.

"I'll have my trust soon, so I'll cover everything. I just really want—no, I need Patty to come with me."

She pursed her lips. Fiddled with the clasp of her handbag and avoided eye contact. Maybe Patty *had* been up to no good. Perhaps she'd fallen in with the wrong crowd. Maybe she let herself break without me. I'd almost lost myself without her.

"San Francisco is… well, I'd need to talk to Henry first. You understand."

"Oh. Well, what do you think about me going, even if Patty can't come?"

"I think it's a fine idea. Just so long as you're well enough for the trip. Let's get you strong first. There'll be plenty of time to work it out later."

"Okay, as soon as I'm feeling well enough."

Patty came in then. We sat together while Mrs. Taylor told stories that made me smile. It hadn't occurred to me how much I missed her voice. The comforting way her smile lit up the room. If my home were built of people, her presence made up one necessary wall.

She leaned down and brushed the hair from my face the same way she did when I was younger. A tiny kiss to my forehead. A lasting stamp of love on my skin. An unmistakable hint of belonging filled the cold spaces inside me. My throat tightened. I blinked fast. It was impossible to remember the last time someone's touch made me feel connected to the rest of the world.

These wounds of mine would heal in time. Despite her best effort, Miss Sally hadn't broken me. I would be whole again, but only after facing a truth I'd yet to learn existed. A truth buried beneath all their goodbyes. Something they'd all seen coming. I'd been too lost between worlds to notice.

Chapter Thirty-Eight

Thirteen days remained until my birthday. Staring out the window to watch the leaves sway in the wind, I thought of the warmth of Pop's voice. In his world, he'd always made things so simple. I ached for his advice now.

I wasn't a little girl anymore. In a lot of ways, I'd never truly been one. Save for the years in the middle with Pop, circumstances outside of my control had consistently tormented my life. Most of my typical childhood experiences had been taken from me in a manner so heinous, it was amazing to realize I'd lived through hell twice.

In adulthood, I knew I'd find the strength to protect myself from further damage. There was resilience in age, but I still mourned the childhood I'd been denied.

The nurses smiled more when they checked on me, their hands lingering on my shoulder or hair as if afraid I might still be hurting. After Mr. Graham showed the police the evidence from the house, everyone knew what Miss Sally had done to me.

I overheard bits of conversation in the halls, whispers and glances, piecing together what they believed happened to her. She'd rushed toward the stairs in a drunken stupor, tripping on a broken chair leg in the hallway. She fell onto the jagged wood, one shard piercing her body, missing her heart by less than an inch.

Three ribs and her right arm were broken. One rib had displaced so severely that it injured her liver, though not fatally. The doctors said the organ was badly bruised but would heal in time.

The hospital contacted Bobbie, asking if she'd come to her

mother's aid. She declined, citing work as her excuse. I doubted the truth of it, but didn't blame her for denying the request.

Patty and Mrs. Taylor came to see me often; sometimes Mr. Taylor came along too. Being with them made my days feel warmer, as if their mere presence could thaw my frigid, broken soul. They asked if I would stay with them once I left the hospital, and I happily accepted the invitation. With them, I'd have the promise of something to look forward to.

As my body healed, time returned to its usual rhythm. A few days before my birthday, my attorney stopped by with Officer Jenkins trailing behind him.

The officer's expression was tight, his pity forced. Beneath it, anger simmered—whether from embarrassment at being wrong or from a sergeant's orders to apologize, I couldn't say.

"Miss Hollings."

"Just Amanda'll do."

Pop's voice echoed in my reply. So much of his spirit lingered in mine. It would be impossible to separate the parts of me that didn't contain him.

"I wanted to see how you're doing."

"I'm okay. Getting stronger every day. The doctor says I should be out by tomorrow. It'll be a long road ahead. Lucky for me to have so many amazing people to help me along the way."

He offered a weak smile. His face flushed as he continued.

"That's good to hear. I'm here to apologize. From where I was standing, it really looked like—"

I cut him off gently. There wasn't any reason I could find to let him go on with his rehearsed speech.

"You don't need to explain. I've already forgiven you."

His surprise was palpable. The red in his cheeks traveled down to his neck. But he softened.

"Why?"

I thought carefully before answering. "We're all flawed. It's what makes us human. Equals. I've had people hurt me for most of my life. Let them damage and bully me. But I don't want to hurt anymore. Don't want to hate anymore either. Letting go is the only way I can reclaim my life. So that's what I have to do."

"I guess I can understand. You're a bright young lady."

Mr. Graham interjected. He'd done his part in allowing the officer a chance to apologize. But he knew nobody in the room was comfortable.

"And she's getting brighter every day. We do appreciate your visit, but I need to speak privately with my client."

"Of course."

He nodded at me and shook the attorney's hand before leaving. My muscles relaxed as the door closed behind him.

Mr. Graham settled into the chair beside my bed. "One more day here. How are you feeling about leaving?"

"I'm more than ready. Mrs. Taylor's picking me up tomorrow. We're going straight to her hairdresser to fix this shaggy mess before we leave for California."

I held up a lock of uneven hair. Jagged, limp ends. A lingering reminder of Miss Sally's cruelty.

"I've prepared the paperwork to release your trust without restrictions. It's dated for March eighteenth, but I'll need you to come by my office to sign it on the sixteenth before you leave for California. Everything should be settled by the time you're home."

"Okay."

"I've booked your tickets for the train. Are you sure you don't want a sleeping room? It's such a long trip. You ladies would have a lot more room to stretch out. And more privacy."

I smiled at his concern but shook my head. I craved the open car full of strangers, each face a piece of life I hadn't touched in so long. "The thought of being shut inside a tiny room on the train would feel like trapping my past in a box with me."

"Yes, I suppose it could bring back some awful memories. If

you'd like, I can pick you up in the morning before you go, so we can get everything squared away, and I'll drive you ladies to Portland to catch your train."

"Mr. Taylor said he wants to drive us. I appreciate your help in planning my trip. I know it sounds crazy to run off to California. It's just something I need to do. I'll study hard for the placement tests and get my diploma when I get back."

"I'm confident you'll pass everything with ease. It's been a long and bumpy road. But it wasn't for nothing. You're stronger for everything you've been through."

"I'll never understand why people choose to reduce their lives to cliches. Maybe not everything has a purpose. Sometimes, things simply happen, and we're left to live with them. I'm not better or stronger because some evil person chose to hurt me, and I refuse to place credit for my strength in undeserving hands. What if the only thing hiding below the surface is pain? It's neither better nor worse; it just *is*. I think the concern should be in how I cope with the aftermath, rather than blaming every situation on some hidden agenda. But I truly am alright, Mr. Graham, and I'm only going to become better from here."

"That was very eloquently worded. I swear sometimes I forget I'm talking to a child," he laughed. "But what you said is right, it doesn't always have to be part of the plan. Though sometimes it's nice to believe there is one."

"I think so too. I suppose I don't want to believe I was destined for such darkness. If what I've endured was the work of a spiritual being, I know it wasn't God. No, what happened to me could have only been created by a more malevolent force."

He nodded, considering my angle before we said our goodbyes. I slumped into my pillows the moment the door clicked shut behind him. My ears buzzed from the conversation. Even the light filtering in through the window felt too bright.

I picked up my copy of *To Kill a Mockingbird* and traced the worn edge of the book with my finger while thinking of Atticus's steady calm and Scout's innocence in a world ready to judge her. They seemed so real, these characters, so close to my own life that it hurt.

I read until after dinner, and then lay down to get some rest. Aside from being tired, I knew sleeping was the best way to pass the time, one of many old habits I'd yet to outgrow.

The rising sun pulled me from my sleep. I got out of bed to watch it come up beyond the field outside my window. Mona's painting from the cafeteria in the orphanage flashed across my mind.

"It's a brand new day, Mona," I whispered into the growing light of morning.

The glass between the world and me was still more like a wall than a window. Each sunrise happened on the other side, while I stayed locked in place. But not anymore.

I returned to my bed to wait for my final checkup. Mrs. Taylor arrived with Patty in tow at eight, and the doctor released me at eight-thirty. When I walked out, I found only excitement in the unknown that lay ahead.

Mrs. Taylor fussed over me all day, straightening my collar, smoothing my hair, and asking if I'd had enough to eat. Each gentle touch was like rediscovering a fragile piece of me I'd lost. At first, I hardly knew what to say. Everything was as foreign as it was familiar.

After a full day of pampering and shopping, we went home. Of all the things Pop told me, only one of them was wrong. His absence hadn't tainted the walls of our once-happy home. Instead, the memory of him lived within the beams crossing the high ceilings, his smile reflected in the fixtures that provided light, his love deeply engraved into each wall. His memory became my home; I took it with me everywhere I went.

We laughed and reminisced around the dinner table. I'd found my way back. I helped clean the kitchen and then asked if it was okay to make a phone call.

"Absolutely, child. You don't have to ask."

I picked up the phone to call Mrs. Donaldson. Slipping my

finger into each number, I let it drag the dial around and waited for it to spin back with a soft whir. An oddly soothing motion, as if I could spin away the memories sure to resurface once I heard her voice.

In a way, I'd been avoiding the call, but I owed it to Buster to offer my condolences to his mother. The telephone rang seven times before I hung up the line.

"I'll try again tomorrow," I whispered to Buster's spirit in the same way I'd done when guarded beneath Miss Sally's control. Could he hear me? Did he know I still spoke to him? Still yearned for him?

Patty and I got out of bed the next morning and inspected the contents of our bags. Confident that everything was in order, we dressed for the day. Mrs. Taylor was making pancakes when we came out of the bedroom.

"Time for breakfast. When are you scheduled to meet with Mr. Graham?"

"We've got about an hour," I replied as I set the table.

"Thank you. I sure do appreciate the help."

"It's better when everybody does their part. A lot of little things can add up to a pretty big whole."

She winked at me as she brought the food to the table. For a moment, I saw Pop standing there behind her. He nodded. He knew I'd found a place where I still believed in tomorrow.

"Are you excited for your next chapter?"

"More like my next life. I've already gotten through three."

"It seems you have," she replied, her vice dropping.

"I'm optimistic. There's a wide open world waiting for me to live free, I just have to go meet it."

"And I'm gonna be here to make sure nobody ever tries to steal your wings again, you can count on it."

We cleaned up the kitchen together. When we were done, I called Mrs. Donaldson's number once more. Again, there was no answer. I dialed Bobbie next to confirm our arrival time and let her know we were on our way. She did nothing to hide the excitement in her voice.

"Not sure what I'm gonna do with myself in this big empty house while y'all are gone," Mr. Taylor joked as he loaded our bags into the car.

"Oh, nonsense, you'll be just fine without us for two weeks," Mrs. Taylor insisted.

I sprang from the car when we pulled up to Mr. Graham's office. "I'll only be a few minutes."

"Good morning. It's a big day today." He flashed me a genuine smile, yet something stirred behind his eyes.

"Indeed, it is," I said slowly. "Is there something wrong? You've got this look about you."

"Sometimes in my line of work, I'm faced with tough decisions. You see, I have something to give you, it's something Pop left behind. He wanted you to have it when you were eighteen, and able to decide for yourself how you would proceed."

A message from Pop shouldn't have made me so nervous. But the shadowed glance Mr. Graham offered, he held back words he didn't want to say. The package became a weight instead of a treasure.

His fingers tapped his desk in a steady rhythm, but his eyes wouldn't meet mine.

"My instructions were clear, and I've done my part. I've spoken to the psychiatrist from the hospital, the one who came to visit you while you were healing, you remember?"

I nodded.

"Well, those visits were part of what was required by Pop. For me to give you the package he left, to be sure you could handle the information inside. The doctor believes you're ready and added the last item to the package to make it complete."

"What is it?"

"That's the thing. I can't tell you what's inside. You have to open it and read through it when you're ready. You don't have to do it alone. I can sit with you if you want, but companionship is all I have to offer."

"Can I take the package and open it with Mrs. Taylor, Patty, and Bobbie when we get to California?"

He flinched at the idea, but nodded. "You can open it wherever you like or never at all, it's yours to do with as you please."

"I'd like to take it with me then."

I should have been more concerned. Should have torn it open right there. A part of me knew whatever waited inside that package might not feel like a gift at all.

"However, you feel most comfortable. It'll only take a second to get your signature. Then I'll let you get on the road so you girls don't miss your train."

As the car wound its way toward the city, a spark inside me shifted. Small and delicate, like the first hint of dawn breaking over the horizon. There was a promise there. Maybe the future held something I'd been too afraid to hope for.

But my world would soon crumble. I couldn't have known, or it was possible I'd known all along.

Chapter Thirty-Nine

The conductor guided us to our seats, tipping his hat with a polite nod before moving on. The low blare of the train echoed as we lurched forward. My stomach flipped. A familiar nervousness spread from my chest and down my arms.

Colors outside the window blurred together. Patches of gold and deep greens made up the fields, with distant gray mountains filling the spacious background. I looked over Patty's shoulder to revel in the moment. Mother Earth stretched out like a quilt stitched by all the colors I'd never noticed before.

The landscape widened as the train continued south, nearing Eugene. I hadn't thought about my birthplace in so long, I'd almost forgotten it existed. Curiosity pulled me to my feet as we passed through.

Patty's head lolled against Mrs. Taylor's shoulder, the two of them lost in twin slumbers. I carefully draped a blanket across them as they settled deeper into sleep.

Still clutching the package from Pop, I made my way to the dining car. While I walked along, I noticed the other passengers immersed in their own worlds. Businessmen muttered into their newspapers, clutching cigars or coffee cups, oblivious to the other passengers around them. A child pressed her nose to the glass. A lone soldier stared off, his expression stretching miles beyond the train. My thoughts drifted to Buster's mother. She'd been so close to having him home before his life was stolen away.

I stopped mid-step, my breath lost. Ahead, a young man with

dark hair and a laugh like a familiar song leaned close to a woman. For a fleeting second, my mind tricked me. I saw Buster's grin, his playful glance. Then the man turned, and his blue eyes shattered the illusion.

A ghost, I thought, regaining my composure.

The dining car was full. I ordered a salad and juice at the counter and turned to leave, but the soft voice of an old man called me back.

"Why don't you join us?"

I turned to find him. A tiny man with ruffled white hair and a matching white beard. Seated across from him was an even smaller woman with kind eyes and a warm smile.

Thank you, Pop and Mona, I thought as I walked over.

"Hello. I'm Dorothy Jean. This is my husband, Paul."

"I'm Amanda. Thanks for letting me sit with you."

We talked for over an hour, and I forgot about losing myself in the passing landscape. Instead, I found comfort in remembering the roots of my happier years.

Dorothy Jean and Paul were celebrating a long-overdue honeymoon. After forty plus years of marriage, they were finally traveling the West Coast for their anniversary.

The old man eyed the package I hadn't let go of. "What you got there?"

"I'm not sure. It was left for me by someone very special, though."

"Why not open it? If they went to the trouble, I'll bet it means a lot to them."

"You're probably right. I'll think about it."

As the hour grew late, I excused myself to go back to my seat. Mrs. Taylor left Patty and me while she went to find a restroom. The package beckoned, tempting me to uncover its secrets.

"What's wrong? You've been quiet," Patty asked as I stared at it.

"It's time to open this. I don't know why I'm so nervous. I'm glad I've got you here with me."

The woman across the aisle glanced at me. Judging eyes. I'd had enough of the stares. Nearly a decade of whispers and sneers came rushing back, overflowing my ability to ignore it this time.

"What? Would you like to say something, ma'am?" I asked, my tone flat, my eyes cold.

She looked away, avoiding my question altogether.

"You didn't have to do that."

Her eyes revealed her pain. She offered a small smile, but I knew it was forced. The woman had affected her in the same way she'd affected me.

She blinked the hurt away. "Are you ready to see what's inside?"

I peeled back the tape with steady hands. The soft tearing echoed loudly. Threatening. A gift from Pop should have been a happy thing. But my gut told me this box held anything but a treasure.

Inside was a worn folder, a pill bottle, and an envelope with Pop's familiar scrawl: *Read this first.*

I lifted the pill bottle, confused. The label was dated only two days before.

"This is weird. Look." I turned the bottle toward Patty.

"I wonder what it's for, didn't you tell me Pop hated the idea of you taking medicine?"

Though I couldn't remember telling her, I must have. How else would she have known?

My fingers trembled as I lifted the envelope's flap. I worried any sudden movement might break its fragile contents. I slipped the letter out, Pop's writing unfolding like a hidden truth I wasn't sure I was ready to see.

Dear Amanda,

I hope this letter finds you whole. You're eighteen now, I'd have given everything to see this day.

There's no good way for me to begin, so I'm just going to get right down to it. I've kept things from you, things I believed would have hurt you more if you knew. My intention in doing so always stemmed from my duty of keeping you protected.

It wasn't always an easy feat, keeping you in the dark, and I needed a lot of help. Luckily, we were blessed to be surrounded by people who adored you almost as much as I.

Miss Sally and Bobbie aided us in preparing you for the world. Ms. Donaldson and Buster kept you safe while you were at school, and Mr. and Mrs. Taylor gave the greatest sacrifice of all by welcoming you into their family and loving you as they would their own child. Of this list, I'm certain you will notice one name is absent. Patricia Taylor. Before I go on, I need you to understand we were aware of your condition long before you came up with her. Your deeper issues were realized when you made friends with Amelia during your stay at the home.

You see, only two girls shared a room with you, and neither was the one you spoke of most—Amelia. At first, we thought you'd made up this friend to cure your loneliness. You were still in shock from losing your parents, after all. But when the Taylors stood on our front porch and you pointed out Patricia, I looked through the window to find no child standing there. I realized then there may be bigger issues.

The difference is that Patricia was once a real person, and the Taylors really were her parents. During an unfortunate incident involving both of the Taylors' children, Patricia lost her life, and their son lost his freedom. It was a lot to ask of them, going along with this manifestation. Mrs. Taylor did so willingly, only hoping to shield you from the insecurity of knowing you were different, as I shielded you from ridicule in school and town.

I stopped reading and turned to Patty. Tears were brimming her eyes. This couldn't be true, she was sitting right next to me. I reached over to hold her hand and went back to the letter.

I'm sorry, Amanda, keeping this from you was no different than telling a lie. Maybe times will have changed by the time you read this. I know the world tends to evolve in ways we cannot predict. The stigma wrapped around your ailment is so heavy, it's taken a village to help me keep it from falling on you.

In this package, you will find the summary report from when you were discharged from the home and all of your psychiatric records. Mr. Graham has been instructed to have you evaluated by a trusted psychiatrist who may prescribe you medication. Please consider that sometimes the risks outweigh the rewards when it comes to psychiatric medicine. Being an adult, those risks are far less than when you were a child, but they are still there.

All of my decisions came after careful consideration. It has always been my sole intention to keep you safe. I can only hope the choices I made were right.

All my love,

Pop

"It's not true." Patty's voice was frantic. "I don't know why Pop wrote those things, but you know it's wrong. There's been some mistake."

"She's right in front of you, you can see and touch her as much as you can hear me speaking to you now. Patty is real, and so am I."

The Unseen didn't exist—a fact I'd been trying to convince myself of for years. But if the Unseen wasn't real, what did it mean for Patty?

Reality cracked, splintering into a silence so thick it felt like wool pressing against my ears. The train tilted off balance, but we didn't fall. I sat glued to my seat, watching the passengers around me with their hair hanging down in strange, disoriented strands. The world itself had flipped on its axis, leaving us helpless, dangling in the absence of time. Nobody noticed that everything was wrong—nobody besides Patty and me.

Patty grabbed my hand and squeezed it tight into hers. Her eyes were wide with a fear I'd never seen in her before. *My* fear.

"I'm scared. Why aren't we falling? Gravity isn't supposed to work this way."

I shook my head. How could I answer when I didn't understand it myself?

"I don't know. Maybe we're dreaming."

A low buzzing crept into my ears. It swelled louder and louder into a roar until my teeth rattled. The walls tore away from the sides of the train. We were exposed now. Vulnerable. Ripping winds thrashing through the inside. Anything not bolted down circled us as we were being pulled into the cyclone. The passengers' hair and clothing flowed in all directions as the train began spinning in full circles. I called out for help, but nobody could hear me. Their bodies remained still. Their faces were lost, almost inhuman.

I gripped the seat and squeezed my eyes closed. My pulse beat through me like thunder until my entire being rattled. Patty's hand squeezed mine even tighter. When I opened my eyes again, the train had returned to normal. The passengers chatted amongst themselves, blind to the turmoil within my world.

"It wasn't real. Nothing's real anymore," I panted, my chest heaving. I had to face whatever this was and find something solid in a world slipping through my fingers. My hands shook. I flipped open the file, hoping and praying its contents could tell me who I really was.

Patty grabbed my arm. She shook me. I watched her frantically try to pull me back to her. But I didn't move. I couldn't.

"Please don't dig into this. Look at me, I'm all you need to see. It's me, your best friend—your sister. Whatever those papers say is a lie. You gotta believe me."

What I'd witnessed happen before me on the train, a trick of my broken mind, proved there had to be some truth in Pop's letter. How many times had I caused reality to twist in front of me without realizing I made it all up?

"I'm sorry, Patty. I have to know."

My eyes darted over cold, clinical terms, words foreign and sharp. But there were phrases buried in the jargon that stood out. Perfectly typed words that even a person with no medical knowledge could understand. *Schizophrenic Reaction/Chronic Undifferentiated Type, Severe Neurotic Depression, Displays inappropriate emotional attachment to imagined figures, Institutional placement may be required.*

I slammed the file shut, stuffing it back into the box as if sealing it away could make it untrue. My hands hovered over the lid, willing it to disappear into some dark corner where I'd never have to see it again.

All of the box's contents were tucked back neatly inside by the time Mrs. Taylor returned to her seat. She didn't have to know I'd looked at it, that I'd brought out a possibility I'd be unable to return. And I refused to sleep, closing my eyes only to sift through the past nine years. The minutes dragged on, each one filled with growing disbelief. Could everything Pop told me be wrong?

"Excuse me," I said to a soldier walking down the aisle after dawn broke.

"Yes, ma'am?"

"Do you have the time?"

He glanced at his watch. "Quarter to eight."

I thanked him, my gaze snagging on a dark-haired man nearby. His easy posture and soft laugh were hauntingly familiar. My heart ached again as I begged to find Buster sitting there.

Patty leaned closer. "I see it too. He looks so much like him. It was a horrible day when I read his name in the paper."

A chill crawled up my spine. I never told her about that. How could she know about the article if she wasn't real?

But real or not, I loved Patty. She'd been there for me, helping me see the world and myself in ways I couldn't have managed alone. I wouldn't be me without her.

How could I face this extraordinary problem?

The train slowed. I pulled myself from my thoughts as the conductor announced our arrival. We shouldered our bags and descended the narrow stairs. Every step I took left me feeling heavier with uncertainty. The station buzzed with voices, the air thick with motion.

"It'll be another twenty minutes before Bobbie gets here," Mrs. Taylor said, motioning to a bench. "You wanna wait over there?"

She was speaking directly to me. I racked my brain, trying to recall one instance of her talking to Patty. There had to be some concrete moment I could remember where anyone had acknowledged her. The memories refused to surface.

"It's as good a spot as any."

I forced a smile to disguise the hurt in my eyes. Pop's words couldn't be true. Mrs. Taylor wouldn't have known about my ailment and continued to perpetuate the lie. Would she? Who did I have left to trust?

When Bobbie arrived, she'd answer the question I didn't want to ask—was Patty real?

Familiar songs weaved their way across the station. *Sittin' on the Dock of the Bay* spilled from a nearby speaker. The melody pulled me in. My foot tapped to the beat as I sang along with Mrs. Taylor. We altered the lyrics to fit our own story.

She played this song for me on the small radio she brought to my hospital room. Special to her for reasons not so dissimilar to my own. She'd run away before, the same as I was doing now. For our tragedies, we were bonded, which only heightened the burn of her dishonesty. I let the music take me away, pulling me from my pain in the same way Mama did.

Before I knew it, I was up on my feet clapping and whistling along with the song. People stopped to stare, but I didn't care. Let them judge. Let them whisper. The rhythm seeped into my bones, lifting a truth buried deep within my soul. With each beat, fragments of my sadness scattered like ashes across the wind.

A few young girls joined in, spinning and singing as their laughter rang out into the crowd. A ripple of joy spread through them. Our worlds threaded together to share a single heartbeat for a moment.

That's when I saw her. A little girl with blonde hair and piercing blue eyes. Amelia. The clapping, the laughter, every person around me fell away until only she remained. She offered me a smile and a quick wave before somebody walked in front of her. Once they passed, she disappeared like smoke in the wind.

I shoved my way through the crowd, a frantic pulse driving me forward. Each time I slipped past someone, two more appeared to block my path. My eyes darted, searching for her in the shifting sea of strangers. But she was gone. Still, the need clawed at me. If I could catch another glimpse of her, I could prove she'd been here, prove she'd been real. The chaos of the crowd swallowed her memory, and doubt seeped into my core, cold and unyielding.

I looked around, for the first time realizing how foreign I still felt in my own skin. Patty danced, her laughter echoing as she tugged me back to her side and back to reality, or maybe further from it. I couldn't tell anymore where I belonged, caught in the fragile space between her world and mine.

Chapter Forty

Time stretched like taffy to amplify the anxiety swirling inside me. I shut my eyes tight, hoping the action would do anything to lighten the war of uncertainty unfolding in my chest. How could I continue when nothing had meaning? With Patty, everything made sense. Who could ever fill the space meant only for her?

I didn't open them again until the sound of the ticking seconds quieted. The train station buzzed with excitement. People rushed about in all directions. As if the scene had been carefully choreographed, nobody collided with each other as they hurried along. I watched them glide around the strangers with ease, like the ants in Mama's kitchen during the warmer months.

A wave of army uniforms surged through the crowd, the crispness of their attire a stark contrast to the chaotic energy around me. The Presidio military base was nearby, where they'd been brought upon their return from Vietnam. They'd get to return to their families soon, the lucky ones still holding onto their lives.

From the corner of my eye, another of Buster's ghosts passed, stirring a painful ache deep within me. My breath halted as I stared at the lonely soldier rushing to catch his train. He had the same walk as Buster. As he boarded, he glanced back in my direction and paused. I looked at my lap so as not to make him uncomfortable by my stare.

"He's got the same eyes as him, too," Patty whispered, stealing the thought right out of my mind.

When I looked up again, he was running toward me. His bags lay where he'd thrown them on the ground.

"Buster," I whispered.

He pulled me into his arms and spun me in a circle, a fantasy I never wished to escape. Patty clapped her hands in excitement.

"I don't understand. Miss Sally said you were… and Patty said so too." My voice cracked from raw emotion. I couldn't bring myself to say the words. I stole a glance at Patty, her head hanging low.

"Miss Sally said what?" While keeping his hands gently on my shoulders, he pushed himself back to get a clear view of my face.

"She showed me your name in the newspaper. She told me you died." I put my hand over my mouth to stifle the sound of my agony.

A flicker of anger ignited in his eyes. He hurried to mask it as he retrieved a crumpled newspaper from his wallet with a steady hand. "I promised you I'd come back for you. Not even the Viet Cong could make me go back on my word. My mother sent me this a few weeks ago. The city honored the local soldiers. Miss Sally is a vicious liar."

"Is this a dream? I'm so happy, I could kiss you right now."

He smiled, mesmerizing me with those mischievous green eyes. Beautiful. Fleeting. Full of stories I begged to read.

"Well, what's stopping you, Mandy?"

When our lips touched, the world stopped turning. Nothing existed but the two of us now. His hand moved to the back of my neck as we shared my first kiss. I expected butterflies. Bobbie said that's what happened when she kissed a boy. But what I got was a sharp contrast to the description of physical touch she'd provided. A symphony of electricity traveled deep into my soul.

I knew my mind was broken. Playing tricks of imagination versus reality. Buster was another mirage in my desert of confusion. But I didn't care. I clung to it with a desperate need to hold onto the clarity it brought. When the moment ended, goosebumps moved throughout my spine. He pulled me in to hold me a little longer when we heard a familiar voice calling out.

"Oh my stars!" Bobbie looked on in wonder, only feet away. A mane of long, windswept waves had replaced her signature strawberry blond straight cut. Her style had changed from the trendy clothes she'd worn in high school, to layered tanks atop a long boho skirt and Birkenstocks.

There was no part of her mother's influence left. No gloss on her lips or rouge on her cheeks. She had blossomed into the beautifully crafted version of the Bobbie she'd kept hidden before. Only her true self existed now.

I might not have recognized her at first glance, except for her welcoming smile, a feature I knew would never change.

"I came for my friend to find she got herself a soldier." She laughed as she playfully punched Buster in the arm.

"You can see him? You see Buster?" I asked, still lost in a whirlwind of confusion.

"Of course I can see him! The sight of you two together is larger than life."

"Oh, Bobbie," I reached out to hug her. He wrapped his arms around the two of us as we cried tears of joy together. "Your mother lied to me. Thank God Miss Sally lied."

Mrs. Taylor smiled at the three of us, true joy in witnessing the gift of healing Buster brought with him. I turned to Patty, isolated on the fringe of our reunion. The realization sliced through me—painful yet undeniable. She told me Buster died because it's what I believed. Every conversation we'd ever had was built from facts I'd already known, or ones I'd inferred. My brain played a horrible trick on me.

My breath caught. Everybody I'd ever cared for had traded honesty for comfort. Pop said they'd done it to protect me, that it came from a place of love. Why did it have to hurt so bad then?

I took a step back to distance myself from all of them. My jaw clenched in an involuntary movement, my fists tightening in frustration. I looked at Patty.

"What's the matter?" Buster reached out for my hand. I pulled away before his fingers could reach my skin.

"You knew. All of you knew, and you hid it from me. Patty's

not real. I must have looked insane for all those years. You *lied* to me."

Bobbie's gaze dropped to the sidewalk, and Buster's shoulders sagged from the emotions neither of them wanted to confront. Bobbie opened her mouth to speak, but I stopped her. Mrs. Taylor rushed to embrace me. I pushed away from everyone, shielding myself from the lot of them with my hands.

An uncontrollable laughter escaped me, a bitter and hollow sound. "So that's it? I just pop some pills, and poof—normal, right? Just like everyone else?" I scoffed. "What then of Patty? It'll be like… like I've *killed* her. She's real to me, she's been there half my life! We've shared secrets, and she stayed by me when Miss Sally locked me away. You don't know her, you don't know what we've shared. She saved me —"

I dropped to my knees. My voice caught in my throat to stifle my cries. Patty reached out to pull me closer to her. Strong and warm. She became a wall between me and the noise of everything else.

"Don't blame them. We were all children back then. Let's give them a chance to explain."

"All those stares, those people whispering about us. It was never about Patty and me; they were looking at me alone. Judging *me*. Oh my God, how I must've looked."

They sat down on the sidewalk. People eyed us, curious about our plight. I wanted to crawl into myself and die alone.

"I'm so confused, you guys. I don't know what's real anymore, what to believe." I sat up straight, determined not to let another tear fall. I didn't want to accept this reality, but I had no choice but to do so.

"I wanted to tell you, so many times I begged my mom to let me try and explain things," Buster insisted. "She said I'd be doing more harm than good because other kids with similar issues had been ostracized, not only at school but by the entire community. So, I did as I was told, but I never felt good about it."

Bobbie chimed in. "Me either. But you know how my mother is. I only asked once. Her answer was the backside of her hand. She said if I ever went against Pop and breathed a word of it to you, I'd get a lot more than a slap. But I didn't keep the secret for her, or even because I was afraid of her. I did it for Pop. I trusted his opinion, and still do. There's no way he'd have kept it from you for any reason other than to keep you protected."

Mrs. Taylor stayed silent, her once fierce eyes holding back tears. She knew the pain of losing Patty was almost too much to carry. There were no words.

"Can you forgive us, Mandy?" Buster pleaded.

I pressed my hands over my ears, but their words bled through my fingers, twisting into whispers from unfamiliar voices. The station warped around me. Tilting. Dropping. A horrific funhouse I couldn't escape. My chest squeezed tight. The truth churned inside me to unravel everything I was. Everything I had been. Patty's laughter echoed from nowhere. From everywhere. My own mind betrayed me once more as I begged for release from this horror. I clamped my eyes shut, but I could still see her smiling, reaching for me. Real. Not real. I didn't know where I ended and the lies began.

I had to breathe, to take control of the situation before it took control of me—in, out, in, out. I forced my breaths into a steady rhythm, slowly replacing fear with calm. I could do this. I could face them, despite what they did to me.

I lowered my hands. Their eyes burned through my barricade and into my fractured soul.

"I don't know. I need time to understand why you lied to me. I'm just not sure if I'm capable of processing all this right now. I need to get out of here. Buster, you've missed your train. I've made you miss your train."

He answered too fast, without even thinking. The light in his eyes, that light that'd shown since the day we first met, melted. Disappeared. In its place, I could only see regret dancing with fear.

"I need to find a payphone so I can call my mom. She's got my train schedule. With all the protests going on against us soldiers, she'll be worried sick when I don't show up. But I can stay a few days, if you'll have me?"

I looked at Bobbie and Mrs. Taylor, unable to make the decision. They both nodded while Buster helped me to my feet.

He ran to pick up his bags still lying on the sidewalk. We loaded them in the trunk and climbed into the car.

"There's a phone at the service station down the road. You can call your mom from there," Bobbie suggested as she pulled onto the roadway. "I can't believe you're alive, Buster. I cried real tears when Amanda told me what she'd heard."

"You always were a softy," he laughed. I could hear the sound clearly. But his eyes didn't turn up at the edges. He'd become me, full of fake smiles and hidden pain. I couldn't let him hurt this way. Not because of me. I'd be big again. For them. For myself. I pushed away the sadness. Pushed away the confusion. And I smiled, soft and quiet. His shoulders relaxed and his eyes crinkled as he grinned back. There he was. Right where he should be.

"Who's up for a beach trip?" Bobbie asked.

I looked at Mrs. Taylor, unsure of myself or my ability to think on my own anymore.

"Well, I sure wouldn't mind sitting in the sand for a bit. I've got a book with me I'd like to finish."

"Let's do it," I replied, grateful for the change of scenery. They were fine. I'd push it down and show them I was fine too. I'd been doing this my entire life.

Grinning when he climbed out of the car, Buster shot us a mischievous look. "The last one to the pier is the rotten egg!"

"Oh no you don't, Buster Donaldson," I called, as Bobbie and I took off running to try and catch him.

Buster's feet hit the pavement first, but he wasn't wearing shoes made for sand. As soon as his soles lost traction, he tumbled backward, landing directly on his backside.

Bobbie and I breezed past him, releasing pure and honest

laughter all the while. For a second, I traveled back in time to the first time I'd ever raced someone. Pop's full belly laugh echoed across my mind.

We reached the pier together, placing our palms against the wood in unison. Looking back, a shoeless Buster came jogging up from behind. Patty stood at the edge of the sand, rooted in place as she watched us from afar.

"Why am I always the rotten egg?"

We sat on the sand and talked for hours, getting up only for an occasional walk to the shore to dip our toes in the cool water. A by-stander wouldn't believe any of us had formed a semblance of a rational thought. Our words tumbled over each other, half memories, half non-sense created by a language only we could understand. Three and a half years apart, but we came back together as if no time had passed.

Bobbie stopped to pick up a pack of firewood from the local hardware store, and we headed to the vineyard. She introduced Mrs. Taylor to her aunt. The two of them became fast friends as they made small talk over a freshly opened bottle of wine.

She grabbed her portable radio while Buster got the fire going. We danced together. Sang together. Our singing voices carried across the hills. Loud. Off-key. Familiar. I couldn't think of anything other than this moment with these people; my people.

A flower child, a soldier fresh out of Vietnam, and me, the orphaned girl who brought us all together. Each of us was laden with sand-coated skin as the chilly night air filled our lungs. We didn't look like the usual trio, but the laughter and love clung to us by the day's end.

Even as Bobbie and Buster talked, I saw Patty by my side. The comfort of her hand rested on my shoulder, steadying me in the way only she could. She'd been the most real, honest, and pure. The irony was not lost upon me.

I tried to cling to the peace of the moment. Prayed for it to overpower the burden of their lies. But it chipped away at my resolve.

Dug into me. Through me. And in the end, I was left feeling hollow.

You Are the Sunshine of My Life came on. They knew every word. The lyrics were as unfamiliar as the feeling of the wind in my hair, or the warmth from the fire's flames dancing in the center of our gathering. I couldn't sing along with them this time. I'd been in the dark for too long. Begged for the sunshine for too many years. Somehow, this song, meant to bring feelings of love and hope, left me falling into in an abyss of loneliness and despair. Their eyes stayed locked on me. I wanted to shrink out of sight, but there was no place for me to hide.

I knew what I needed to do.

"Is there a phone I can use to call my attorney? I promised I'd let him know I made it here all right."

"There's a phone inside, straight down the hall in the den," Bobbie replied, still breathless from her excitement of the evening.

I closed the door behind me. Flipped the lock. Sealed the secrecy of my plan away from unwelcome ears.

Chapter Forty-One

Bobbie set Buster and Mrs. Taylor up in the guest rooms, sharing her suite with me for the night.

"Are you still awake?" Her voice traveled through the dark bedroom. Haunted. Full of unnamed torture.

"Uh-huh. You can't sleep either?"

She switched on the lamp beside her and turned to face me on her pillows. "I haven't slept right in weeks. I keep thinking about what she did. And how I left you behind."

Her fingers traced invisible patterns on the blanket. Nervous energy coursed through her fingers with no place for her to send it..

"Your mother has a crippled moral compass, and she's chosen to weaponize it. There's no way you could've known she'd—"

She cut me off. "No. Nobody could've guessed, but I've known what a terrible person she is my whole life. I abandoned you. There's no simpler way to say it."

"I wanted you to go, Bobbie. You needed to get away from her. Knowing I helped you escape made me feel good about myself for once. I've never blamed you."

"Well, that makes one of us."

"Look, we both knew the same thing, your mother treated you poorly because she blamed you for your dad's death. She hadn't hurt me like she did you back then. Even when she was upset, she never raised a hand at me."

"No, she just tried to have you arrested instead!"

"The fact is, we both thought she'd be stern, but neither of us believed she'd be cruel. You're better for leaving. Nothing will make me see it any other way."

"Thank you for saying so. I still feel responsible for all those years you lost, but at least the world can see what a monster she is now."

"Believe me, the whole town knows, and justice is coming."

She remained quiet for a long moment. I thought she was absorbing what I said, but she was searching for the right words to express it.

"She killed my father. I know for a fact now, and so does my aunt. We found the proof a couple of weeks ago while going through some boxes from my old house. After Dad died, my mother didn't even bother checking that she'd gotten rid of all the evidence before dumping the stuff we couldn't bring in my aunt's barn."

"Proof? What kind of proof?"

"Two small glass vials buried deep in an old box. One empty, one half full. My aunt had her suspicions, so she sent them to a friend in the city. Turns out they were filled with a powdered form of lead paint."

"How would she even have gotten it?"

"She must have chipped it off something and ground it down. And then she poisoned him by sneaking it into his food or drinks, I think. My aunt always thought it strange that they never tested the paint on my dollhouse. My mother threw it out before they confirmed how he died."

"Can you take the vials to the police?"

"There's no point. It's been so long, and they were found here. Without a way to prove they came from her, there's no case. It doesn't matter; she's going to jail anyway. I hope they throw away the key."

"Same here. One good thing came out of it, though."

"What?"

"Now you can get rid of those dark clouds chasing you."

"I suppose I can."

The guilt consuming me since the night I escaped Miss Sally lifted. Her false accusation from all those years before came to a reality when she tried to keep me from getting out. This time, I really *had* pushed her down. Watched her writhe in pain from the wood piercing through her. I found no desire to save her life at that moment. Did it make me evil like my father? My instinct of self-preservation had driven the act itself even though I knew it was wrong. When I saw the blood pooling around her, I turned and ran. If given the chance to redo the night, I knew my actions wouldn't change.

This time I'd done it on my own, without any urging from the Unseen, only fueled by fear and panic. But I guess it was the same with my father. The Unseen had always been an extension of me, the dark side of my thoughts. I could see now Patty had been the light. Two forces, both born from the desperation of a broken mind. I couldn't have one without the other, the roses without the thorns.

Miss Sally was no victim. She'd have killed me at some point when she couldn't subdue her anger with rationality. Her shallow breathing, a rattle I'd been certain meant her death would come soon after, hadn't stopped me from leaving her there. The same way I ran after I killed my father. But she didn't die, and I hadn't proved to be a monster. My conscience was clear.

I looked at Bobbie sleeping next to me while praying for answers, hoping for some sign that would tell me the right thing to do. No imaginary friend or words from a faceless entity could lay out my path for me. This was something I had to conquer alone while facing my biggest fear—the buried parts of my mind.

When sleep found me, it was light, and I woke before the sun crossed the horizon. I pushed the covers aside and tiptoed to the bathroom to dress, quiet as a shadow. I became the ghosts I'd been running from. My suitcases waited in the front room where I'd left them the night before. If I tried to explain, they'd talk me out of it. I wasn't strong enough to hear them ask me to stay.

But I couldn't disappear without a trace, so I wrote them a note.

Placing the letter on the table near the door, I grabbed my bags and hurried outside to wait for the car my attorney arranged. It was 4:45—fifteen minutes early.

The driver arrived right on time, pulling up in a dark sedan. He got out to load my bags into the trunk, introducing himself with a cautious voice. "Morning, Miss Amanda, my name's Francis."

His movements were careful, almost rehearsed. My attorney made it clear this was my getaway, and keeping quiet was imperative.

We pulled away, and I glanced back at the dark house, the heartbreak I was leaving behind. All I'd ever done was try to make others happy, but now I had no choice but to care for myself.

Patty sat beside me as the highway stretched ahead.

"Happy birthday, it's your golden one," she whispered.

"Thank you," I whispered back.

Francis glanced at me in the rearview mirror. "Oh, no trouble at all. I take clients on these drives all the time."

I blushed. He'd caught me. But at least he thought I was talking to him.

Deflect. Get it together. Relax.

"Have you been a driver long?"

He chuckled lightly, his voice warm. "When I was a boy, I thought I'd be someone important, maybe even break the mold. Not many options for Black men back then, but my mama swore I could be president. That woman saw things in me I didn't see in myself." He smiled at the memory.

"Sometimes mothers know us better than we know ourselves."

I thought of Mrs. Taylor rather than Mama. Her warm smile. Her arms shielding me when I couldn't find my footing. She always knew what I needed, whether I asked for help or not.

Francis nodded. "Got my license right outta high school. Never felt so free. I've been driving ever since. Guess it's been about twenty-five years now."

"It's good you found something you love and stuck with it.

Getting people where they need to go can mean a lot. This ride means the world to me."

"Thanks. Not as fancy as being president, but it pays the bills. Plus, meeting folks and hearing their stories is something I've grown to enjoy just as much as the driving."

We continued down the highway in companionable silence until Francis offered, "Let me know if you get hungry. I know all the good spots along this route. Just say what you're in the mood for."

"I'm not picky. Whatever you recommend works for me."

He grinned. "Yes, ma'am. I've got just the place. Want some music in the meantime?"

"That'd be nice. Thank you."

I turned to Patty, her quiet presence beside me. I'd taken the first pill when I woke up, but her image hadn't dimmed. Saying goodbye to her would take time—a curse as much as a blessing.

With my parents, as with Pop, there were no warnings. One moment they were there, the next, gone. The shock was sharp and sudden. But with Patty, I'd see the goodbye coming, feel it tear through me bit by bit. Isn't stepping on glass, fast and without warning, less painful than knowing it's under your foot and pressing down slowly anyway? I didn't know if I was strong enough to apply the pressure, but I had to at least try.

"Here we are." He parked outside a small cafe, stepping out to open my door.

"Thank you. Time feels so unnatural this morning, like it's moving too fast," I said, immediately regretting it. Why would I say something like that? This may be the only person on Earth not convinced of my insanity, yet I'd opened my mouth and revealed evidence to the contrary.

Francis didn't seem to mind. "You were pretty deep in thought, makes the time slip right by." He held the cafe door open for me. "Want me to walk you inside or wait out here for you to get seated before I go in and make my order?"

"Oh, you're not eating with me?"

"You don't need to sit with hired help. I can eat outside and give you some privacy."

"Nonsense, I'd enjoy the company, unless you'd rather not?"

He hesitated but then smiled back. "Well, I suppose I'll accept the invite. Thank you, Miss Amanda."

"Just Amanda'll do," I said as we walked inside.

The waitress handed us menus, her gaze lingering a moment too long. "You folks know what you wanna drink?"

"Do you have Coke floats?" I asked.

"Yes, ma'am. Vanilla or chocolate?"

"Vanilla, please."

I opened my menu, painfully aware of the eyes on us.

"When will they learn?" Patty asked quietly.

I scoffed, replying under my breath, "Ignorance must be in their bones."

Francis looked up, catching my tone. He scanned the room briefly, meeting the stares until they dropped away. "They just don't know any better. Folks get raised one way, and here we are, showing them another. Most don't take kindly to different."

I nodded. "Believe me, I know how being considered different gets treated. People go to great lengths to disguise the pieces of themselves that others wouldn't understand."

He tilted his head, curious but polite. "Well, you seem like a normal young lady to me."

I wanted to keep talking, to scream out every horrible truth of who I was and who I wasn't, but the approaching waitress silenced me. I bit my tongue, saving us both from the brewing storm.

We ordered our meals and chatted while waiting for our food to arrive. By the time we left, I'd calmed down some, though a bitter edge remained.

Back in the car, Francis thanked me again for inviting him to breakfast.

"And thank you for coming. I don't do well alone," I admitted. "Lately, I've realized things about myself, about my mind. Things everyone I love knew and never told me. Turns out, I've been alone my whole life without even knowing it."

He turned the radio down. "I don't know your story or the people in it. If you need to talk, I'm all ears."

I wanted to. I wanted someone to hear me and tell me what to do. But my story carried too much judgment, especially from a stranger.

"What does it matter if he judges you?" Patty said. "You'll never see him again after this. I say, tell him."

"*And I say keep quiet,*" the Unseen countered, catching me off guard.

The Unseen's words, once constant in my life, had become rare since finding Patty, and he rarely spoke in her presence. This was his desperate attempt to stay relevant, but nothing could shake my resolve to silence them both.

I covered my ears. Why was this always my defense? Pointless. It never worked to drown them out. My breath came shallow. Erratic. Chest heaving. Every inhale entered my body jagged and unsatisfying. With a spinning head, the world tilted as my body struggled to work. A tingling numbness spread from my fingers to my arms until every limb tingled.

My heart slammed against my ribs so fast that I couldn't catch my breath. I couldn't see. I felt my hands drop, falling to my sides as I sagged into the seat. I'd lost control.

Patty's voice broke through the chaos. "I'm here, Amanda." Her hand stroked my hair, grounding me, pulling me back.

Francis called my name, his voice distant and garbled like a shout carried through water. I squeezed my eyes shut, willing it all to stop, praying to be normal, to be anyone else.

A cool, damp pressure touched my forehead, startling me. My eyes snapped open to find Francis leaning over me. A wet cloth covered my forehead.

"You alright? We'd better get you to a hospital."

My pulse began to settle, my breath slowing. "No, I'm okay. I don't need a hospital. I think I'm starting to feel better now."

"What happened?"

"It felt like my lungs were gonna burst out of my chest. I couldn't breathe."

"Have you had this happen before?"

I nodded.

"Think you can sit up? I've got some water up front."

With his help, I sat upright, still shaky but improving. "I'm sorry for worrying you."

"No need to apologize. Let's just focus on feeling better, sound good?"

I nodded weakly. "These episodes don't last long."

He seemed relieved. "Good. My sister had something like this happen a while back. It looked a lot like what just happened to you. Only, she didn't bounce back so quickly."

"Your offer to talk still good? I think I might need to get some of this off my chest."

Francis smiled. "Yes, ma'am. That's an offer with no expiration."

Once I was steady, we got back on the road. In a perfect world, with a perfect narrator, my story would've come out clear and concise. But what Francis got was a tangled, chaotic version of a short life wrapped in trauma and confusion.

He kept his eyes on the road, glancing at me only during the most horrific parts. I didn't know if my words made sense or if he was genuinely listening. It didn't matter. I needed to say it out loud, to make it real instead of a half-forgotten nightmare.

When I finished, I sat still with my hands folded in my lap. Even Patty and the Unseen had nothing to say.

I stared out the window, waiting for him to look at me like

everyone else had. But he didn't. He tapped the steering wheel while mulling it over.

His voice was soft but sure. "I wasn't expecting anything like that. I just—wow. Now, do you want advice, or did you just need to vent?"

I thought about it. I'd wanted to purge a piece of the plague, but maybe his perspective could help. "I'd appreciate your input."

He nodded thoughtfully. "You've had a lot thrown at you all at once. Getting away makes sense. Gives you time to sort through it. But I hope you'll try to understand why they lied. I don't think you've been alone your whole life. Not really. But this next part? You'll have to face it on your own. Whether or not you're with your friends."

"I'm not ready to say goodbye to Patty. She's not just some imaginary friend. I couldn't have survived without her."

"But you did survive. Patty's a part of you. Always will be, whether you see her or not."

His words landed. Patty had only ever told me what I already knew. Her voice, her stories, her jokes—they'd all come from me. I realized it during a moment of clarity at the train station, but pushed the thought out of my mind. I needed Francis's gentle reminder.

It wasn't the lies that caused the most pain, but rather knowing they didn't believe in my strength and didn't trust me to decide which truths I could handle. I harbored no shame. Not for loving Patty or tolerating the Unseen. To reject them would be to abandon true pieces of myself.

I hesitated, then asked the question I feared most. "Do you think they were ashamed of me? Is that why they lied?"

Francis shook his head. "I can't say, but I doubt it. I think they just loved you. They didn't know any other way to look out for you."

He could have been right about them. Maybe. It did nothing to lesson the betrayal. This time though, I knew I had to look out for myself.

No more running. No more hiding. This time, I was choosing.

Chapter Forty-Two

We pulled into Stonehaven around dusk. I couldn't shake the feeling that there was something here for me to find. A purpose? Belonging? Given my past, anything unknown left me with a certain amount of unease. But maybe this time I'd see the path that would lead me toward a better road.

Francis helped carry my bags up the front steps of The Inn. Turning toward the orphanage down the street, I paused, admiring the sunset tucking itself behind its high roof.

The building once filled me with terror, but now I sensed the love seeping from its core. Pop and Mona's legacy lived on in the pieces of their hearts scattered throughout this town—a comforting realization that calmed the tender parts of my psyche.

After confirming I had a room, Francis pulled a card from his pocket. "You can call me anytime."

"Thank you. I'll keep in touch."

He reached out to shake my hand, and I grasped his firmly. What I really craved was to feel the warmth of another human's embrace. The handshake would have to do. I waited until he left before retreating to my room to welcome the unfamiliar space.

For the first time, I craved solitude, and solitude was what I found. I spent the next week holding it close, becoming one with the thing I'd feared for so long.

I learned a lot about myself during my stay at The Inn. I'd never truly been afraid of being alone. My fear came from the forcible control lingering in the corners of my bedroom as a child. It hid in the lost minutes and dark shadows lurking during every moment of Miss Sally's care. Like a monster hiding beneath the bed—I'd cowered at the idea of isolation.

When Miss Sally locked me away, she'd taken from me the greatest gift I'd received from Pop. Freedom. I wasn't a prisoner anymore, not to my abusers and not to my past. My life held the promise of a new beginning, and I'd find it on my own terms, under no control of outside forces.

I would do those things alone.

The Unseen's words began to fade. I knew Patty soon would, too. Some days were more challenging than others, but each morning I swallowed the pill, determined to mend what had long been broken.

I woke up reaching for her, my hand landing on empty sheets. No warmth. No breath. Nothing remained but a quiet so loud it burrowed deep into my soul. I waited a second, kept my eyes closed, and prayed to see her smiling face when I opened them.

It wasn't supposed to end like this. She was supposed to say goodbye. To laugh with me one last time. Or maybe even cry. But instead, she left the same way she came—out of nowhere, into nothing.

I opened my eyes and sat up slowly. The walls stared back at me like they too knew the air had changed. I wanted to scream, except there was no place in my body left to hold sound.

Find your normalcy. You can do this.

I willed my thoughts to take on her voice, but I couldn't hear her anymore. Only the suffocating silence coupled with the sound of my sorrow surrounded me.

Steam poured from the faucet as I filled the tub with hot water, the same as I'd done a hundred times before. But I didn't take my clothes off. Didn't pull the tie from my hair. I couldn't find normalcy. Not today. I'd been teasing myself by pretending I could.

I stepped in, the water soaking my socks and weighing down my nightgown as I sank deeper into its warmth. My head broke the surface until every part of me became submerged in the unforgiving truth. Let it rise. Let it take the parts of me that still believed in her. At first, I didn't cry, I only trembled. Then it came.

It took four words to break my mother. For me, though, it took only three.

Patty was gone.

She slipped away, no matter how hard I tried to hold on. Every essence of her left me.

The grief I experienced for Patty differed from what I'd endured for Pop or Mama. I'd known it would be hard, but I also knew I had to face it before I could reconnect with others.

Nobody knew I'd returned, except for my attorney, my psychiatrist, and the keeper at The Inn. Every evening, I told myself, soon. And each morning, I found I still wasn't ready.

Weeks passed before I woke up, sure that it was time. I called Mrs. Taylor first, hoping she'd already be awake. She cried real tears at the sound of my voice. A pang of guilt struck me, but I pushed it down. I'd done nothing wrong in taking time to heal.

"Won't you call Bobbie? She's been worried sick. Calling and coming by nearly every day asking about you."

"Bobbie's here? She came home?"

"Oh yes, child. We all drove up together the same day you left California. They thought you'd taken the train, so we tried to meet you in Portland. We split up, hoping one of us would find you."

"Mr. Graham sent a car for me," I explained. "But I'll call her when we hang up. I'm ready now. Is she staying at Miss Sally's?"

"Yes, and she's not leaving until after the trial."

Mrs. Taylor invited me for lunch and insisted Bobbie come too. After we hung up, I dialed Bobbie's number.

Her voice sounded different—aged. Again, guilt stirred. Though she didn't say it, I knew my disappearance hurt her.

I gave her the address of The Inn and agreed to ride with her to visit Buster.

When he saw me, he lifted me in his arms, nearly tumbling over from excitement.

Where there'd once been four, now there were only three. In moments like these, I grieved Patty on my own, but I'd gotten better at the alone part.

Buster looked at me, worry in his eyes. "You're staying, right? You're not going anywhere?"

I let him lace his fingers through mine, butterflies stirring at the touch.

"I'm staying. This is home for now."

"Can I see you later? Dinner? A movie? Whatever you want. Bobbie can come too."

"I'd like that. Dinner and a show."

Bobbie chimed in. "Sorry, guys, I've got plans. Rain check?"

We ironed out the details, Buster leaving me with a light kiss on the cheek.

Excitement tickled my bones. A real date? The feelings coursing through me were otherworldly.

"We're almost there."

Bobbie squeezed my knee when we neared the Taylors'. Warm. Real. A touch given without request. She knew my heart, watched me succumb to my pain, and witnessed my dysfunction. Yet she decided to keep me anyway.

Mrs. Taylor waited on the porch, a tall young man and a young woman beside her.

"Girls, this is my son, Marcus, and his wife, Denise," Mrs. Taylor said.

"I'm so happy to meet you."

Just then, the door swung open. A little girl with golden eyes and pigtail braids barreled outside.

"Slow down, Patty Mae," Mr. Taylor called as he followed.

"Are you my Aunt Amanda?"

Her face was full of conquest. Playful and childlike. But something lingered behind her eyes. Something familiar and unrecognizable at the same time.

"I am, and I've been waiting a long time to meet you."

"I got a swing set out back. Paw said I can play on it whenever I feel like, even after we move next door. Wanna see?"

Her excitement was contagious. Soon, we were in the backyard, her laughter ringing out like music.

And there I was, nine years old again. Not the broken version of myself, but the girl Pop always believed hid beneath the surface.

Mrs. Taylor called us in for lunch.

"Will you swing with me after we eat?" Patty Mae asked.

"I can't today, but I'll come visit every chance I get."

"Promise?"

"My pinky promises." We wrapped our little fingers around each other's, sealing my words with an unbreakable tradition.

At the table, laughter and stories warmed the room. Marcus and Denise began to relax. I silently vowed to help them navigate any hurdles ahead.

I helped Mrs. Taylor clean the dishes. We finished putting everything away before I pulled her aside for a moment of privacy.

"Thank you for everything you've done for me. I'm sorry for any pain I caused. It couldn't have been easy going along with it all."

She smiled. "At first, it was hard. Your light knocks at our door, reminding me of my baby girl every day. But your presence became a gift. Through you, I glimpsed the life Patricia could've had, and I came to look forward to you coming around. I love you like my own."

Her words sank into the place where I kept my grief, filling the cracks like Mama's torn bits of fabric. She was a mother without a daughter, and I was a daughter with no mother. Our shared pain bonded us, igniting the places we didn't realize were still frozen.

"You have no idea what that means to me. I love you too."

Maybe for the first time, I believed I was worthy of it all. Of friendship. Of family.

"You always have a home here. We'll see you girls this Sunday morning."

How had I ever doubted this? The Taylors' home was more than a house, it was a haven where love filled every corner. Where people chose to welcome me regardless of my flaws. For the first time, I knew I belonged somewhere, a moment to keep with me always.

At Bobbie's house, I hesitated at the door, but knowing Miss Sally was gone gave me the strength to enter.

We found all of my things she'd removed from my bedroom while I was drugged. Too lazy to spend the effort destroying them, she'd thrown everything in boxes and shoved them in the corner of the den. The artwork on my walls showed proof of Miss Sally's lies; each piece was in perfect condition, absent her claims that I'd destroyed them with scissors.

Repairing the space Miss Sally took from me was a form of therapy I hadn't anticipated. I removed the remaining screw from the window. The symbolism of the moment coursed through me. I stood by it, clasping Buster's quarter in my hand as the fresh air streamed inside. For the first time in this room, my fear lifted. It wasn't a cage anymore, but a space I could breathe in.

The months spent working on my room and myself began to shape me. I studied for my high school diploma and spent evenings with Buster. Bobbie and I joined the Taylors at church on Sundays. Along with Denise, we made up the one percent of fair-skinned attendees. The congregation welcomed us with open arms.

I revived our old tradition of spending early Saturday afternoons wandering through downtown Hillsboro. Sometimes Bobbie and Denise came along. On other days meant for just Patty Mae and me, we often walked the streets of Stonehaven for a change of scenery. Even after several trips, her eyes never lost the excitement of being included.

We paused in front of the art gallery window. The glass was clean enough to double as a mirror, and behind it hung a canvas of wild blue brushstrokes. I leaned in closer, hoping that getting nearer might explain its meaning.

Movement to our right caught my attention. I stiffened at the sight of a not-so-dear old friend. Linda.

I turned back toward the painting, willing her to continue on her way. But the air shifted, and there was no mistaking the sugary voice behind me.

"Well, if it isn't Amanda Hollings," Linda said. "I thought that was you."

I forced myself to meet her eyes. Her smile was wider than I remembered. Years of rehearsing, I knew the look well.

"It's been a long time," she went on, rocking lightly on her heels. "You look… different. Grown, I guess."

Patty Mae looked up at me, curiosity resting in her young eyes. Could she sense the danger? I swallowed the dry taste in my mouth before responding. "Yeah. Time does that."

For a moment, it almost seemed normal. We could have been nothing more than two old friends catching up on a sidewalk. No pain in our history. No disjointed memories of harsh words or bloodied noses.

Linda gestured toward the painting. "That one's strange, isn't it? I don't get it, but maybe that's the point. The world changes. People do too."

I studied her. Waiting. Wondering. Maybe this was someone new.

Then her voice dipped, and the girl I remembered seeped through. "'Course, some things don't change. Like how your kind never fit in. You can dress yourself up or stand in front of fancy paintings, but you're still the same underneath, aren't you?"

Patty Mae laced her fingers through mine, taking a small step back. She'd picked up on this vile girl's spirit, the same as I would have at her age.

Linda pushed out her left hand, a diamond on her ring finger. "When you're normal, you get to enjoy the things that *really* matter. You know love, marriage, belonging. David and I will be married by this time next month. Our happily ever after. I doubt very much you'll ever be so lucky. Crazy's still crazy, the same as Black's still Black." Her eyes darted between Patty Mae and me. "Don't expect the world to make room for people like you. Maybe then you won't be let down."

I held strong to Patty Mae with my left hand, but my right one balled into a fist. And then I saw her, only a glimpse of a reflection in the window. Patty. She shook her head as if to say, "It's okay, just walk away."

So I smiled, but it never reached my eyes. "We've still got several shops to look at. Congratulations on your engagement. I'm sure you and David will find nothing more than the lives you deserve."

We left her standing there as we made our way down the street toward the Dairy Bar. My hands were shaking, but I couldn't let Patty Mae know how much Linda had riled me. We'd have a well-earned dessert while I worked on letting go of Linda's hateful speech. If I'd learned anything from Mrs. Taylor, it was that sometimes a sweet treat could take away the bitter flavor of painful words.

"What did that girl mean? Was she talking about me?" Patty Mae looked up, eyes filled with questions I didn't want to answer.

"She's a very confused woman. It's sad, really, but some people live in a bubble and never try to break free from it. You just have to remember that those people don't know how to love. But we do. And we always will."

She nodded, though I had a feeling she didn't quite understand what I was telling her. One day she would, a fact that didn't make me feel any better.

We laughed and carried on as though the moment was endless. The space around us became ours, and we chose to keep it. Nobody's eyes lingered too long. Nobody whispered.

For my own sanctity, I'd found the strength to walk away from Linda. Nothing could have been gained in entertaining the ill nature of a dark-hearted woman anyway. My life was finally my own. I looked down at Patty Mae, so innocent and special, and I knew the future belonged to her. Her world would be a beautiful canvas, painted by her own hand.

And I'd use every ounce of love I owned to make sure of it.

Chapter Forty-Three

That summer, I grew up. My stolen firsts found their way into my life, even if they were a little late.

My friends-turned-family helped shape me into the woman waiting behind the walls I'd built around myself. They trusted me. *Believed* in me. I knew I'd taken the brunt of the work for myself, but without their guiding hands, I couldn't even imagine coming so far.

Mr. Taylor welcomed the role that had been taken from Pop's grasp in his death. He ushered me into the driver's seat of his old truck, ready for my first lesson behind the wheel.

"You're gonna do just fine, child. But I gotta say, I don't think I've ever seen your eyes so wide!"

He laughed, that deep, warm laugh he always had. His eyes crinkled at the corners, and I relaxed my grip on the wheel.

And then I put the truck in gear. We rolled forward at least three feet before the truck jerked and stalled. There were so many things to remember. Which pedal to stop, which one to go, and that other oddball one on the end. I had to know the precise moment to push it in or let it out, all while steering and shifting between gears. Thank goodness there were no cars around on the quiet back road he chose, or we'd have found ourselves in real trouble.

When the lesson ended, I'd succeeded in moving the truck down the entire road at a speed no greater than fifteen miles per hour. And boy was I tired. Who knew driving could be so exhausting?

But weeks later, I had it down. By the next month, Mr. Taylor informed me that I was ready to hit the ground running. An odd turn of phrase, but I think it was his way of letting me know he trusted me to try for my license.

And I passed the exam on my first attempt.

Bobbie and Buster joined me on the day I went to pick out my car. I was finally a real person, doing real things—a dream I never knew could come true.

"Oh, look at that red Beetle," Bobbie pointed out. "It's even a convertible."

I cringed at the memory of that day on the way to court, all those years before. I'd told myself I was trapped. That the car could have been responsible for my imprisonment, for the impending doom I feared I'd find upon our arrival. And even though I'd made it out, the thought of climbing inside that monster made my palms sweat and my pulse pick up a beat.

"Uh-uh, no thank you," I said with a crinkled nose. "Something with four doors that doesn't make me feel like I might bounce right off the road."

And then I saw it. A new Plymouth Valiant in a sensible shade of blue. Not too dark, not too bright. The sticker on the window showed twenty-six hundred dollars; the most significant purchase I'd ever made. A pang of guilt stirred, but it quieted by the glaring prices plastered on the other cars' windows. This one was hundreds less than most of the others on the lot, including that ghastly Bug.

I drove myself downtown the following week to try to earn my high school diploma. My nerves had been climbing almost daily over the prior weeks. But for some reason, they'd calmed that morning. Deep down, I knew I was ready to take what was mine and show the world who I was—a normal girl deserving of the same things as everyone else.

I walked out of the testing center with the certificate in my hand, clutching it tightly as if it might disappear at any moment. A song nobody else could hear played in my mind as I looked up at the sky. The weight of years of pain lifted. Sunshine warmed my face, and I knew I belonged in its light.

"I did it," I whispered. But I wanted to shout it to the world. Amanda Hollings had done something right. Something real. This was proof that my past would no longer define me.

The next morning, I made the drive to the cemetery outside Stonehaven, parking in my usual spot.

My shoes lay on the passenger seat as the soft grass invited my bare feet to revel in the cool, lush earth.

The fence line, typically speckled with sparrows or robins, lay bare. I couldn't remember a day when they didn't watch my quiet steps lead me to where my family rested. But then I saw them, several Western Meadowlarks sitting atop the silent stones. Our state bird, yet one I rarely saw in person.

Their melody came like a greeting as I continued toward my family's corner. They waited until I was close, eyeing me with the same curiosity I gave them. My approach inspired their silence. I slowed my pace to admire them before they decided to retreat. And when they flew, I could almost feel the wind beneath their wings, carrying them away to someplace safe.

I could have been a bird back then, but I'd found my own version of flying high. And I knew it would take more than a weak-minded villain to ever make me come back down.

Leaves had settled on Pop and Mona's tombstone. I brushed them away and replaced them with a bouquet of tulips. Despite the sounds of nature, the cemetery was shrouded in a serene silence. When I spoke aloud, my words resonated like a symphony, not a whisper.

Talking to Pop and Mona had become a ritual for me. Every morning, after breakfast, I drove to the cemetery. Most days, I came empty-handed, but today was special. July 5, 1973—nine years since I wandered onto Pop's porch.

I closed my eyes to remember. The creak of the door. The first glimpse I caught of him through the small crack. I'd been a terrified little girl wearing a big girl's face. But looking back now, I know he saw the parts of me I tried desperately to conceal. He chose to welcome me into his world. The good parts. The broken parts. Everything I truly was, he accepted without condition.

Pop taught me how to love with ferocity, without bounds. He'd needed me too, though I didn't see it then. In so many ways, we'd rescued each other, healed each other even. He truly was my angel. I'd always celebrate the day he saved me.

"I passed all my tests yesterday," I said, kneeling before his grave. "I wish you could've been there. No big ceremony, no cap and gown. But I did it. Summer's almost over, and I've signed up to begin college next month in Portland. I'm big now, Pop, but I haven't forgotten how to be small. I love you—give Mona a hug for me."

Whether my words reached him or were scattered by the wind didn't matter. Saying them lifted some of the ache from my final locked room. For so long, I'd ached to confide in him. Then one day I did. I hadn't missed a morning visit in nearly two weeks. These moments would dwindle as life carried me forward, but for now, they were my favorite part of each day.

I glanced at my parents' tombstone. The sunflowers I'd left three days ago were wilting, their brightness fading; sunflowers, symbols of hope. On the ninth anniversary of Mama's death, that word —hope—filled my thoughts. My mother hoped I'd find freedom. Now that I had, I knew she'd found peace.

The sun warmed my cheeks as a breeze stirred my amber-streaked hair. She was in everything around me, urging me forward. Smiling, I stepped closer to their grave, letting the silence enfold me.

My fingers traced the engraved letters of her name. The necklace at my throat held the small lock of her hair. She'd been alone too long. I'd never again leave her waiting years for my return.

The wind picked up, and a hint of lemon greeted my senses. I inhaled, deep and hungry for the essence of someone long gone. I let myself live in the memory. And when the leaves began to rustle in the trees above, I heard Pop's voice. Calm and free, like the gifts he left for me.

A giggle came from somewhere in the distance. A shared moment between friends as close as sisters. As real in that moment as Patty had always been. I laughed with her one last time, refusing to allow the moment to turn to grief. There was strength in that laughter, a sound to remind the world I'd survived the fight.

My symphony had arrived at last. It was never meant to be quiet. Never meant to be unnoticed. The bittersweet pieces of them haunted me, and I was strong enough to let go of the pain. But not these pieces, these were the ones that were mine to keep.

I stood and brushed the grass from my dress, then kissed my hand to press it to Mama's name. There was no darkness in a phrase both Pop and Mama had said countless times. The words only scarred me once they weren't true. But I'd return tomorrow, so I made a promise I knew I could keep.

As I turned to leave, I whispered, "I'll be right back, my dear."

The Music Within

Roy Orbison — *Crying*

Martha and the Vandellas — *Dancing in the Street*

The Beach Boys — *I Get Around*

The Rascals — *People Got to Be Free*

Billie Holiday — *I'll Be Seeing You*

Billie Holiday — *He's Funny That Way*

Bob Dylan — *Pick one, their ride to the creek had room for them all.*

Simon & Garfunkel — *The Sound of Silence*

Otis Redding — *Sittin' on the Dock of the Bay*

Stevie Wonder — *You Are the Sunshine of My Life*

Coming In 2026

MISPLACED SHADOW

Warren holds tightly to what he believes he can control. He needs Grace Marie to stay exactly where she belongs—by his side where he can protect her. But the line separating protector and captor is thinner than he ever imagined, and some shadows refuse to stay hidden from the light.

The secrets they've shared, the hurdles they've climbed, none of it means anything when she vanishes. All fingers point to him—judging, blaming, dissecting every piece of their life up until the night she walked away. And now he's desperate to clear his name, or allow himself to fade into the dark with her.

In a world built on fragile trust, desire turns to anger, loyalties shatter without warning, and the one person he was trying to save may have been the one person he should have feared the most. Now the question lingers: *Where the hell is Grace Marie?*

About the Author

Cassady Rhodes lives in a suburb of Charleston, South Carolina with her husband and their dog, Baby, who curls beneath a blanket at her side while she writes. The mother of seven mostly grown children, six daughters and one son, she's learned that family teaches you as much about resilience as it does about love. Born the daughter of a traveler, she spent her childhood moving from coast to coast, though Safford, Arizona is the place she considers her hometown. Writing has been a part of her life as far back as she can remember, shaped by lived experiences and the chaos she's found in the truths of the world.

"Find the love that lingers when the person is gone, for that is what will guide you forward when you believe you can't take another step."

—Cassady Rhodes

www.ingramcontent.com/pod-product-compliance
Lightning Source LLC
Chambersburg PA
CBHW071530110726
47908CB00007B/1828